RITUAL

Nine feet under water, police diver Flea
Marley closes her gloved fingers around a
human hand. Disturbingly, there is no body
attached. Even more disturbing is the
discovery, a day later, of the matching hand
. . . Seconded to the Major Crime Investigation Unit in Bristol, is DI Jack Caffery. He
is looking for a man recently released from
prison, who sleeps rough and walks the
country roads as he relives the memories of
a terrifying crime. Caffery and Flea soon
establish that the hands belong to a boy who
has recently disappeared. Their investigation
leads them into the darkest recesses of
Bristol's underworld, where drug addiction is
rife, and where an ancient evil lurks: an evil
that feeds off the blood — and flesh — of
others . . .

MO HAYDER

RITUAL

Complete and Unabridged

CHARNWOOD
Leicester

First published in Great Britain in 2008 by
Bantam Press
an imprint of Transworld Publishers, London

First Charnwood Edition
published 2008
by arrangement with Transworld Publishers
The Random House Group Limited, London

The moral right of the author has been asserted

This book is a work of fiction and, except in the case of historical fact, any resemblance to actual persons, living or dead, is purely coincidental.

British Library CIP Data

Hayder, Mo
   Ritual.—Large print ed.—
   Charnwood library series
   1. Caffery, Jack (Fictitious character)—Fiction
   2. Police—England—Bristol—Fiction 3. Police
   divers—England—Bristol—Fiction 4. Missing
   persons—Investigation—England—Bristol—
   Fiction 5. Detective and mystery stories
   6. Large type books
   I. Title
   823.9′2 [F]

   ISBN 978–1–84782–463–9

Published by
F. A. Thorpe (Publishing)
Anstey, Leicestershire

Set by Words & Graphics Ltd.
Anstey, Leicestershire
Printed and bound in Great Britain by
T. J. International Ltd., Padstow, Cornwall

This book is printed on acid-free paper

To 'Adam'

Somewhere in the middle of the remote Kalahari desert in South Africa, nestling among the dry ochre veld, is a small weed-covered pool at the bottom of a crater. Ordinary except for its stillness — the casual observer wouldn't pay it much attention, wouldn't give it a second thought. Unless they were to swim in it. Or dip a toe into it. Then they'd notice something wrong. Something different.

First they'd notice the water was cold. Freezing, in fact. The sort of cold that doesn't belong to this planet. The sort of cold that comes from centuries and centuries of silence, from the most ancient recesses of the universe. And, second, they'd notice that it was almost empty of life, only a few colourless canefish living in it. Last, if they were foolish enough to try to swim in it they'd discover its fatal secret: there are no sides to this pool and no bottom — just a straight, cold line to the heart of the earth. Maybe that's when it would come to them, repeated over and over again over in the whispered ancestral languages of the Kalahari people, *This is the path to hell*.

This is Bushman's Hole. This is Boesmansgat.

1

13 May

Just after lunch on a Tuesday in May and nine feet under water in Bristol's 'floating harbour', police diver Sergeant 'Flea' Marley closed her gloved fingers round a human hand. She was half taken off-guard to find it so easily and her legs kicked a bit, whirring up silt and engine oil from the bottom, tipping her bodyweight back and upping her buoyancy so she started to rise. She had to tilt down and wedge her left hand under the pontoon tanks, then dump a little air from her suit so she was stabilized enough to get to the bottom and take a little time to feel the object.

It was pitch dark down there, like having her face in mud, no point in trying to see what she was holding. With most river and harbour diving everything had to be done by touch, so she had to be patient, allow the thing to feed its shape from her fingers up her arm, download an image in her mind. She palpated it gently, closing her eyes, counting the fingers to reassure herself it was human, then worked out which digit was which: the ring finger first, bent away from her, and from that she could figure out which way the hand was lying — palm upward. Her thoughts raced, as she tried to picture how the body

3

would be — on its side probably. She gave the hand an experimental tug. Instead of there being a weight behind it, it floated free of the silt, coming away easily. At the place where a wrist should be there was just raw bone and gristle.

'Sarge?' PC Rich Dundas said, into her earpiece. His voice seemed so close in the claustrophobic darkness that she startled. He was up on the quay, tracking her progress with her surface attendant who was meting out her lifeline and controlling the coms panel. 'How you doing there? You're bang over the hotspot. See anything?'

The witness had reported a hand, just a hand, no body, and that had bothered everyone in the team. No one had ever known a corpse to float on its back — decomposition saw to that, made them float face down, arms and legs dangling downwards in the water. The last thing to be visible would be a hand. But now she was getting a different picture: at its weakest point, the wrist, this hand had been severed. It was just a hand, no body. So there hadn't been a corpse floating, against all physical laws, on its back. But there was still something wrong about the witness statement. She turned the hand over, settling the mental picture of the way it was lying — little details she'd need for her own witness statement. It hadn't been buried. She couldn't even say it was buried in the silt. It was just lying on top of it.

'Sarge? You hear me?'

'Yeah,' she said. 'I hear you.'

She picked up the hand. She cupped it gently, and slowly let herself sink to hover above the silt

4

at the bottom of the harbour.

'Sarge?'

'Yeah, Dundas. Yeah. I'm with you.'

'Got anything?'

She swallowed. She turned the hand round so its fingers lay across her own. She should tell Dundas it was 'five bells'. A find. But she didn't. 'No,' she said, instead. 'Nothing yet. Not yet.'

'What's happening?'

'Nothing. I'm going to move along a bit here. I'll let you know when I've got something.'

'OK.'

She dug one arm into the muck at the bottom and forced herself to think clearly. First she pulled gently at the lifeline, dragging it down, feeling for the next three-metre tag. On the surface it would appear to be paying out naturally — it would look as if she was sculling along the bottom. When she got to the tag she sandwiched the line between her knees to keep up the pressure and lay down in the silt the way she taught the team to rest if they got a CO_2 overload, face down so the mask didn't lift, knees lightly in the sludge. The hand she held close to her forehead, as if she was praying. In her coms helmet there was silence, just a hiss of static. Now she'd got to the target she had time. She unplugged the mike from her mask, took a second to close her eyes and check her balance. She focused on a red spot in her mind's eye, watched it, waited for it to dance. But it didn't. Stayed steady. She kept herself very, very still, waiting, as she always did, for something to come to her.

'Mum?' she whispered, hating the way her voice sounded so hopeful, so hissy in the helmet. 'Mum?'

She waited. Nothing. As it always was. She concentrated hard, pressing lightly on the bones of the hand, making this stranger's piece of flesh seem half familiar.

'Mum?'

Something came into her eyes, stinging. She opened them, but there was nothing: just the usual stuffy blackness of the mask, the vague brownish light of silt dancing in front of the face-plate, and the all-enveloping sound of her breathing. She fought the tears, wanting to say it aloud: Mum, please help. I saw you last night. I did see you. And I know you're trying to tell me something — I just can't hear it properly. Please, tell me what you were trying to say.

'Mum?' she whispered, and then, feeling ashamed of herself, 'Mummy?'

Her own voice came back, echoing round her head, except this time, instead of *Mummy*, it sounded like *Idiot, you idiot.* She put her head back, breathing hard, trying hard not to let any tears come. What was she expecting? Why was it always here, under water, that she came to cry, the worst place — crying in a mask she couldn't pull off like sport divers could. Maybe it was obvious she'd feel closer to Mum somewhere like this, but there was more to it than that. Ever since she could remember, the water had been the place she could concentrate, feel a sort of peace floating up, as if she could open channels down here that she couldn't open on the surface.

She waited for a few minutes longer, until the tears had gone somewhere safe, and she knew she wouldn't blind herself or make a fool of herself when she surfaced. Then she sighed and help up the severed hand. She had to bring it close to her mask, had to let it brush the Perspex visor, because that was how close you had to get to things in this sort of visibility. And then, looking at the hand close up, she realized what else was worrying her.

She plugged in the coms lead. 'Dundas? You there?'

'What's up?'

She turned the hand, less than a centimetre from the visor, examining its greying flesh, its ragged ends. It had been an old guy who'd seen the hand. Just for a second. He'd been out with his toddler granddaughter who'd wanted to test-run new pink wellies in the storm. They'd been huddled under an umbrella, watching the rain land in the water when he'd seen it. And here it was — at the exact same hotspot he'd told the team it would be, tucked up under the pontoon. No way could he have seen it down here in this visibility. You couldn't see down five inches from the pontoon.

'Flea?'

'Yeah, I was thinking — anyone up there ever known it be anything other than nil vis down here?'

A pause while Dundas consulted the team on the quayside. Then he came back. 'Negative, Sarge. No one.'

'Definitely nil vis about a hundred per cent of the time, then?'

'I'd say that's a high likelihood, Sarge. Why?'

She placed the hand back on the floor of the harbour. She'd come back to it with a limb kit — no way could she swim to the surface with it and lose forensic evidence — but now she held on to the search line and tried to think. She tried to catch an idea of how the witness had been able to see it, tried to hold on to the idea and work it out, but she couldn't nail it. Probably something to do with what she'd got up to last night. That or she was getting older. Twenty-nine next month. Hey, Mum, how about that. I'm nearly twenty-nine. Never thought I'd get this far, did you?

'Sarge?'

She paid out the rope slowly, working against the surface attendant's pressure, making it look as if she was crawling back along the base of the quay. She adjusted the coms lead so the connection was secure.

'Yeah, sorry,' she said. 'Zoned out a bit there. Five bells, Rich. I've got the target. Coming up now.'

⋆　⋆　⋆

She stood on the harbour in the freezing cold, mask in her hand, her breath white in the air, and shivered while Dundas hosed her down. She'd been back down to recover the hand with the limb kit, the dive was over and this was the bit she hated, the shock of coming out of the water, the shock of being back with the sounds and the light and the people — and the air, like a slap in the face. It made her teeth chatter. And the harbour was dismal even though it was spring. The rain had stopped and now the weak afternoon sun picked out windows, the spiky cranes in the Great Western Dock opposite, oily rainbows floating on the water. They'd screened off an area of treated pine deck at the rear of a waterfront restaurant, the Moat, and her team in their fluorescent yellow surface jackets moved round the outdoor tables, sorting their gear: air cylinders, communications system, standby raft, body board — all laid out between the standing pools of rainwater on the deck.

'He was agreeing with you.' Dundas turned off the hose and nodded to the restaurant's plate-glass window where, his reflection smudged and dull, the crime-scene manager was looking down to where the hand lay at his feet in the opened yellow limb bag. 'He thinks you're right.'

'I know.' Flea sighed, putting down her mask and pulling off the two pairs of gloves all police divers wore for protection. 'But you'd never know it to look at him, eh?'

It wasn't the first, nor would it be the last body part she would fish out of the mud around Bristol, and except for what it said about the sadness and loneliness of death, usually a severed hand wasn't remarkable. There'd be an explanation for it, something depressing and mundane, probably suicide. The press often watched the police operation with their zoom lenses from the other side of the harbour, but today there was no one at Redcliffe wharf. It was just too commonplace even for them. Only she, Dundas

9

and the CSM knew that this hand wasn't commonplace at all, that when the press heard what had slipped by them they'd be tying themselves in knots to get an interview.

It wasn't decomposed. In fact, it was completely uninjured apart from the separation wound. So damn fresh all the alarm bells had gone off at once. She'd pointed it out to the CSM, asked how on earth it could have got separated from its owner when to look at it there was no way it had just come apart from the body, not without some very particular injury, and if she had to take a guess those didn't look like fish bites but blade marks on the bones. And he'd said he couldn't possibly comment before the post-mortem, but wasn't she clever? Too clever by half to be spending her life under the water.

'Anyone spoken to the harbour master?' Flea asked now, as her surface attendant helped her off with her harness and cylinders. 'Asked what flow's been through here today?'

'Yes,' said Dundas, bending to coil away the jetwash hose. She looked at the top of his head, at the vivid red beanie he always wore — otherwise, he said, he could heat a stadium with the warmth that came off his bald scalp. Under his fluorescent all-weather gear she knew he was tall and heftily built. Sometimes it was hard being a woman on her own, making decisions for nine men, half of them older than she was, but Dundas she never doubted. He was on her side through it all. A genius technician, he had a father's way with the staff and the gear, and, at times, a filthy, filthy mouth on him. Just now he was concentrating, and when he did that he was so good she could kiss him.

'There's been flow today, but not until after the sighting,' he said.

'The sluices?'

'Yeah. Open this afternoon for twenty minutes at fourteen hundred. The harbour master had the dredger come down from the feeder canal to offload for a bit.'

'And the call came in at?'

'Thirteen fifty-five. Just as they were opening the sluices. Otherwise the harbour master would've waited. In fact, I'm sure he'd have waited, when I think how much they love us down here. How they're always trying to bend over backwards for us.'

Flea hooked her fingers under the neoprene dry hood and rolled it up her neck, going gently over her face and head so it didn't snag too much, because whenever she inspected her hoods they always seemed to be full of hairs pulled out by the roots, little pearls of skin attached. Sometimes she wondered why she wasn't as bald as Dundas. She dropped the hood, wiped her nose and looked sideways across the water, up to Perrot's bridge, the sunlight splashing gold on the twin horns, beyond it St Augustine's Reach where the river Frome rose from underground and let into the harbour.

'I dunno,' she muttered. 'It sounds backwards to me.'

'What's that?'

11

She shrugged, looked at the piece of grey flesh on the deck between the two men's feet and tried to work out how the witness could have seen the hand. But it wasn't happening. Her head kept seesawing — trying to take her with it. She reached out and sank on to one of the chairs, her hand to her forehead, knowing the blood had gone out of her face.

'All right there, Flea, old girl? Christ, you're really not looking much of it.'

She laughed and ran her fingers down her face. 'Yeah, well, don't feel much of it.'

Dundas squatted down in front of her. 'What's going on?'

She shook her head, looked down at her legs in the black dry suit, at the pools of water gathering round her dive boots. She had more diving hours under her belt than any of the team, and she was supposed to be in charge so it was wrong, all wrong, what she'd done last night.

'Oh, nothing,' she said, trying to keep it light. 'Nothing, really. The usual — I just can't sleep.'

'Still crap, then?'

She smiled at him, feeling the light catch at the raindrops in her eyes. As the unit leader she was a trainer too, and that meant sometimes putting herself in the water, at the bottom of the chain of command, giving the others a chance to be dive supervisor. In her heart she didn't like it. In her heart she was only really happy on days like today when she'd put Dundas in as dive supervisor. He had a son — Jonah — a grown-up son who stole money from him and his ex-wife to feed a drug habit, yet gave his father all the feelings of guilt that Flea's brother Thom gave her, always. She and Dundas had a lot in common.

'Yeah,' she said eventually. 'It's still crap. Even after all this time.'

'Two years,' he said, putting a hand under her arm and helping her to stand up, 'is not a long time. But I can tell you one thing that'd help.'

'What?'

'*Eating* something for a change. Stupid thought, I know, but maybe it'd help you sleep.'

She gave him a weak smile and put a hand on his shoulder, letting him pick her up. 'You're right. I'd better eat. Is there anything in the van?'

2

The Station had been the police boathouse before it was sold and renovated, and because of that the new owner said it'd be all wrong if he couldn't return the favour now and let the police use it in their hour of need. He'd given them a room at the back of the restaurant, next to the kitchens, and it was warmer in there than in the van. It used to be the police locker room; now it was the staff's changing area. Their street clothes hung on hooks, outdoor boots and bags tucked underneath the bench that ran all the way round.

While Dundas went off to ferret in the kitchens, Flea slung down her black holdall and began to get undressed. She peeled the dry suit and the force-issue navy thermals down to her waist. Keeping the thermals on, she rolled the dry suit down to her ankles, kicking off the dive boots. She paused and stared at her feet because she was alone and could afford to. She flexed them and inspected the little part between her toes, rubbing at the flaps of skin, making them go red. Webs. Webbing on her feet like a frog. 'Frog girl', they should call her. She took the piece of skin between the big toe and the next one and dug in her nails. Pain bolted up her body and lit her brain white, but she held on. She closed her eyes and concentrated on it, letting the heat move round her veins. The force counsellor at their six-month meeting had told

14

Flea she needed to show someone her feet and talk about the way this problem had developed — and just remind me now? When did this skin appear? Was it about the time of the accident?

But she hadn't shown anyone. Not the counsellor, not the doctor. One day she'd need an operation, she supposed. She'd wait, though, until there was pain, or loss of movement, or something that might stop her diving.

A sound behind her, and she fumbled her socks out of her holdall and pulled them on quickly. Dundas came in holding a ciabatta wrapped in a flower-sprigged paper napkin, raising an eyebrow when he saw her sitting in her bra and rolled-down thermals, her hands wrapped protectively round her feet.

'Uh — maybe get some clothes on? The deputy SIO's coming down to tie things up. Told him where to find us.'

She pulled on a T-shirt, picked up a towel and began to rub her hair vigorously. 'Where's the SIO, then?'

'Got a meeting about Operation Atrium — not interested in us lollygagging around with a hand on the harbour front. Doesn't think the Major Crime Unit should be bothering with us. He was off twenty minutes ago.'

'I'm glad. Don't like him,' she said, thinking about the briefing earlier on. The on-call senior investigating officer had been okayish, but she'd never forgotten the look on his face when he'd first seen her at a dive briefing three years ago: just like all the other SIOs, sort of depressed because there he was, waiting for someone with a bit of authority, someone who'd answer the questions about the water, and what he got instead of reassurance was Flea — twenty-six and skinny, with lots of hair and these blue child's eyes that were so wide spaced she looked as if she wouldn't be able to open a bank account, let alone pull a dead body out of the mud under four metres of water. But they mostly did that to her, the senior ranks. At first it had been a challenge. Now it just pissed her off.

'Well?' She dropped the towel. 'Who's his deputy, then? Someone out of Kingswood?'

'Someone new. No one I've heard of.'

'What's his name?'

'Can't remember. One of those who sounds like a wasted old Irish soak. Old-school — beer and takeways. High blood pressure. Type who every year sends someone younger with a snide ID to do his bleep test for him.'

She smiled and peered down at her arms, flexing her biceps. 'Don't say the bleep word. Annual medical in two weeks' time.'

'Up to Napier Miles, is it, Sarge? Need to start eating, then.' He pushed the ciabatta at her. 'Protein drinks. Ice-cream. McDonald's. Look at you. Underweight is the new overweight — didn't you know?'

She took the sandwich and began to eat. Dundas watched her. It was funny the way he seemed protective of her when she was his boss. Dundas never wasted time lecturing his son. Instead he saved it for Flea. She chewed, thinking he was someone she could tell — explain what was really going on, explain what

16

had happened last night.

She was trying to sort out the words, get them into a line, when behind them the door opened and a voice said, 'You the divers? The ones pulled the hand up?'

A man in his mid-thirties, medium height, wearing a grey suit, stood in the doorway holding a cup of machine coffee. He had a determined sort of face and lots of dark hair cut short. 'Where is it, then?' he said, leaning inwards, one hand on the doorframe, looking round the changing room. 'There's no one on the quayside except your team.'

Neither of them spoke.

'Hello?'

Flea came back to herself with a jolt. She swallowed her mouthful and hastily wiped crumbs from her mouth with the back of her hand. 'Yeah, sorry. You are?'

'DI Jack Caffery. Deputy SIO. Who are you?'

'She's Flea,' Dundas said. 'Sergeant Flea Marley.'

Caffery gave him a strange look. Then he studied her, and she could see right away he was holding something in under his expression. She thought she knew what. Men didn't like working alongside a girl who just squeaked in at under five five in her diving boots. Either that or she had crumbs on her T-shirt.

'Flea?' he said. '*Flea?*'

'It's a nickname.' She got to her feet, holding out her hand to shake. 'The name's Phoebe Marley. Unit Sergeant Phoebe Marley.'

He looked down at her hand, as if it was

17

something alien. Then, as if he'd remembered where he was, he shook it firmly. He released it quickly, and the moment he did Flea stepped away, out of his space. She sat down and self-consciously brushed the front of her T-shirt, off balance again. That was something else that pissed her off. She wasn't very good around men. At least, not this sort of man. They made her think about things she'd put behind her.

'So?' he said. '*Flea*. Where's this hand you pulled out of the water?'

'Coroner's let it go,' said Dundas. 'Didn't anyone say?'

'No.'

'Well, he did. The CSM sent someone to Southmeads with it. But it won't be done till tomorrow.'

'Pull a lot of hands out of the water round here, then?'

'Yup,' said Dundas. 'Got a collection up at Southmeads. Feet, hands, a leg or two.'

'And where are they coming from?'

'Suicides, mostly. Down in the Avon nine times out of ten. She's got a tidal race on her like you've never seen — things get bashed around a bit, hit with trees, debris. Get pieces turning up round here, right, left and arsenal.'

Caffery shot his hand out from his suit sleeve and checked his watch. 'OK, then. I'm done here.'

He had the door open and was halfway out when he went a little still, his back to them, his hand on the door, facing out into the kitchen corridor, maybe feeling the two of them watching him silently.

He took a few beats, then turned back.

'What?' he said, looking from Dundas to Flea and back again. 'It's a suicide. What do you usually do with a suicide?'

'If we haven't got a hotspot? If we haven't got a witness?'

'Yeah?'

'We, uh, wait for it to float.' Flea went softly on the word 'float': in the team they used it so often they'd got easy with it, forgot sometimes what it meant: that a corpse had to get so full of decomposition gases it rose to the surface. 'We let it float, then do a surface snatch. In this weather that'd be in a couple of weeks' time.'

'That's what I thought. It's what they do in London.' He started to go again, but this time he must have seen Dundas throw a glance across at Flea, because he paused. He closed the door and came back into the room. 'OK,' he said slowly. 'You're trying to explain something to me. Only problem is, I haven't a clue what.'

Flea took a breath. She turned her chair, put her elbows on her knees and sat canted forward, meeting his eye. 'Didn't the CSM tell you? Didn't he say we don't think it's a suicide?'

'You just said you get a million suicides out here.'

'Yes — in the Avon. If it was in the Avon we'd understand it. But it's not. This was in the harbour.'

She got up and stood, half holding the chair as if it would protect her. She didn't show it, but

19

she was conscious of the way he was tall and sort of lean under his suit. She knew if she got closer she'd stare or something, because she'd already noticed a few things about him — like the point above his collar where his five o'clock shadow started. 'We're not the pathologists,' she said. 'We shouldn't be telling you anything. But something's not right.' She licked her lips and glanced sideways at Dundas. 'I mean, first off it's been in the water less than a day. A body's not ready to come to bits in rough water until a long, long time after it's floated. This one's way too fresh for that.'

Caffery put his head on one side, raised his eyebrows.

'Yes. And if it was wildlife chewed it off — fish, the harbour rats, maybe — there'd be bites all over it. There aren't any. The only injury is . . . ' she held up her hand and circled a thumb and finger round her wrist ' . . . is here. Right here where it came away from the arm. The CSM's with me on all of this.'

Caffery stood in front of her, looking at her hair and her thin arms in the thermals. She hated it. She never quite felt her skin was on properly when she was surface-side, where other people did sophisticated things with their relationships — and that was why she'd always be better under the water. Mum, she thought, Mum, you'd know how to do this. You'd know to look normal, not surly like me.

'Well?' he said, studying her thoughtfully. 'What could have made an injury like that?'

'Could have been a boating accident, maybe.

But those happen further out — in the estuary. Then there's people coming off Clifton Bridge. Suicide Bridge, we call it. If someone takes a dive round here, nine times out of ten it's off there. They can get dragged up and down the river and sometimes, *sometimes*, if the tide's right, they'll get washed quite a long way upstream.' She shrugged. 'I suppose theoretically if they'd come off the bridge, got cut by a boat out in the river, a stray hand might've *just* got past the stop gates, ended up in the harbour. Or come up through the Cut.' She pushed her hair behind her ears. 'But no. That's impossible.'

'Impossible,' said Dundas. 'It's about a million to one. And even if it came from the Frome River or higher up the Avon, down through Netham lock and into the feeder canal . . . '

' . . . it would only have happened if there was flow in the harbour, which is usually when the sluice gates are open.'

'Which happened only once in the last two days. After the sighting was called in. We checked.'

'You're saying it was dumped?'

'We're not saying anything. Not our job.'

'But it was dumped?'

They exchanged a glance. 'It's not our job,' they said simultaneously.

Caffery looked from Flea to Dundas and back. 'OK,' he said. 'It was dumped.' He checked his watch again. 'Right — so what shifts are you two on today? What do I need to do to keep you in the water?'

'Oh, I shouldn't worry about that if I were

you.' Dundas smiled, getting his all-weather gear off the hook and pulling it on. 'We haven't signed off with the harbour master yet. And, anyway, we're always interested in overtime. Aren't we, Sarge?'

3

25 November

All he's ever wanted to do is get off the gear. It'd sound crazy to anyone who's seen him spending 100 per cent of his time and energy on scoring to hear that actually what he wants, what he really wants more than anything, is to see a way through it all and get clean. It's November and he's standing with Bag Man, the one they call 'BM', in the shadow of the tower block, over by the waste disposals where most of the dealing is done. A grey autumn wind is whipping up the litter and the plastic bags. BM is wearing a grey hoodie with 'Malcolm X' written on the breast pocket, even though he's white, and Mossy is raging because BM's just told him there's no more credit.

'What?' Mossy says, because he and BM have serious history and there's no reason for him to go cold like this so suddenly. 'What the fuck're you talking about?'

'Sorry,' BM says, looking at him really straight. ''S all gone too far. Can't help you this time, man, not any more. This is the end of the line.' He pinches Mossy's arm and pulls him closer. 'It's time you got yourself into counselling.'

'Counselling? What d'you mean, counselling?'

'Don't push me, mate. Given you a tip. Don't push me more.'

Mossy does try, though, just a bit more, tries to convince BM to give him something, just a little something. But BM's determined and digs in his heels, and in the end the only avenue for Mossy is to slouch away, half thinking about killing BM and half thinking about what he's said about counselling. He surprises himself to find that by the afternoon he's in the West of the City, going into a counselling session in a weird little clinic with an old woman receptionist who is honestly totally scary. One day this action alone, the action of walking into that clinic, will be enough for Mossy to blame everything on BM.

The session's weird. Everyone dotted around the room — not meeting each other's eyes. One of them's got a two-litre bottle of spring water and keeps sucking it like it'll save his life. Mossy sits there with his elbows on his knees and pretends to be interested in them, talking in their monotones about how life isn't fair, because that's what he's noticed about people on H. They always feel self-pity and he hopes he doesn't sound like that. But all the time he's looking at them, what he's really wondering is whether one has some gear and which one'll feel sorry enough for him to share a bit. So he wheels out the story — like how he was abused by his uncle, how he learned to jack up when he was thirteen, and all the stuff with the drug treatment and testing orders he's served and the prostitution and how that came really early, when he wasn't even fifteen, and he rambles on, even though he can feel the moderator, a worked-out guy who got clean years ago and owes something to society, staring at him, staring into his eyes, and Mossy thinks he's getting sympathy here, thinks he's maybe the only one here who has a really good reason to be this hooked. But then, when he's finished, the moderator goes: 'Mossy? Mossy? Where'd you get a name like that?'

He shrugs. 'Dunno. Mates made it up. Cos I'm skin and bones, me, like that model. Y'know, Kate Moss.'

There's a bit of a silence and no one looks at him, except the moderator, who stares a bit more.

'You don't think that could be considered offensive?' he goes, and there's sort of a note in his voice that Mossy knows is all wrong, like a warning. So it's time to get out, and he mumbles something about not meaning to offend no one, and waits for the subject to change. Then he gets up, quiet as he can, stashes the plastic chair against the wall, and goes outside. He walks away from the clinic, lights a roll-up and finds a place a little down the road where he can see the front of the clinic and everyone coming out of the doors, and he waits, feeling the cramps coming slowly through him from front to back. They're the worst of the agonies, the cramps, the first to come and the last to leave. He sits down and hugs his belly, wondering if there's a karsi round here. It's a warm day and that helps, and if he keeps humming it'll take his mind off it.

After a while the doors open. He can feel the moderator staring at him, but he's not going to be intimidated, so he waits while the others come out. He's like a hyena, picking off the softest-looking ones who go round the edge of the pack, the ones who'll fall for a story — you can spot them, something about the hope in their eyes: like they really believe people can be redeemed. Mossy waits till they pass, then falls into stride next to them, hands in his pockets, head down a little so he can sway it a little sideways and mutter, 'Got anything to help me, there? Hmm? Just a little? I'll pay you back. Can promise you that.' But they mutter and cross the road heads down, like they don't want to be seen with him, leaving him standing there, the sweats starting, and the itching, and when he walks back to his spot he can feel his kneebones rubbing each other raw. Is that because he's too thin or is it something else? Is it because of something weird his skin is doing?

When they've disappeared he tries to bum some money from a passer-by, but she walks past, eyes on the distance, so after a while he decides to go down the docks, see if there's anything happening down there. Maybe one of them from the Barton Hill estate'll be there in a good mood. If not, he'll think again.

He's just got up and is ambling along when it happens. One minute he's on his own thinking bad thoughts, next minute, walking next to him is this tiny, skinny black guy with his hair real tight against his skull and a bit of a moustache. He's wearing jeans that've been factory faded

down the front of the legs and an olive-green
Kappa jacket, the hood sort of draped round
his head, and Mossy recognizes him from
the counselling session — he was sitting in the
corner. But the main thing Mossy notices is
the way he walks: like he's oiled. Like he wasn't
born here on the dry Bristol streets, but in a
better place. Like he's used to walking the bush
day after day after day.

'You looking for something?' he goes. 'You
looking for something?'

Mossy stops. 'Yeah,' he goes, 'but I'm skint.'

And what's weird is that instead of the whack
to the head he expects the skinny guy looks
Mossy in the eyes and says, 'No worries about
the money. No worries. I know someone who
can help you.'

And that, of course, is how it all starts.

4

13 May

The late sun had come out from behind the clouds, red and a bit swollen, but in the Station restaurant the table lights were already on. The place was filling up, people coming in, taking off coats, ordering drinks. It was too cool to sit outside and the deck was deserted, so Caffery went out to make his phone calls. There was the super to push a bit, talk him into taking seriously what the dive unit and the CSM were saying, assign a level to the case before the post-mortem — because there was going to be a postmortem for the hand, all on its own — and there were the two DSs over at Kingswood to move around a bit. They'd been given to him to work on an armed-robbery case so now he threw in a little extra: hospital casualty and mortuary duty. Any male corpses turned up missing a right hand?

When he'd rattled a couple of Bristol's cages he put his phone into his pocket and went to the point on the deck where he could see round the police screens to the dive crew readying themselves on the deck of the neighbouring restaurant. The Moat, it was called. He liked that — the *Moat* — as if it was something medieval and not just a spivved-up boathouse with a bit of fake taxidermy on the walls. Someone had talked

28

the manager into not opening for the evening, and the team had dumped their gear on the deck. It lay around in pools of water. Picking her way among it, bending to hook up a dive mask, stopping to talk to her surface attendant and check the harness, was Sergeant Marley.

He leaned on the balustrade, rolled a ciggy — a habit he still hadn't been able to break, in spite of the way the government sat on his head about it whenever he switched on the TV — and lit it, watching her carefully. 'Flea' — stupid nickname, except that he sort of understood where it had come from. Even in the force-issue dry suit she had something kind of kinetic about her, something in her face that suggested her thoughts didn't stay still for long. He hated the way he'd noticed these things about her. He hated the way, when he'd gone into the staff room and she'd been sitting there with her dry suit crumpled down and her thin brown arms bare, and her wayward stack of blonde hair all tough as if she'd washed it in sea water, he hated the way he'd wanted to leave, because suddenly all he could feel was his body. The way it made contact with his clothes, the way his trousers scratched against his thighs, the brush of his waistband against his stomach and the places his shirt touched his neck. He had to stop himself. That was for someone else. Another person in a different place, a long time ago.

''Scuse me?'

He looked over his shoulder. A small woman was standing behind him. She had bright red hair tied with multicoloured rags into lots of little bunches all over her head. A waitress from the Station, by the apron round her waist.

'Yes?'

'Uh — ' She wiped her nose and glanced over her shoulder into the restaurant to make sure she wasn't being watched. 'Am I allowed to ask what's happening?'

'You're allowed.'

She crossed her arms and shivered, even though it wasn't that cold out here, really not cold enough to make you shiver. 'Well, then . . . have they found anything?'

Something about her voice made him turn and look at her a little more carefully. She was small and thin, wearing under the apron black combats and a T-shirt that said, *I love you more when you're more like me.*

'Yes,' he said. 'They have.'

'Under the pontoon?'

'Yes.'

She pulled a chair off the table and sat down on it, putting her hands on the table. Caffery watched her. There were two rings in her nose and from the way the holes were inflamed he guessed she fiddled with them when she was anxious. 'You all right?' he said. He stubbed out the roll-up, pulled up a chair and sat opposite her, his back to the Moat. 'Something on your mind?'

'You wouldn't believe me if I told you,' she said. 'I mean, I can see by your face you wouldn't believe me.'

'Try me?'

She twisted her mouth and regarded him

30

thoughtfully. She had very pale eyes, anaemic lashes. A cluster of spots round her nose had been covered with make-up. 'God.' She put her hands to her face, suddenly embarrassed. 'I mean, even *I* know it sounds *mental*.'

'But you want to tell me. Don't you?'

There was a pause. Then, as he'd expected, she put her hand up and started twiddling one of the rings in her nose, round and round and round, until he thought she was going to make it bleed. The only sounds were the water lapping at the quay, the dive crew clinking harnesses and cylinders. After a long time she dropped her hand and lifted her chin in the direction of the pontoon outside the Moat.

'I saw something. Really late one night. Standing over in front of the Moat. Just where those divers are now.'

'Something?'

'OK. Some*one*. I suppose you'd say *someone*, although I really don't know for sure.' She shivered again. 'I mean, it was really dark. Not like it is now. Late. And I mean really late. We'd closed and someone'd puked all over the ladies' floor and who d'you suppose gets to clean up when that happens? I was walking through the restaurant with a bucket, on the way to the broom cupboard, and I was just crossing inside there, near the window . . . ' She pointed into the Station restaurant to where a few diners had noticed the police screens and were craning their necks to work out what was happening. The sun was nearly touching the horizon now and he could see his and the girl's reflections on top of them, silhouetted in a blaze of red. 'And as I get to that table something makes me stop. And that's when I see him.'

Caffery could hear the thickened clicking of the girl's breathing in her throat.

'He was naked — I saw that straight away.'

'He?'

'My boyfriend reckons it was some traveller's kid. Sometimes they find their way down to the banks of the Cut. You can see them from the road, camped behind the warehouses with their washing out. My boyfriend said a kid because he was so tiny. He'd of only come up to here.' She held out her hand in mid-air to indicate a height of just over a metre. 'And he was black. Really, y'know, jet black, which is why I can't see it. Can't see him being a pikey.'

'How old, then? Five? Six?'

But she was shaking her head. 'No. That's just it. That's just what I told my BF. He wasn't young. Not at all. I mean, he was small, like a kid. But he wasn't a child. I saw his face. Just a glimpse, but it was enough for me to see that he wasn't a child. He was a man,' she said. 'A weird, weird-looking man. That's what's so effing freaky about it — that's why I know you're not going to believe me. That and . . . '

'That and?'

'And what he was doing.'

'What was he doing?'

'Oh . . . ' She fiddled with the ring again. Moved her head from side to side, not looking at him. 'Oh, you know . . . '

'No.'

'The usual — you know — what men do. Had his thing — you know.' She cupped her hand on the table. 'Had it out like this.' She gave an embarrassed laugh. 'But he wasn't just — you know, just some old wanker. I mean it must've been some kind of a trick, because this *thing* he had ... it must have been something he'd strapped on cos it was ... *ridiculous*. Ridiculously big.' She looked at him now, sort of angry, as if he'd said he didn't believe her. 'I'm not joking, you know. And I could tell he wanted whoever was in the Moat to look at it. Like he was trying to shock them.'

'And was anyone in there? Any lights on?'

'No. It was, like, two in the morning. Later I was sort of thinking about it and I thought maybe he was looking at himself in the reflection. You know — in the window? With the lights off inside he'd have been able to watch himself.'

'Maybe.'

In his head Caffery played it back: the restaurant deserted, the only illumination the coloured light of the optics and the Coors sign above the bar; outside the lights from Redcliffe Quay and the reflections in the water; a section of darkness between the river and the restaurant. He imagined the girl's blurred outline in the window as she walked across the floor with the bucket. He saw her face, white and shocked, ears tuning in to a small sound, eyes swivelling to focus out into the dark night. He saw a child's silhouette against the orange sky watching itself naked in a plate-glass window. A Priapus.

'Where do you think he came from?'

'Oh, the water,' she said, sounding surprised he hadn't figured that out yet. 'Yeah — that was where he came from. The water.'

'You mean in a boat?'

'No. He came out of the water. Swam.'

'To the pontoon?'

'I didn't see him arrive, but I knew that's where he'd come from because he was wet — just dripping. And that's where he went afterwards. Back in the water over there. There, where that red thing is now. Really quick it was, *he* was — like an eel.'

Caffery turned. She was pointing to the red marker buoy in the water. Sergeant Marley — Flea — must be underneath it by now, because the surface crew were standing on the pontoon peering down into the water. There was a life line snaking up out of the water to the surface attendant and Dundas was talking in a low voice into the coms panel, but it was a struggle to imagine anyone was down there: the water was smooth, featureless, reflecting the red sky. Someone had brought out a 'dead stretcher', a rigid orange polyurethane block, and it lay expectantly on the decking ready to be thrown in. There was a weird silence hanging over the scene in the fading light — as if they were all listening to the water, waiting to see something shoot out of it. A human that looked like a man but was small enough to be a child, maybe. A human that moved like an eel.

Caffery turned back to the girl with the red hair. Her eyes were watering now, as if she was reliving the fear, as if she was remembering something dark and wet slipping silently into the water.

'I know,' she said, seeing his expression. 'I know. It was the weirdest thing I've ever seen. I watched it for a while, moving along the wall and then . . . '

'And then?'

'It went under. Under the water without leaving a ripple. And I never saw it again.'

★   ★   ★

Flea and her unit did more than just dive: along with normal support-unit duties, riot control and warrant enforcement, they were trained in confined-space searches and chemical and biological clear-up. The spin-off of knowing how to use all that protective clothing was that if ever a rotting corpse turned up in the area — in or out of the water — Flea's team was drafted in to remove it. They'd got so good at moving decomposed corpses that in December 2004 they'd been sent to Thailand to work on the disaster-victim identification exercise: in ten days the team recovered almost two hundred bodies.

People couldn't believe she coped with it. Especially after the tsunami, they said. Didn't she have nightmares? Not really, she replied. And, anyway, we get counselling. Then they asked if she needed to do it, and wasn't pulling rotting bodies out of pipes and drains just wasting her talent? Surely, if she only had a word with her inspector and put in for her 'aide'

35

transfer to CID, she could be in plain clothes. Wouldn't that be nice?

She didn't answer. They didn't know she couldn't give it up. They didn't know that since her parents' accident the only time she could think straight was when she'd been able to return someone's body to the family, knowing that somewhere some mother or father or son or daughter could get a bit further along their recovery. And the diving — over everything it was the diving. Without the diving — which she'd been doing all her life with her family — she'd never get up in the morning. Under water was the only place she was herself.

Except now, because this evening even under water she was uneasy. The water in the harbour had settled a bit and she was getting vague visual references if she used her torch. Submerged shapes began to appear in the murk; landmarks she recognized; a submerged heating tank chucked off one of the boats a month ago; a car about ten metres to her left — a Peugeot with its windscreen and tax disc still visible in the murk if you got close enough. It was an insurance jobbie, pushed in near the Ostrich Inn before the slip had been blocked. It had been there for almost six months before the dredger arm clunked against it one February morning. She'd searched and stropped it as a favour for the harbour master — now he was waiting for the crane to be serviced so he could lift it.

But even though it was all familiar and straightforward — like a hundred other speculative searches she'd done — it didn't stop a weird apprehension settling round her as she worked. Some people said the harbour was strange: they talked about weird entrances that led from the bed out into a deeper underworld, like the bricked-over ancient moat that disappeared under Castle Green, joining the river Frome a quarter of a mile away in a dark, secret junction ten feet underground. But she'd dived it a hundred times before and she knew it wasn't that making her shaky. And it wasn't the deputy SIO either, even though she hated the way he looked at her, as if she was a kid, going straight through all her professional stuff and reminding her just how scary life was and how stupidly *young* she'd felt since the accident — even that wasn't enough to make her feel like this. No. In her heart she knew where this creepy feeling was coming from: it was from what she'd done last night in Dad's study.

She tried not to think about it, working in the soupy water. They'd chosen a jackstay search pattern, pinning a shot line at each side of the harbour because it was narrow enough at this point, then stringing a diagonal line between the two and moving along it, sweeping with a free hand. She'd been working the pattern for almost forty minutes — too long, really. Not that she cared, but it was dark surface-side, she could tell that from the colour of the water, and Dundas should have pulled her out by now. She wasn't going to undermine the authority she'd given him, but she was tired now of swimming to and fro, moving the jackstay weight a metre along the harbour wall, then turning, keeping the line on her left as she sculled her way back, working slowly, hugging the bottom, dredging with her hands in a one-metre arc.

A defensive tactile search it was called, tactile because you did everything by touch, and defensive because you expected any minute to find something hazardous — broken glass, fishing line. Sometimes the last thing you expected to find was what you were looking for. A foot. Or hair. Once, the first contact she'd had with a corpse had been its nostrils — both fingers up them. You couldn't have managed that if you'd tried, said Dundas. Another time she'd dragged a piece of industrial-pipe lagging to the surface, sweating and swearing, one hundred per cent certain it was the leg of a thirty-year-old gym instructor who'd gone off Clifton Bridge a week earlier. Everything got upside down when you were weighted to neutral buoyancy and could see only a few inches in front of you. When she hit the shotline under the pontoon, only two metres from where she'd found the hand, it was a weird relief.

Moving slowly because she was starting to tire now, she hauled the weight out of the mud, moved it along a metre and dropped it again. She had made it secure and was checking the line was tight ready for the return journey when something happened that made goosebumps break out all over her. It was the weirdest thing. She didn't see anything, and afterwards she wouldn't even be able to swear she'd felt anything, but suddenly, for a reason she couldn't explain, she was certain someone else was in the water with her.

She twisted round, ripping out her ankle knife and jamming her back against the wall. Breathing hard she clutched the shotline and, moving her feet a little, steadied herself with the knife out in front of her, ready for something to come hurtling at her.

'Rich?' she said shakily, into the coms mic.

'Yeah?'

'See anyone else in the water?'

'Uh — no. Don't think so. Why?'

'I dunno.' She kept herself upright by sculling her hand a little, stopping the water twisting her back to the wall. The air in her suit tried to rise to the surface, gathering round her neck, pressing on her and making her light-headed. 'Think I've seen a ghost.'

'What's up?'

'Nothing. Nothing,' she said. Her head was thudding now. The shot buoy was meant to take a human's weight and she could haul herself up it in a second if anything came at her. But her training stopped her bolting for the surface and she waited, breathing hard, eyes scanning the gloom, moving the knife in a defensive circle around her. Bristol harbour, she told herself. Only Bristol harbour. And she hadn't actually seen a thing. Minutes ticked by. The needle on her SPG contents gauge moved minutely, and slowly, slowly, when nothing happened and her pulse and breathing began to return to normal, she pushed the knife back into her ankle garter. It was last night and Dad's study catching up with her again. This wasn't funny. Not at all. She steadied herself and tipped down from the waist so the air returned to her legs and she wasn't being squeezed any more round the neck. She let a moment or two pass, the silt swirling round her.

'Dundas?' she said. 'You there?'

'You all right, Sarge?'

'No. No, I'm not.' *I'm having hallucinations, Rich. Paranoia. The whole works.* 'You've dived me for forty minutes,' she said at last. 'I think it's time to pull me out. Don't you?'

5

Dad's study had been locked since the accident. Flea had always known where the key was — hanging on the nail in the pantry — it was just that she'd never found the courage to use it. Two years had passed since the accident and still she couldn't bring herself to go into the place Dad used to retreat to think. In the early days after the accident, her brother Thom would go in there to think, to reflect on what had happened, but now he wouldn't come near it, wouldn't even go in and help her sort everything out. Everyone knew how hard Thom had taken their parents' loss, even harder than Flea had, and maybe, when you thought about what had happened to him in the accident, it wasn't a surprise he refused even to say the words: *Mum and Dad . . .*

In the end she'd had to do it alone. It was a sunny Tuesday morning two days before the hand was found in the harbour. The television was on in the kitchen and she was in the pantry searching the back of the shelves for an old flour canister, a blue and white bakeware tin with a sieve in the lid that Mum always used for making sponges. She was stretching forward when something made her look sideways, and there, glinting at her, was the key. She stood for a moment, her arms pushed into the back of the cool darkness, her eyes rolled sideways, looking at it. For a moment it seemed to be communicating something to her — fanciful, she knew. Nevertheless she decided right there and then that it was telling her the time had come.

The house her parents had lived in for thirty years was ramshackle, spreadeagled. Four eighteenth-century stone-workers' dwellings joined together, it rambled along the side of a remote country road for almost sixty feet, a stone-flagged corridor running down its spine. The study was at the end of the corridor, and when she got there she was a little shaky on her feet. She stopped at the door, feeling like Alice in Wonderland with the key lodged in her palm, the other hand resting on the door, her nose pressing against it, breathing in the smoky waxed musk of the wood. Dad never encouraged the children to go in, but she knew what the room on the other side of the door looked like: stone-built, open beams, her father's books covering all three walls from floor to ceiling. There was an old-fashioned librarian's stool he'd push along with his foot — she could see him now, the spectacles he'd mended with Araldite sliding down his nose as he peered at the spines of his books.

With all this in her head that morning she was prepared for what happened when she put the key in the lock and turned it. She was prepared for the way she was picked up by the scruff of her neck and thrown back to her childhood. It was the air: warm and sweat-stained, tinted with turpentine and resin, pipe tobacco and heather coming out of the books, the way Dad'd always smell when he came in from the garden on an autumn day. Inhaling it was like inhaling her father's last breath. Then she saw the librarian's stool against the bottom shelf and the way the battered wing chair was pushed slightly back from the desk as if he'd stood up only a few moments ago, and she leaned into the doorframe, pressing her teeth together until they creaked to stop the tears.

Eventually she pushed herself away from the door and went to the desk, halting briefly as if Dad might be there, saying, 'Not when I'm working, Flea. Go and help your mother.' The sun was coming through the gaps in the shutters, striking the back of the chair, and when she put her hands there the leather was slightly greasy and warm, like the skin of her hands. The old draughts set, its cheap balsa wood pieces painted in scagliola to resemble marble, sat in the centre of the desk where Dad used to play against himself late into the night.

She wasn't methodical by nature — it was how she'd got her nickname, jumping at things — but her training in the job had helped and when she began to search Dad's study she did it as she'd do a forensic retrieval with the unit: systematically, in silence, cross-legged on the floor as the grandfather clock ticked in the hallway outside and the neighbours' horses whickered from the fields. In every corner of the room there were boxes crammed with journals, notes and projector slides, faculty photographs of Dad, owlish in a corduroy jacket; four sealed boxes of books marked with his best friend Kaiser Nduka's name. When she'd finished searching, almost everything she'd found was exactly what she'd have expected of Dad.

Almost everything.

Because among the detritus and dust there were two things she hadn't expected. Two things she couldn't explain.

The first was a small safe. Pushed under the desk so it was hard up against the wall, it was the old-fashioned sort with a brass Yale dial lock. Unopenable. She tried every number sequence she could think of — Mum's birthday, Dad's birthday, her birthday, Thom's, her parents' wedding anniversary. She even got an old mathematical book down from the shelves and leafed her way through integer sequences, trying them at random: the Wythoff Array, the Para-Fibonacci sequence. But the safe wouldn't budge, so in the end she pushed it aside and turned back to the other thing she'd found: a purple brocade jewellery roll of her mother's pushed into the back of the desk drawer.

Inside, there was a ziplock freezer bag, and the second she unwrapped it she knew what it contained — she recognized them from the drugs warrants she'd executed over the years. Mushrooms, wispy shrivelled things huddled together like tiny dry ghosts. There must have been hundreds — enough to give real weight to the jewellery roll. She opened the bag and tipped them out into her skirt. They came with a scattering of small fibres, spreading across the fabric, and as they did a memory lifted into her head.

It was a picture of Dad, lying on his back on

the sofa, his hands resting on his chest, a cushion on his face to shut out the light. He'd lie like that for hours on end, not speaking or moving, as if he was sleeping. Except he wasn't sleeping. There was something too unsettled about him for sleep. It was something else. Now, poking the mushrooms, she wondered if she was beginning to understand. So, Dad, she thought, was *this* what it was for you all that time? And I never guessed.

She sat looking at the mushrooms for a long time. Then, when the grandfather clock struck eleven, something big locked into place in the back of her head. She got to her feet and shovelled them back into the ziplock bag, put it into the velvet jewellery roll and got to her feet. Picking up the safe she went to the kitchen, put everything on the shelf, then stood for a few moments at the window, staring out. Her mouth was dry, her head was thudding, because she knew, as sure as she knew the smell of her own father, that she was going to take the mushrooms too.

★   ★   ★

Now, standing next to the underwater recovery unit's Mercedes van at the head of the slip, the arc-lights fizzing and popping as the team wandered around, Flea could still feel the sickly psilocybin moving through her system. Even when, at eight, they called a halt because everyone was too knackered and the Health and Safety lot would tap her on the shoulder if they got wind she'd worked the men these hours, even then she found it difficult to turn away from the harbour — from the mesmerizing pull of the water and the eerie sense that something nasty was going to come out of it.

The team had gathered at the van and were coiling the yellow and blue umbilicals, packing up the surface supply panel. DI Caffery stood a few feet away, just inside the shadows, arguing on his mobile: she could hear most of the conversation — he was speaking with the SIO who was already pissed off that he'd taken all this extra dive unit time without waiting for the pathologist to confirm that the hand had been cut off.

She turned away tiredly, a bit irritated. Her team had knocked themselves out. They'd searched the whole of Welshback: under the houseboats, even into the vaulted foundations of the bonded warehouses opposite, finding every-thing down there from mobile phones, pairs of knickers, tables and chairs from the bars on the front to a decommissioned gun. Four divers had clocked up ninety minutes each; they'd covered a sixty-metre section of the harbour. But, and she knew she was the only one who noticed this, it wasn't enough for DI Caffery. She could tell he was disappointed in her, let down that she couldn't work a miracle when it was her unit who'd set him out on this wild-goose chase. When at last she'd closed the doors of the Mercedes and seen the team on their way, she couldn't help it — she couldn't let him go away thinking she'd failed: she caught up with him as he made his way back to the car.

'Look,' she said, in a voice more apologetic-sounding than she'd meant it to be, 'I suppose there's a chance the rest of the body could have shifted.'

'Yeah?' he said. She had to walk fast to keep up with him, splashing through foul-smelling puddles at the front of the restaurant because he didn't break step. 'Meaning?'

'Uh, meaning there was flow-through here today — they had the sluices open — so I suppose theoretically it could have shifted down into the upper harbour.' As she said it she knew it was bullshit. She'd never in her six years in the unit known a body to do that. It was pretty much physically impossible. 'It's a big jump to make, I grant you, but if you really want to keep at it we could be back here in the morning.'

'Sure,' he said, without even taking time to think about it. He swung into a junky old car, badly parked across the entrance to the restaurant and put the key into the ignition. 'That's good,' he said, through the open window. 'See you at first light, then.'

He started the engine and he was off. No goodbye, just a quick swerve out into the deserted road. The headlights disappeared and then she was alone on the quayside, except for the two uniforms out of Broadbury patrolling the sealed-off area in the distance. She stood for a moment, in the silence, realizing that her feet were wet and greasy from the puddle, that she was shivering and tired, but most of all realizing how totally pissed off she was. Not so much

47

pissed off with DI Caffery as with herself. A body shifting along the harbour floor? Yeah, right. Christ, what a sap.

★ ★ ★

The hallucinations the day before had come on like an electrical storm. At first there had been nothing. Not even the elevated pulse she'd expected. Flea had taken the mushrooms at eleven thirty. A full hour had gone by and she was about to get up from her father's sofa and go into the kitchen to make toast, when something made her start. She'd had the impression of a firework exploding outside the window, somewhere in the blue sky high over the spires of Bath.

She sat up and turned to the window, and as she did, she spotted something else, a movement behind her in the shadow: a vague smear of colour, as if something in the study was reaching out a hand for the back of her neck. When she turned there was nothing, only the patches of sunlight dancing on the wall. For a while she sat looking stupidly at it. And then, suddenly, she was laughing. She leaned back, the laughter huge in her mouth, bigger than her tongue, bigger than her throat. And that was how it started.

She couldn't have said when the hallucinations reached their peak, how long into the trip it was, but at one point she knew who she was and where she was and that she'd taken a drug and that things were happening, and the next moment her face was hard against the sofa, and the fabric, so close to her eyes, was magnified a hundred times, the weave like the trunks of trees. She could smell mothballs and see a small dot of white, probably a stray thread in the sofa, but suddenly it was big and she could see it wasn't a thread, it was her mother in the trees, dressed in jeans and a T-shirt, a floral scarf round her head, squatting down to inspect a patch of dog violet.

Flea's mouth moved against the rough fabric, a word coming out: '*Mum?*' It sounded so far off, her own voice — as if it was coming from a distant hill — but Jill Marley heard it. She turned, looking into the trees questioningly, not quite seeing her daughter. Her expression was unmistakably sad — Flea could tell from the straight set to her mouth, the reflection in her eyes.

'Oh, Mum.' Her throat tightened. She reached up a hand to touch the image. 'Mum? What is it?'

Jill stared into the trees. Then, slowly, cautiously, because still she couldn't see her daughter, she began to speak. Flea knew what she was saying was very important, and she strained forward to listen, but at that moment the image faded and Flea was back where she remembered being before, on the sofa, the fabric against her cheek and nothing left of the hallucination but the notion, so clear it was like the wind or the swell of the sea, that the words Mum had been about to say were: 'You looked in the wrong place. We went the other way.'

We went the other way.

Lying on the sofa, the late sun streaming

through the gaps in the shutters on to her red eyelids, she knew, without having to question it, that her mother could only have been talking about one thing.

She was talking about the accident.

6

25 November

Turns out not to be a blow-job that Skinny's after. Turns out he's got other things on his mind. He takes Mossy to a small car park next to a row of garages and they get into a beat-up old Peugeot where Skinny gives him a hit of gear so good it makes him want to cry.

'Let me put this on?' Skinny asks, after a while, when he can see the H is working on Mossy. He holds up an eye mask, the sort you see them wearing in ads for long-haul airlines. 'I'm going to take you somewhere — take you to meet someone who can help you. But him want you to wear this thing. Him not want you see where him live. What do you want? Do you want to wear it or not?'

Mossy takes it from Skinny and dangles it from his finger, smiling at it. One thing everyone always says about Mossy is that he's not afraid to take a chance. 'Someone's going to 'help' me?'

'Yes. What you want? Money? Or more H? Plenty good H, eh?'

Mossy has this picture suddenly, of being driven off to a wasteland and having a bullet in the back of his head. Then he thinks about money, and the suicidal part of him thinks, What the fuck? He snaps the mask round his head and lies back in the seat. 'Go on, then,' he says, still smiling. 'Start the show.'

There's a few moments' silence, and he wonders whether to take the mask off, then the car shifts and the door opens and slams and the other door opens and he realizes Skinny has got out of the front and into the back with him. 'Hey? What're you doing?' But he feels Skinny's hands on his face, he can feel the calloused fingertips like they're made out of hemp rope, and the fingers smoothing the mask down, holding it tight. He doesn't reach up to stop Skinny. He just waits in the silence, and there they sit until he hears footsteps and someone else gets into the car. The chassis shifts and groans and someone's adjusting the front seat, but no one speaks. Then the car engine fires and Mossy licks his lips. The adventure is about to start.

'Bring it on,' he goes, laughing. 'Bring it on.'

★ ★ ★

It's like being in one of those gangsterland New York movies, the sort Ray Liotta'd be in, and Mossy wonders seriously once or twice if his number's up. Even with the smack his head is keen enough to feel out the little details. The scent of aftershave — that comes from the driver, not the little black guy who sits next to him holding the mask in place, and smells of something different, something bitter, like roots or soil.

They bump along and he can hear other cars, buses, motorbikes passing them in both directions. He can hear the indicator clicking, but still no one speaks. He's lost track of where they're going and when they pull up and pitch him gently out on to cold ground his heart speeds up. This is it? The end?

But it isn't. There's a bit of walking and a voice from somewhere: a bloke, but he can't really hear what he says because it's not a local accent. Then Mossy hears a key in a door and he's led into a building — he can feel the change of temperature. It's warm in here with carpet underfoot and it smells worse than the car. It smells like the old crackhouse that started up last year on the estate, a bastard of a place it was, with people in there half dead — once someone completely dead and in a weird shape, bent over a table with his drawers down and everyone whispered how he was being fucked when his heart suddenly decided to stop, and everyone bet there was some frightened old John somewhere out in the city waiting for the filth to knock on the door. Somewhere a TV's playing. Mossy's guided round furniture, and then there's a long corridor, and Skinny's still guiding him, with the driver walking in front. There's the sound of a door being opened, a curtain being pulled back and keys, heavy and metal like a gaoler's keys, and a rusty squeak of a gate opening. But this time Mossy balks.

He pulls back, suddenly unsure. 'Nah. Don't like this.'

'It's OK, son,' goes a voice he hasn't heard before. The driver? 'D'you want us to take you back?'

Already Mossy can feel that the hit's got to its

best. There's that faint sinking of something in the back of his neck that's telling him the turning-point isn't far. That in a few hours he'll be back in the agonies, wanting to die.

'You've got something for me? There'd better be something for me.'

'Come through,' goes the voice. 'You can see it. As soon as you step through.'

There's a bitter taste in his mouth, but he steps through anyway. He has to lift his feet because the opening is smaller than a normal door and he wonders what the fuck sort of a place he's in. Behind him he hears the door being locked and again he pulls a little, but he can feel Skinny's small scratchy hands on his arms, leading him, pushing him forward. The air's better in here, just a faint smell of burning and damp, but better than it was in the other place.

'Here,' goes Skinny. 'We's here.' And he pushes him down on to a seat.

Mossy gropes for the mask and drags it off. He blinks. They're on their own, no driver, in a room with no daylight coming in — the only light is a lopsided standard lamp next to the sofa — and a three-bar electric fire plugged into an extension lead that trails off into the darkness. There's old wallpaper on the walls, but it's been scribbled on like this is where kids have been living and someone's pinned up teenagers' magazine posters of Russell Crowe in *Gladiator*, Brad Pitt in *Troy* — another one of Will Smith and Tommy Lee Jones wearing shades, the words *Protecting the World From the Scum of the*

Universe blazing above them. Mossy shuffles his feet. The carpet is worn out, a sort of sickly purple colour, you can see the foam backing in places, and in the corner a ghetto-blaster, a kettle, a box of tea-bags and a packet of sugar.

'Where's this place to, then?' He turns to look over his shoulder. There's a little corridor with a window behind them, but the glass is broken and it's covered with a grille, 'SITEX' stamped on it like the stuff the council used to cover up the ones in the crackhouse after the dead body on the table. It feels like someone's started to convert this place into something then got bored, because bare wires are poking out of the plaster in places and holes are bashed in walls and Mossy knows that the only way out is through the gate they just came through. 'This where you live then, is it?'

'Yes'm,' goes Skinny. He's standing at a wooden unit that's been torn out of a nameless kitchen and stranded here in this fuck-awful place. 'I live here. This be my home.' He gets something out of the drawer and brings it to Mossy, whose heart jumps. He knows what's in it even before Skinny opens it. He can feel his legs and stomach go a bit fluid.

'Well?' he says. 'What've I got to do for it?'

Skinny doesn't answer. He rubs his brown finger over his top lip and doesn't meet Mossy's eyes. Mossy makes a grab for the bag, just misses. Skinny steps out of reach and stands a few feet away. Something in his eyes has closed off and gone all evasive.

Mossy sits back in the sofa, breathing hard. 'Come on — spit it out. What do you want? No weird shit, OK, no 'red' or anything. But fists is OK and you don't need to wear nothing.' He rubs his crotch a little, gives Skinny a sly look. 'And there's lots of me if it's you wants the fucking. I'd fill you up, little thing like you.'

Skinny sits down on the sofa next to Mossy and gives him such a sad look that Mossy has another flash that they're about to kill him.

'What?' he goes, trying to make it sound light. 'What's that look for?'

'Blood,' says Skinny. 'Just a little blood. A little blood and you get plenty H. Plenty money too.'

'*Blood?* I just told you, I don't do no weird shit. No 'red'. You ain't going to knock me around, sweetheart, not for all the gear in the world.'

'A needle.' Skinny taps the inside of Mossy's arm, just where the H went in. 'I is put little needle in here, and take a little of yours blood.'

There's a long silence. Mossy stares at his arm, then looks up into Skinny's liquidy eyes. They meet his, and Mossy can see blood in the whites, like he's ill. But he's not being threatening and, anyway, there isn't enough of him to put up much of a fight — though he's wiry and doesn't look like he's a user so he'd have the edge if anything did kick off.

'You a vampire, then?' He laughs hoarsely, a little nervous. But Skinny keeps on looking into his eyes, all serious. So Mossy stops. He swallows. This is so fucking freaky. He uncurls

56

Skinny's fingers from his arm.

'What're you going to do with my blood, then?' he asks tightly, because something about this is making him feel sick. 'What're you going to do with it? Drink it?'

7

13 May

Caffery came quicker than he'd meant to. Maybe it was the stress of the day, maybe the long hours, or maybe something else, but almost as soon as he was inside Keelie, her legs hooked up over his shoulders, it was over. She was lying on the back seat of the car with her skirt hitched up, holding the back of his head in both hands and pulling his face down so it was pressed against hers, and maybe she didn't want it to have been that quick because it took him a minute or two to get her to loosen her grip on him, untangling her fingers from his hair and moving her shoulders back. He knelt up in the well of the car, moved her legs and fell sideways on to the seat, one hand loosening the collar of his shirt, the other resting on his chest.

She didn't say anything so neither did he, just stared blankly out of the window, feeling his heart thudding under his ribcage, his pulse making him vaguely aware of a conversation he'd had three months ago. It was the day he'd left London, and when one of his colleagues had asked him, 'What the hell do you think you're going to do out there in the middle of nowhere with the woollies?' he'd answered, with no trace of a smile, 'Don't know. Probably fuck myself to death.'

A joke, of course, but now the words came back to him because he didn't know how else to explain what he was doing, seeing girls like Keelie week after week. He hadn't wanted to tell the truth: that he'd left London, the city he'd lived in most of his life, because one day he'd woken up to find he'd lost the only connection he had to the place — the disappearance, thirty years ago, of his only brother Ewan, age just nine. The question of what had happened to Ewan had been the only question in Caffery's life. Ever since he remembered, it had coloured everything he did, and for a long time he was sure the answers were in London, across the railway cutting at the back of the family garden, in the house of the ageing paedophile, Penderecki. Caffery obsessed about that house, the place he was sure Ewan had died, for years. Then suddenly, overnight, it had gone. Vanished into nothing. Yes, he still dreamed and thought about his brother. Yes, he still had the drive to find his body, but it wasn't London he felt connected to any more. He'd stopped wanting to stare out of his window at Penderecki's house, and he couldn't remember why he'd once thought he'd get an answer out of the damned place.

But he still wanted his job. He'd gone into the Metropolitan Police force because every case he solved felt a little bit more like balancing out what had happened to Ewan. And although he wasn't a ladder-climber — he'd got a jumpstart on the HPD scheme in the Met but at thirty-seven he didn't want to think about Chief

Inspector exams — every conviction helped nail down the thing in his chest that kept him awake at night. His connection to London might be weakening, but the link to the firm stayed hard. He could do the job anywhere — even here, in Bristol. And, anyway, there was someone out here in the west that he hoped would help him untangle the Ewan equation a little further.

Next to him Keelie coughed and put her fingers to her throat, rubbing it a little as if it was sore. Then she put her index fingers into the corners of her eyes and wiped them, clearing out the caked make up. She pulled her skirt down from where it was rucked up round her waist and leaned over the front seat, clicking the passenger side sun-visor down to check her face in the mirror. The skirt was tight across her backside so the dents of her knickers and suspenders were visible.

Suddenly out of nowhere Caffery felt his throat get tighter, his eyes sting. He sat up a bit, putting his hand out, resting it on her calf, wanting to speak to her suddenly, ask her if she had kids, ask her just to say one human thing to him. But Keelie took the touch the wrong way. She raised her eyebrows at her reflection in the mirror and gave a small smile. 'What's that for?' she said, and was about to say something else when the car dipped violently. There was a *boom* of metal, and out of the corner of Caffery's eye something dark seemed to cross in front of the windscreen.

'*Fuck!*' Keelie grabbed the back of the seat, hanging on as the vehicle bounced. '*What was that?*'

Caffery fumbled his zip closed, shouldered the door open and leaped out into the deserted alley. 'Hey!' he shouted into the darkness. He looked behind him, his back to the car, scanning the shadows. 'What the *fuck* was all that about?'

Hey, the echo came back, *fuck was all that . . .*

Silence. The only sound was traffic and the distant ring of women laughing on City Road. The alley was empty — just a carrier-bag spilling out rubbish on to the pavement and the reflection of a few neon lights on the stone kerb. He walked the length of it, up to the road, inspecting every doorway, every dip in the contour of the old brick walls. He turned back to the car. Keelie had switched on the interior light and was staring out at him, white-faced and scared. He knew what she was thinking — that it had been like someone flying past them, bouncing once on the bonnet and disappearing into thin air. Or — because the idea of someone flying was crazy — it was as if someone had been sitting on the bonnet the whole time, and when the sex was over had jumped off and run away, hiding somewhere neither of them could see.

Caffery had a thought. Carefully, moving quietly, he fastened his belt. *Don't go to war with your trousers undone.* He rolled up his sleeves, got down on the cold pavement and tipped on to his side, lying close enough to the wheels of the car that he could see under there, but not so close that if something rushed out at him he wouldn't have somewhere to go. He lowered his face on to the kerb, levering it forward so he could see under the car. There was

61

nothing — just the smell of petrol and the faint burr of orange streetlight reflected on the road. He used his heel to push himself further under the car so he could see behind the wheels but, again, there was nothing. He rolled back and turned his face up to the sky, the clouds lit orange by the city, the stars beyond. He studied the tops of the buildings and thought hard about the feeling he had that they were being watched. Even now.

After a while he got to his feet and brushed himself down, thinking about suspension systems and whether they could get latched down. Maybe a car could stay caught that way for a while, waiting for a movement inside to release it like a coiled spring, then unexpectedly bounce itself free.

Keelie was still staring at him and he raised a hand to her. The need to have her again had gone, but he knew he'd have to speak to her, and the thought made him feel tired. There'd been more to the move to Bristol than just wanting to get away from London. There'd been a giving up, an acceptance that he'd never meet the human being who'd understand how guilt and loss can take a person and squeeze the life out of them. A long time ago he'd stopped looking at women and thinking one of them might bring it back for him.

Yes, he thought now, feeling in his pocket for a smoke and checking the walls for anything he'd missed, he'd got over that one long ago. And life was all the better for it.

8

After the dive in the harbour Flea's legs were like lead. She felt every second of twenty-nine years weighing on her. Coming out of Bristol she let the car slow. She pulled into a lay-by, switched off the engine and got the bag of mushrooms out of the glove compartment. She sat for a moment, studying them, feeling the last exhausted scraps of imagery tinker in the back of her head. *We went the other way.* She wanted to open the bag and shovel them into her mouth. More than anything she wanted to be back in those woods, going down the path where she knew her mother was still crouching, examining dog violets.

But she didn't. She put the mushrooms back into the glove compartment and fumbled out her phone. Earlier this evening, when she'd checked her texts, there'd been one from Tig. She liked the irony there: Tig, one of the few people in her life who would understand everything about her hankering for those mushrooms, literally *everything*, and after three months of silence he'd chosen tonight of all nights to text her. As if he was reading her mind. His flat was on the Hopewell estate, not far — with the streets this quiet she could be there in twenty minutes. It would be easy, and comfortable, to tell him about Dad and the drugs, and the trip, about how she wanted to take the drugs again and slip back into that forest where Mum was waiting.

But then she thought about the way the mushrooms had been so carefully coiled into the jewellery roll, she thought about her father lying on the sofa with a cushion on his face, and right away she knew there *was* someone else who could unravel it for her even better than Tig. One person who could really set her straight.

She shovelled the mobile back into her pocket, fired the engine and swung the car into the road, heading south. Quickly the houses on either side of the road thinned. Soon she was past the last of the streetlamps and on to the dark roads that would take her into the lonely Mendip Hills.

Kaiser Nduka.

If Dad had ever admitted to having a close friend it would have been Kaiser Nduka. They'd been undergraduates together at Corpus, and at first sight two more different people you couldn't imagine: Dad with his Swedish heritage, papery, bruisable skin and delicate hands like a child's, and Kaiser, the eldest son of an Ibo chieftain, a spectrally tall man with shinbones thinner than walking-sticks, a greying halo of curly hair, and a face so heavy it looked as if it might unbalance his body. Kaiser had been sent in the nineteen seventies from Nigeria by his oil-rich family to study in England and had arrived wearing an *abeti-aja* dog-ear cap and a Western suit. Somehow the two misfits — Kaiser and Dad — had found a common ground in their studies, applying philosophy and psychology to world religion. A professor of comparative religion, Kaiser's speciality was hallucinogenic experience in shamanic ritual. His career path was smooth until, with a chair at a Nigerian university, he'd become involved in a research project that had gone disastrously wrong and had been thrown off the faculty. At the same time his fiancée had left him.

'They probably worked it out . . . ' Mum had said darkly. 'His girlfriend and the university probably worked out that he was only half human . . . '

Kaiser always made Mum edgy. She never said why but she'd find excuses to stay at home when Dad came out to the Mendips. Thom was afraid of Kaiser too — he said he looked like the devil and that he'd had nightmares about him hunting people in the streets. Flea tried to imagine where he'd got that idea from, and what he'd seen in those fevered childhood dreams: the greasy half-lit streets of Ibadan, the hawkers and never-ending traffic, a silent shape slipping through the alleys: Kaiser. It struck her as almost humorous, Kaiser, his big head wrapped in a cloak, prowling the streets for human beings. She laughed at the idea, but Thom wasn't swayed. He was terrified of the house, the way it was always being worked on, boarded up, tarpaulined, sometimes unexpected parts of it peeled open and exposed to the sky.

Pulling into the long, darkened track now, the only illumination the moon cutting a sharp circle against the sky in front of her, Flea sort of knew what Thom meant. The place did have a remote, forgotten feel you could think of as spooky, isolated out here in the rainy limestone forests of the Mendips. Wet weeds hung over the car as she

65

drove, trailing long fingers on it until she had to turn on the wipers to clear them. Up and up she went, the headlight beams bumping all over the place, almost a mile, until the driveway opened to a pocked field that stretched out silver under the open sky. At the furthest end the land dropped away to nothing — the furthest ridge of the valley was two miles distant — and it was there, at the edge of the drop, poised as if ready to tumble, that Kaiser's house stood, built from the local blue lias, once pretty but scarred by his perpetual renovations and changes. A single light was on in the living room, dim, barely visible behind a tacked-up blanket. He'd be in there, in his usual place — slouched in his reclining chair in the corner.

She parked, shoved the bag of mushrooms into her fleece pocket, and crossed to the back door, arms folded, shivering because suddenly it seemed so late. She went inside, into the kitchen, closing the door carefully, and breathed in the heat and the good spicy smells.

Kaiser's house was full of clutter. Every surface in the kitchen was piled with dusty stacks of journals and letters and oddities he'd collected from around the world. Just like Dad's study. So it always seemed utterly improbable that Kaiser's biggest hobby was cooking. Over the years he'd singled out Flea for his attention. It was always her he took aside, telling her stories, showing her secret places in the garden, letting her put her fingers through the eyeholes of his family's traditional masks. But, most of all, he showed his affection by cooking. His recipes were borrowed from every nation and tradition. Sometimes it was coconut pie, sometimes it was couscous sweetened with condensed milk served in chipped bowls from Woolworths. Tonight it was sticky date loaves — two were cooling on a wire tray. Flea sliced one, arranged the pieces on a plate, and carried it through into the draughty corridor.

'Just me,' she said, lowering her head and pushing through the plastic sheeting hanging over the living-room doorway. 'Only me.'

The room was dimly lit and chaotic with its stacked shelves and lumpy furniture, a tattered standard lamp on in the corner. Kaiser was exactly where she'd known he'd be: in the chair in the corner, his legs elevated and lightly crossed, his hands steepled contemplatively. He didn't move when she came in, didn't look surprised or pleased. Instead he seemed to be concentrating on a space a few inches in front of his nose. He was dressed in pyjamas that ended mid-calf, ridiculous blue Turkish slippers on his long feet.

She put the date loaf on the coffee-table. He stared ahead, his long yellow nails positioned just under the tip of his wide nose as if it was too heavy for his face and he was trying to stop it falling. Next to his chair, on top of a small cabinet, the computer was open at divenet, the international sport divers' forum, and next to that a photo of his African ex-fiancée, Maya. He'd lost Maya thirty years ago but said he still loved her. Maya's mouth, Flea noticed, was exactly level with Kaiser's right ear.

'Kaiser?' she said eventually. 'Kaiser, the door was open.'

He nodded.

'Kaiser? Can you hear me?'

He shook himself, glancing at the computer screen. 'Yes, Phoebe,' he said wearily. 'I can hear you. But I am so sad. So sad about your parents. Still. After all this time.'

Ordinarily she might have sat down then, perhaps at his feet, or maybe she'd have hugged him. But she had to speak to him seriously. She sat in the chair opposite and tipped forward, elbows on her knees.

'Kaiser,' she said. 'Remember whenever you cooked us anything Dad always used to nudge you? Remember? Nudge you and say, 'Kaiser, old man, you sure there's nothing in this cake we should know about?''

Kaiser smiled. He dipped his chin, half laughing at the memory.

'Except,' she said seriously, 'this time it's not a joke.'

His smile faded. 'I beg your pardon?'

'This time, Kaiser, it's not anywhere near as funny as I used to think it was.' She gave him a long, level look. His eyes were pus-coloured, a bit bloodshot. Something about his big-boned face had always made her think of a hairless goat. 'See, now I realize it wasn't ever really a joke. Not to the people who mattered.'

'What on earth do you mean?'

She turned to the cupboards in the recesses on either side of the fireplace. They were locked and, now she thought about it, there had always been things in Kaiser's house that were locked away, places she and Thom weren't allowed. People were always contacting Kaiser to ask about his shamanic skills and it made him laugh: 'I'm hardly a shaman. Just a dusty old lecturer.' But there was something hidden about Kaiser, something in the sinewy body, quite strong in spite of his age, something in the way he would stare fixedly at a person. Dad said Kaiser knew 'whereof he spoke' and that the cupboards were where he kept the ritual drugs. Flea'd always thought it was one of Dad's jokes. She wasn't sure she'd ever believed it or given it much thought. Until now.

'Phoebe? I asked you a question.'

She sighed. Picking up a piece of date loaf she sank back into the chair, sticking her feet out in front of her, her hands on her stomach, looking morosely at the cake between her fingers. 'I went into Dad's study, Kaiser. The place he keeps all his books. Some of your things are in there.'

'Yes?'

'Yes, and there's a safe too — I couldn't open it. The code's not in the study.' She fiddled with the cake, not giving in to the temptation to look at him. 'I searched everywhere but I couldn't find it so I wondered if you'd know what it is. Or if you know where he might keep it.'

'Is that what you came here to talk to me about?'

'Do you know where he'd keep it?'

Kaiser took in a deep impatient breath, and let the air out slowly through his nose. 'I don't know anything about a safe or a code. And I repeat, is that what you came here to ask?'

Flea put the cake back on the plate, and rotated her head, as if she had a crick in her neck. 'Kaiser,' she said, after a while. 'Kaiser, do you know why Dad used to lock himself in the study for days on end?'

Kaiser levered the footrest down with a clunk so he was sitting forward. There were a few moments' silence. 'Let me ask you, Phoebe. Do you know why? Do you know why your father did it?'

'I think so. Yes. I think I probably do.'

'Your father's drive to understand was greater than anyone's I've known. He must have talked to you about Secondary Attention.'

'The places in our heads — places we can't always get to except if we're dreaming or fainting. Or maybe hypnotized. That's what he used to talk about. A place that holds keys to things we've buried. And his way of getting there . . . ' She lifted her eyes and met his. 'Was with drugs?'

'Your father had many different routes. Sometimes it was meditation, but, yes, often it was drugs.'

'I knew it.'

'Don't judge him too quickly. David always had the need to uncover, to strip down his head — pull things out.'

Flea let a moment pass. Then she took the bag of mushrooms out of her fleece pocket and dropped it on the floor between their feet. 'Psilocybin,' she said. 'I looked it up. It means 'baldhead'. The Aztecs called them *teonancatls*

70

— flesh of the gods.' She was silent for a while, looking down at them. 'They could lose me my job.'

Kaiser made a clicking sound in his throat. It was a sound she remembered him making years ago and had always thought you might hear it on the plateaus of Nigeria, a herdsman calling the shorthorn cattle to his side. But now she understood it was his way of marking the moment an idea came together. 'And you've taken them. I know you, Phoebe, I can hear it in your voice. You've taken them. Without consulting me.'

'Yes,' she said slowly. 'And I want to take them again.'

He snorted. 'Don't be an idiot.'

'You said Dad used them to pull things out of his head?'

'Yes.'

'Don't laugh at this, Kaiser, but in all your research have you ever — ' She let her voice drop to a whisper. 'Have you ever heard anyone say drugs can let them communicate with people who've died?'

Kaiser sighed. 'Your parents, you mean?'

'Mum.'

He shook his head and got up, standing facing the locked cupboards. He put one hand in the small of his back. That fragility — it was a lie, she thought, not for the first time that night. There was something strong in his long muscles and his claw-like hands. 'Phoebe,' he said, in a low voice, 'there are some things you have to let rest — you can't keep going back and raking it over.'

71

'Would Dad have let it rest?'

'No.'

'Then you know I'm never going to.' She sat forward a little. 'It could lose me my job, but that doesn't change anything. I want to go back where I went last night.' She paused. Her voice had been getting quieter and quieter. 'I saw her, Kaiser, I saw her. She was trying to say something about the accident.' Flea shook her head and screwed her hand into a fist. 'But I couldn't quite . . . couldn't quite understand what she meant.'

Kaiser's face was grave. 'What did you say?'

'I said, something about the accident — something in the way we're thinking about it — is all wrong. We've been looking in the wrong place.' She held his eyes. 'Kaiser, I'm going to do it — I'm going to take them again. Find out what she meant.'

A long, long silence rolled out between them. Something was happening behind his eyes — she could almost see the computations he was making. Then, when it seemed they'd be locked there for ever, Kaiser broke away, and went back to his chair. He sat for a moment, hands on the armrests, head turned sideways, looking at his ex-fiancée's face. 'If you want to communicate with people who've gone,' he said quietly, 'there is something. A hallucinogen you can control, a drug that is legal. Your father introduced me to it.'

'But you don't believe it, do you? You don't really believe it's all true?'

'There'll be some literature about it in your

father's study.' Kaiser pretended not to have heard the question. 'Please, read it, then come back to me. Throw away the baldheads — they won't take you any further. But this will.'

' "This?" ' She sat forward, creeped and excited all at once, as if her skin had been brushed the wrong way. 'What's 'this', Kaiser?'

'What's 'this'?' He smiled to himself, a little sadly, as if it was a secret he'd known he'd have to give up one day — that he had to be big about letting it go. ' 'This' is called ibogaine.'

'Ibogaine?' She whispered the word. It put pictures in her head of firelight and people dancing ancient dances in the dark.

'Ibogaine,' Kaiser said. 'And if you really want to speak to your mother again . . . '

'Yes?'

' . . . then it's the only route to take.'

9

14 May

The morning of the second day of the case, drinking coffee on Bristol harbour and watching the dive team assemble their kit, Jack Caffery was thinking about a direction: he was thinking about west. For a long time it wasn't going to be west for him when he left London, it was going to be east — the direction that for an Englishman means cold winds and invaders. At about the same time that his sense of a connection with Ewan had disappeared he'd been doing a job in Norfolk, and maybe that was why he'd felt pieces of him had got stuck there. For a while after the abrupt ending of his sense of Ewan, he'd looked for a position in East Anglia, monitoring vacancies on the web. But when months had gone by with none coming up, he'd turned his attention to the west where something more interesting was happening.

A prisoner had been released from an open jail. A man who understood a particular species of violence. The more Caffery thought about it, the more he knew he needed to meet him. Then, almost like an omen, a position came up in the Major Crime Investigation Unit in Bristol. The wait for Norfolk was shelved and it was west that Caffery came: to smugglers and apple orchards and Somerset, the land of the summer people.

It was odd how things had worked out because there was something about working in the west he liked: a straightforwardness instead of the freakiness of London where, whatever you did, it all ended up a bit warped. Now, as the sun sparkled off the boats and the restaurant windows and the courting swans in the harbour making heart shapes with their necks, he told himself he was liking the west. Yes, he thought, looking down to where the dive unit had finished loading the boat and Flea was standing in its bow zipping up her dry suit, if it wasn't for some promises he'd made himself, if it wasn't for the bad way he felt inside about women, he could get to like this place.

She was only a couple of feet below him, her hair pinned up wildly round her small tanned face, her feet planted wide to balance as the boat rocked. Now that he looked at her closely he saw her pause, her hand at her collarbone. She wasn't facing the harbour, the part they were going to dive this morning, but the opposite direction, back towards the quay — at the point where the pontoon met the wall a few feet beneath his feet. It was the exact place the waitress had pointed to when she'd described seeing the odd creature coming out of the water.

It was a moment or two before anyone noticed her expression, then PC Dundas, who was about to throttle up the motor, glanced at her and saw that something was wrong. He let go of the tiller. 'Sarge?'

'Yeah — hang on.' She held up a hand. 'Hang on.'

She was staring at the harbour wall, as if she was trying hard to remember something important — something just out of reach. Caffery remembered a snatch of tourist blurb he'd read: the harbour and the Cut had been built by prisoners of the Napoleonic wars and still stood, almost two hundred years later, mossed, slimed and blackened from decades of engine oil and pollution. To him they were unfamiliar and weird, like a dungeon, but Flea must know them back to front so her sudden interest made no sense.

'Sarge?' Dundas said, frowning. 'Sarge? You all right?'

She didn't turn to him. Instead she raised her head to Caffery. 'It was raining yesterday morning,' she said. 'Wasn't it?'

He gathered himself quickly — a bit unprepared for the direct way she was looking at him. He put his elbow on the handrail and leaned over. 'Yeah. Yeah, it was. Why?'

She stared at him a bit more, sort of blankly, as if she was still trying to work an idea out of an awkward corner of her head. Then, a passing boat sent up a swell that rocked the little launch and her concentration was gone. She shook her head and finished zipping the dry suit. She pulled on her harness, then her fins. 'Come on,' she called, signalling Dundas to start the engine. 'Let's do it.'

Caffery watched the boat set off, leaving a foamy trail in the muddy water. Flea was bending over, checking her cylinders, tapping gauges, clipping the lifeline to the harness with a D-ring. He was in a way glad to see her go — she had a way of looking at him as if she knew all his secrets, not just the ordinary ones but the dirty ones too. As if she knew where he'd gone after he left the harbour last night. Now he couldn't tell if the bad taste in his mouth was from the bottle of wine he'd drunk or the memory of what he'd done in the back of his car, parked in the alley next to the dumpsters.

He watched till the boat had gone round the corner, then finished his coffee — the third cup, because whatever happened he couldn't allow a hangover into his day. The fingerprints on the hand hadn't come back. The IDENT1 computer wasn't as bad as the old NAFIS system but it could be slow and overnight it had only pulled up one of the five prints needed for comparison. But the path report was complete and made disturbing reading. The pathologist had recovered some fibres from the hand, purply blue ones that she'd sent to the lab at HQ, and she'd agreed that the marks on the bones had been made by a saw. She also said that the hand had probably been removed when the victim had still been alive.

All of which had brought the superintendent down a bit on his fury with Caffery. He'd assigned a level to the case and the Major Crime Investigation Unit had sent a staffing quota of a three-man HOLMES team for the incident room at Kingswood, two more DCs, a DS and a civvy investigator — a retired officer — plus a crime-scene manager and a scene liaison officer.

It lit Caffery up to have decent manpower — there were another four men due at the quayside by eight a.m., ready to start interviewing anyone who worked in or frequented the area. Today the harbour would be running with police.

He crumpled the coffee cup and was about to head back to the road to meet his team when the sound of the utility craft made him stop. It was heading back towards the pontoon fast, Flea in the bows wearing her dive hood, no mask, staring at the same part of the harbour wall she'd been pulled by five minutes ago. As the boat came nearer and Dundas killed the engine, the stern came round so it lay alongside the wall. She leaned forward and, grabbing the buddleia trunks that grew out of the mossy quayside wall, dragged the boat sideways, stopping every few inches to press her hands against the stone, inspecting it with a frown.

'What's up?' Caffery peered at her head — shiny and dark like that of a small seal. 'Found something?'

'Nope. I've worked something out.'

'What?'

'The witness statement,' she said, breathing hard now. 'Did you read it?'

'Only in outline. They took it at New Bridewell. Why?'

'I got most of it from your super in the briefing. Right from the beginning it bothered me.' She squinted down at the harbour wall. She brushed aside some algae, squinted again and shook her head, dismissing whatever had caught

78

her attention. 'It bothered me that he could see the hand at all. Bothered all of us.'

She stepped her hands further along the wall, digging her nails in. Caffery took a few steps along to keep up with her. 'And it still bothers you?'

'It was nil vis in the water yesterday. I just couldn't square it — how he could have seen the bloody thing.'

Something caught her eye and she stopped again. She swung her legs round so she was sitting on the stern of the boat, fingers digging into one of the mossed old stones of the quayside, her feet wedged against the pontoon so she could push the craft into the wall and get her face close to it. Dundas had found a mooring pin and was holding on to it, steadying the boat. She made a small, satisfied noise and pushed her right hand at the wall. Caffery leaned over as far as he could but all he could see was her head, her shoulders, her face, turned sideways and screwed up in concentration, and her arm disappearing deep into the wall.

'I said, is it bothering you now?'

She nodded. Her eyes had the shortened focus of someone who is working by feel alone. 'Yes. And he said there wasn't . . . ' She pushed her arm a little further in. 'He said there wasn't anyone else on the quayside. Didn't he?'

'Far as I know. Maybe it was floating.'

She glanced up at him. Blue eyes that gave him a jolt because he hadn't noticed before that there was something a bit wild about them. Then she dropped them again and all he could see was the top of her dive hood, and her arm burrowing into the wall.

'A hand on its own doesn't float,' she said. 'It just wouldn't. Even if it had started to decompose . . .'

She broke off. She pulled her arm out of the hole and looked at what she held in her fist. A lump of congealed black slime with pieces of leaf and stick in it. She rolled backwards a little and dropped the mess on to the pontoon, giving it a cursory examination with a finger, her face tight with the strain of holding herself up.

Then she glanced back at Caffery — that flash of blue light in her eyes again. 'Even if it's decomposed, which this one wasn't, a hand still wouldn't *float*.'

'Why not?'

'Because it's too heavy, so much bone, not much soft tissue. And even if there was enough gas the skin's broken, so the gases would've escaped. No gases, no floating.' She inserted her hand back into whatever hole she'd found. He could smell it — the foul odour of drains and dark places. This time her arm went in all the way up to the shoulder. Her face was pressed against the wall, squashing her cheek forward. 'Which means he's either lying. Or . . .'

'Yes?'

'Or it got washed into the water by a current and he happened to see it going down. It was raining yesterday morning. So, for example, it could have come out of a storm drain.' She grimaced as she tried to get a grip on something. With a little grunt she wedged her free hand

80

against the wall and levered herself backwards, pulling her right hand out and delivering the second wet handful of slime on to the pontoon. Then she pulled back, both hands either side of the hole and peered into it. The sleeves of her dry suit were covered with green moss and slime. 'A storm drain. Like this one.'

10

25 November

It takes some time — and some getting desperate on Mossy's part — but in the end he decides they're not asking much of him.

The deal goes like this: they'll take some blood, bleed him a little. It's not the same as 'red' — they won't fuck him until he bleeds — they're going to use a needle instead. Skinny's got the equipment ready, a syringe and a tube leading to something that looks like a catheter bag. They're going to take it from one of the veins that isn't burned out, fill the bag, it'll take twenty minutes maybe, then he can have a lie-down, another hit, a cup of tea or a Tennants Extra if he wants. Anyway, he's free to go. There'll be two hundred nicker in it and the whole bag of gear Skinny's been flashing around. He's got to go back out of the building in the blindfold and they'll drop him anywhere in Bristol he wants to go. And what keeps going through his head is why wouldn't he trust them? People give their blood for free, don't they? And what's the deal? Selling a little piece of himself that he doesn't need and, fuck's sake, it's not like he hasn't been selling his hole for long enough. Think of this as a variation on a theme, even if it is a bit off its head. Anyway, it's so warm in here, and there's a smell somewhere of food cooking and suddenly he remembers he hasn't eaten since last night.

He lies on the couch and smokes a thin little J while Skinny gets the needle in. It takes two tries and when he checks the blood's coming up he botches it, pulls too quick making Mossy swear.

'You're an expert,' goes Mossy, watching him stick it down with Sellotape and attach a tube to it. 'Ain't you?'

There's a little plastic tap on the tube and Skinny's about to turn it when it's as if something occurs to him. He pauses and looks over his shoulder into the darkness, just long enough for Mossy to wonder if someone's watching them. He lifts his head off the sofa a little and tries to peer into the gloom where Skinny's looking. There's another of those gates there, locked, and beyond it a room in darkness.

Skinny makes a little sound in the back of his throat. He lets go of the tube and, moving daintily, like a girl dancer, he lies on the sofa next to Mossy, his hand draped over Mossy's bony ribcage. Surprised, Mossy lifts his chin and squints down at the top of Skinny's head, at the curls and snags and bits of fluff tangled there, and feels an unexpected tenderness. It's like this guy is trying to comfort him, or warm him. It feels like the way a kid curls up with a parent.

'What?' he says, and his voice comes out a little hoarse because all of a sudden he wants to touch Skinny's hair. 'What do you want?'

'I'm sorry. Plenty sorry.'

'What you talking about?'

83

He feels Skinny swallow. He can actually feel the cartilage in the man's throat move up and down against his arm.

'Them's wanting you to scream.'

Mossy can feel the thick beat of the hash going through his veins and, for a moment, he thinks he's going to laugh. 'Scream?' he goes, half smiling. 'You fucking joking? Why've I got to scream?'

'It's all I ask you. When I pull out your blood you scream. OK?'

Mossy cranes his neck, trying to see into the adjoining room, looking for a pair of eyes in the dark, trying to catch out whoever's watching. He can't see anything, only the glint of the metal gate, which he's one hundred per cent is locked. He laughs, deep and knowing. Now he gets it.

'Hey, sweetheart,' he calls, his voice echoing into the dark spaces. 'I know you're out there. Can't see you, like, but I know you're there. And let me just tell you — I *like* perverts. I do. I love you all. I'll do the best show you've ever seen. Got your video running, have you?'

As if in answer, from out of the darkness comes a click and a whirr and a red light blinks on and off. Mossy puts his head back and laughs. He's on home ground now. He's been videoed by them all — the ones who want to watch themselves and the ones who are so ashamed, either because of what they're doing or because they know their dick size will humiliate them, that they have to video him and get off later when he's gone and can't laugh. Now he gets why the price is so good, and it's something he doesn't care about. He can relax.

Skinny shifts. He sits up and turns on the tap. His face is close, and Mossy wonders if they could be friends. 'Scream,' whispers Skinny. 'Now. Scream.'

And Mossy does. He drops his head back on the scratchy sofa and screams.

11

14 May

'Don't need to ask what this is about.' The council subcontractors, three men in bright red jackets marked SITA, were manoeuvring their inflatable raft against the edge of the pontoon, one of them assembling a jetting machine, snapping on the jet head to the orange flexipipe. One was holding his finger under the drain, watching the steady dribble of water on to it while his colleague was testing the jet. 'Only question is, how far up.'

Caffery was on the pontoon, looking down thoughtfully at the handfuls of sludge Flea'd pulled out of the drain. 'You what?'

The contractor was a big red-faced man with a shaved head and three piercings in his right ear. 'He's blocked, isn't he? The drain. See, a trickle like this on a sunny day and it means 'e's blocked somewhere.'

'How far up?'

'Wales?' He laughed. 'Cardiff? Don't worry. When we hit it you'll be the first to know.'

As they inserted the jet head Caffery studied the entrance to the drain and the long green tail of slime under it. Then he peered at the stuff on the pontoon between his feet. It was black, but ever since it had been pulled out he'd been thinking of the fatty white residue that had been clogging up Dennis Nilsen's drains back in the nineteen eighties. Everyone in the Met knew that story — the story of what the drain people had found. Human fat, as it turned out, from the sixteen bodies Nilsen had dismembered in his bed-sit, boiled and flushed down the toilet.

'Figured out where the drain comes from yet?' he asked Flea. She had showered in the Station and was dressed in a navy fleece and combats, and now she was kneeling on the pontoon, inspecting the blueprint they'd had biked over from the Environment Agency. He came and crouched next to her, trying not to be conscious of the way the air changed near her, the way the smell of the drains was replaced by baby lotion and toothpaste.

'Where do these things lead?'

'Some of the drains let into the harbour, some into underground rivers — the Frome, or the moat — but just to confuse things some let back into the sewer system.' She gestured downstream to where the Clifton Suspension Bridge stood cold and remote, spanning the dark gorge. The contractors turned on the sluice and dirty water gushed out of the opening, splashing into the harbour, moving the boat round with its force. She raised her voice above the noise. 'The pumping station for the northern interceptor is right over there. Just up under the bridge.'

'The northern what?'

'One of the sewage systems. We've got two in Bristol — one's the southern ring, the other's in the north. We're on the north one here. But that doesn't mean anything because most of the storm-drain system is separate, like in most cities. This one . . . ' She ran a finger along the route shown. It led from the harbour back past the restaurant entrance, terminating about three metres further along, by the road. There was one open drain cover shown at its head. 'This one's not connected underground.' She tapped the map at the head of the drain. 'It only looks it because it's flowing in that direction.'

'We're there,' shouted one of the men on the boat. 'We've found him.' Caffery and Flea looked up. The contractor with the earring was holding the jet hose above his head, both hands on it, eyes narrowed, face turned away from the water that was fountaining out, soaking everything. 'Got him.'

'What've you got?' Caffery came forward, shouting above the sound of the water. 'Do you know what it is?'

'Can't tell,' he yelled back. 'It's a long way up — ten metres at least. We're going to have to have a look inside.'

★   ★   ★

Caffery watched Dundas assemble the search unit's drain cam: a gyroscopically mounted camera on a wheeled probe. It was attached by a fifty-metre cable to a portable screen zipped inside a yellow waterproofed casing and when the contractors had moved their boat out of the way and the dive team had manoeuvred their launch into position, Flea began carefully to insert the camera head into the hole.

She switched on the remote-control toggle, and the wheeled camera trundled off on its long journey into the drain. There was silence as everyone watched the screen, the only sound the squeak of the cable winding gently off the spool. The camera had two lights mounted on it and the picture was in full colour — an eerie, twisting journey into the earth, brushed by hanging knots of plant roots, passing through the blinding whiteness of sunlight from an overhead grille, water sloshing over the lens. There had been drains in the railway banks at the back of Caffery's house that the police had searched for Ewan's body and Caffery had problems with drains to this day.

'Lookit that,' murmured one of the contractors, studying the inside of the drain. 'Bloody thing's cracked to buggery. Radials everywhere.'

Flea worked slowly, glancing back and forth between the drainage charts, the screen and the entrance to the drain. 'That's five metres,' she said, checking the read-out on the monitor. 'And what? You hit something at ten?'

'Ten and a half.'

They lapsed into silence, the team glued to the screen, expecting at any minute the camera to turn a corner and the screen to be filled with an image. Maybe everyone was expecting to see something different, but for Caffery it was eyes. All through his childhood he'd lie awake at night, thinking of the railway cutting outside his bedroom window, wondering where Penderecki had buried Ewan. He always pictured Ewan on his back, his face turned upwards, so even now he expected the eyes to come first, looming out of the darkness, the light hardly reflecting off flat, dried-out corneas.

'Nine,' Flea murmured. 'Nine and a half. Ten. Ten and a . . . '

She stopped the camera. The screen had filled with an image. Everyone crowded round, hardly breathing.

'What's that?' murmured Caffery.

It wasn't the distorted body part everyone had in their heads. It took them a moment or two to see what it was instead: an accumulation of rock, silt, root and soil.

'That's your blockage,' she said.

'Looks like a fall,' said one of the contractors. 'You've had a cave-in there.'

'Can you get past it?'

'Think so.' She was toggling the controls. On screen the camera head lunged into the rock, climbed and fell. 'If I can just . . . ' She made three attempts at it. On the fourth the little remote camera climbed to the top of the fall and trundled down the other side into standing water. The picture got blurry under water, the lights picking up swirls of silt. On it went, Flea stopping it to inspect every anomaly, swivelling the camera head at every crack or bump. After about five minutes it butted up against a blank wall and came to a stop.

'What's that?'

She shook her head. 'The end?' she suggested. Then, a little surprised, 'There's nothing.'

There was a short, disappointed silence. Flea

let the camera nose up against the wall, turned it, let it make a final inspection of the fall from the opposite side. But nothing. The length of the drain behind the fall was clear. She switched off the camera, and the image on screen died, dwindling to a point.

'Oh, well,' said Dundas. He put his hand on Flea's back. 'It was about the only half-logical explanation anyone could have come up with.'

'Yeah.' She shrugged. 'I suppose. Even so . . . ' Biting her lip, she spooled in the camera, setting it into reverse mode, lights off.

The sub-contractors began to disband, a little disappointed not to have seen a dead body rammed into a drain, a horror story to tell their mates in the pub. Only Caffery didn't move. He was standing quite still, his thoughts racing, staring at the blank screen. Something was ticking away, something that had to do with direction and intent, and the sudden conviction that whoever was responsible for cutting off the hand had never intended it to end up in the harbour. He turned to the harbour wall, trying to estimate the distance from the opening to the surface. About five feet, he reckoned.

'Hey,' he said to Flea. 'The camera was going up, wasn't it? On an incline?'

'Yes. Because the drain is at a pitch. Why?'

He picked up the chart and studied it. 'How deep does the drain run? Can we follow the path overground?'

She stopped winding in the camera and glanced dubiously at the chart in his hands. 'It depends how accurate that is. S'pose you could put ground-probing radar on it, but that's a trip to HQ for us.'

'Come on, then.' He stepped off the pontoon. 'Let's give the chart a try.'

'But there's nothing in the drain,' she called from behind, putting down the control and coming after him. 'I covered it all. I didn't miss a thing.'

'Didn't say you did, Sergeant. Didn't say you did.'

Caffery bunched the map in his hand, so he could see the dotted line, and headed up the quayside, out through the privacy screens to where one or two people hovered inquisitively next to the unit van, its Underwater Search sign an open invitation to every ghoul in the city.

'Hey,' Flea was saying breathlessly, hurrying to keep pace with him, 'don't worry. I'm not going to cry about being wrong, you know.'

He halted a few feet from the restaurant and she stopped next to him. There was a pause. Then, at exactly the same time, some instinct made them both look down. They were standing at either side of a puddle that stretched round the drain grille between their feet. There was a moment's silence while they considered the puddle, wondered what it meant.

'This was here yesterday,' she said, staring at her feet, at her regulation boots just touching the edge of the water. 'I got my shoes wet in it.'

'Because the drain's blocked. It's not draining away.' Caffery looked at the cobbles that stretched to the stairs leading into the restaurant entrance. If he was reading the chart right, this grille was at the head of the drain. From here it ran back towards the harbour in a straight line. About two metres from where they stood it would have to run under an area cordoned off by timber palings where the dumpsters were. He followed the imaginary line back, going round the palings until he came to the opening.

'What're you doing?'

He held up his hand to quiet her and stepped round the fence into the enclosure. There was a smell here, flies gathering round the piled-up bin-liners bulging with waste from the kitchens. A dozen or so crates of empty beer bottles stood against the steps up to fire doors leading into the kitchen. He pushed away one of the dumpsters and used his foot to move the bin-liners, clearing the ground in the direction of the entrance. At the wall, where the drain must have run briefly under the porch of the building, he stopped, peering down at what was between his feet.

'What're you — ' Flea broke off when she saw what he was looking at. The last cobble, the one that should have met the underside of the steps, was missing. Others, surrounding it, had been cut, crudely, maybe with a pickaxe. 'Oh,' she said softly. 'I think I know what you're thinking.'

'Yeah. I reckon we're standing right over the cave-in. Don't you?'

12

And so the team discovered that not one but two hands had been buried under the entrance to the Moat restaurant. Whoever had done it had dug a fraction too deep, making the earth give way, dropping one hand into the drain below from where it was carried out into the harbour. The second, covered with earth and debris, had hung on — it was lodged precariously above the cave-in, its fingers stretched out above the water. Just out of view of Flea's camera.

It wasn't as if Caffery'd never seen a severed hand — if there was one thing he'd been around the block with it was the mutilation of the human body and he'd known more distressing combinations of the way the familiar can become the unfamiliar than he cared to remember. In fact, he really wasn't sure why finding a second human hand buried under the entrance to the Moat was giving him this apprehensive little buzz.

Overnight his head had kept going back to the waitress at the Station, her voice sounding as if she didn't expect to be believed: subdued and sort of pleading, knowing what she was saying was a bit weird, a bit sick. He'd dreamed of shadows, of things moving around at waist height. He'd got a HOLMES operator in Kingswood to search the force network for flashers in the area and a list had come back not in tens but in hundreds. It could take weeks — and there was nothing concrete to which he could connect this character exposing himself — not to the case and certainly not to what had happened with Keelie in the car last night. So why did he keep making those links?

But it didn't matter how illogically his head was behaving, he knew enough about the system to appear at least to be doing things methodically. The owner of the restaurant was out of the country on holiday — Caffery had someone trying to track him down — but the rest of the staff had begun to arrive for work and were taken aback to be stopped at the entrance and led across to the Station to be interviewed. Caffery had taken all the core team off door-to-dooring the marina so now almost all his manpower was in there, sitting at tables in the restaurant drinking bitter-smelling black coffee from tiny cups. The place looked like a job centre, interviewer and interviewee gazing intently at one another across the tables. On top of the usual questions, he'd told each investigator to ask if anyone had seen anything unexpected on the pontoon late at night, after the place closed.

Caffery stood at the side of the restaurant, waiting for the CSI team to unearth the hand — they were doing it as slowly as archaeologists so that no evidence was lost. The sun had crossed the harbour, and in the distance you could see it sparkling on the masts in the marina, but close up the pontoon was dark and cold-looking. Somehow he couldn't picture the sun on it, whatever time of day it was. The police search adviser, the POLSA, had set up parameters, and teams from Portishead had been bussed in to comb the restaurant, using ground-probing radar and scanning the quayside around the Moat while the sub-contractors rodded every drain in the area. But everyone was coming up empty. They still couldn't find the rest of the body.

The CSM thought it was very funny, the way they were all knocking themselves out. 'Call yourself a detective?' he said, placing the hand in an evidence bag and coming up to Caffery. He was a little man, with a pinched nose and red bags under his eyes, expressionless and grey, and if Caffery had to guess he wouldn't place him as city. He'd place him as coming from one of those ribbon towns south-west of Bristol he had to drive through to get home. Nailsea maybe.

'I'm sorry?' Caffery said, looking down at the grey flesh in the bag. 'What did you say?'

The CSM regarded him with his slightly runny eyes. 'I said, 'Call yourself a detective?' I thought the idea of being a detective was never to make assumptions.'

'What am I assuming?'

'That there's a corpse.'

'Look, I know this sounds stupid, but if there's a hand — two hands — there has to be a corpse.'

The CSM snapped the bag closed and ran his nail across the top to seal it, then initialled and dated it. 'I'm not a doctor, mind, but you pick things up in my job and,' he said, placing the bag in a polystyrene cool box, 'the simple laws of physics and bio-medicine tell us that a severed hand does not necessarily turn a human body into a corpse.'

'You mean this guy might still be *alive*?'

The CSM fumbled in his case and pulled out a bundle of pens wrapped in a piece of red elastic. He unpicked the knot and let them clatter back into the case. 'See this?' He held up the elastic. 'This is the human artery.'

'OK. Whatever you say,' Caffery said patiently.

The CSM fumbled for a Stanley blade in a plastic container. 'You know how suicides get it wrong.' He ran a hand at right angles across the elastic. 'Slash their wrists this way.'

'Yeah. Doesn't work.'

'If they did it lengthways . . . ' He made a longitudinal cut in the elastic. A few ends frayed but the elastic remained in one piece. ' . . . they'd make a better job of it — cut an artery like this and it keeps bleeding — out of here. It's still intact so it can keep pumping blood. But cut it completely this way . . . ' He laid the elastic on the wooden railing at the edge of the deck, sliced across it horizontally with a bit of effort and held it up, twisting and writhing, ' . . . and it springs back, up into the arm like this.' He gave the nylon a tug and it jumped in the air like a live eel. 'Stops the blood pumping, seals the whole circuit off. One pleased patient. Or, rather, not pleased, if it was intended to be a suicide.'

In the distance, above the sun-tipped buildings of Bristol, dusty old flocks of birds rose in the blue. Caffery watched them thoughtfully. 'You mean,' he said, 'there's someone out there? Someone walking around with no hands?'

The CSM snorted. 'Now, I didn't say he'd be *walking around*, did I? But I didn't say he'd be a corpse either. Anyway . . . ' He caught up the elastic and shovelled it back into his case. ' . . . I'm only here to release this bloody thing to Southmeads. I'm not the pathologist and I'm certainly not the detective. In fact, you know what?'

'What?'

'The detective part? There's a rumour going round that's *you*, Mr Caffery.'

13

7 May

Mossy's heard about a programme over in Glastonbury that'll get you off the gear in a weekend — herbal and non-addictive, you don't remember a thing — and he supposes he should use the money Skinny gives him to get clean. But willpower's hard to come by in Mossy's world, and it's not long before the idea is a memory and his money's back out on the streets, in the Bag Man's pocket.

Day after day goes by, the winter comes and goes, Mossy gets an infected sore on his leg and spends a week in hospital going through a meth programme that does absolutely fuck-all, just leaves him thirstier for the real gear when he gets out. Spring is coming and times on the street get a bit easier because the sad divorcees and old poofter farmers from Gloucestershire get the sun on their heads and decide they can't think straight till they've driven down to Bristol and had their dicks sucked. On the days when business is slow Mossy sometimes meanders back — back to the place Skinny picked him up. He mopes around a bit, hoping to see him again because, as he told BM, they're going to need more where he came from. There's someone in that place's got an appetite for the bad stuff and it's not like they're asking for a quick tug-off. This is a bit more and a bit less. Selling his body but not selling his soul, in a way.

But it's early May by the time he sees Skinny again. It's like before — one minute Mossy's shuffling along, kicking at the butts on the pavement, wondering if there's enough here to put together a ciggy, next thing he knows Skinny's next to him, doing that oiled-walk thing, hands in his pockets. This time Mossy stops and looks at him. He's forgotten that this man is *pretty*. Really pretty, with long dark eyelashes and hair that curls down his elegant neck. And he's cleaner somehow, like the dust of Africa's been washed off him.

'Hey,' goes Mossy, taking him in slowly, from his trainers to his brown leather jacket that's too big because they don't make things to fit someone this small. The clothes are almost smart — neat straight jeans and a sweater under the jacket — but hanging off him, the sleeves and trouser cuffs rolled up. 'It's been a while.'

Skinny doesn't answer. He puts a hand on Mossy's wrist, holding it with his thumb and forefinger, and squeezes gently, reassuringly. That rush of tenderness comes back into Mossy and he gets an ache somewhere that he can't bear. He pulls his hand away.

'He wants some more, don't he? Wants to hurt me some more?'

'Him wants more.'

But this time Mossy has a plan. It's a good plan and a brave one too. He takes Skinny to the herbal clinic to find out how much the cure will cost. The clinic's upmarket, and they both feel a bit out of place — especially when they hear how much it's going to cost. But this is Mossy's plan. He says he'll go with Skinny, give them what they want, if they pay him enough to cover the treatment. Skinny goes outside and makes some phonecalls. He's secretive about them, a bit anxious, but something he says must work somewhere up the line, because eventually they head back to Bristol and end up in the car park again. It's nightfall when they get there and the filthy old Peugeot is waiting.

To start with, the routine's the same — a hit in the back of the car, then the blindfold and the bumpy drive. The doors opening and closing and the crackling, salty feel of the old sofa as he sits down, a broken spring in it now, digging into the back of his legs until he shifts a little. But when he takes off his blindfold he sees Skinny is crying.

'What?' Mossy gets a little knot of anxiety in his voice. 'What's the matter?'

Skinny averts his eyes. He runs his thumb and forefinger up the long column of his throat and Mossy remembers the way he could feel the muscle moving in that throat last time. A pulse starts in his belly.

'What?' he goes again. 'Come on, man, what is it? What do they want this time?'

Skinny turns his watering eyes to him. 'I'm sorry,' he says, in a small voice. 'I am very, very sorry.'

14

14 May

That afternoon, as she and the team unloaded the DUC — the durable utility craft — jet-washed the equipment and pulled in the Alpha flag boards, Flea noticed that every time she turned DI Jack Caffery seemed to be somewhere in her vision. For a few minutes she thought someone was playing a joke on her, that Caffery and Dundas had struck up some strange friendship and were messing her around. Then she wondered whether the mushrooms were still in her system, flashing images at her. The truth, when it came to her, was worse: that part of her had unexpectedly, and completely involuntarily, become hyper-tuned to someone she didn't know, someone who had no understanding of her, or any connection in her life, except that he happened to be the deputy SIO on one of her jobs.

The moment she realized what was happening she walked away from the harbour, opened the doors of the van, pushed all the cylinders in, headed back across the car park and clambered into her car. She slammed the door, pulled out her phone and scrolled up the day's texts: a 'hi' from Thom, a list of shift changes from the resource department, an upgrade notice from the mobile company, until she found another text from Tig. She sat with her head in her hand and read it again.

Txtd u yesterday. Need 2 talk. Just 4 a catch up. Things shite here as per. Got time? I'm @ home all night. Call & I'll come out & meet u if OK? Tig x

She deleted it, then sat for a bit more, thinking about how different she felt from the days when she would fuck freely and happily. Before the accident, when she had her own flat and only went home at weekends, she'd liked the things she could do with sex — the way a man's face would change when he saw her in her underwear, the way his voice was different when he said her name. But since the accident all she'd had for company was lonely masturbation and vague fantasies about some or other film actor. She told herself it was because she would never take her shoes off in front of anyone, but there was more to it than that. She knew she'd never again speak openly about life and death, and she'd never find a way to talk about the other things that had come into her life. Now the only men she was close to were either much older, like Kaiser or Dundas, or gay. Like Tig.

She pushed the key into the ignition and dialled his number. The answerphone was on, so she started the car and drove out into the street. She shouldn't be close to Tig, it was another of those unprofessional things she did, but tonight only Tig would understand what was happening to her.

Tig, then. She was going to see Tig.

★ ★ ★

The photo was the only framed thing Caffery possessed, and he supposed that after two months in the little rented cottage it was time he made a token effort to call the place home and hang the damn thing up. The walls in the old part of the house were porous and uneven, probably made of ancient lime and horsehair or something, so he chose one in the extension where they were modern and should have easily held a little frame like this. But somehow the photo wouldn't stay on the wall. It kept pulling the tacks out even though it wasn't heavy.

After the discovery of the second hand he'd spent a long time at his desk, tying up ends, putting out feelers. The fibres on the first had been sent to Chepstow for tests the in-house lab at Portishead HQ couldn't do, and IDENT1 was still crunching those dabs. Meanwhile the team had contacted staff at the Moat who'd been on leave and they'd tracked down the owner, who'd agreed to cut his holiday short and come home the day after tomorrow. But apart from that there wasn't much he could do, so he'd worked out that the smart thing, the normal thing, would be to go home. He'd stopped at a hardware shop in Hartcliffe and bought a set of Rawlplugs and some screws.

'And that,' he said, through clenched teeth,

giving the screw a final turn, 'is the end of that.'

He stood back, checking it was straight, using the ceiling and the skirting-board as a guide. It looked ridiculous on the bare wall, a tiny rectangular frame marooned there. It was a picture of his passing-out parade at Hendon back in the eighties and he had been placed at the back and at the far end. He went close and peered at the faces. He'd bumped into some of the guys over the years, watched them get promoted, get married, turn into fathers — grandfathers some of them already. He'd seen them get fat, lose their hair, develop police-diet diabetes. And there he was, the only one who hadn't changed, weighing pretty much what he had then and still with all his hair. He should think himself lucky. People were always telling him so, lucky bastard, still with his own hair. He'd nod, make a joke about it, but in his heart he hated what he saw in the mirror. He hated it because his reflection told him one thing: life, real life, had never touched him.

He put his finger on his face in the photo, seeing quite clearly in black and white the thing that had set him aside all these years. Even back then, when he was only twenty, his eyes'd had that one-track determination, the same anger even then. They weren't the eyes of a killer yet — that part was still to come — but they were the eyes of someone who could think only of revenge and violence. He'd once been given a book for Christmas by Rebecca, his ex-girlfriend. It was a collection of sayings and she'd highlighted one of them for him. He couldn't remember who'd written it, but he'd never forget what it said, though the book was long lost: 'Little, vicious minds abound with anger and revenge, and are incapable of feeling the pleasure of forgiving their enemies.'

'Little and vicious,' he murmured now, looking at his photograph. Little and vicious because he didn't understand the concept of forgiveness, because it was still a word that made no sense to him. He went to the window, put his hand on the pane and stared out, thinking about what he'd come to. The cottage sat on karst land, on a lonely slope leading down to a minor country road, pocked with natural sinkholes and open-cast mines where the Romans had once quarried for lead, the depressions lined with wetland plants like sedge and marsh marigold. Half a mile down the road there was a pig farm and just a few hundred yards past the cottage boundary the furthest edge of the Priddy Circles — four Neolithic circles, scarred by sinkholes, remembered by some for the mysterious rumours of ancient ritual. A strange, remote place to come to understand the violence in him, to try to let this thing stuck inside him all these years dislodge itself and work itself out of his system.

Something in the corner of his eye moved. He didn't do anything, just stood, hearing his own heartbeat thudding. Then he turned slowly towards the television. It was switched off but the room was reflected in it: the open door with the carpeted passageway going back into the house; his face, eyes a little hollow; the windows

106

with the orange ball of the sun going down. From the reflection it was difficult to tell if the movement had been inside the room or in the garden. His nerves on alert, he waited for it to happen again. A minute or more ticked by, and just as he was about to put it down to his imagination, he heard, behind him, a small flurry of clatters, then a crash.

He turned. The photo lay on the floor. Shards of glass everywhere, the frame cracked open, its little screws exposed. After all the work he'd put in it still wouldn't stay on the wall. He went and pushed his fingers into the hole. The Rawlplug had fallen out, taking plaster with it. He looked around at the silent room, at the late sun falling on the floor, at the TV, then back at the photograph. He breathed in and out, in and out, telling himself he was being an idiot. Really an idiot, because the thought that had popped into his head was ridiculous. The thought that the house, inanimate and blank though it was, had somehow found a way to dislike him.

* * *

Tig lived in one of the tallest blocks in Bristol, a windswept crumbling tower painted in red and blue on the Hopewell estate. It had views all across the town, but half of the flats weren't occupied: boarded up and vandalized. As she got out of the car she noticed how deserted the place felt. A small black guy passed her, his hands in his pockets, his eyes averted the way they all did round here. But he was the only person she saw as she crossed the car park to the tower.

When Tig opened the door he had the chain on and seemed a bit shaken, as if maybe he'd been asleep. He was rubbing his eye with his knuckles, his compact body worked and toned in a black weightlifter's vest.

'Hi.'

'Hi.'

'I'm sorry it took so long. Had a bad couple of days at work. You OK?'

When he was in jail his cellmate had poured bleach into Tig's eyes. The left had recovered, but in the right he'd developed secondary glaucoma, swelling the eyeball and swivelling the pupil to the side. It was always this eye he rubbed when he was on edge. She waited a minute while he went on digging his knuckle into it. Then she shivered, crossing her arms tightly and looking round at the deserted estate. 'Tig? Can you let me in?'

He hesitated, glanced over his shoulder into the flat. There were piles and piles of belongings crammed into the hallway and she knew he was embarrassed. Fifteen years ago Tig had been done for the attempted murder of an eighty-year-old woman while burgling her house. He'd been a heroin addict in those days, but he was a rare one: he'd cleaned up in jail and since his release he'd founded his own charity offering advice and sanctuary to street people trying to get clean. Through his work he'd developed contacts in the ethnic and refugee groups in the area, and had even, for a while, been felt out by Operation Atrium. An intelligence-led anti-crime operation, Atrium was targeting drugs-trafficking among Jamaican gangs, and white though he was, they'd researched Tig's connections and decided they'd like him as a 'CHIS' — the new word for an informant. The interest didn't last long: they backed off when it came to them loud and clear that if there was one thing you couldn't call Tommy Baines it was a snout. They'd have lost it completely if they'd found out that one of his closest friends was a support-unit sergeant.

She'd met him through the diving. Somehow he'd got the money together to take four of his clients on a basic PADI course where she was finishing her dive master's qualification. Forced together for two days, they'd hit it off. But it wasn't the diving that held them together, it was something less definable than that: a shared sense of being damaged, maybe — and, more important, a sense they were both meeting their debts by acting responsibly. For Flea the responsibility was about work and about Thom, for Tig it was work and his mum.

His mum was a bit dotty — nothing official, but Tig's prison sentence had been the last straw for her. When he'd got out of jail a year ago he'd moved straight in here as her carer and ever since had been dealing with the junk she amassed. Everyone knew it was slowly driving him mad.

'The idea was for me to come out and meet you,' he said now.

'I tried to call — and even if there was somewhere to go in this part of the world, I haven't got any money and, anyway, *you* said you wanted to talk.' Her nose was running. She wiped it impatiently. 'Look, Tig, for God's sake, I'm cold. I don't care about your mum if that's what's on your mind.'

He studied her for a while and she knew what he was seeing. She looked a mess. He pressed his face into the gap and examined her face, his right eye lagging behind the left. 'You're shaking,' he said. 'What's wrong with you?'

'I'm cold. Look, I came to talk to you. *You* asked *me*. Remember?'

He pointed down to her feet. 'You stay there. Right there. I'll be back when I've checked we're all decent.'

He disappeared into the dimly lit corridor with its peeling wallpaper and stained paintwork, leaving her on the doorstep. She waited, stepping from foot to foot, pulling her coat close. There was a cold, stale draught coming from the corridor and the sound of a badly tuned radio scanner from one of the rooms. That would be Tig's mum. Ever since Flea could remember his mother had been addicted to listening to the police. Always said she wanted to steal a march on them if they decided to come and get her, because that was how it was for her now, imaginary armies and men from the institution coming through the streets. Now that the police signals were encrypted she listened to the static instead. That was how out of the box she was.

After a few minutes Tig reappeared in the hallway, switching on the light and unlocking the chain.

110

'Mum's not sleeping. It's always worse when she doesn't sleep.' He stood back to let her in, waving his hand a little sorrowfully into the depths of the hallway. The narrow corridor of carpet was filthy, stains trodden in over years. 'It's always about now I want to use. When she can't sleep.'

They went into the kitchen with its piles of laundry, its cheap laminate table, salt and pepper and ketchup bottle on a stained plastic mat in the middle. Tig put the kettle on, turned the gas burners on the stove up high to warm the place up, and moved a pile of clothing off one of the chairs, gesturing for her to take a seat. She sat in silence at the table, the smells of neglect, decay and gas filling her head, the little bag of mushrooms still in her fleece pocket, hard and lumpy against her breast, reminding her of Mum and the dog violets. Tig made her a cup of milky tea, then found a packet of peanuts and opened it with his teeth, poured them into a bowl and pushed it in front of her.

'What is it? Work? Something horrible happen? It's funny — when you come here you don't smell of dead bodies.'

'I don't spend my whole life moving bodies around, you know.'

'Just most of it.'

Well, Tig, she wanted to say, these days the main thing I need my protective gear for is sitting in this flat. But she didn't. She pulled the coat tighter round herself. It really was cold in here, draughty. 'But you're right. I've had a couple of body days. Except not a yuck one

— well, it was sort of yuck, sort of not.'

He picked up a handful of nuts and began idly to sort them in his palm. 'How can something be sort of yuck?'

'It was a pair of hands.'

He looked up. 'A pair of hands?'

'Under a restaurant in the floating harbour.'

'Without a body?'

'Without a body.'

'In Bristol harbour?'

'That's what I said.'

'Well, how in fuck's name did they get there?'

'Wish we knew.'

'Do they know whose hands they were?'

'Nope.'

'So which restaurant?'

'Down opposite Redcliffe Quay.' She poked at the peanuts, wondering if it was safe to eat anything in this place. 'The Moat.'

'The Moat?' He gave a low whistle. 'I know the fucking Moat. I know the guy who runs it. African guy — gave me a huge chunk of my start-up capital.'

'Well,' she said, popping a couple of peanuts into her mouth. 'That's a good enough reason for me not to talk to you about it, isn't it?'

He sighed. 'Just showing interest, that's all.'

She took another peanut from the bowl and split it in half. Tig's hand was resting on the table, short nails, fading blue prison tattoos on the knuckles: *Love* and *Hate*. Not *Mum* and *Dad*. 'Tig?' she said, after small silence. 'You know when you used to take drugs?'

'I ain't about to forget it, am I?'

112

'Did you ever feel . . . ' She ran her hands down her face, trying to find the words. 'Did you feel like a whole — a whole *universe* was opening up . . . in here, in your head?'

He gave a short laugh. 'A whole universe? Oh, yeah. That's how it feels to start with, like there are whole new worlds in there you'd never've got to any other way. But then later, when it turns itself round — because it always does turn itself round — suddenly the universe is what opens up when you're *not* using. But this time it's a universe of pain. And the only escape is more gear.'

'But at first, when you're in that universe, did you ever think you could . . . I don't know, that you could *connect*, maybe? Connect with people who've died?'

'Oh please, Flea. *I see dead people*, is that what this is? Give me a break, there isn't a moonchild, white witch or guru who doesn't tit around with gear and convince themselves they're getting some sort of super vision — some sort of clairvoyance or whatever the fuck they want to call it. I've heard it chapter, verse and fucking book. Think they're going to speak to the dead because they inject some shit into their arm.'

Speak to the dead, Flea thought, picturing her mother, crouched among the trees. Speak to the dead.

'Now, if you're asking me can you uncover things you've witnessed,' Tig went on, 'things you've forgotten, things you don't even know you know, then to that the answer's yes. Of

113

course. But it can't tell you things you haven't already learned.'

She rubbed her arms and avoided his eyes. 'I found mushrooms in my dad's stuff. And I took them.'

Tig looked at her intently. 'You of all people,' he muttered. 'You of *all* people.' He drummed his tattooed fingers on the table. *Love. Hate. Love. Hate.* 'Stupid effing cow. Stupid cow.'

She gazed at him steadily now, at his weird, fucked-up face, with the eye that went the wrong way and his nose that looked as if it had been punched. The problem with this situation, here with Tig, was clear: she wanted to use drugs to go deeper into her memory, to find the answers she knew were just out of her reach. She was going to use drugs to find the voices. With him it was the other way round. He'd used drugs to shut the voices up. He'd used them to quell the anger. And that was the hitch. He might understand better than others, but he'd never fully see what she wanted.

After a while he shrugged. 'Oh, well. You've done it now. It's happened.' He sat back, slumping a little. 'So what's worrying you?'

'I saw my mum. And she was trying to tell me something.' Flea leaned back in the chair, pulling her hair off her face, holding it in a knot and concentrating on the ceiling. 'But I can't quite get at it so I want . . . '

'You want to do it again?'

'Not the mushrooms.'

'Oh, don't tell me you want to be a smackhead like me?'

114

She dropped the chair down and met his eyes. 'Do you remember my friend Kaiser?'

'Yeah. Weird old shit. Friend of your old man's.'

'He says I won't get there with the mushrooms.'

Tig nodded, his bad eye droopy now, as if this was too tiring. 'And?'

'He's come up with something else — told me about it last night. Ibogaine.'

'Yeah, yeah, I know it. Organic, legal, from Africa. Some places are using it to get people off the gear.'

'Kaiser says I could spend months using the mushrooms and get nowhere but this'll get me where I want to be. It gets inside and . . . ' she made a flicking motion next to her temple, ' . . . maybe I'll be able to speak to Mum again. Find out what she was trying to say.'

'And you believe him?'

She put her hands between her knees and studied the untouched cup of tea. The sound of the scanner in the bedroom next door hissed through the walls. No, she thought. No, I don't really believe him but it's better than nothing.

'Ah, well,' Tig said, when he saw she wasn't going to speak. 'Looks like there's nothing I can say. Is there? And people like you, well, you never get hooked anyway. Not in the way people like me do.'

She gave a sad smile. 'I've got four days' annual starting Friday, no standby.'

Tig swung out of his chair and got another bag of peanuts from the cupboard. He poured them into the bowl, a little puff of salt coming off them, and gave a sad laugh. 'Friday it is, then. I won't try to talk you out of it.'

She sat looking at the peanuts and knew then that things would always be like this, some people getting away with it and some people not. Some people gilded by life, some not. And in spite of everything, in spite of her loss and her anxiety, in spite of the things she believed she shared with Tig, she knew in her heart that she was gilded. That she was gilded and Tig wasn't.

15

Now that the sun was going down it was getting cold and the Walking Man had stopped walking. He'd squeezed through a hedge on the roadside on the tiny B route in Somerset, and was preparing his camp for the night in the field on the other side, making a pile of the paper scraps he'd gathered from the roadside that day. At half past eight Jack Caffery pulled up his car opposite, his headlights on.

At first he didn't get out, just switched off the engine and watched. This was someone he'd been thinking about for months. It was bizarre to be here at last.

The Walking Man was used to drivers and their ways and paid no attention. When he turned to gather more wood for the fire Caffery caught sight of his face. Here, he thought, is a man who was born at the bottom of a firepit. He was soot-covered from head to toe: the thick socks he wore over his walking boots, tied in place with a piece of cloth at each calf, were blackened and the three-quarter length jacket he wore, tied with washing-line round his waist, was so grimy you wouldn't know what colour it had once been. He was in his late forties — Caffery knew this from his Criminal Records Bureau entry — but to look at him now you'd never have been able to guess his age. His hair hung past his shoulders and a black beard rambled from just below his eyes to his chest, covering him like a cowl.

Caffery dragged his coat from the back seat and got out of the car. It was one of those deserted Somerset lanes so narrow the trees link overhead and turn themselves into a tunnel: the only light was a little evening sun coming from the gap in the hedgerow that opened on to the Walking Man's field. Caffery shut the car door, buttoned the coat and crossed the lane, pushing himself through the dead remains of a hawthorn bush, getting his old trousers torn, scraping his right sleeve.

In the field he pulled a beanie from his pocket and pulled it down over his ears. It was freezing now it was evening; you'd think it was winter again. He stood on the hard, ploughed ground and waited. The Walking Man continued what he was doing, fishing out a filthy cigarette lighter and putting it to the bottom of the pile of twigs. It flared almost instantaneously, years of firebuilding practice. Flames bit and crackled inside the sticks, casting shadows across the twilit earth.

Caffery came a few steps closer. 'You're the Walking Man.'

He didn't look up. He threw a log on the fire and gathered another two in his gloved hands.

'I said, you're the Walking Man. Aren't you?'

'It's not what I was christened. Not what my mother called me.'

Caffery folded his arms. The Walking Man's voice was educated, sort of polite, but he didn't seem to care who he was speaking to or what they thought. It was as if he'd known Caffery was coming and wasn't bothered whether they talked or not. He dropped the logs on to the fire and watched them for a few moments. Then, satisfied it was going to catch properly, he forced two sticks into the ground next to it, unwrapped the bedroll from his back and draped it over them — spreading it out to warm. His clothing steamed, his breath hung white in the darkening air.

'I've been looking for you for a long time,' Caffery said, after a while.

'And how did you find me?' His voice was light, almost amused. 'I'm not an easy man to find. I move. I walk. That's what I do.'

'And what I do is find people. I'm the police.'

The Walking Man stopped what he was doing and, for the first time, looked up. His eyes were dark-lashed and blue and Caffery had a weird moment of recognition: the same eyes. He and the Walking Man had exactly the same eyes. As if somewhere back down the line they'd shared a relative. Someone as far back as Donegal, maybe.

'I don't like the police.' The Walking Man squinted a little, studying Caffery. He took his time, looking at the beanie, the rough donkey jacket, the Dr Martens. Maybe he was thinking Caffery didn't look like a copper. Or maybe he'd noticed the eyes thing too.

'So,' he said, after a while, 'my old friends. The police. They know where I am, do they?'

'They have an idea. A general idea. You don't stray much out of Somerset and Wiltshire.'

119

The Walking Man laughed. 'Do they think I didn't spend long enough inside? Or that I'm going to do it again? That I'm going to hurt someone else?'

'Sightings of you get called in. From the public, from people who don't know who you are, maybe see you sleeping rough and think you're ill.'

'Or a danger to them?'

'We don't throw anything away in this job. You're somewhere on an intelligence file.'

'Intelligence,' the Walking Man said to himself, as if it was the wrong word to use for the police. He turned his back on Caffery to organize his dinner. '*In-tell-igence*.'

With the bottle-opener hanging on a tape round his neck, he made holes in the lids of four cans and placed each in the centre of the fire. Then he sat down, moving slowly for the bulk of his clothes, and pulled at the pieces of cloth wrapped round his feet. He removed his boots carefully, taking each lace with caution, and placed them on the ground next to his bedroll. Then he took off his socks, three pairs, and inspected his feet. Caffery saw that in the places his own feet were calloused and red, the Walking Man's were black — as if his body was exuding a kind of protective tar. He used the cloth to rub and dry them, then put on two pairs of dry socks and what looked like sheep-skin slippers, which he bound at the ankles with the cloth. After that he took care of his boots: running his hands inside each one, tapping them together at the heels, rubbing a thin line of Vaseline from a tiny

120

pot inside each and setting them near the fire to dry. The Walking Man spent every waking hour of every day walking and his boots needed all the attention he could give them.

'I've come a long way to see you.'

'Have you now?'

'It's taken me a long time to get here.'

'Well, it's taken me a lifetime to get where I am.'

'I know.' Caffery shifted his weight. It was cold out here, really bitter. 'I'm here because I want you to tell me things. I want you to talk about what you did.'

The Walking Man laughed again, mild and polite, as if he had told him a gentle joke. 'And where,' he said, 'does it say I talk for nothing? Hmm? Is there a notice on my back says I'm ready to talk to anybody?' He was still laughing. 'You're not the boss of me. Po-lice-man.'

Caffery unzipped the donkey jacket and pulled out a litre of Scotch from inside his sweater. He held it out. 'Brought you something.'

The Walking Man stared at it, then at Caffery's face. After a few moments he came over and took the bottle, turning it round and round in his hands. Close up his fingernails were raised and yellow, as if they had something bad brewing under them and might fall off at any time. He smelled of firelighters and smoke.

'In nineteen eighty,' he said thoughtfully, looking at the whisky label, with its gold and white picture of a tea clipper, 'an average house in Bristol was worth twenty grand. Did you know that?'

Caffery was never put off track when someone changed direction without warning. It was part of being a cop. 'I didn't. I could maybe hazard a guess about what it was like in London. But not out here. This is new territory to me.'

'Well, now you're in on the secret. Twenty grand. Now, my parents, see, were doctors — both dead now, of course — and they had one of the biggest houses in Clifton. They paid sixty K for it in nineteen eighty and it came straight to me when they died. Course, I couldn't use it because I was in a high-security wing at Long Lartin until — ' He made a sound in the back of his throat and rolled his dark blue eyes. 'But you already know that, don't you?'

'I've seen the file.'

'The executors paid off the tax and lodged the house with a management company. They banked the rent for the last ten years of my sentence. It was a beauty of a house — even I could see that. It had six bedrooms and a coach-house, one of the finest examples of Georgian architecture in Bristol, so said the estate agents. When I came out of the nick last year I sold it. What do you think they gave me?'

'I just sold a house in London. It wasn't much but my parents gave fifteen for it in the seventies and I got back more than three fifty. I don't know? Five hundred?'

'Try four times that. Almost two million. Every month I get more than eight grand interest paid into my account. Do they have that on my intelligence file?' He threw the bottle into the air, let it spin round, light moving against the navy blue sky, and caught it with a neat smile.

'Here,' he said, jamming it into Caffery's chest. 'I drink cider. But thanks anyway.'

★ ★ ★

Flea stayed with Tig until eight. They got fish and chips from the only shop in Bristol that still wrapped it in newspapers. They took it back to his flat, shared a bottle of wine and talked, and all the time she kept prodding herself to ask him about the text — about what he'd wanted to talk about. But the idea kept slipping away and when she did remember, when she was getting up to leave at the end of the evening, he waved it aside. No, he said, it was nothing. Just missed seeing you, that's all.

She buttoned her coat, found her keys and kissed Tig's cheek — he always froze when she came near him, as if he'd gone into spasm, his arms out at his sides as if he'd been petrified, but she did it anyway. She was turning away, half smiling to herself at the way she could immobilize him with embarrassment, when she saw his mother standing in the doorway. She was dressed in a pink quilted housecoat and her long grey hair was loose round her shoulders. She looked older than fifty, as if only half of her was actually in the world, the rest somewhere else. A skeleton in a nightgown.

'Mum,' Tig said. 'Mum. Go back to bed. It's late.'

But she held on to the doorframe, her face confused, looking from one of them to the other,

her mouth opening and closing as if she was trying to speak. Tig got up and took her arm.

'Oh, Tommy,' she muttered. 'Please. Tell them to go away, will you, love? Tell them to leave me alone.'

'Come on, Mum, you're dreaming again. Back to bed.'

'Tell them to leave me alone — the blacks.'

'Mum, please.' Tig put his arm round her and tried to coax her back down the corridor. 'Come on, darling, back to bed.'

But she resisted. She clung to the doorframe, and turned her head to Flea, as if she might help. All the veins under her yellow skin were standing out blue and sick-looking. 'Oh, dearie,' she whispered. 'Oh, my love, I'm in so much trouble.'

'Mrs Baines, do you remember me? I'm Flea. I met you before. Remember?'

'Ask them, dear, will you? Ask them to leave me alone with their bang-bang music and their smells. Tell them to stop running up and down my corridor and putting their faces through my walls.'

'Don't worry, Mrs Baines.' Flea stepped forward and put a hand on her arm. It was cold and as fragile as a matchstick. 'I'm sure Tommy's got it all organized.'

Mrs Baines blinked at her. Then she began to cry. It was a thin, confused sound, no energy in it. She reached out for Tig. 'Tommy, stop the little one putting his face through my wall again.'

'Mum. It's a television programme. You've watched too much television.'

'I *know* it's a television programme, Tommy. I know. Have you got that butter knife?' She twisted away from him, peering blearily round the kitchen. 'Where's the butter knife? Your dad's butter knife with the bone handle? Give it to me so I can defend myself.'

Tig glanced despairingly at Flea and she knew he was asking her to help him through this. But all she could do was wrinkle her face sympathetically. Maybe she was kidding herself that because of Thom she could understand what Tig went through with his mum. But this was much worse than having a brother who was out of work and depressed. What Tig dealt with daily was beyond her. And, somehow, he still managed not to use.

'Come on, Mum, I'll get you back to bed. Then I'll bring you some hot milk. You'd like that, wouldn't you?'

'What about the butter knife?'

'I'll bring that too. As soon as you're in bed I'll bring it. I promise.'

'And you'll stop them looking at me? When I'm in my bed?'

'I will. I promise. I'll switch the TV off.'

And he eased her away through the door, his hands on her shoulder-blades, two beaten people, moving slowly down the crowded hallway, leaving Flea alone to stare blankly at the kitchen door swinging on its hinges, thinking that whatever your relationship with your parents somewhere along the line there was always pain.

* * *

It was turning out that the Walking Man wasn't like everyone thought. Apart from the cider and the money — Caffery was sure no one knew about the money — there was more. For one thing he didn't stop in the place he found himself when the sun went down. It was more planned than that. He had pit-stops all over the West Country, little hidey-holes just off the road where he knew he wouldn't be bothered. He left things hidden there, under rocks, under cattle troughs, tucked into crumbling walls. On this pit-stop he had tins, a pile of foam-rubber mats and four jars of scrumpy buried in the loose earth next to the hedgerow.

'Should always drink the alcohol produced by the land you're standing on.' He uncorked the glass jar with his teeth. 'You go to Cuba, you drink rum. You go to Mexico, you drink tequila. Never get a hangover if you do that. Generations of wisdom've gone into making these drinks. Generations learning how a body rubs up against the climate and the soil and the water.'

Caffery unscrewed the bottle of Scotch and tipped the contents onto the frozen earth. He leaned forward and held it out to the Walking Man, who carefully filled it with cloudy scrumpy, holding the glass mason jar to the bottle neck.

'And in Somerset you drink apples. Cider.'

The fire was blazing well now, throwing its light into the faces of the two men. They sat on the corrugated squares of foam and watched the night fall. As the last of the daylight faded, the glow of the lights of Bristol came on to the north-west, misty and distant under a grey sky

126

like a fabled living city, as if dragons lived there, not students and drugs-dealers and people gone bad enough to hack off someone's hands and bury them under a restaurant.

Caffery sat back and put the bottle to his lips. The scrumpy was cold, but it brought such a hit of autumn and childhood apple orchards that he almost drank it all at once, just to stay in that memory and not think about buried hands.

'Farmer I get that from,' said the Walking Man, 'until nineteen ninety he was still putting a carcass into the vat. A pig or a chicken. Said it sweetened the mixture and since the inspectors stopped him the scrumpy's not a shadow of what it used to be.'

Caffery drank some more, straight down, not caring about the car parked on the lane and whether he'd need to drive home. This was how farmers and workers had lived for years and there was something comforting about that. Now, with the cider in his mouth and the honest coldness of a ploughed field on his backside, he let the weirdness of the day fall away from him, let himself stop worrying about some poor bastard with no hands, dead or dying. He wiped his mouth and pulled up his knees, rested his elbows on them and leaned forward.

'What do I have to give you?' he said. 'I can't give you money and I can't see what you need.'

The Walking Man gave a wry smile. 'I need you to give me two things.'

'Two?'

'The first is I need you to tell me who it is who's come here out of nowhere, off the road like a ghost, asking me to turn my past over to him.'

'I'm Jack.' He held out his hand, straight in front of him, waiting for him to shake it.

The Walking Man didn't raise his own. 'Jack? And there's another name comes along with that one? A second name?'

'Caffery.' He lowered his hand and put it on the ground next to him, half embarrassed by it. 'Jack Caffery.'

'Jack Caffery.' The Walking Man laughed a little. 'Jack Caffery, Policeman.'

He stoked the fire and moved the cans expertly around in the bottom. A thin line of steam came from two and these he set aside in the embers. The sun had gone now and the white puffs of old man's beard caught in the top branches had taken on a blue haze, like tiny night-time clouds.

'London, then? Is that where you live?'

'No. I live here. In the Mendips.'

'But you're a London boy. I can tell it from looking at you even before you open that policeman's mouth of yours.'

'Family's Liverpool, Donegal before that — but me, yes, I'm London. And now I'm here. I got a transfer two months ago.'

'To the west?'

'Because I wanted to talk to you.'

'You could've just got an off-peak supersaver. Spent the day with me. Gone back to the Smoke where life is so much better, eh?'

Caffery gave a dry laugh.

'But that's not it,' said the Walking Man. 'Is it?

There's more than just wanting to see me.'

'There's always more.'

'There's a woman?' A smile twitched under his beard. 'Jack Caffery, Policeman, don't smokescreen me. There's always a woman.'

'Was. There was a woman. Yes.'

The Walking Man watched his face, waited for him to speak. Caffery sighed. 'She wanted children. The harder she asked for it the more I couldn't. Until we get ourselves into this pressure-cooker of a life, and before we know what's happening . . . ' He clapped his hands, sending out a puff of air that made the flames waver. 'Hey,' he said, dropping his hands and smiling. 'I suppose I didn't love her enough. But whatever happened I couldn't do it. I just couldn't have a child. Not after what I've seen happen. To children.'

There was a silence. The lights of a plane from Bristol airport rose up from the horizon and glinted, cold and silent, and both men looked at it, both maybe pretending not to be thinking about that word, 'children', and the different things it meant to them. When Rebecca had talked about having children she referred to the C-word, because she knew, for Caffery, it was one of the most dangerous words she could utter. She said that without a child the energy he was putting into life was wasted — going into a dead hole. When he asked her what that meant she'd said: 'The energy you put into finding out what happened to Ewan — the same energy you put into the job — means nothing. Absolutely nothing. It goes nowhere and creates nothing.'

Which was funny, because he'd never thought of his job and finding an answer as wasted energy. But whenever he thought of a child, a family, the only thing he could imagine was something loose and ethereal, something you could lose in a second. Like trying to gather mist with your bare hands.

After a while the Walking Man got painfully to his feet. He pulled tin plates from the store under the hedgerow and brought them back to the fire. He used a stick to roll the tins out, squeezing one between his feet to hold it still while he cut into the lid with a Swiss Army knife. 'We're going to eat in a minute.' Sweat appeared on his forehead. It ran through the grime and into his beard. 'We'll eat. And then we'll talk some more.'

Caffery held the bottle between both hands and looked up at him. There was only ten years between them but, for a reason that probably had something to do with the scrumpy, this felt as natural and reassuring as looking up at a father. More, maybe. The Walking Man put food on the plates and they ate: steak pudding, little potatoes and some herbs the Walking Man had produced from a pocket. Caffery didn't know why it should be — maybe it was the cold, maybe it was the wake-up call of the scrumpy — but that meat and vegetable from burned tins tasted like the only meal he'd remember when he died. He wiped the plate clean with his fingers and licked them. The Walking Man had finished his meal and was watching him. 'Well, Jack Caffery,' he said, 'you left one woman behind, and what about now? There's no woman here? With you?'

Caffery smiled. 'No. No woman.'

'What do you do, then? For a woman?'

Caffery put the plate down and reached inside his jacket for his tobacco. A habit he hadn't broken, even after all these years. He took his time rolling the cigarette. He couldn't help the way when he heard the word 'woman' the first picture he got was of Flea on the harbour that morning, dirty-blonde hair and her arms tanned under the force's navy T-shirt. When he licked the paper he didn't raise his eyes to the Walking Man. He kept them on the lights of Bristol.

'Prostitutes,' he said. 'I go to prostitutes. Over there. In Bristol.'

'Prostitutes? Or a prostitute?'

'More than one. I hardly ever go to the same one twice.'

'How often?'

'Not often enough.'

'How often's not often enough?'

He lit the cigarette, took a couple of draws, thinking about the bodies and the faces and the streetlights. He thought about the cold void in his chest he must be imagining women like Keelie could close. 'Once a week. Why? What do you do for a woman?'

The Walking Man showed his teeth a little, like bone, and the red edge of his tongue. 'That's over. With me that's been over since it happened. Belongs to another life. Don't miss it when you think of it being something other people do in another life.' He got to his feet and collected the plates, wiped them with a cloth and stacked them next to the ditch. He corked the cider, pushing the jar back under the hedgerow. Then he pulled out a long roll of rubber matting and tossed it into a ditch. 'It's time for me to sleep.'

'The second thing. You haven't told me the second thing you want from me.'

'In the spring I go to sleep an hour after dark,' said the Walking Man, as if he hadn't heard. 'Always have done, ever since they let me out of Long Lartin. You can stay if you want, but you don't want to sleep out here under the stars. For one thing it's cold. And for another . . . ' He shovelled his clothing into the ditch, arranging it on the mat so he'd sleep on it and give it some of his heat for the morning. He took the sleeping-bag from where it hung next to the fire, rolled it up quickly to conserve the heat it had soaked in and laid it on top of the clothes. 'For another you won't want to sleep out in the open with me. I mean . . . ' He clicked his tongue up behind his teeth as if he had something tasty there. 'I mean, how do you know what you'll look like when you wake up?'

Caffery stood. 'There were *two* things. I've done one — what's the other?'

The Walking Man came a little closer, and this time Caffery saw something infirm about him. Like a limp. Or a hesitation. 'There is one more thing you can do, Jack Caffery. And after that we can talk.'

'Name it.'

'The Snowbunting and the Remembrance.

132

That's my price. A clutch of Snowbuntings and Remembrances.'

'Snowbunting? It's a bird?'

'No. Not a bird. It's a flower. A crocus. A little white spring flower.'

'Where do I get a crocus at this time of year?'

'You get the bulbs so I can plant them. But when you bring them you come to listen to me — you don't come with a lecture in your mouth, or an idea in your head of converting me and making me a productive member of society. I am who I am and you must not try to make me believe in redemption. Understand?'

'I understand. No redemption.'

'Good. The Remembrance is not so popular now, not like it used to be. Out of fashion and not easy to find. But . . . ' He straightened and put his hand on Caffery's chest, holding it there as his hand rose and fell with Caffery's breathing. As if he was testing his heart. 'But you'll find them. You'll find my crocuses. I know you will.'

16

Car-jacking had arrived in the West Country. In 2006 the young professional owners of a Scénic MPV, driven in for the day from Wellington to see a show, had their car stolen as they parked near the Bristol Hippodrome. The car-jacker was wearing a red fullface ski mask and R&B jeans, and he'd waited until the wife was out and the husband was pulling on the parking brake before he struck.

He dragged the driver out on to the pavement, breaking his wrist, jumped into the car and drove off at thirty miles an hour, causing ten thousand pounds' worth of damage to other vehicles in the car park. He took the road up towards Clifton, and no one knew how far he'd have got if it hadn't been that in stealing the car he'd also stolen a passenger. The couple's six-year-old daughter was in the back seat. When he realized this he dumped the car double quick, leaving it on the pavement in Whiteladies Road with the motor still running, the child unharmed. He disappeared into the grey afternoon, never to be seen again.

Flea'd paid a passing interest to the case because she sometimes used the car park. She asked a friend in Intelligence for the details and when she went over what had happened one thing stuck in her mind: *the child was sitting in a booster seat*. Flea spent the next few days wandering parking lots, looking through the window of any Renault Scénic, looking especially for booster seats, until she was convinced of one thing: whichever angle the guy had come from he would have seen the child before he'd stolen the car. And when she looked at the witness statements she found the child reported that the first thing the offender had said was: 'Shut the fucking crying.' It didn't sound like someone who was surprised to find she was in the car: 'Shut the fucking crying . . . '

What if, Flea wondered, they'd got it wrong? The police thought the car-jacker'd dumped the car when he realized the child was there. But how about if you turned it round? What if it wasn't the child's presence that had made him *dump* the car? What if the child — and the thought made her cold — what if the child being there had *made him steal it in the first place?*

She became obsessed with the idea that he'd targeted the car for the little girl, and had got frightened into abandoning the kidnap. She started fishing, asking questions, offering theories. She made friends with a proactive intelligence officer in the vehicle-crime unit at Trinity Road and dropped by, asking what they thought. Then one day she got a call from her inspector. The first time she'd ever had to stand in his office, instead of sitting comfortably. He was to the point. 'I'm going to say this once and then we'll pretend I never said it. Marley, wind your neck in.'

And so she'd learned caution. Even though the little girl crying in the back seat of the MPV haunted her, Flea would never again get involved in something that wasn't her business. She made a self-pact: next time she found herself playing detective she was going straight to her inspector, putting her name down for the trainee programme and getting started on the CID 'aide' course. But that, of course, would mean an end to the diving. And because she was never going to give up the diving she went on doing her job, pulling out the bodies, searching for the knives and guns that had created the corpses, standing in the front line whenever the force needed muscle. But one thing she never did was think about the cases. No curiosity, no theorizing. It was a rule she had.

Which was why that night, driving along the little country lanes that skirted the northern outskirts of Bath, the lighted abbey and the church spires glimmering against the dark hills, Flea deliberately wasn't having any ideas about how a pair of severed hands had come to be buried under the entrance to the Moat restaurant. Instead she was thinking about Tig, about whether he was the only one who understood how she felt about her parents. Whether he understood the guilt and whether he still carried a dark hole inside him for what he'd done to that old lady. She was still thinking about him when she got home, and she might not have given the hands another thought for the rest of the night if it hadn't been for the accidental discovery she made inside her father's study.

★　★　★

It was late, the cottage in darkness, only the little lantern hanging over the door to guide her as she pulled the Ford Focus off the road on to the gravel driveway. The wisteria that twined round the lamp was dislodging the stones above the front door and, without the money to hire a stonemason, a couple of months ago she'd had to climb up a ladder herself with a plasterer's float full of mortar. She'd mixed it too hard, and now, only two months on, the soft Bath stone was cracking in a long, depressing line over the lintel.

She let herself in, picked up the mail, and sorted it as she headed to the kitchen. On the top was a copy of the local property paper, a scaremongering headline in red: *House Prices Drop in Second Quarter*. Stuck on the front page was a pink Post-it with one sentence scrawled on it: 'But we would always honour our original offer, of course. Best wishes, Katherine Oscar.'

Centuries ago, the Marleys' garden hadn't belonged to the cottage but to the neighbouring Charlcombe Hall. And now Katherine and Giles Oscar, the new owners of Charlcombe, wanted to reinstate the garden, wanted a clean sweep down to the valley from the back of their overbuilt, over-decorated house. Sometimes Flea thought selling her section of the land was the smart thing to do, release a bit of equity. After the accident Thom hadn't wanted to stay there, 'with the ghosts', so they'd agreed she'd keep the house and give him a loan against her share of the life-insurance money that would come after the statutory seven years. The Oscars' money would make life easier.

But no. She crumpled the paper and shoved it into the belly of the Aga. She wasn't going to budge, no matter how hard it got to maintain her parents' house. It was the closest she could get to her childhood — and maybe that made her soft, but she needed it. She'd been born here, grown up knowing every inch of the ageing lawns that dropped in terraces out of sight, past ponds and a lake, ending somewhere vague among the fields. She'd grown up with the distant views of Bath, hazy mist settling in the valley in the autumn mornings so only the church spires were visible like sunken trees in a lake.

She waited for the newspaper to catch, then kicked off her shoes and went down to Dad's study. In the electric light all the belongings looked a little frozen, as if she'd forced them to sit in unnatural positions. Kaiser's boxes stood in a row under the table, untouched. She went to the shelves and ran her fingers along the book spines until she found the bound thesis her father had done at Cambridge. She pulled it out and opened it, looking inside the cover. It was typical of Dad to write in books — he didn't revere them, he used them. The only good book, he said, was one that had been added to by the reader and the inside cover of the dissertation was covered with scribblings — tiny notes to himself. She stood under the light and studied the list, looking for anything, anything, that could be a list of digits for the safe.

After a while, when she couldn't find any

numbers and she couldn't think of any other place he might have hidden the code, she put the dissertation back, crouched on the floor and pulled out the three boxes of Kaiser's stuff, each secured with thick parcel tape. She slit them, using the sharp edge of a ruler from her father's desk and began pulling out the contents — three stacks of periodicals bound with rubber bands, a sketch of what looked like an African tribal dance, book after book on religion and psychology — all covered with plaster dust; at some point they must have spent time in Kaiser's house.

The book Kaiser had been talking about was at the bottom, another dissertation, it seemed, produced on a dot-matrix printer. The cover illustration was a line drawing of a plant root photocopied. The pages were bound with a red plastic spiral. *The Use of the Tabernanthe Iboga Root in Shamanic Initiation*, it said, above the author's name and the University of California, Berkeley's copyright line. She pulled it out and sat down in her father's chair to leaf through the pages of graphs and research methodology sections.

By the time she'd got to the end of it she understood more. Ibogaine was root bark. It was used by the Bwiti believers in Cameroon and Gabon to give them what they believed was access to their ancestors — they described using it as 'cutting open the head to allow the light in'. The book was dotted with poor-quality black-and-white photographs of an African tribe, some dressed in raffia skirts, some in cat fur, a tribal

139

elder holding a torch made of tree bark. There was a section about fatalities from ibogaine. The book's author said he had no reliable way to estimate the number of those who died as a result of using it: it was sometimes used to treat withdrawal symptoms after chronic heroin addiction so there was little documentation of a participant's physical health at the outset. Anecdotal evidence suggested up to one in a hundred users may have died as a result; the heart and the liver were the two organs most commonly affected.

Flea put the book under her arm and was about to switch off the light and take it back to her bedroom when something on the floor caught her eye. In the litter of books at her feet some had fallen open. One photo in particular made her stop, a photo that showed a pair of severed hands — shrivelled and black in colour. She turned the book over and read the title. The back of her skull crawled.

She put the dissertation down, sat on the floor and, slightly dazed, turned the pages of the book, looking at the photos, reading slowly. In the corridor the grandfather clock ticked patiently, but she was numb to time passing: the words in the book crept slowly, nastily, into her thoughts, freezing everything else.

When she'd finished she raised her eyes to the window, the moonlit garden with the ghostly creepers hanging round the window. She should be rolling safely into bed now. Instead she was sweating. The windows were open but she was hot — sitting upright and alert on the floor, pulling unconsciously at the neck of her T-shirt. Suddenly she'd forgotten Kaiser and ibogaine and Tig. Suddenly she'd forgotten her self-pact — her promise never, ever to get involved again in theorizing about a case. Suddenly she couldn't think about anything except hands buried under a restaurant. And, most of all, that the owner of the restaurant was African.

17

8 May

He's never fought like this in his life. He's fought and fought, half killed himself, and still he can't get out. No matter how many times he's rammed himself into the locked iron gates, blundering like a darted animal at the walls, no matter how much he's bellowed and tugged at the grating on the window, in the end he can't find the strength and he gives up. He lies down on the sofa, face in his hands, and begins to sob. 'Please,' he cries, 'I've changed my mind. I don't want the fucking money.'

Skinny is sitting against the wall watching this. His knees are up and his eyes are wide. He looks scared. He looks as desperate as Mossy feels.

'Please, I mean, really fucking seriously *please*, let me out of this place. I swear I won't tell a soul — I swear.' He breaks off, tears running down his cheeks, his hands up in the air in front of his face, half ashamed of his fear. His hands. His fucking hands. It's his hands they want to take, and it's all too un-fucking-believable, this place, with the bars and the locks. This insanity. He goes on crying for a while. Then Skinny makes a strange noise. He gets to his feet and turns to the gate. He taps three times on the bars — a signal.

Mossy drops his hands. 'What you doing?' he

yells. 'Where're you going? Don't fucking go.'

'Uncle,' he says quietly. His voice is thick, a little embarrassed. He doesn't turn to him. 'I'm going to speak to Uncle.'

'Who?' Mossy says. 'Who the fuck's . . . ' There's a noise in the corridor. A shaft of light, a figure appears in silhouette and the words stick in Mossy's mouth. He goes really quiet. Moving very quietly, not taking his eyes off Skinny, he gets up and picks his way to the back of the sofa, squatting in the corner, sitting on his hands like that will protect him. It's too dark to see who this new person is but it looks like a man. The driver? There's a moment when he can see gloved hands unlocking the gate, then Skinny slips out. There's a clang as the gate is closed, locked, and Mossy is left on his own in the silence.

He doesn't move for a long time, just stares at the closed gate expecting someone to come back through it. But minutes tick by and nothing happens. After what seems like an hour, when no one reappears, he gets up cautiously and moves around, breathing fast, like an athlete, which is a joke for someone with a body like his, trying to keep his legs springy, half bent, facing the gate so he never has to take his eyes off it for more than a few seconds. He goes round the place checking every corner half by feel.

The room is perfectly square. It must have been a bedroom because there is girls' wallpaper in some places: a frieze of ballerinas. At one end there is a small corridor and at the end of that a bathroom. Briefly he takes his eyes off the gate to check it out. And then he wishes he hadn't.

There's some heavy-duty S&M equipment riveted to the walls — no doubt what's gone on in here in the past. Coiled on the floor is a yellow, industrial hose, the type used for cleaning factory equipment. The hose says more than anything: it says that what happens in here, or what's meant to happen, needs to be cleaned up after. There's a half-broken bog with a window above it. It's barred, the window, with SITEX again, no getting out of that, but back in the corridor there's another window, and on this one the grille, which is oversized and goes all the way down to the floor, is bent, just at the bottom, as if something has squeezed through it.

He gets down on the floor with his back to the wall and tries to push his head up into the gap. He gets his shoulders in — and if he turns his head he can see the grey daylight above. This must lead outside, but as he tries to push a little higher he realizes he's stuck. He can't go any further. He kicks a bit, tries to push it that last inch, but the grille is digging into his spine so hard it feels like it's going to break his back. Someone could be coming in through the gate any second and find him trapped here, so he shuffles himself down, pulling back into the room, inch by inch, the grille digging into his skin. He comes out with his T-shirt over his head and the skin scraped off his back.

He stands and pulls the T-shirt down, shivering now. He hates this room. Apart from the gate and the two windows there is only one other entrance. He remembers this from last time because then it reminded him of an animal's cage. It's a hole in the wall, hacked roughly into the breeze blocks, the shape and position of a fireplace. An iron gate is set into the sides so it's barred too, like the one Skinny's just gone through. You could imagine a lion in there, or a tiger. He squats and on the other side of the grille sees a pile of clothing. He's just about to reach for it when the gate to his right opens.

Mossy darts behind the sofa, cowering, starting to cry again in his fear, but it's only Skinny. There's a figure behind him, locking the gate, but now Skinny's standing on his own in the room. His eyes are bright, he isn't smiling, but he hasn't got that sad look on his face any more. The other person moves off down the little hallway and when they've gone Skinny comes forward and kneels on the sofa.

'What?' hisses Mossy. 'What is it?'

'Do you have a friend?'

'A friend?'

'Someone who needs money too?'

'What're you talking about?'

'Uncle. He say maybe you have a friend who can come instead. And then you can go free.'

Mossy stares at him. 'What?'

'Someone to come here in your place. Someone to have *his* hands cut off.'

'You mean if I do that he won't cut my hands off?'

'That's right.'

Mossy lets out his breath. He's having trouble keeping up with this. 'You mean,' he says, looking intently at Skinny, because now, more

145

than ever, he needs the truth from this person, 'you mean the moment someone else turns up I can go?'

'Yes. You can go.'

Mossy eyes Skinny. His heart is thumping now. He's trying to think fast because he knows this is his chance. There are people all over Bristol he'd like to see with their hands cut off — some he'd cut off himself given half a chance — but none of them are stupid enough to get themselves into the position he's in right now.

But then he realizes there is one person: one person nasty *and* stupid. In fact, dopey as shit. Jonah. Jonah Dundas from the Hopewell estate. He raises his eyes to Skinny, a smile twitching at his mouth, because he's just about to save himself by sacrificing someone else.

And, to tell the truth, it feels good.

18

15 May

At seven a.m. the following day the big IDENT1 computer, having kicked up five comparisons, had whittled the prints from the severed hand down to one person: Ian Mallows. A twenty-two-year-old drug addict from the Knowle West housing estate. By the time the good residents of Knowle West had started breakfast and looked out of their windows the place was crawling with uniformed cops: nine of Avon and Somerset's finest, knocking on doors.

Caffery, feeling the effects of last night's scrumpy, was standing in the doorway of the Community Contact van in his shirtsleeves. He was tired and his back ached. But he knew the case was squeezing a little, a bit less ragged round the edges, and he had an idea that if he stepped on it they might even get the crucial evidence by the end of the day — the rest of Mallows's body. Or even Mallows alive, if the CSM was right. He had a DS interviewing Ian Mallows's probation officer, and some of the support unit had forced an entry into Mallows's flat, but it was empty and the CSM was doing a forensic search of that now. The other officers were crawling over the estate, each waving a picture of Ian Mallows, and the same comment had come up over and over. 'Ask BM. BM knows everyone round here. Ask BM.' And, from looking casually around the estate, from the squat brick buildings to the skanky bits of grass covered with dog shit, within five minutes Caffery could see exactly who 'BM' was.

He was standing at the bottom of a flight of stairs, his hands in his pockets, one foot up against the wall, dog-tags jangling round his neck. He was wearing a grey hoodie under a black blazer-type jacket and his face was white, sort of upper-class English, with a Roman nose and slightly pink cheeks that looked as if he might have got them on the rugby pitches at Harrow. But close up you could see he was a Knowle West boy right to the core: it was the way his eyes kept going from side to side, the way his body was already soft and spreading, the tops of his thighs rubbing together.

'Wha'?' said BM, when Caffery approached, warrant card extended between the thumb and fingers of his right hand. He pushed himself away from the wall and eyed it suspiciously. 'What's going on?'

'Got a minute, son?'

'No. No, I haven't.'

'Suit yourself.' Caffery put the card back into his pocket. He pulled up his collar and stood for a moment, contemplating the stairwell with graffiti and water running down the walls. BM glared at him, waiting for him to speak, waiting for him either to go or to start a row. But Caffery didn't. He coughed loudly, smiled at the lad, then went back to gazing up the stairwell, as if

148

they were two people standing at a bus stop, waiting for the same thing. As if he had all the time in the world and could wait for ever if he wanted to, and maybe had the most patience of the two of them. Somewhere in his head he really didn't care if BM spoke to him or not.

Since last night all he'd been able to think about was what the Walking Man could tell him. Still, he thought, he had to concentrate: he still had a duty to the sorry drug-prowling dropout who'd got his hands cut off.

BM took his own hands out of his pockets, sucked his teeth at Caffery, the way the Jamaicans used to in Deptford, and swung himself on to the stairs, heading up.

'BM,' Caffery said calmly. 'Used to know someone called BM in London. D'you know how he got that name?'

On the stairs BM hesitated. Caffery could see the dirty bottoms of his Ice Cream Reeboks. 'He got that name because he was someone's Bag Man. BM. Bag Man. Don't suppose that's how you got your name. Or should I be asking your probation officer?'

There was a silence. Somewhere a television was playing the theme to *This Morning*. After a moment or two BM crouched and put his face through the railings. 'Don't have a probation officer,' he hissed. 'Haven't got a record.'

'Do you want one?'

There was another long silence. Then BM sat down. There was the sound of him breathing, then of him surreptitiously taking a baggie from his pocket and squeezing it under someone's front door. Caffery heard it, noted where the door was, but didn't move. The thing was to let BM keep face. After a few moments his trainers squeaked as he came back down the stairs, hands in the pockets of his low-slung jeans.

'What?' he said sullenly. 'What you going to do?'

Caffery showed him the photograph. BM rubbed his nose with the back of his hand, stepping from side to side in his Reeboks. 'That's Mossy. Innit? Where's 'e to, then? Got himself in the nick, has he?'

'He's missing.'

'And you think maybe I took him?'

Caffery put the photograph back in his pocket. 'Someone cut his hands off. They used a hacksaw; sort of thing you could pick up in a hardware shop at the end of the road. Probably killed him, but we don't know for sure because his body never turned up.'

BM lost all the pink in his schoolboy cheeks. He sat down suddenly on the bottom step, his feet planted wide. For a moment his hand wavered, as if he was trying to reach the banister for some support, but Caffery was watching so he stopped himself and shakily rested his elbows on his knees. 'All right there, son?'

'That's what he meant,' he muttered. 'That's what he meant.' A little line of perspiration beaded his lip. 'Ages ago he said something to me. He was in the agonies when he said it and I just thought it was him going crazy, you know, saying stupid shit.'

'What did he say?'

150

'Said he'd met someone. He'd been at one of those charity dry-out places, places that're supposed to get you off the gear but don't. Everyone just hangs around reckoning they're going to meet someone and score.'

'You remember which one?'

'Could have been any in about a hundred. They're all over the place. The only one it wasn't was the Knowle West one. I can tell you that straight away, because no one on the estate who's still using would show their face there.'

'So, who did Mallows meet?'

'Dunno.' BM put his hands in his pockets and went to look out of the stairwell at the bleak estate, police everywhere, going along the alleys and balconies, from door to door. Then he came back into the stairwell, shrinking into the shadows, making sure no one was listening. When he turned to Caffery his face was drawn, none of the rosy-cheeked schoolboy left. 'He said something weird. He said people were going to get hurt. I remember him saying it now — said, 'There are some sickos out there, BM, and I don't know who they'd go out and hurt if it wasn't for people like me, stupid fuckers who give it up without a fight.'

'OK,' Caffery said, taking BM's arm and lifting him to his feet. 'Your gear's not going anywhere for a minute or two. Nice and safe under that old lady's doormat. Let's have a little sit-down and get this on paper.'

★ ★ ★

The thing about Flea, Caffery thought, was get her out of the water and she always seemed a little on edge. Sort of guarded, as if she expected you to tell her some really bad news. It was the first thing he'd thought when he'd seen her in the car park at HQ that afternoon.

It had been a dry day for the investigation. In the statement BM hadn't been able to give them much more than he'd told Caffery in the first five minutes in the stairwell: Mossy, he said, was the kind to take up with anyone he met — an idiot, really. He'd go off with anyone who looked at him, and there wasn't any more to the conversation about the sickos than he'd already told Caffery. He gave them about forty names, about twenty locations he knew Mossy some- times hung out, and the names of seventeen drugs-counselling sessions, but no, apart from that time a long time ago he was just guessing really. He didn't have any idea if Mossy had been to any of them recently, and actually, what he wanted to know was how the fuck had those people kept Mossy still long enough to cut his hands off? Not much to go on for Caffery, but the SIO wanted 'afternoon prayers' — the afternoon round-up of the day's events at HQ, where he'd got another meeting. So it was off to Portishead.

He had just parked the staff X5 and was heading for the chrome and glass atrium, batting out the creases in his suit jacket for his meeting with the SIO, when he saw her coming purposefully across the grass towards him. Her hair was wet and slicked off her face and she was dressed in civvies, old jeans and a grey tank top, with her arms bare.

'Inspector Caffery,' she called. 'How are you?'

She looked on edge, from the way she was trying to catch up with him, the way she had her hands pushed into her jeans pockets, as if she didn't trust them not to wave around. Everything in the West Country was different, he thought. He didn't remember a patch of grass like this at Scotland Yard or anyone like her in the force. She fell into step next to him, as if she'd been invited to and they were on their way to the same meeting.

'Any news,' she said, 'about the case?'

'Yeah.' He watched her sideways as they walked, a little wary of her. 'We've got an ID. We know who owned the hands.'

'An ID?'

'From the dabs. Ian Mallows, a.k.a. Mossy. A smackhead from one of the estates.'

'Anything else?'

'Fibres under the nails. You must've bagged the hand well because they were still there. Purple fibres. Like a carpet.'

'Hey,' she said casually, glancing at the glass building they were heading towards, 'you don't — you don't know why someone cut off his hands?'

He stopped. 'No,' he said. 'I don't know why.'

'Such a weird thing to do.' She halted and looked at him in a way that made him stop too. It was as if there was something she wanted to say but was keeping back. She held his eyes seriously. 'I mean, why would someone do that?'

She moved a little closer. 'Did you know he's African?'

'What?'

'The owner of the Moat. He's African. Do you think that might be something to look at?'

Caffery frowned, taking in the shock of blonde hair. There was nothing about her face, he thought, that suggested she could take all the hard knocks in the job. Except maybe her nose, which had a slight wideness that didn't quite fit, as if she might have broken it years ago. To him she had the look of something too fanciful, not quite real. A bit like the way she was talking now.

'Sorry,' he said. 'Do I think *what* might be something to look at?'

'Only that he's African and there might be a connection. Between him being African and there being hands buried so close to the entrance.'

Caffery laughed. He wondered if he was being had. 'This is a joke, yeah? I'm supposed to try to work out what you're saying.'

There was a few moments' silence, then something in Flea's face cleared. 'It's none of my business,' she murmured, scratching her head distractedly. 'But I'm trying to work out how those hands came to be under the restaurant.'

'I don't think we're going to have to look much further than the nearest drug deal gone wrong. We're not going to be letting the location lead the investigation any more.'

'No?'

'No. The victim's where we're taking it from

154

now. He had serious smack history, always trying to get clean, you know the story — DTTOs stacked up so high. The only witness statement we could pull out today has him being pretty bloody scared about something that happened to him at some drugs counsellor's. So that's being actioned even as we speak. About a hundred drugs charities to sift through and I think — ' He broke off. Flea's expression had changed. Her eyes were suddenly hard and guarded, flashing something he wondered if he'd be stupid to mess with. 'And I think that's where we'll find the lead,' he finished thoughtfully. She was still staring at him. 'What? Why you looking at me like that?'

'Nothing,' she said. 'I should let you get on with it.' And she took a step backwards, still holding his eyes as if she expected him to jump her. Then she began to walk away, pulling her phone out of her pocket and banging out a text with her thumb.

Somewhere Caffery'd heard that teenagers were getting over-developed thumbs from all the texting they were doing — he'd've liked to say something to her about it.

'Flea?'

She stopped, pocketing the phone as if she'd been caught holding a bomb. 'Yes?'

'I'm new here. New to the area.'

'I know that.'

'I'm hoping someone could give me some pointers. To Bristol. You know.' And then, quickly, because it sounded as if he was asking for a date, he said, 'I want a nursery. Just wondering if you could tell me where to look for a good nursery.'

He wasn't sure but he thought her eyes flickered towards his hand, his ring finger. 'I could ask around,' she said. 'How old's your . . . son? Daughter?'

He smiled. Half at the absurdity of the mistake, and half because he felt stupid because he couldn't claim children when everyone else at his age could. 'No,' he said slowly. 'I didn't mean that. I meant plants. I want to buy some plants. Some bulbs. That's all.'

★ ★ ★

It was Tig she'd been texting. With this itch in her head about the picture in Kaiser's book, with the way that whatever she did she couldn't get away from the thought of those hands under the restaurant, she'd spent most of the day trying to talk Tig into introducing her to the owner of the Moat. Although at first he'd been appalled, had blustered for a while about professional ethics, 'Mine and *yours*, Flea, by the way,' in the end he said he'd see, grudgingly, what the owner said, and why didn't she come down to see him at work? Which would have been fine, until what Caffery had just told her about Mallows. Now she was worried.

If CID were looking at drugs charities, sooner or later Tig would come up on their radar — and what the hell were they going to make of his history, especially if it came out that he knew the owner of the Moat? Plus, if the suits went

156

knocking on his door, no way was he going to believe she hadn't somehow set the ball rolling in his direction. It was going to be two-way nastiness. And if Mallows turned out to be a client of User Friendly, Tig's charity, well, then the shit was really going to hit the proverbial. Still, she thought, swinging into her car and firing off the text — *Hi Tig, Be there in an hour* — DI Caffery wasn't showing much sign of doing anything about what she'd said. Cryptic though she'd been, he could have shown some interest in the restaurant owner being African. Because, she was absolutely bloody certain, someone *ought* to be interested.

She drove quickly to the community centre where Tig took his Wednesday sessions. It was a Victorian schoolhouse, cleaned up and fitted with laminate flooring and disabled toilets with dangling alarm cords. By the time she arrived his group had finished and he was alone in the echoey building. He opened the door to her, wearing a black sweatshirt, camouflage combats tucked into his boots. He was carrying a stack of folders under one arm.

'Well?' she said, as he led her down the corridor to the little office that smelled of new carpets and cleaning fluid. She went fast, trying to keep up with him. 'Have you spoken to him — your friend? The owner?'

'I have.' He threw down the folders on the desk and dropped into a swivel chair, his hands linked on his stomach, spinning round to face at her. He gave her the sort of measured smile he'd give an interviewee.

'OK.' She dumped her holdall and her fleece and shoved her hands into her pockets. 'I'm going to have to beg you.'

Tig gave a dry laugh. 'He's been away,' he said, 'with his wife in Portugal — they've only been back since lunchtime. We can go for a cup of coffee, but it's not exactly open arms. I'm pretending I want to schmooze some more dosh from him for the charity. So for fuck's sake, girl, don't you be going in there and asking police questions, get it?'

'I get it.'

'No digging. You sit and keep schtum. Whatever you want to talk about you let him introduce the subject, and if he doesn't introduce it you just walk straight away from it, Flea. Straight away. I'm doing this as a major, major favour, OK? And if it goes tits up, if he gets wind tonight you're filth, then . . . ' He swiped a hand across his throat. 'I'm finished. And it'll be your fault.'

'God, Tig.' She sat down, folding her arms. 'That'll be me, then, well and truly told, eh?'

'That's the way it is. And that's the deal. OK?'

She looked at him for a while, at his hard body and the grey-blue scalp where the hair was shaved. She was thinking about the photo in her bag — the photo of Ian Mallows she'd printed off back at Almondsbury.

She took a breath and was turning to get the photo from her bag when Tig said suddenly, 'So, tell me, how's the professor? Have you spoken to him again?'

'Kaiser, you mean? No. Why?'

158

'But you're still going there tomorrow?'

'Yes. In the afternoon.'

Tig gazed up at the ceiling, as if he was trying to remember something. 'Just remind me — what's his job again?'

'He's . . . ' Flea paused. 'I don't know — comparative religion. The hallucinations — that's a corner of his job . . . Why?'

'Why?' Tig fiddled with the collar of his sweatshirt as if he was too hot. 'Just wonder who you hang out with sometimes. The lowlifes you know.'

'*Lowlifes?*'

'Just wondering if maybe it's time I paid a bit more attention to the men you see.'

'I don't 'see' men, Tig. You know that.'

'Maybe you don't.' His face was suddenly serious. 'Maybe you don't. But maybe it's still time for me to pay some attention.'

'What?'

'I should have done it a long time ago, Flea. I should have always shown more of an interest in you.'

'Stop it, for Christ's sake. I don't know what you're talking about.'

'Don't you?' He held her eyes. 'Don't you know?'

Flea gave a tentative laugh. 'Tig?' she said woodenly. 'You're gay.'

There was a beat of shocked silence. Then Tig started to laugh. 'Gay?' he said. 'Oh, give me a fucking break. *Gay?*'

'Yes, I mean you . . . ' She trailed off, suddenly seeing where this was going. 'Tig,' she said.

159

'Come on. Tell me you're not serious.'

'I am,' he said quietly. 'I'm very serious.'

She blinked. This was insane. Tig was gay. Had always been. Always would be. That was the only way they'd been able to be friends so long. Maybe she wasn't the most perceptive person in the world — she could find a nail in a lake blindfolded, but when it came to other people she was a blunt instrument — but *this?* This was weird and unbelievable.

'Well,' Tig said, 'what do you think?'

'What do I think? I think . . . ' she shook her head ' . . . that if you're saying what I think you're saying, which is pretty weird, to be honest, but if you mean it I've got to say no.'

'No?'

'Look, you *know* what it's been like for me, Tig. I'm just . . . ' She searched for the word. 'I'm *cut off*. Since the accident I can't think like that. I'm just . . . ' She sighed. Fuck. This was all so bloody clumsy. 'I mean, Tig, for God's sake, you're supposed to be *gay*.'

He pushed back his chair and held up his hands, giving a laugh, a sort of 'I knew this would happen and I'm laughing at how good I am at predicting things.' There was tension in his jaw, but his eyes weren't angry. 'Listen. Don't worry about it. I swear — you have a think about it.' His tongue moved around inside his mouth as if an object was in there, or a taste he was trying to push out. 'You think about it and when you're ready you tell me. OK?'

'OK,' she murmured, still staring, shell-shocked, at his weird offset eyes. 'OK. I will.'

160

And then, to cover her discomfort, she turned away, looking for something to do. She picked up her bag and shuffled through it, taking longer than she needed. After a few moments, when her face felt a bit cooler, she closed her fingers over the crumpled photo. For a moment she considered leaving it in her bag. Get the meeting with the restaurant owner over and tell Tig about Ian Mallows another day. But no. It had to be done. There was a world of trouble in it if she didn't. She placed the photo face down next to him on the desk, not meeting Tig's eyes.

He paused. 'What's this?'

She took a deep breath. She knew what he was going to say: 'That's one of my clients. Why're you showing me his photo — think I don't see the ugly bastard enough?' She turned the photo over.

Tig's face went blank. There was a long, long silence. Then he shrugged. 'What? What am I supposed to be saying? Show me a geezer's photo and what're you waiting for me to say?'

'You've never seen him before?'

'No. Am I supposed to have?'

'He's not one of your clients?'

'No.'

She let her breath out and gave a small laugh, feeling a bit better now. 'Thank fuck,' she muttered. 'At least *something*'s going right today.' She zipped the photo back into the holdall and picked up her fleece. And that was when the community centre's doorbell began to echo round the building.

19

At the community-centre door in Mangotsfield Caffery was tired. A niggling ache had started in his legs, and while he waited for someone to answer the bell he pushed two ibuprofen into his mouth and dry-swallowed them. He'd have liked a cigarette and to lie down somewhere. Or to be with one of the City Road girls — anywhere except here, waiting to sit through another interview with a reluctant drugs counsellor.

The meeting at HQ that afternoon had turned into a sterile exercise in man management. Now that drugs were in the equation, the steam had gone out of the inquiry. He'd spent the time gazing at the sprinklers and trimmed lawns of Valley Road HQ, half listening to the SIO and half thinking about those forty names, twenty locations and seventeen counselling services waiting to be visited. For a moment his spirits had been raised when he heard from Kingswood that there'd been a message about the purple fibres found in Ian Mallows's fingernails. But it was just a memo to let him know the Chepstow lab had agreed with the Portishead lab that the fibres were from a carpet and wanted to do expensive gas chromatography tests before they gave him any more information.

There was a few moments' silence before someone came to the door. The chief counsellor of the charity, Tommy Baines, wasn't what

Caffery had expected on paper. He was in his late twenties, with the faint blue of a laser-treated tattoo on his neck and his hair closely shaved in a way that Caffery read as shorthand for aggression, past and present. There was something wrong with one of his eyes too, something that could have come from a fight. As Caffery flashed his warrant card he thought he saw, or imagined, a beat of anger in Baines's eyes — almost as if Caffery was an old mate who'd promised not to bother him at work but had turned up anyway. It was as if he'd been interrupted, and for a moment Caffery wondered if he'd blundered into something personal. As Baines unlocked the door, showed Caffery inside and locked up, Caffery got the clear idea there was someone else in the building, someone hiding in one of the darkened rooms. A woman maybe? He thought he could smell something. A perfume that might have been familiar. He scanned the corridor they walked up, registering where each door was, where it claimed to lead.

'You can call me Tig,' Baines said, as he took him into the office. 'Name I got in prison. Don't ask why.' He picked up a stack of twelve-step sheets and threw them on to the photocopier, jamming his code in with his thumb, not looking at Caffery as if he wasn't much interested in him — as if he was used to the Bill turning up on his doorstep. 'We're hand to mouth at the moment. Small. No permanent beneficiaries so we're getting by on a donation here and there, and whatever fees we can pick up from the clients. The ones who can afford it, which is about none of them.' He spoke in a measured way, thinking every word through before he let it out of his mouth. 'It's me does everything. I'm the managing trustee, the only counsellor employed, and until we can afford it I'm housing-support officer too. This centre,' he raised a hand to indicate the building, 'is one of our donors. I get six free hours a week here.' He took the sheets from the feeder and put them into a transparent folder. He glanced at the vertical blinds, the industrial blue carpet, the impersonal chipboard desk and filing cabinets. 'Yeah, this is as near as I get to official premises. Apart from this and some relapse counselling for a residential programme over in Keynsham I basically run the charity out of my mum's flat. And she's a fruit, my mum.'

It was getting dark outside, and except for the office the old Victorian school was deserted. Caffery put his hand on a chair. 'Can I sit down?' he said. 'I need to have a few minutes' chat if that's OK. Not in a hurry, are you?'

At the copy machine Tig hesitated. Caffery thought his eyes flicked briefly to the door and he got the impression again that someone else was in the darkened building. Unfinished business. But it didn't go anywhere. Instead Tig gestured to the chair. 'Sure, sure. There's no one else using the place tonight. Sit, mate. I'll get the kettle on.'

Caffery sat and watched him busy around, making tea, wiping out coffee cups with a green paper towel, scouting cupboards for a biscuit tin. While he waited he got out his notebook and the

164

photo of Mossy, putting it face down on the big desk. This kind of interview drove him crazy: he'd never met anyone in drugs counselling who wasn't as closed as an arsehole, who didn't act like the police were asking for arterial blood when they asked to know about clients, and *what* was their *problem*? Didn't they *get* the *concept* of client *confidentiality*? The voluntary sector could be a bit easier than the statutories, not as hidebound, but even they didn't pipe out information for free.

'You never get tired of it?' Caffery asked, as Tig handed him a mug of tea. 'Never want to tell them to go and get a life?'

Tig gave a short laugh. He rolled up the sleeves of his sweat-shirt and sat down, legs crossed so his foot was resting on the other knee, balancing the tea mug on his ankle. 'Listen, mate, I know the police. You don't really give a shit how I feel about my clients. You're not here for that. So what are you here for? What do you want to know from me?'

Caffery didn't speak for a second or two. He looked at Tig's eyes. The bad one was sort of grey and cloudy. A bit like a shitty London day. Caffery had a second of disorientation. A second or two where he couldn't read the guy at all. He turned over the photo of Mossy and held it out.

'Recognize him?'

Tig didn't hurry. He put the cup calmly on the desk, the handle to the side. He lifted his foot off his knee and put both feet on the floor, his hands on his thighs as he stood up and took the photo. As he examined it, Caffery thought he saw a

165

contraction in the muscles at the corners of his eyes, no more than a millimetre's change. It came to him that Tig had already known exactly whose picture he was going to see.

'No,' he said, holding it to the light, squinting. 'Nah, sorry, mate. Never seen him.'

He held the photo out for Caffery to take, but he didn't. He was still watching Tig's face. 'You sure you don't know him?'

'A hundred per cent. Never seen him in my life. Here — take it back.'

Caffery waited a moment more. He was trying to get in under this bloke's cloudy eye, trying to get a flicker out of it, just a dilation in the pupil, anything to tell him he was lying. But there was nothing. Just this sort of weird evenness he didn't know how to interpret.

In the end he took the photo, tucking it into his folder. He left his hand on it and thought about the next question he had to ask. And then, because he hated the question and because he knew where it would lead, he thought for a few moments about the girls on City Road and what he could be doing now instead of this. What he could be doing to forget. The thought made him want to sigh again. He took his hand off the folder.

'Your clients,' he said. 'Do you s'pose any of them would recognize him? Maybe I could have one of my lads come out and have a chat to them?'

Tig snorted. Gave him that look Caffery knew from years and years of doing the exact same thing in south-east London. 'I shouldn't have to tell *you* about client confidentiality. It's the backbone of the whole set-up. We'd be ruined if we ran around opening our arms to the police every five minutes.'

'Yes. I know. But . . . ' Caffery spoke slowly, ponderously, studying the backs of his own hands as if he was more interested in them than in the words coming out of his mouth. 'But do you know what I'm picturing?'

'What?'

'I'm picturing your future, Tig. I'm picturing your future and all the steps you can take to change it. And then, on the tail of that, I'm picturing all the people out there now, all the people this same thing might happen to in the future. The victims that aren't victims yet . . . ' He let that hang in the air — *the victims that aren't victims yet* — so that its implication sank down a little. This was the best lever he had, to move the responsibility away from the police and on to the interviewee. 'Maybe even someone you care about. I'm picturing them, and I'm picturing their lives going ahead, happily, maybe having a house, a family. And then I'm seeing the opposite. I'm seeing them murdered. Mutilated. Hands taken off. With a hacksaw. An ordinary hacksaw you can buy in a hardware shop. What sort of a future is that?'

He saw that Tig was caving. A little patch of white had started on his forehead, as if the blood had stopped flowing.

'Look,' Tig said, 'I've got a responsibility to these lads.'

'And to their futures. This guy on the photo

167

— he's got to be a lot like some of your clients, same lifestyle. What that tells us is that if it happens again, it's likely to happen to someone a bit like him.'

'But I can't have your people down here, can't do that. My clients'll never trust me again.'

'It's your decision. It's only you who can decide to do the right thing.'

There was another pause. 'Tell you what,' Tig said at last. 'If you leave the photo I'll let the guys see it. Maybe something'll come out of it like that.'

'Can I rely on you for that?' Caffery wanted to play the game out a little further. 'The *future victims* . . . can they rely on you?'

'Mate, listen now. I'm giving you a promise. OK? I make you a promise. You take it or you leave it.'

Caffery slid Mossy's photo back out of his folder and passed it over. Tig picked it up, his face tight, contained. He put it on the photocopier and ran off copies, standing with his back to Caffery, who sat for a while, not speaking, wondering if there was something else he should be asking. On the floor near the photocopier was a bag he hadn't noticed before, a holdall with a fleece draped over it. He vaguely registered something familiar about its logo. It was making him drift a bit when Tig said, 'Do you know about me?'

'What?'

'You didn't look at my record before you come here?'

'What would I've found if I had?'

168

Tig handed him the photo and sat down. He rubbed his hand across his shaved scalp. 'What you said earlier — don't I ever get tired of it. Do you know how come I don't?'

'No.' Caffery looked down at the bag again, then back at Tig. 'No, I don't.'

'Because it's me. I'm one of them. Or I was. That's why I never get tired of them or of the shit they're going through — the self-hatred, the misery, the awful fucking hole you fall into when you're an addict. I know what it's like to break a car window for a ten-pence piece on the dashboard, to rob my mum's pension, to pick someone else's stash out of a pool of their puke. I know what it's like to be down there.'

'Why're you telling me this?'

'Because I nearly killed someone.' He paused to let that sink in. 'I've done my time, but I can see you finding out about that and coming back, getting a bit tasty with me, maybe pointing fingers. Better tell you now so it's no surprise.'

Caffery sat back in his chair. For a while the only noise was the photocopier whirring and flashing, sending the smell of copying ink into the air. Then he said, 'Well? What happened?'

'An old lady. I was high. Went into her house to rob her and ended up half killing her — tied her up with the bedside-lamp cord and smashed both legs with an iron.'

Caffery smiled slowly. Something cold was creeping into his skull. 'And you're telling me you regret it? That you're straight, learned your lesson? That you're a productive member of society? That we should be having a soft little

169

session about rehabilitation?'

Tig smiled back nastily. 'Ah, yes. I should have known. I should have seen in your eyes. You don't believe people can change. Forgiveness isn't a word you use in a hurry.'

Caffery tried to imagine what it'd be like to wrap electric cord round an old lady, then hit her so hard with an iron that the bones in her legs shattered. He tried to imagine what Penderecki had done to Ewan. What it would be like to rape a nine-year-old boy. How loud would someone have to scream to make you stop? Penderecki had had his shot at redemption — he never did time for Ewan, and he could have made anything he wanted out of his life. But he had died, alone and penniless with no family or friends, just a pile of children's underwear catalogues in his council house. And even that was about a million times better than he deserved.

Tig stood up and took the huge bunch of keys from the desk. He went to the door, and turned. 'Is that it, then?'

Caffery got to his feet, snapped closed the leather folder and went to the door. He stopped next to Tig and looked into his eyes. 'Just one thing,' he said softly. 'If you took my legs away from me do you know what I'd want?'

'No. What would you want?'

'I'd want to pay you back.' He smiled, feeling as if there was blood on his teeth. 'I'd want to take your legs in return.'

20

Tig wasn't in the mood to talk about what he'd said. *I'm not gay.* When he came to find Flea, sitting quietly in the unlit kitchen downstairs, waiting for Caffery to go, his face was red and patchy, his eyes were hard. She asked him what was the matter, what had been said, but he shook his head and was silent as they drove to the restaurant owner's house. It was only when they were standing on the doorstep, waiting for the door to be answered, that he spoke.

'They don't make them any different from the way they made them fifteen years ago. Something out of *The Sweeney*, that one.'

Flea didn't answer. She was staring at the little window in the restaurant owner's front door. Several times on the way over here she'd almost said to Tig, 'Look, let's forget it. Let's just turn round and pretend I never said anything.' She knew she was getting in too deep and now she was light-headed, as if an elastic band had been wrapped round her skull and was being tightened. If she was right, this innocuous-seeming house could hold the key to how Mallows got his hands cut off.

'Hey, you with us?' Tig said.

She blinked. 'What?'

'I just said — that cop. Jack Caffery. Gave me a little Fascist-police-state spiel. Aggressive. Only word for it.'

'He's not that bad.'

Tig looked her up and down in a way that made her uncomfortable. Then he gave her a tight grin. 'See? You gave the game away. You fancy him.'

She was about to answer when the sound of locks being opened from inside stopped her. She straightened her shoulders and ran her hands self-consciously down her jeans to iron out the creases. She wished she could see herself in a mirror — she knew she'd be pale in the face.

The man who opened the door had a faintly anxious, scholarly look about him. He was thin with close-cropped greying hair and skin so dark it seemed almost to have an ashy dust over it. He was dressed unassumingly in lightweight belted trousers and his pale green checked shirt had its sleeves rolled up. She noticed that the skin on his forearms was shiny — as if it had been greased.

'Mr Mabuza.' Tig extended his hand. 'Good of you to see me. Short notice, I know.'

Mabuza forced a smile. 'Don't worry, my old friend.' He took the hand carefully, almost delicately, and shook it. Then he inclined his head to Flea. 'Gift Mabuza. And you are?'

'This is Flea, my — my girlfriend. Hope you don't mind.'

Girlfriend? When the hell was that okayed? she thought, but Mabuza was looking at her so she removed her sunglasses and held out her hand. There was a slight beat — just a split second when she thought something crossed his face — then he took it and shook it lightly. When he let go she could feel a thin residue left on her hand — something faintly pungent, faintly unpleasant.

'Come in,' he said. He spoke in a stiff, clipped way — only a trace of an accent, a bit like Kaiser spoke sometimes. Sort of Eliza Doolittle-ish — a bit *too* English to be real. 'Come in, come in.'

She stepped inside and instantly felt a drag on her — as if the gloom was pulling energy from her. There was a smell in here, of meals cooked many months ago, of sadness. When Mabuza took them in and left them in the living room while he went to get coffee, it was a few moments before her eyes got used to the light, but when she did she saw the interior was decorated like an English guesthouse: horse brasses on the walls, purple carpets on the floor, overstuffed floral sofas with arm protectors, embroidered cushions plumped up and propped in a row. There were trimmed lampshades, a cheap carriage clock on the television, twin china spaniels on either side of the mantelpiece with a wooden crucifix on a small base between them. Without waiting to be asked she went to the mantelpiece and studied the cross, thinking there was something strange about it, something she couldn't quite put her finger on.

'Do you like it?'

She jumped. Mabuza stood next to her, holding a tray with cups and a coffee pot. His eyes were going from the cross to her face and back again. 'Very nice wood, do you think?'

'Yes,' she said, holding her face very still. 'Very nice.'

'I will leave the house in twenty minutes.' He

set the tray down, then bent to pour coffee into thin rosebud-patterned china cups. Flea sat down on the sofa and Mabuza put a cup in front of her. Tig sat in a leather armchair, his head back, his hands on the chair's arms. 'My wife and I will go to a meeting at our church,' said Mabuza, 'so, my friends, I am sorry, we cannot talk all night.'

'We understand.' Tig pinched up the knees of his combats and sat forward, elbows on his knees. 'We'll try not to keep you.'

'And I should tell you now,' said Mabuza, 'I don't know why you are here, but I am very afraid you will be disappointed by our meeting, my friend. Today of all days I fear for my business.' He put his hands together, as if in prayer, and pointed the fingers at Tig. 'With the best will in the world my work for charities will become limited.'

Flea sat in silence while the men talked about business, the charity. She fiddled with the spoon in the saucer, letting her eyes flit round, first to the crucifix, then to the cupboards, the walls, trying to decide what it was about this room that bothered her. There was a painting of a cat washing its face under a picture light in the alcove. It was on nailed-together boards and seemed out of place. She studied it for a while, wondering if that was what worried her. Or maybe it was the bay window, with its heavy curtains that would stop any light getting in or out. Or the wallpaper — striped up to the waist-height dado rail, with a plain dark ochre base that might have been washable. She thought there was a faint sheen to it and tried to pick out areas that had been cleaned, where the colour was paler. And then it struck her. It wasn't the walls or the curtains that were setting off alarms. It was the carpet.

She stared at it, her pulse thudding. Slightly dusty-looking, its pile was too deep to be fashionable, but otherwise it wasn't anything out of the ordinary. Except for one thing. The colour. It was a dark, slightly pinkish purple. The same colour as the fibres on the hands.

'Flea,' Tig said sharply, next to her, making her jolt upright. She looked up to find Mabuza in front of her, offering her a plate of biscuits.

'I'm sorry,' she said, her mouth dry. 'I'm . . . '

'Miles away,' Mabuza said. 'That's the expression, isn't it?'

She looked at the biscuits, then back at his face. Was this the face of a man who had cut another human being to pieces — here in this room? 'I don't know much about charity work, the voluntary sector. It's not my thing.'

'Don't apologize. Did you want a biscuit?' He smiled and pointed at the plate. 'My wife made these ones. The others, I'm afraid, are from the shop.'

'Thank you.' She leaned forward, her cup and saucer balanced in one hand. Hesitating — thinking of the carpet, the heavy curtains — she put her finger on the edge of the plate and applied just enough pressure to pull the rim down. Mabuza tried to catch it but it fell out of his hands, landing face down on the carpet, scattering the biscuits.

She put her cup down with a clatter. 'Damn, I'm — Here, let me.' Before Mabuza could do anything she had pushed back the coffee-table and was on her hands and knees, collecting up the biscuits, piling them back on the plate, raking through the carpet for crumbs. 'Clumsy.' She lifted her face to the two men, giving them the blankest of smiles. 'Clumsy and stupid.'

When the floor was almost clear she took a deep breath. With her left hand she picked up the last couple of biscuits, the right she closed round a chunk of the carpet. She pulled. There was a faint, ripping sound, but she kept her eyes pinned on the men, still smiling. In one movement she tipped back on her heels, putting the biscuit on the plate, picking up her cup and sitting back on the sofa, her right hand folded round the clump of carpet and tucked under her left arm.

The two men didn't say anything but looked at her silently. She found herself speaking, saying anything to cover the silence. 'Where are you from, Mr Mabuza?' It was out of her mouth before she'd even thought what to say. She forced herself to hold his eyes and keep the smile there. 'Tig'll tell you,' she said, trying to make her voice calm. 'I'm about as nosy as they get. Sorry.'

'Don't be sorry.' Mabuza inclined his head with a polite smile. 'No apologies necessary in this house. I'm from South Africa — thank you for asking.'

'South Africa?'

'Do you know it?'

A picture came into her head. A picture of dark, freezing water, a picture of human screams echoing into the desert air. 'No,' she said quietly. 'Not really.'

'I know what you're thinking.' His eyes were slightly yellow round the pupils as if he was jaundiced.

'Do you? What am I thinking, then?'

Mabuza laughed. 'You're thinking I'm black. You're thinking the only South Africans you meet are white, and here I am sitting in front of you, large as life, and I'm black.'

'That's right,' she said, not moving her eyes from his. 'That's exactly what I was thinking.'

'I'm one lucky South African black, believe me.'

He went on holding her gaze in a way that made her uncomfortable. It was just as if he'd seen her grab the carpet and was trying to spook her into saying something. Slowly he began to talk, his eyes not leaving hers as if he wanted every word to sink in. At first the words meant nothing to her, drowned by her pulse pounding, but slowly she realized he was telling her his story — how he'd been born in Johannesburg, how when the white-owned drilling company he worked for had wanted to look good and fill their quotas, as if they belonged to the new South Africa, they'd gone hunting down the company's ranks and taken a long-standing black forklift driver, moving him quickly and artificially up the ranks until he was appointed CEO and taken to Cape Town. Gift Mabuza had never made a decision in his three years as CEO. He'd spent the days in his oak-panelled office in the shadow of Table Mountain, playing Internet poker and signing cheques until the whole scam was cracked apart by the press. Then he had taken the pay-off, come to the UK and, with what he'd learned, had opened the Moat.

'And so,' he said, 'my new friend, Flea. Tell me, what do *you* know about my country?'

'Very little.'

'You see, what's on my mind is what on earth the police in England think of my country.'

'I beg your pardon?'

'There has been a terrible business at my restaurant — I'm sure you've followed it on the news. The police, you see, interviewing my staff, keeping my business closed. Even I'm not allowed inside, they tell me. Now, I don't know, my friend, what beast or inhuman brought this terrible ungodly thing to my door, but I have lived long enough to know that it is a slur — an attempt to sabotage me.' He opened his hands and held them out. 'You see the colour of my skin. You hear my voice. I'm an African, Flea, and the African will always be the leper of the world.'

Flea sniffed. She patted her jeans, pretending to feel for a tissue. She pushed her left hand into the front pocket and, with a surreptitious flick of the finger, released the chunk of carpet. Then she rested her hand on her thigh. Mabuza's eyes followed the movement.

'You see,' he said, after a while, letting his eyes linger on her hand. 'I am not wanted in this society — so someone . . . ' He slowed down and

178

repeated the word, ' . . . *someone* has taken the most appalling risk to discredit me. But . . . ' He gave her an unexpected smile. His teeth were white. One was missing, next to his right canine. 'My enemies have taken a wrong turn here. That is the joke. No one can point a finger at me — I am not a savage.'

'Mr Mabuza,' she said levelly, 'you're talking in riddles.'

'Riddles? Hardly. What I'm trying to explain is that I have never had any dealing with the police.' He said the word very deliberately, enunciating every syllable. 'The *police*. I don't know what they must be thinking about this black South African.' He raised his eyes and locked them on hers again. 'And you? Do you know what they're thinking?'

He knows, Flea thought. *Damn and fuck, he knows who I am.* 'No,' she said steadily. 'I have no idea what they might be thinking.'

There was a long silence. Next to her on the sofa Tig was fidgeting, clearing his throat. She was about to say something to him when the carriage clock chimed. Immediately he was on his feet. 'We should be going,' he said, holding out his hand to Flea. 'Come on. Let's go. *Now.*'

She got to her feet a little shakily, setting the cup down so hard the spoon fell off the saucer. 'I need to use the toilet, Mr Mabuza. I just want a bit of tissue to blow my nose.'

There was a moment's hesitation. She didn't imagine it — she knew she didn't. Mabuza's eyes flickered to Tig's, came back to hers, then returned to Tig's. And then he smiled, graciously, holding up his hand to show her out of the room. 'Of course,' he said calmly. 'Of course you must.'

★ ★ ★

The toilet was on the first floor directly above the hallway. She climbed slowly, the stairs curling round above the hallway where the two men waited for her. On the staircase she passed four or five niches in the wall. In each stood a crucifix, some small, some big, all clean and new in spite of the dust that lay everywhere else. The walls were panelled below waist height and she couldn't say what it was, but something about the panels made her uncomfortable — she held her hands across her chest so she didn't have to touch them. They made her think of things being shut away — of shadows snapping at her heels.

She got to the landing, with its low lighting and faintly clinical smell. The feeling was still there — that someone or something was watching her. At the top of the staircase a door faced her, just where Mabuza had said it would be. She pushed it open, pulled the cord and the little room lit up — primrose-yellow porcelain, a box of Kleenex tissues on the cistern, and her reflection staring back at her from the mirror above the sink. She held the door handle tightly, studied her face, the hair that hung in hard coils round her forehead, the circles under her eyes. After a moment or two she stretched up on tiptoe so that she could look at the reflection behind her, down at the panels behind her

180

calves. There was nothing. Why had she thought there would be?

Just as she was debating what to do a noise to her right made her turn. A few feet across the landing a door was half open. She hadn't noticed the room because the light was off, but now she couldn't take her eyes off it. The sound was coming from inside, of someone sniffling, as if they'd been crying.

She pulled the toilet door closed, shutting it tightly so it would be heard downstairs. The two men were at the foot of the stairs, talking, in low, confidential voices, and their tone didn't change so she took an experimental step across the landing towards the open door. The floorboards were solid — no creaking or sagging — and in a few short steps she was standing just to the side of the door. The men went on talking below. From here she could crane her neck and see most of the room beyond.

It was an odd bedroom, lit only by two standard lamps in the corners. It made her think of a pioneer home with bare floorboards, gingham check and a lollipop flower-stitched quilt. There was a suitcase on the floor and a few feet away from it a white woman on her knees in the middle of the room, facing the bed. She was a little younger than Mabuza, blonde and enormously fat — her body seemed to flow out of the plain white dress she wore. Her chest heaved and shuddered with the crying: a strange sound that Flea somehow knew wasn't connected with sadness.

The woman put both hands on the floor and

bent, her enormous arms dimpling, dipping her head so that she could see under the bed. Even from the doorway Flea could see the tears shivering in her eyes as she squinted into the dark, and at that moment it struck her what was odd about the crying. It was the sound of fear. The woman was crying because she was afraid of what she thought she would see under the bed.

She craned her neck to peep into the far corners, and when she seemed to have found nothing she tilted back on her heels and turned, very slowly, to look directly at Flea. The tears were standing on her cheeks, but she didn't speak, or seem surprised to find someone watching her. She just gazed at her steadily as if she'd known she was there all along.

Without a word Flea went back to the stairs, expecting any second to be shouted after. Ignoring the charade about the toilet — she'd meant to open and close the door, run a tap or something — she headed down the stairs as quickly as her legs would carry her. At the bottom the two men stopped talking.

'It was nice to meet you,' she said to Mabuza. She didn't stop walking or offer her hand to him, just went straight to the door, ignoring Tig coming up behind her. 'Very nice. I'll see myself out.'

Outside she went fast, going in a straight line, her arms folded. The air was warm, but she couldn't help shivering, glad to have the feel of the house off her. What she'd seen was enough. In the morning she would go straight to Jack Caffery.

'Hey.' She'd got halfway down the street by the time Tig caught up with her. He grabbed her arm and swung her round to face him. 'What the fuck do you think you're doing?'

'He knows who I am, Tig.' She swept her hair off her face and held his eyes angrily. 'Couldn't you tell? Didn't you see the way he was looking at me? It was weird.'

'The only thing that was weird was you forcing him to talk about the case. That was weird.'

'I didn't *force* him. He wanted to talk about it. And anyway — there's something wrong in that house.'

'Flea. Flea.' He pulled her a little further down the road so they were completely hidden from Mabuza's front gates. It was nearly seven o'clock in the evening, but the sky was still blue, and the businessmen who owned the houses in this community were returning home in their Audis and Mercedes. Some eyed Tig and Flea. One parked his car, then stood in the driveway, his sunglasses in his hand, watching them. 'Listen,' Tig said. 'Don't you think you're being paranoid? You went in there worried — you didn't say anything but I could tell you weren't comfortable. You're making things up.'

'I'm not making up the way he was *staring* at me. When he asked what the police would be thinking.'

'Flea, look, I'm not saying I know him well, that'd be a lie, but I know enough to tell you he doesn't do things in weird ways. He's not underhand.'

'Oh, yeah?' She wasn't convinced. 'You sure?'

'Yes,' he said, and walked towards the car. 'I'm sure.'

She waited a while, watching him leave, her heart still thumping. The man in the driveway lost interest and aimed the remote control at the garage door. Eventually, when there was nothing else to do, she followed Tig to the car, getting out her keys. She opened the door for him, then got into the driver's seat, sinking down with a sigh.

'I'll tell you something else,' she said, pulling on the seatbelt. She could still feel the thin layer of grease on her hand from Mabuza's handshake. 'They're not going to church this evening — at least, not to any church you or I would go to.'

'Oh, come on. What're you talking about?'

She stared back in the direction of the house — an ordinary enough house on the face of it. She thought about the idea she'd had that shadows were running round the panelling at knee height. She thought about the woman searching under the bed, the fear on her face. She thought about the crucifixes. And then, in a second, she realized what was wrong with the house.

She turned back to Tig, her eyes stinging. 'I'm just telling you, Tig, those people aren't Christian.'

21

By eight o'clock, when Caffery got back to the office, the HOLMES team had finished entering their actions for the day and had packed up. One of the team wanted some overtime so Caffery gave him the only drugs groups on the list that had evening sessions. Soon the place was deserted.

Enjoying the silence, Caffery footled around for a bit, pretending to himself he was being efficient, reading his messages, looking up biogs on some of the newer team members and doing a lackadaisical search on the force intelligence network for key words in the waitress's statement: *River. Juvenile.* When he typed in *exposure* the screen filled up so quickly the scroll-bar tab shrank to the size of a nailhead. The HOLMES operator had been right — just about a thousand guys in Bristol waggling their knobs at local girls in the dead of night. He didn't have the stomach for that list of entries.

He went to the window, pulled apart the blinds and a weird wave of despondency came over him. The halal butcher's opposite was closed, but the takeaway next door hadn't opened yet. He checked his watch. Eight thirty p.m. Kind of early. But it wasn't long before sunset. And that meant the girls would be out on City Road if you knew where to go. His fingers tightened on the blind, harder and harder, until he thought he'd break it if he stood there any longer. He got out his mobile and pulled up the number Flea'd given him — an old friend of her mother, she'd said, who ran his business from home.

The phone rang a few times and he was about to put it down, thinking he shouldn't be calling so late, when the nurseryman answered and said, rather slowly, that the Remembrance, well, now, she was getting on a bit, the Remembrance, in terms of what was popular, but he might be able to get 'some of she' ordered in the next couple of days, if Caffery didn't mind waiting, but Caffery'd have to drive out to Bishop Sutton to pick them up because he didn't do deliveries, mind. And while he had Caffery on the phone how *was* Flea Marley, love her? Wasn't it a tragedy what turned around and happened to that poor girl, her not even thirty yet?

'I think . . . ' Caffery tapped a finger on the desk, feeling strange to be the only one not in on a story that everyone else knew. 'I think,' he said, 'considering everything, she's getting on OK . . . but I'll tell her you were asking.'

They talked a bit more about inconsequential stuff, payment, and Caffery didn't sound like he was from around here and just how did he like it in the West Country? Caffery talked calmly, but when he finished the call he was frowning, tapping his finger a little harder, wondering about what the nurseryman had said. A tragedy in Flea Marley's life. What sort of tragedy? he thought, and then he found himself wondering if she'd had a boyfriend to help her through it. And that was where he had to stop himself. Normal to be curious, old man, he thought, it's what made you a detective. That and the drinking. But don't let it go any further. There was a lot of damage he could do with thinking like that.

He went to the area map on the wall and put his thumb on Bishop Sutton, then stretched his hand until his little finger sat on Shepton Mallet. At first the Walking Man's routes had seemed random. But since the other night, when Caffery'd seen the stash of cider in the hedgerow, he'd come round to thinking there was something planned about where he went each day. He'd plotted out all that he could, using the few reports the intelligence database had hung on to, adding in the other night's stopover near Vobster quarry and now, standing in the badly lit office, he began to see a shape. It was like a half-open fan, or a slice of pie, its base at Shepton Mallet, the top arcing from Congresbury almost as far as Keynsham, the A37 marking the flat, leading edge. He stared at the shape a little longer, then pulled his jacket off the back of the chair and felt for his keys.

The thing about the Walking Man was that he moved all day long, every day. To find him you had to move too. Either that or you had to know what he was thinking. Keeping the fan shape in his head, Caffery drove out to the A37, an old route used by the Knight's Templars, one of the oldest in Britain. He passed Farrington Gurney and into Ston Easton, the hamlet's steep, dripping walls rising directly up either side of the road, slimy clumps of vegetation in the stones making it feel as if he was driving through the drained bed of an old canal. Outside the hamlet he slowed. There was no other traffic on the road, so he dawdled along, the headlights making icy filigree domes of the branches above. He kept his window open, leaning out on his elbow and searching the inky blackness on either side of the road for signs of the Walking Man's fire.

After a while he passed a small track on his right. He'd gone on a hundred yards when something made him stop and swing the car round in a U-turn. He pulled it well over on to the verge so that both wheels were off the road and he didn't need to use his hazards. Then he got out and climbed over the low fence into the neighbouring field. The countryside was black and unfathomable, only the greyish shape of a tree or hillock disturbing the darkness. Suddenly it was cold. He pulled on his jacket and stood with his hands buried in his armpits, letting the darkness come down over his head and round the back of his neck. He strained to hear the crack of a twig or to smell campfire smoke.

The Walking Man had cut off a man's nose using an Exacto blade from a craft kit. It had happened in the back of his garage in Shepton Mallet and he'd kept the guy still — Craig Evans, his name was — by taping him to an ironing-board using red and white 'Handle With Care' parcel tape. After the nose, which had made Evans puke blood for a bit, the Walking Man had used his thumbs — his *thumbs*, that bit got to Caffery more than anything — to press

188

the man's eyes so hard into his head that they'd slipped out of the sockets. When he'd finished he'd propped the ironing-board against the wall and nailed his hands to the breeze blocks. Crucified him.

The police knew everything because he'd videotaped it so he could watch it later for his pleasure. They knew that he'd put both eyes, and the long slippery red trails that hung from them, on to a shelf, then he'd smashed both kneecaps with a crowbar, cut Evans's dick off, gone inside the house and coolly put the bits and pieces — the eyes, the nose and the dick — into a Cadbury's Selection biscuit tin. When the police found it, they'd decomposed so much they'd popped the lid.

Caffery breathed in, letting the cold sting his nostrils, thinking about the darkness. He listened to the silence a bit more, watched the mothy-grey spectre of an owl hurtle across the sky. Then, when he couldn't hear anything in the dark he went back to the car. He got in and sat there, looking at the clouds through the lattice of branches, shredding and sliding round the moon.

There was that faint ache in his limbs again, and it struck him that this time it was connected not to tension but to tiredness — and that the tiredness, in turn, was connected to the conversation he'd had with the nurseryman. *Wasn't it a tragedy what happened to that poor girl?*

It took a while for him to put his finger on it, to remember the feeling he'd had — of being on the outside of something. That he was the new one, the outsider looking in. Maybe he'd do some asking around about what had happened to her. Nothing so obvious that he'd look like a twat, though. And then he heard the Walking Man's voice: *Don't miss it when you start thinking of it as something other people do in another life.* Yeah, he thought, he's right, forget it. You'd've done it once — gone down every route to find out about her, about her secret, about what happened to her. But not now. Your world's a changed place now.

He switched on the engine and swung the car into the road. It was gone ten and by the time he got to City Road it'd be near enough eleven, which was the time Keelie came out on the street. He opened the window and the bitter smell of fumes and earth came into the car. Even if he really concentrated he couldn't remember Keelie's face, couldn't remember what colour her hair was. But what he could remember was she had the grace never, ever to look him in the eye when he was fucking her. And that, he supposed, had to count for something.

22

9 May

A day later, and Mossy's lying on the sofa with one foot dangling above the floor, his lower lip resting on his upturned thumb, watching the gate and waiting for Jonah to appear.

But day becomes night and night becomes day and nothing happens and no one comes. Sometimes he thinks the sun's got stuck in the sky because every time he opens his eyes, for what seems like years and years, daylight comes through the grille. Then other times he thinks he's in a time machine on fast-forward, with the sun crossing the sky rapidly like in a silent movie, because one minute he feels sure it's morning and the next he opens his eyes to see a sunset sending red fingers of light through the boarding, lighting up the filthy, dusty room that has become his torture chamber.

They live on sugary coffee and Cup-a-Soup and Skinny sneaks him a little scag every now and then. He gets it from 'Uncle', who always seems to be on the other side of the iron gate. Uncle must have a room out there, Mossy thinks, because whenever Skinny wants to speak to him, or leave the room, he goes to the gate and knocks on it three times. There's usually silence for a bit, then a shaft of light in the corridor, and a figure in silhouette fills the passageway, bringing with it keys and a whiff of cold. Mossy can never quite see Uncle properly, but he knows he must be wearing something on his face because his head always looks wrong on his body: too dark and too big.

Mossy spends hours studying that gate, trying to bore through it with his thoughts. There's a passageway beyond: he can see the walls and the woodchip paper on them that has been gouged and ripped and is hanging off in sheets. Somewhere he can hear a tap dripping. Most of the time it's dark in the corridor because there's no light-bulb, but he gets a sense of how long the corridor is when someone moves along it: Skinny or Uncle. Sometimes he can hear strange voices — electronic and very clipped — but these sounds come only in bursts and he's never quite sure if he's imagining it or not.

Skinny has become everything to Mossy: yes, his jailer, but more than that, his anchor, the person who brings relief in a needle. He's always there, a hot little bundle that fits round Mossy's torso: like an animal he digs in his dry hands. And, like an animal taking comfort in the presence of another, for a moment or two Mossy's fear dissolves. He feels like it's him who should be protecting Skinny, the one who brought him here and is planning to cut his hands off. Even though inside he wants to cry, something about this person makes Mossy feel like a man. He feels bigger when Skinny's around: he doesn't see him as a tormentor but as a victim, and he thinks it's because this little

African child-man is being used too.

Skinny works for Uncle and that work is varied: sometimes it's taking blood out of people, sometimes it's selling drugs, and sometimes he has to go out on the street and sell his body. Nothing much to surprise Mossy there: Skinny is small — so small — and they both know there's a market for that sort of thing. There's one guy in particular, a fat guy in a scruffy car who sits outside the local supermarket, and sometimes when Skinny goes out he's wearing stupid things that make him look like a kid — little caps and schoolboyish blazers.

'It's for the fat man,' he says. 'He like me to wear it.'

Mossy can't understand why it should matter to him what Skinny does when he goes out of this place. He can't understand why he hates the idea of some fat bastard's cock up Skinny's arse, except that in all this horror he's somehow got fond of the guy. He can't say anything about it, of course, because that's the way it goes in this life: when it comes down to it he and Skinny are the same creature. Both of them have been scraped from the arsehole of the world. The only currency they've got is their own bodies and you don't question it when a friend has to turn to the trade.

Anyway, it's probably even worse for Skinny because he's an illegal in this country. Mossy's got a feeling there are other illegals too, living in this place: sometimes he sees shadows in the cage thing opposite and hears strange noises — like someone scuttling in there. When it's really dark sometimes and Skinny is out, Mossy can convince himself there's someone weird living in the place with them. Sometimes, on the rare occasions he can get to sleep in this hell-hole, he wakes up with the idea that whatever it is has slipped silently into the room from under the window grille and, without making a sound, has slid across it and into the cage.

Well, he thinks, if a long streak of piss like him can't fit through that window grille how the hell would anyone else get through? Unless, he thinks sometimes, late in the night when he's been on his own all day, unless it wasn't someone but some*thing*. Something inhuman.

But that thought makes him cold all over. So he turns away from the window whenever he can and tries his hardest not to think about it.

23

16 May

Katherine Oscar was dressed in a white shirt with beige men's jodhpurs tucked into riding boots, her hair tied back in a knot, loosely arranged as if she really hadn't spent much time on it. It was a fine and clever art being Mrs Oscar, and she worked hard to make sure no one would ever get away with calling her mannered. Or a snob for that matter. On this Wednesday morning, very early, she was standing on the Marleys' gravel driveway, irritation on her face. Her hands were on her hips, the early sun picking out the stray wisps of hair round her face, and her head was tilted back so she could stare up at the first-floor windows of the Marleys' cottage. Wondering, probably, why no one was answering the door.

Flea, just out of the shower and wrapped in a towel, stood quite still and watched her from the bathroom window. Ever since she could remember there had been one problem with living here: Katherine Oscar and her family. The steep walls of the Oscars' house abutted the Marleys' garden so there was always a sense of being overlooked — the Oscar children could lean out of the bedroom windows and watch the Marleys in the garden that had once belonged to the Oscars' house. The manor had other gardens on the far side, acres of them with a swimming-pool, stables and a knot garden, but the Oscars found it hard to accept that they no longer had sovereignty over the Marleys' garden too, and quite often they wandered on to Flea's property without asking, as if they had the right simply by virtue of their wealth.

The worst offender was the youngest boy, Toby, a stocky child with a pudding-basin haircut and close-together eyes. The crunch had come one autumn afternoon when Flea happened to look out of a window at the front to see him in the road below her peeing happily and copiously against her wall. She threw open the window and yelled at him, but he pretended not to hear, calmly zipping himself up and wandering back along the road towards the manor, scratching his head as he went, as if he was trying to remember something. By the time she had her shoes on and had got to the manor, the front door was closed. It took three rings to get anyone to answer.

'A place this *cavernous* we need two doorbells!' Katherine Oscar always had a joke to make about how enormous her house was — but when Flea explained what had happened her smile faded. She stepped outside and peered carefully down the road, as if she didn't believe it was possible that a child of hers had done something like that. She stepped back into the hallway, and closed her eyes. 'You know, it makes my blood run cold to think of the children being out there on this road. Thank you for telling me.'

She started to close the door but Flea got her foot inside. 'I'm not interested in the road, Katherine. I'm interested in whether you're going to speak to him.'

Katherine Oscar coloured. 'I'm sorry?'

'Are you going to speak to your son?'

'Of course I'm going to speak to him. What do you take me for?'

I take you for trash, Flea thought, looking at the blonde hair, the expensive blouse, the stud earrings. In fact, you know what, Katherine? I hate you. I hate the way you look down your nose at me, I hate the way you respect power and money, the way you swing your SUV round corners and force other cars to stop for you. I hate the way the other day you left your car blocking the road, got out and had a long conversation with your gardener not caring that three other cars had to wait five minutes so you could talk about fertilizer and bedding plants. I hate the way your chimneys belch smoke, the way you put out twenty bags of rubbish a week, and the way you speak differently to people who come to the manor to work for you. You'd scream the place down if a criminal came near you, and yet your husband is a pig in a Barbour who spends his life at a computer stealing from other people and is the biggest criminal I've ever met in my life.

She'd have liked to say it all. She'd have liked to pin Katherine Oscar to the wall and say it into her face. But, of course, she didn't. She knew how to hit someone, she knew how to do it efficiently and fast, but she knew how to hold herself together too, so instead she nodded. 'Good,' she said calmly. 'You speak to him, then. And speak to him properly, because if it happens again I'll have him done. Get it?'

After that the Oscars left her alone. From time to time she'd catch the boys glaring at her from behind the smoked glass of the SUV on their way to school and she'd hear them laughing at her from the windows of the house, but that didn't matter. The less she saw of them the better. For a while the only thing she heard from the Oscars was the faint sound of the horses in the stables on long summer evenings. But if she thought it would stop there she was wrong because Katherine simply couldn't let the garden idea go. About six months later she started leaving voice messages on Flea's phone, telling her how much the Oscars would still like to buy back the garden, in spite of their differences, and how they were going to speak to the council, to English Heritage, to local residents' groups and the National Trust about reinstating it as part of the manor. She posted notes through the door two or three times a month and dropped by every week just to 'say hello and see if you've had any more thoughts'. Keeping up the pressure.

Now, as the doorbell echoed through the cottage again, Flea knew she was here to ask about the note: *Did you get it? Have you thought about what I said? About property prices?* So she stood quite still, knowing she couldn't be seen, until Katherine got fed up with waiting and, with an impatient shake of her head — as if to say she never had been able to understand the Marleys, and why did they spend their money diving in stupid parts of the world when they could have bought a decent vehicle so their shabby cars didn't mess up the neighbourhood — she turned and walked stiffly up the drive. Even the sound of her footsteps crunching in the gravel had a specific note to it — as if her feet struck the stones more sharply than other people's would.

Flea waited for her footsteps to go and then, when she was sure she was alone again, she turned back to the opened bathroom cabinet, quickly scanning all the familiar things: spare toothbrush, nail scissors, her contraceptive cap in its case — years since she'd needed that, she should throw it away — moisturizer, hair clippers. She'd forgotten now what she was looking for — her head was too hot and full with all the things that had happened last night, as if an infection was starting.

Tucked at the back of the cabinet behind the vitamins she took, thinking they would boost her immune system and fight off the bugs and germs she was always immersing herself in, was a packet of Kwells, kept there for Thom's travel sickness. She was probably going to be sick this evening. Kaiser had warned her that the psychoactive ingredient in ibogaine would give her the symptoms of travel sickness. She hooked the packet out — probably years out of date, but better than nothing — and propped it on the sink for later. Then she closed the cabinet and dried off, throwing on loose trousers, a T-shirt and an old Chinese workers' cap over her wet hair. Finally she found her keys and jumped into the car. Holding the steering wheel, she studied the veins in her arm, standing blue and cold against the skin. Later today she was going to put a poison into her bloodstream, something to let her speak to the dead. And to do that she needed as much peace in her head as she could gather. So she didn't care what her line manager said about interfering with inquiries, it was very simple: the things she'd seen and felt last night had to go. They had to be passed on before she took the ibogaine.

As she left the driveway she let the old Ford spin its wheels in the gravel a couple of times. Then she sailed past the manor, sounding the horn a couple of times. Just enough so that Katherine Oscar heard and knew she'd been there all along.

★ ★ ★

It was the dust marks that had really got into Flea's thoughts. Mrs Mabuza — if the woman in the bedroom had been Mrs Mabuza — might have been a good cook but she was a bad housekeeper. The crucifixes dotted around the house were all perfectly clean, but each one stood in a larger dust mark. The crosses were clean because they were brand new, not because they'd been polished. And they stood in dust marks because they had very recently replaced something that had been there for a long time. The crucifixes were for show, Flea was sure of it. They were to make the world believe this was the house of a Christian.

When she knocked on the deputy SIO's door no one answered so she pushed it open a fraction. Caffery was alone, in shirtsleeves, standing with his hands shoved into his trouser pockets, his feet slightly apart, and absorbed in something outside the window. She studied him from behind, getting the clear impression he hadn't been home the night before. If it didn't sound so crazy she'd say he'd spent the night in the office. Or sleeping in the car. She wondered if he even had a home here, or if he was living in an HQ training-wing bedsit until he got settled.

Then, as she looked at the way his hair was cut short, clipped at the back of his neck, a picture flashed into her head of him in bed. He was asleep, one hand pushed out at his side. He was tanned and his face was squashed against the pillow so she could see the muscles in his shoulders slightly flexed. She cleared her throat, making the picture go.

'Hello.'

He turned. Something blank and half angry came into his eyes and for a moment it was as if he didn't recognize her. Then his face cleared. He took a breath and smiled. 'Oh, hi. Sorry — miles away.' He pulled out a chair and gestured for her to sit. 'You caught me on a daydream.'

She took off her cap, shuffled her fingers in her hair, and sat. 'What about?'

He leaned back against the desk, his arms crossed over his chest, one hand fiddling with a paperclip, and studied her. She didn't let herself think about it too much but a big part of her had registered lots of things about him — for example, that he didn't have brown eyes, as she'd originally thought, but blue, with very dark lashes. As dark as his hair. 'I wasn't expecting you,' he said, 'wasn't planning on working with your unit today. You must know something I don't.'

She took her eyes off his face and pretended to look at the tiny office, with its dull paintwork and faded area map on the wall.

'Flea? What's on your mind?'

'Right,' she said slowly. 'I want you to promise you won't let what I'm going to say leave this room.'

He raised an eyebrow. 'OK.' He half smiled. 'Try me.'

'OK. I'll be honest. I've done something stupid.'

'I see.'

'I went to talk to Gift Mabuza. The owner of the Moat.'

Caffery laughed as if he didn't believe her.

'Seriously. I went to his house last night.'

'He's not even in the country. Not until this afternoon.'

'He came back early. Maybe he knew you were looking for him.'

Caffery's expression went flat. He dropped his arms to his sides. 'You're serious. You really went to speak to him.'

'I didn't say I was job.'

'So who did you say you were?'

'I didn't. I went with a friend of mine who knows him.'

He flicked the paperclip into the bin. 'Pretty stupid, if you don't mind me saying. Pretty fucking stupid.'

'I know.' She shook her head. 'But he's not going anywhere — I'm sure of that. He's waiting for you. And . . . on the subject of being pretty fucking stupid I did something else.' In spite of the look he was giving her she felt in her pocket and found the ziplock bag full of fibers. She held it out on her flat palm, under his eyes. 'They're from his carpet.'

He took the bag from her. 'What, these?'

'You said there were carpet fibres on the hands. So I thought . . . I thought maybe this would help.'

Caffery turned the bag over and over. Then he went to the filing cabinet, took out a paper evidence bag and put it inside. He uncapped a pen, seemed to be thinking about what to write on it. Then he changed his mind, scribbled a note to himself and stuck it on the bag.

'I didn't force my way in. I was there legitimately.'

'You know the section nineteen stuff well enough. It's an issue of consent versus true consent. You didn't tell anyone who you were and you used the relationship to get information,' he said, in a patient monotone. 'Let's hope the defence isn't awake, or can't be bothered to check, or they could say you've made yourself UC without authorization.'

Flea's jaw got tight. She'd told herself she wouldn't, but she felt like walking out. UC stood for 'undercover' and Caffery was probably right:

the defence could get them for it. But she wasn't going to let him put her off. She forced herself to straighten up. It was a physical thing. Put her shoulders back — it made her feel stronger.

'What about the fibres?' she said. 'Do they look like the ones on the hands?'

At first she thought he hadn't heard. He was still looking at the paper bag, an expression on his face as if the fibres were communicating something to him. 'Are they the ones on the hand?' she repeated.

Caffery said, as if he hadn't heard her, 'You kept telling me yesterday — 'He's African.' What did that mean — *he's African*?'

'Are you sure you want to know?'

'I'm sure.'

'OK.' She gestured at the computer. 'May I?'

'It's slow. May as well still be on dial-up — Avon and Somerset's finest, and if the traffic's bad it can take five minutes for a page to download.'

She rolled the seat forward, using her heels to pull herself across the floor, and gave the mouse a shake on the mat. When the screen came up she waited for the connection, did the search — he was right, the server took ages — and went to the page she wanted. 'There,' she said, pointing to the photo.

Caffery came to stand next to her, bending a little to peer at the screen. If he hadn't gone home last night he had at least found somewhere to shower. He was close to her and he smelled clean. 'What am I looking at?' he said slowly. 'What's this?'

She was thinking of something she knew he'd remember: the headless, limbless corpse of a small boy found floating in the Thames. 'Adam', they'd called him, because the only clues to his ID were the orange shorts his remains had been dressed in, the contents of his stomach and that the killer had deliberately removed the first vertebra. 'When you were in London,' she said carefully, 'did you have anything to do with Adam?'

'Adam?'

'The little boy in the Thames. The torso.'

'Yeah,' he said. 'Couple of my colleagues worked on it. But why . . . ' He trailed off, his eyes on hers, his face suddenly drawn. 'Oh, Christ,' he said tightly. 'I see what you're talking about.'

She didn't answer. Eventually 'Adam's' trail had led the Metropolitan Police to Africa, where their worst suspicions were confirmed: the colour of the shorts and the missing bone, the Atlas bone, held by many African religions to be the centre of the body . . . everything had pointed to one thing.

'*Muti*,' Caffery murmured. 'That's what you're saying. This is a *muti* killing?'

'Yes,' she said, and for a moment they were both silent. *Muti* — black magic, witchcraft. The word was enough to make the room feel cold. African magic medicine: sometimes it included the killing and dismemberment of a human for use in a religious ritual. In the last decade there'd been signs it had wound its sheltered way into Britain.

'It was in a book I saw.' She said it quietly, as if it was rude to be talking about it aloud. 'A book about African witchcraft and shamans. It had a picture of severed hands — a guy in Johannesburg got done for it. He'd cut them off a corpse and sold them to a local businessman.'

'What was he going to do with them?'

'They're supposed to entice customers into the business. That's the idea. You bury them or put them into the walls and they beckon people in. And from what I could work out from the book, the place to put them . . . ' she paused, ' . . . is at the entrance.'

Caffery's eyes were slightly distant as if he was concentrating on the thought processes unravelling in his head. Then he looked at the screen again, and said, a little more quietly, 'And this?' An object, brown, about the size of a sleeping-bag crumpled up, was displayed in a glass case.

'This? Oh, God, I don't know why I had to show you this, but it made me realize just how far people will go.'

Caffery leaned into the monitor, studying the obscene folds, the edges yellowing and frayed. 'What is it?'

'What do you think it is?'

'I don't know . . . ' Neither of them said it but something dark had crept into the room, as if the sun had gone behind a cloud. 'I think, and don't ask me how, but I think I'm looking at someone's skin.'

24

10 May

Mossy wakes to find Skinny squatting a few feet away from him on the floor. At first he's confused. The room is bathed in a weird blue-white light that gives the smallest things shadows, making the dust and bits of tobacco and hairs on the floor appear to crackle like electricity. Skinny is dressed in some sort of robe in chequered red, black and white with symbols on it like an African mask. On his head is a wig, long black hair beaded with white shells. For a moment he is frozen, like a lion about to spring, then suddenly he's in motion, going quickly round the floor. There's something nasty about the movement that makes Mossy sit up on the sofa, because it's fast and unnatural and a bit like a wounded spider, the way he's half using his hands and half using his feet. The beads in his hair click together.

Skinny hisses, baring his teeth like a snake, but Mossy knows this isn't for real: he's watching a performance. It takes him no time at all to work out that it's being done for the camera, which he sees has appeared in its sly way in the corridor. The gate stands open and that's where the light is coming from — from a mini spotlight stuck above the lens.

Mossy knows who's there. Uncle is behind the camera, and Mossy's not going to draw attention to himself, so he tips his forehead down like he's still asleep and rolls his eyes up to watch.

Skinny stops scurrying round the floor and takes from under the robes a small cloth bag. Mossy's seen it before. Sometimes Skinny leaves it lying on the purple carpet — he says it contains his 'divining bones' but he's never let Mossy look at them. Now he tips them out and hunkers next to them, waving his hands over them, murmuring under his breath.

Mossy can see them scattered on the filthy carpet, not just bones but other things too: shells, two playing-cards, a domino, a folded pocket knife, and a chunk of yellowish rind that Mossy thinks could be from a butcher's. He watches in silence as Skinny points at the playing-cards, muttering something in a language he's never heard before but brings with it the strong smell of Africa.

The performance goes on for a long time. When it is finished Skinny leaves the room and goes into the corridor. The gate is locked for a moment or two and he can hear muttering. The light goes out and after a while there is the sound of the far door opening and closing. Then Skinny is coming back into the room, locking the gate behind him. He comes to sit near Mossy. 'You watch me?'

'Yeah.' He puts one hand on his forehead and peers at him closely. 'I watch you. What the fuck was all that about?'

'I throw the bones.'

'You what?'

'Throw the bones. I am *sangoma*.'

'*San*-what?'

'*Sangoma*. Diviner, guide, doctor. My bones are my guide — I can see into the future, I can find thieves. They give me the truth about many things, many problems of health and fortune.'

Mossy gives a hoarse laugh. 'You telling me you're a fucking witch doctor?'

'It's like witch doctor. Not the same, but almost the same.'

Mossy laughs again. 'No, you ain't. You ain't no fucking witch doctor. That was the worst acting I've ever seen.'

'Yes, I am.'

'No, you're not.'

Skinny looks at him for a long time. His eyes are sad. Then he goes to the gate. He peers through it, listens. Then, when he seems satisfied they're not being watched, he takes off the robes and puts them in a pile on the floor. Underneath it he's wearing old-fashioned Y-fronts and nothing else, and his slight body is dark and slick next to the saggy material. He comes to the sofa and eases himself on to it next to Mossy. He cups a hand round his ear and upper neck and presses his face close, as if he's going to kiss him. But he doesn't. Instead his hot cracked mouth comes up against Mossy's ear and he whispers, 'You don't tell Uncle, you don't tell him.'

'I ain't going to talk to him, am I?'

'Me and my brother. We is runners in Africa. The gang we worked for — we took they money to come here.'

'Runners?'

'Trafficking. You understand.'

'I know what fucking trafficking is. What did you traffic?'

'Skins. Carry them through borders. They is taken in Natal or in Mozambique and they is sold in Tanzania.'

Mossy pulls away from him and drops his chin to peer at Skinny's face. 'What kind of skins?'

'Of people.'

'Human skins, you mean.'

'Yes,' Skinny says, as if it's nothing. 'That is our business, me and my brother. People skins. They make very powerful medicine.'

Mossy feels the watery vomit come into his mouth. He has to lean his head back and swallow while his stomach heaves. He's heard of people selling their kidneys — a friend of his reckoned he'd sold a kidney in India to buy his airfare home, had everyone believing him. But all of that was supposed to belong to another world.

'Fuck,' he mutters, his body going hot and cold. 'Fucking shit. Is that what you did with my blood? Is that what — oh, Jesus — what you want to do with my *hands*?' He pushes Skinny off the sofa. He's shaking now. 'It wasn't just someone wanted to watch me — it was you wanted to *sell* the fucking things?'

Skinny crouches next to him on the floor, his eyes bright. 'Not me. *Uncle*. Uncle is the man who makes the money. Me — I don't have no choice. I don't have no proper visa — you know? Uncle, him tell me all the time, him can send police to me any time him choose.'

210

Mossy closes his eyes, and gulps a few more times, getting himself under control. He's always thought that the world he inhabited meant he understood the sickest things people could do to each other. He thought he knew how bad people could get. But now he sees how dense he's been. Now he sees there's a whole universe out there, a universe he's ignorant about, a universe of horror and despair darker than he's ever dreamed possible.

25

16 May

The grandfather clock said twelve and at the back of the house the sun shone directly along the line of trees, casting their shadows on the gravel. Spring was here. Already the wisteria was hanging its long racemes at the windows, fingering the pane as if it'd like to get inside. The Marleys used to do the gardening together, but since the accident Flea had never had the time or the inclination and certainly couldn't afford a gardener, so now the gardens sprang up in the summer, jungly and throbbing with insect life. Two years on and you couldn't get down the terraces to the bottom of the valley without a hacksaw. There was a folly down there too, meant to look like the Bridge of Sighs in Venice. It spanned a small ornamental lake, but the limestone mortar had weakened and last winter the stone had sunk into the lake until only the very top of the arch was visible. The sensible thing would be to sell the garden to the Oscars, but she couldn't bear it. She couldn't bear the thought of the Oscar children running up and down the lawns she and Thom had grown up on.

'Falling in around my ears, Mum,' she muttered, standing in the kitchen that lunch-time. She could see the solar panels Dad had

212

fitted in a line outside the garage. They had broken months ago and there wasn't any money to repair them, and on top of everything moss was covering the tiles and grass was growing in the gutters. From a distance the roof looked like another lawn. 'I'm so sorry. I never meant it to get like this.'

She lifted the pasta off the stove, dumped it in a colander, and, squinting in the steam, set it on the counter next to Dad's safe. Kaiser had told her she was going to be hungry, that she would probably be on the trip for more than twenty-four hours and when it was over she would want carbohydrate and vitamins. Preparing food afterwards — or doing anything that needed concentration — would be difficult. Pasta was the thing, Mum's favourite. She could save it in Tupperware and microwave it tomorrow. She peeled the skin off the beef tomatoes she'd been scalding in boiling water, running her fingers under the tap when they got too hot. She took the skin to the bin and paused, her foot on the pedal, the lid open, looking at the slippery pile in her hands, the juice leaking down between her fingers. Into her head came the mound of human skin she'd shown Caffery that morning. It stayed for a moment or two, then she dropped the tomato peel into the bin, wiped her hands on a tea-towel, and let the image go.

'Flea?'

She turned. Thom was in the doorway, standing in that nervous way of his with his feet placed at an odd angle, like a foal, not sure its legs would support its weight. 'I'm sorry,' he said apologetically. 'The door was open.'

'Oh, sweetpea. That's OK.' She came forward, reaching to touch his face. Her little brother. Poor, poor Thom. 'It's so nice to see you.' He smiled. His skin was still as pale and fragile as it had been when they were children, and the bags under his blue eyes, which always made him look as if he was too scared to sleep, were pronounced today. 'Here. Sit down,' she said, pulling out a chair and patting it.

He sat, his awkward hands resting on his knees.

'I'll put the kettle on — make you tea.'

'What are you doing?' he asked, gesturing at the things she'd been cooking with — the olive oil, the garlic, the jar of pasta.

She took the heavy frying pan from the stove and scraped the garlic and onions into the tomatoes. Then she set the pan in the sink, running water on it.

'Flea?'

'Yes,' she said. 'What?'

'What are you doing?'

'What does it look like?'

'Cooking. But you're acting strange.'

She paused, standing at the sink with one hand on her hip, the other on the tap, and watched the yellow circles of fat float to the top of the water. She could hear the crows cawing in the cedars along the edge of the garden, she could feel her tongue sticking to the roof of her mouth. She thought about Mum staring at her from the path in the trees, whispering, *We went the other way.*

'Flea? What is it? You're scaring me.'

She turned. 'Thom, I know you don't like to talk about it.'

'About what?'

'About — about, you know, the way it all happened. The accident.'

There was a moment's silence, while they both stared at each other. Slowly Thom's cheeks went red. The rest of his face stayed pale.

'The accident,' she repeated, more softly this time. 'One day we're going to have to talk about it. About what you remember.'

There were a few more seconds where he didn't do anything, just went on staring. Then he began to drum his fingers on the table. A little humming noise started in the back of his throat. There was a scar in Thom that no one should mess with, things he couldn't bear to think about. Guilt he carried everywhere. He scraped his chair back and got up. He went to the stove and stood with his back to her, looking down at the pan of tomatoes. He shook the pan, moving things around, collecting spoons and spatulas, as if he had purpose. His hair was so fine and blond you could see the tanned scalp underneath, the back of his neck so vulnerable where the hair hung away from it.

'You know what?' he said conversationally. 'I'm not doing well in my job. I'm really not getting on in it.'

'Thom, I just want to — '

'If I'm honest, I'd say it's even starting to affect us. Me and Mandy.'

'Please listen to me — '

'And if I'm telling the truth, I feel trapped. Trapped like I've never been before. All because of the job.'

Flea closed her mouth. She knew people could go into denial, but she'd still imagined, in some corner of her conscious mind, that one day Thom would talk about the accident if he was forced to. She thought that by now he'd have worked the guilt through, rationalized it. But no, there he was, blanking her, as if he hadn't heard a word she had said. She sighed and sat down at the table.

'I can't bear it any longer.' He poked at the tomatoes. 'I'm trapped.'

'Are you?' she said flatly, half annoyed with him, half pissed off with herself for bringing that subject up in the first place. 'I had no idea.'

There was a long silence while Thom stirred the tomatoes and Flea sat watching him.

'Anyway,' he said, after a few minutes. He tore off kitchen towel, put the spoon on it, and cleared his throat. 'Anyway, I think I've got a new thing going.'

'What sort of new thing?'

'Some people I know. They import chandeliers from the Czech Republic. They're beautiful, better than any you've seen in the antique shops round here.'

Flea pressed the bridge of her nose with her thumb and forefinger because she could feel a headache starting. Since what happened in Bushman's Hole, Thom had lost every job he'd had. He'd worked for travel agents and magazines selling advertising space, he'd worked as a telephone researcher for seven pounds an hour. When he wasn't employed he'd used the loan on his insurance money to start businesses. In two years he'd been involved in no less than six failed ventures. From selling slimming pills he'd imported from the US to selling pixels on a web page, to investing in a piece of land for which he later found he couldn't get planning permission. All had gone wrong, leaving him almost broke.

'Thom, we've talked about this. You said you'd stick with a job. You can't keep taking these risks.'

'It's not a risk, it'll be fine. I just need an alibi.'

'An *alibi*?' Flea dropped her hand. 'What sort of alibi?'

He pushed aside the pan and came back to the table, sitting opposite her, elbows on the table. She could see in his eyes that he had wiped the accident from his mind. It was weird, the way he could do that.

'It's a really good venture but I've kept it from Mandy — '

'Because she'd say exactly what I'm saying and — '

'No, because I want it to be a surprise when it works.' He looked at her anxiously. 'But I need your help. Things have gone a bit wrong.'

'What?'

'I keep going off to meet them and Mandy's starting to think I'm seeing someone else.' Flea raised an eyebrow. 'I know,' he said, and suddenly the pallor had gone and his voice was excited. 'I know — she's even been following me. Brilliant, isn't it?'

217

'*Brilliant?*'

'I've seen her sneaking along the road behind me. You know what it means.'

'No,' Flea said. 'I don't.'

'It means she *loves* me. She's *jealous*! She really, really loves me.'

Flea shook her head wearily. She looked at the smooth skin of Thom's throat, faintly transparent and white where it covered the Adam's apple. Mandy was his first serious girlfriend. There had been a series of women he'd imagined he was having a relationship with — he'd fall ridiculously, childishly in love and end up devastated when they didn't return the attention. Until Mandy. And, like a child, he mistook Mandy's possessiveness for true love.

'She thinks I don't know she's following, but I do. So, now I've got an important meeting with these people, make-or-break. If I'm not there I can say goodbye to the whole thing.'

'And you want me to lie for you?'

'If I tell Mandy I'm here she'll believe me.'

'Here? No, she'd come and check.'

'Probably. But she'd never knock on the door because she thinks I don't know she's on to me. I'll take your Focus — I'm insured — and leave my car out the front on the road. That way if she follows or drives past I'm covered.'

'When do you want to do this?'

'Monday night.'

Monday was the day after tomorrow. Flea's last night off work. Kaiser had promised her the ibogaine would be out of her system by then.

She stood, picked up the pan and ladled the

218

tomatoes into the pasta. She dropped in some olives, some sliced sausage and left the lid off to let the sauce give up its moisture. Then she spent some time wiping the surfaces.

Thom watched her, his eyes fixed on her. 'Well,' he said eventually, 'will you do it?'

'You know the answer to that, Thom.' She sealed the Tupperware box and put it into the fridge, closing the door hard. She didn't know why but she felt angrier than she should. 'Because you know I'd do absolutely bloody anything for you.'

26

When Flea had gone the office was quiet. He sat for a while in thought, thinking about the word '*muti*', wondering why he hadn't thought about it before. He took the time to read the web page carefully. The human skin, he realized with a jolt, wasn't some*one*'s skin but the skin of *two* people — two teenage boys. They hadn't known each other in life, but in death their existences had been inextricably combined, displayed in a box as an exhibit about smuggling in Dar es Salaam. The skins had been confiscated from smugglers whose trade was to flay people in Tanzania, then export the skins — sometimes to Nigeria, sometimes to South Africa — for huge sums.

He stared at the picture for a long time, conscious of his own skin, of its shape, its inadequacy. *Muti.* Even the sound of the word was bad. The owner of the Moat, Gift Mabuza, had come back into town without telling the police. He was African, and in some countries it was a superstition to bury hands under the entrances to businesses. A basic equation.

Caffery thought about Mabuza for a few minutes, tried to imagine what species of human he was. He was ready to bring him in right off, but when he thought about it he saw it would be a mistake: he wouldn't have the PACE adviser on hand if they needed to make an arrest. Best to build some intel, get the fibres back from

Chepstow and know how to hit him. He'd called the immigration officer attached to Operation Atrium and asked him to look into Mabuza's immigration status. Then he'd got on to his SIO and talked him into okaying directed surveillance for twenty-four hours, just to know that the guy was staying put. But as he was putting the landline down, his work mobile began to ring in his pocket. He flipped it open. 'DI Caffery, MCIU. How can I help?'

There was a moment's silence, then a stiffly polite voice, slightly accented, said, 'My name is Gift Mabuza.'

Caffery was quite still, his pulse coming back at him in the earpiece. 'I know who you are,' he said quietly. 'What can I do for you?'

'Your men spoke to me on my holiday. I have come home because I have heard about the trouble at my restaurant.'

Caffery hesitated. Then he said, 'Yes. There's been some trouble.'

'I would like it if I could come and talk to you.'

'You'd like to come and talk to . . . ?' He let the sentence trail off, still hearing his heart thumping. 'OK. Good. That's no problem. How does . . . ' He tried to think what to do. He'd like to know what the lab had to say about the fibres before he interviewed Mabuza. 'How does . . . tomorrow morning sound?'

'Yes — good. I would like to get to the bottom of this business.' There was another pause. Then, in that over-educated way, Mabuza said, 'Thank you, sir. Thank you and goodbye.'

The line went dead. After a while he put the phone into his pocket and used his index finger to push the little bag of carpet fibres around on his desk, thinking about Mabuza. Had he sounded like someone with something to hide? Then he thought about Flea in the office, the way she kept fiddling with the zip on her fleece as she talked, the way her fingernails were clean and white, her limbs straight and slim under the force regulation overalls. If she'd looked like a regular Support Unit sergeant he might have laughed her out of the office. *Muti?* Was he being walked into a theory he wouldn't have come to himself?

Technically he should record Flea's visit to Mabuza's house in his policy book, his decision log and his pocket book. He should state quite clearly that he'd advised her of the ways she'd breached the Regulation of Investigatory Powers Act 2000. He should have done all of that — but he didn't. Instead he put away all his logs, cradled the phone receiver against his shoulder and tapped in a number. Marilyn Kryotos, the woman who'd managed the HOLMES computerized investigation system in his old Metropolitan Police unit. She was up at the Yard now, detailed to a specialist team advising on ritual abuse and witchcraft. It'd been set up as a reaction to the cases of Victoria Climbié and Adam. Adam, the pathologist reckoned, had been between four and seven when he'd been ritually dismembered. All the intelligence indicated he'd been alive while it was happening. No one had been done for it yet.

The line hummed and clicked on the third ring. 'PC Kryotos.'

He hesitated. The familiar calm voice. It took him back to the way things used to be in the Area Major Investigation Team in London; to the daily whirlwind of a chaotic investigation. The only thing to ground it, stop it spinning out of control, had been Marilyn Kryotos. No ego, no grandstanding from her. In spite of himself he smiled. 'Hey, Marilyn. Guess who. Blast from the past.'

There was a silence. Then a small, sarcastic laugh. 'Not so distant past, Jack. It's only been a couple of months.'

His smile faded. 'Not happy to hear me, then? What? Am I on your shit list or something?'

She didn't answer. She let the line hum a little.

He sighed. 'I know what you're thinking.'

'Do you?'

'Yeah — like everyone else. You're thinking I'm a tosser.'

'Are you?'

'Marilyn, haven't you ever left anyone?'

'Course I have. Years ago. Before the kids.'

'Well, then.'

'It's not that you *left* her. I mean, she was nuts, Jack. Pretty, but nuts. Last week she was in the paper — looks like she's got her medications, used make-up and blister packs and stuff, and stuck it in an acrylic block and called it art. Me, I never had time for her, you know that. So it's not that you left exactly — it's the *reason* you left. I mean, what sort of reason was that? Jack, I never said this to you before because of the

223

situation, but you're not my line manager now and — '

'And now you can give me a piece of your mind?'

'Jack, you're not getting any younger. I hate to say it, but you're staring forty in the face, aren't you?'

'I don't want kids, Marilyn. Not now, not ever.'

'Jack, *everyone* should have kids. Everyone. Even walking disasters like you. You're not a complete human being until you have kids. Please trust me on this. And, Jack, I've never said it, but the truth is you'd make a — '

'Let's change the subject here, it's getting — '

'No. Listen to me . . . ' He could picture her face at the other end of the line. Sort of cross but patient too, as if he was her son. 'You, Jack, whether you like it or not, would make a brilliant dad. OK?' She gave a little puff of air, like he'd forced her to do something she didn't want to do. 'There, I've said it.'

In his cramped little office, with the dying plant on the windowsill and the view of the halal butcher's, Caffery moved the phone from one ear to the other. The computer had popped up one or two search results, but the reflection of his face was superimposed over them and he really didn't want to look at his own eyes. He turned the chair to face the wall.

'OK, Marilyn,' he said. 'I'm bleeding on the floor. You finished with me now?'

'I s'pose so.'

'Can we have a professional conversation?'

224

'S'pose.'

He gave a dry laugh. 'Queen of my conscience. Never abandon me, Marilyn.' He dug at the vinyl armrest with his thumbnail. 'Look, I've only been here five minutes and already I've stumbled on something I don't know how to handle. Whichever way I turn, one word keeps coming up. Witchcraft. That's why I called you.'

'Then fire.'

'Hands. Severed hands, near or under the entrance to a business. I'm being told from elsewhere it's a witchcraft thing. African.'

'Well, whoever 'elsewhere' is, they're right.'

'Rings some bells, then?'

'Got any African connections to it?'

'Maybe. The owner of the property is African — but the hands, well, they're white.'

'Except white flesh is considered more powerful by some people. That's still how it is in some parts of Africa, the old colonial thing. White man makes more money, white man is more powerful, his flesh makes better medicine. Stronger *muti*.'

'You mean witchcraft.'

'No. Medicine — everyone gets *muti* and witchcraft tangled up. And just to make it more bloody complicated the name changes from tribe to tribe. One word you see a lot in the press along with *muti* is *ndoki*. Now *ndoki* really does mean 'witchcraft', but it's what they call it further up the continent, West Africa. It's the area our team's studying at the moment.'

'You're enjoying it, aren't you, Marilyn? I can hear it in your voice. You like this job.'

She laughed. 'Jack, I'm finding out about the world. I'm not just plugging in data on every sordid south London nonce. And you know what?'

'What?'

'The more I look at it, the more I think it's not that weird after all. It's not that different from Chinese medicine, and nobody screams voodoo about that. Everyone assumes Adam was murdered to use his body parts for *muti* — somehow that name got attached to his case. But we think he was murdered for black magic, which isn't the same as medicine.'

'Subtle difference.'

'Subtle, yes, but still different. For *muti*, we don't automatically think about human body parts. The place we start mostly, Jack, is with the Endangered Species Act.'

'How come?'

'*Muti*'s usually about animal parts. Every animal's got a different power. I mean baboons. I never even knew what a baboon was, Jack, until I was in this job — can you believe it? — but now I do. No one likes the baboon in Africa. They're like foxes, really cunning and nasty, and no one thinks twice about killing them. But because football's a rising thing over there you can sell a baboon's hands on the open market. They're supposed to help a goalkeeper stop goals.'

Caffery turned his chair round, pulled up the Guardian intelligence database and entered Endangered Species as a search term. He waited for the computer to crank its way through the millions of entries. 'Marilyn,' he said, pulling his chair nearer the screen. 'Have you got anything

226

you can send over to me?'

'I'm doing it as I talk. I'm sending you an info pack we've made up for distribution. Nottingham's got one from us already and Manchester — this thing's really picking up across the country. I won't put it through the registry, I'll courier it today. There's a couple of bibliographies in it, contacts for academics, practitioners, that sort of thing. But most of all there are press releases and cuttings.' She paused. 'And, Jack?'

'What?'

'You're going to be really careful, aren't you, how you tread? In London this is a seriously hot issue right now. The right-wing press — you can picture it, can't you? — they've made it a race thing, like every African, every black church, every Pentecostal minister is doing ritual abuse, exorcisms, the works. Truth is, there've been maybe a handful of cases in the last couple of years, two or three that've stuck, but because there've been kids involved, the press are getting all their hot buttons pushed.'

Caffery nodded slowly. There was so much tension in the country's big cities, the streets felt like any spark could take the whole lid off. In front of him the computer was stacking up results: there were already five entries. He put his glasses on and pulled the chair closer to the screen. 'Marilyn,' he said, 'you get that info pack off with the couriers and you say hello to everyone at home. OK?'

'Yeah,' she said drily. 'I mean, it's not like you've got any family of your own to say hello to.'

'Marilyn,' he sighed, half smiling at her cheek, 'it's always so good to talk to you. Thank you for your support.'

When they'd said goodbye he returned to the screen. The searching had stopped and of the ten in the list he could see immediately which entry was going to interest him. The report was sketchy, just the bare minimum because the case had never got to court, but it must have set off alarm bells for the intelligence officer who had logged it, because the attachments were detailed. Caffery scrolled through it. It had been originated nine months ago by a traffic officer near the Clifton Suspension Bridge. He'd stopped someone for dodgy brake lights and when he came round to speak to the driver, there, hanging from a ribbon on the rear-view, was a decaying vulture's head.

Caffery opened the photograph attached: a grizzled head like an outsized, misshapen chicken. Its thin neck was carefully tied with red ribbon, and there was a National Lottery ticket lodged in its beak. At great expense the police had sent the vulture to be identified by Bristol Zoo, who'd sent back a series of pictures along with, he could guess, a sneery note. The 'vulture' was a fake. The dissection photos were attached to the report showing how, once the skin was peeled back, it turned out to be the skull of a small sheep filed down at the snout to resemble a beak and wrapped in shavings of chicken meat. Big laughs all round, but the point here was that the *driver* had thought it was a vulture. He refused to say where or why he'd got it. Said it had been in the car when he'd bought it and he'd never got round to removing it, but the police officer, who'd been watching a programme the night before about witchcraft, guessed he was looking at a fetish.

Caffery scrolled through the report for the name of the driver. Kwanele Dlamini. He half closed his eyes and read it again, a little smile at the edges of his mouth. Dlamini. It sounded the way he imagined a Zulu chieftain to sound. African.

So, then — he pushed his chair back and got his jacket — it seemed there was a little visiting to do. Just a little visiting.

27

Thom wanted to write Flea a note so she didn't forget he was going to borrow her car. He needed to be reminded of appointments like this, and it made him think she would too, so he insisted on sitting at the table and putting it on a Post-it in his laborious handwriting. Flea stood at the sink, her arms crossed, studying his faintly bruised-looking eyes, the dark lashes lying diagonally across the pale skin, the way he crabbed himself over the paper to write. His colour had come back, but somehow she knew it would never return properly. If someone had asked her when she'd last seen her brother, she'd have answered truthfully: on the day of the accident two years ago.

It wasn't that she hadn't seen him physically since; in fact, she hadn't left his side, not through all the hospitalization in Danielskuil when they'd told her he might die, or during the dreadful journey home via Cape Town with the air hostess who wouldn't give her a paracetamol for him because the airline was afraid of being sued, or during the eight weeks of the investigation into their parents' death. She'd seen the physical Thom, his body, the shell he was in, but her brother was gone. You could look into his eyes and see nothing. So she would say that the last time she had seen him was that day at Boesmansgat when he emerged from the sinkhole crying and vomiting, thrashing his arms in the water.

Under him yawned the dark hole, a hundred and fifty metres wide, and three hundred metres deep. Like an oubliette for a sleeping predator. It was a grave too. Bushman's Hole had taken three divers in the last decade, and now two more: David and Jill Marley. Dad had gone first, heading straight down into the dark. Mum followed. Thom had made desperate grabs for them, and for a few moments he'd even had a precarious grip on Mum's right ankle, but he couldn't keep hold. It was as if, determined to get to the bottom, they had both turned face down into the gloom. Which was unthinkable because the bottom was a hundred and fifty metres deeper than they'd intended and they had both known it was suicide to go even ten metres deeper than the dive plan.

They'd planned it scientifically, because if David and Jill Marley knew anything it was respect for the water. Bushman's Hole was the pinnacle for them, the height of a lifetime's addiction to extreme sport diving. It had started a long time before the kids came along, so long ago that Flea didn't know the exact equation it had sprung from. But she did know one thing: it was Dad's gig. Mum had gone along with it, had got an enthusiasm of sorts going, but Dad was the addict, fatally attracted to it, and Dad who, in his quiet moments in the study, dreamed he was in the deep.

He'd been wearing a video camera on his helmet in Bushman's Hole. He'd have filmed his descent, and his own death. But the South African investigators had never found the bodies or the camera, and with only Thom's fractured memories to go on they couldn't do much more than put the Marleys' death down to either 'narcosis' from a miscalculation in the deep-dive gas content or possibly a hyperoxic blackout. The British coroner, who'd got permission from the home secretary to hold an inquest without the bodies, ruled out narcosis — the disorienting euphoric effect nitrogen can have at too much pressure. Because the 'Trimix' combination of gases the Marleys were using was specifically designed to combat narcosis, the coroner guessed instead that David Marley had begun to breathe too fast and deeply, shutting down the sensitive carbon-dioxide receptor in the back of his neck, which had knocked him out. When he'd started to drop Jill had tried to stop him — that much they knew — and maybe descending so quickly she'd held her breath, causing the Trimix system's oxygen sensor to over-deliver oxygen. In effect she'd died in exactly the same way as David had: from hyperoxia, too much oxygen.

He'd been a kind man, the coroner, and had added in his summing up that the Marleys' son Thom had done the right thing to let them go. As difficult as it was, it was one of the most important rules in technical diving and he'd stuck to it. He should be commended for it — should be proud. Instead, of course, it was destroying him. He'd let his parents die.

Flea didn't know what she felt guiltiest about. That she hadn't been with Thom in Bushman's

Hole when it had happened, or that, deep down, she'd been glad that Thom had gone along on the trip to Danielskuil. It used to be her Dad pushed, always urging her on — 'See that tree, the big one? Bet you can climb *that*, Flea Marley!' She'd never thought of saying no, just done as she was told — knowing in some dark corner of her heart that if she didn't it would mark her out as different. Weak, somehow. Not a true Marley. But then Thom had come along, a shy little thing who didn't walk until he was nearly two, and Dad's focus shifted away from her and on to Thom. The message from Dad was clear: *Never show fear. There is no place in this family for cowardice.* It became instinct, the same instinct that had driven Thom years later when he had climbed with his parents into the cold, motionless eye of Boesmansgat.

After his parents had disappeared, Thom had had to spend six hours coming back to the surface, stopping every few metres to decompress and allow the concentrated gases to expand and leave his body because helium lodged not in the soft tissue like nitrogen but in the bony cavities and took longer to dissipate. Tears filled his mask and a helium bubble had formed in his inner ear making his head spin. One of the police divers who'd come in when the alarm was raised had had to clip him to the shot line D-ring with a karabiner and stay with him because he'd lost the feeling in his hands and didn't know any longer which way was up. The last ten metres were the worst, the most dangerous of all, and the most frustrating because each stop was for more than an hour and he could see the surface, could see the sun filtering down, but had to wait, had to stay there in the cold, with only one thing to think about: how he'd failed and, worse, what was happening three hundred metres below him.

As far as anyone knew, and the truth was no one did know for sure, there wasn't a big enough outlet at the bottom of the sink-hole for a body to pass through, so Mum and Dad would have settled, unmoving, on the bottom. Using Thom's statement, the investigators had worked out the approximate area they'd have ended, and sent a remote-operated vehicle, a small submarine mounted with a camera, down to search the side and the very deepest corner of Bushman's. But the ROV could see nothing. There was no point in waiting for the bodies to float. As they began to decompose, when most bodies would lift to the surface, the Marleys never would; the gases of decomposition would be under too much pressure to float them and, anyway, the diving equipment would keep them weighted down until they rotted where they lay and all that was left of them was the bony pickings. The investigators had run out of resources. There was nothing more that could be done to recover them.

There were other bodies around the world suspended in their own silence, nosed and buffeted by currents and fish, divers who'd died in places so treacherous that it would cost the lives of other divers to rescue them. She'd been lectured on it by the South African police, by her counsellor, by Kaiser, to accept that Mum and

Dad's last resting place was on the floor of Bushman's Hole. And she'd made a kind of peace with it. But she never stopped thinking about it.

Sometimes Flea got pictures of them on her inner eye, fleshless, eyeless armatures floating on an axis. She'd turn them over and over in her idle hours, trying to place them, trying to imagine how they'd be lying. Thom said Dad had gone first, but she hadn't needed to hear it from him. In a way somehow connected to his meditation in the study, and somehow to the long hours he had spent with Kaiser, she knew instinctively it would have been that way: Dad going first. And so her mind had settled on a picture with Dad lying face down, arms plunged into the sand up to the shoulders, as if he was embracing the floor of the cave, while Mum was always lying on her back, facing the surface with her arms up, as if she was still hoping someone might notice her mistake and pull her back to the world.

But now, standing at the sink, the midday sun coming through and picking out all the dust and details in the kitchen, Flea thought more about the way they'd sunk. Could they have gone down in the opposite direction, away from the corner of the hole that had been searched? Was that what Mum had been trying to say?

At the table Thom was writing fastidiously. She imagined saying to him: *Could there be something wrong in what you remember about the accident? Maybe we should sit down and go through it all again?*

But no. No point in upsetting him over something flimsy. An hallucination. She turned on the tap and let the sink fill, soap bubbles swirling and catching the sunlight. She looked again at the way the greyish veins meandered down her inner arms. The ibogaine was going to open her skull, pour light in — and maybe by this evening she might be able to explain what she was missing. She wasn't going to talk to Thom about it, but one thing was sure: she was going to ask Mum on which side of the hole they'd ended up.

28

Kwanele Dlamini's last known address was in Nailsea: a brick-built Georgian-style detached three-bedroom house on a nineteen-nineties gated development. The houses were almost identical in their textured sandstone, each had a portion of lawn, a garage and a US-style mailbox at the front. Dlamini's house was at the end of the road, with a view of the airport control tower at Backwell Hill, but when Caffery rang the bell the door was answered not by Dlamini but by a blonde woman in belted low-rider jeans and a pink T-shirt that said 'PORN STAR' in glittering letters.

'Long gone,' she said, when he asked for Dlamini, 'back where he come from, and I won't be hearing from him again. Don't ask me to contact him — I've tried, believe me.'

But she invited Caffery in anyway. She seemed to want the company, and he knew from the look she gave him, checking out his body through his open jacket to see if he was in shape — from that and from the way she walked in front of him, moving herself carefully, conscious of her hips — he knew right then that he could if he wanted.

They went to the back of the house into the living room where two little girls in identical pink trackies, their blonde hair scrunched on their heads in pink silk flowers, lay on the floor watching *Bratz* on a plasma-screen TV. The tracksuits had 'Barbie' spelled out across the bottoms. Caffery thought the girls couldn't have been more than ten or eleven.

'Hey,' the woman aimed a tanned foot in a pink tennis sock at one child's feet, 'keep the volume down. I'm going to be in here and I don't want no interrupting.'

They didn't answer, but one held up a remote control and turned the volume down a few notches. The woman took him through etched-glass double doors into a palm-filled conservatory looking out over a fenced garden with a pink and lavender swing seat in the centre of the patio.

'Nice kids,' he said.

'Yeah.'

She pushed a Dobermann from where it sat on a wicker sofa. It loped away into the living room, its claws ticker-tickering on the tiles, and she bent over to plump up the cushions, blowing off dog hairs.

'He was importing stuff, gave the business his best shot, and when that didn't work out it was like everything fell apart.' She pressed the cushion on to the sofa and stood back to allow Caffery to sit. 'I can't tell you where he is. I tried to get in touch with him, but he's disappeared. Back home.'

'This his house, then?'

She snorted. 'Oh, please. Do me a favour. It was my ex's, before Kwanele, but now it's mine and the girls'. And long may it last.'

'The girls aren't his?'

She gave him a look, as if she thought he was joking. 'You winding me up? Do they look like his?'

'I don't know — I've never seen a photo.'

'Well, he's black,' she said, condescendingly. 'Very black. South African.' She sat at a small glass table, crossing her legs prettily. The long blonde ponytail hung down over her shoulder. She looked as if she spent a lot of money in tanning salons. 'What do you want to know about him? See, me, I don't care how much trouble I get him in. I'll tell you anything you want.'

Caffery took his jacket off, draped it over the arm of the chair and sat down, rolling up his sleeves. It was hot in here. Still only May, but the conservatory soaked up the sun. 'Who are you?'

'Rochelle,' she said, offering him a well-manicured hand. 'Rochelle Adams.'

He shook it. 'Rochelle,' he said. 'What I'm thinking about here is about religion. Mostly that's the question I have about Kwanele. I'm wondering about his beliefs.'

'He didn't have none. No church, if that's what you're asking.'

'What about other beliefs? Beliefs from his old country.'

'Oh, *that*.' She put a long nail into her flossy hair and itched, her eyes half closed. 'Yeah — that was part of our problem. I mean, he loved me and he loved the girls, but he never really gave up all the shit from back home.' She dropped her hand and looked at him as if a lightbulb had just come on. 'It's that vulture, isn't it? That's why you're here. I hated that thing — it stank like someone'd died in that car. I wouldn't let the girls in there, not with that thing dangling like it was watching you.'

'So why the vulture? Do you know what it meant to him?'

'The lottery, weren't it? The vulture, you know, sees into the distance. So the idea goes, according to Kwanele, you get the vulture's vision. You can see into the future, see the numbers or something. And the worst thing is, two weeks after he got the bloody thing, he only turns round and wins. Just like he said, nearly a grand, so I'm, like, not a leg to stand on. And he's like, 'This is great — I'm going to make it into soup — drink it, get even more power out of it.' And I'm 'No way, Kwanele, no way.' So he doesn't make it into soup, but he won't take it out of the car either. Except then you lot have it off him and turns out it's not a vulture after all, and there's me, laughing my knickers off. You can imagine, can't you?'

'Is that the only superstition he brought from his country?'

'God, no. It was everything with him. There was this bit of dolphin tail on a gold chain round his neck. Only little.' She held out her fingers, showing him how big, a gap of about an inch between the thick-polished nails. Her bracelets jingled and collided with each other down her tanned arm. 'He was like, 'It's for sociability', and when I asked him why a dolphin, because I love dolphins, me, he goes on about how dolphins swim in a pack and how this bit of bling is *somehow* going to make sure he's always swimming in a pack, and I'm just livid, me, because I love dolphins, and I'm like that.' She held up her hand so her palm was facing the

240

imaginary Dlamini, and cocked her head, suddenly all sass. ''It's me or the charm, Kwanele.'' She sighed and dropped her hand, half smiling, half exasperated. 'And you hear all these stories, don't you? About how the blacks are repressed in South Africa or whatever, but you meet someone like Kwanele and, honestly, you can't help thinking, Yeah, I'd bleeding repress you, mate, with that crap coming out of your mouth. I mean, *dolphins*, for Christ's sake. What did they ever do to hurt him?'

She stood, went to the long low sill that ran round the conservatory and picked up an earthenware jar painted with geometric designs. It was about as big as a large grapefruit and it had a little lid that she took off delicately. 'This was what he picked up last November after he got it into his head there was a devil following him.' She brought it over to show Caffery, holding it out on her flat palm. He looked inside. It was dark and stained. 'Meant to be a charm. Defence. He said it was all right for a woman, she only had to sleep with the Tokoloshe to stop it, but a man, well, it was harder for him to get rid of it.'

'Get rid of the what?'

'The Tok-o-loshe. Don't ask me how they spell it — some African word, innit?'

'What's the Tokoloshe?'

'Name of the devil he reckoned was after him. Always crapping himself about the Tokoloshe — said he'd do anything to stop it.' She put the lid back on the pot. 'I kept it 'cause I like the pot.' She held it up and admired it. 'Pretty, isn't it? I like all these ethnic things, me.'

'Can I see it?'

She handed it to him. He weighed it in both hands. It was heavy, and weirdly warm, as if it had trapped the heat of the spring sunshine on the windowsill. He lifted the lid again.

'What're the stains?'

'Blood. That's what a man has to offer the Tokoloshe. A bowl of blood.'

Caffery looked up. 'Blood?'

'Only chicken blood or something,' she said. 'Smelled effing awful after a day, so I made him put it in the garden, and the next morning the pot was on its side and the blood was gone, and all we could think was an animal came in the night. That, or the dog.' She gave the Dobermann a dubious look where it lay in a patch of sun, blinking. 'Course Kwanele told me it was human blood, trying to scare me, but I'm like, yeah, where'd *you* get human blood? The same place you got your so-called vulture?'

'He said it was human blood?'

She snorted. 'Yeah, as if. But Kwanele? One hundred per cent convinced. Pays a shitload for it, says he knows it's true because he's seen the video of the blood being taken.'

'There's a video?'

'Nah. He was just saying it, weren't he? I mean, if it existed it'd be like a snuff movie, wouldn't it? And there's no way I believe snuff movies exist.' She scratched the tip of her nose thoughtfully. 'What about you? You're police. You ever seen a snuff movie?'

'No,' Caffery said quietly. 'At least, not the

type you're talking about.'

She smiled. As her lips parted the frosted lipstick held them together a fraction longer than they would naturally, then popped to reveal perfect teeth. 'Yeah, I bet you've seen some things in your time. I bet you have.'

* * *

When Caffery had arranged for someone from Portishead to come and pick up the earthenware jar, he stayed with Rochelle for another thirty minutes, asking her questions. She was polite, co-operative, but he wasn't stupid. He knew what was happening in her head — he could tell from the way she pulled her feet up under her on the sofa, the way her fingernails made little circles on her collarbone while she was talking. He left open in his head the idea of whether he'd try to take her to bed. He was easy about it. Either he did or he didn't. As it worked out, by the time they'd finished talking he decided he liked her a little more now than he had when he'd walked in and that she didn't deserve the shit he'd bring to her doorstep so he dropped the idea. After half an hour he got up and thanked her. They were almost at the front door and he could see she was irritated he hadn't made a move. When he hesitated, he knew she thought this was the moment when he would ask her.

'Yeah?' She rested her hand on the hall radiator and cocked one knee a little in front of the other, pushing her hip out to the side. 'You forgot something?'

He looked at her neck, at the bangles on her tanned arms, then back at her face. 'In case you're wondering, I think you're very pretty.'

She blushed. He hadn't thought it was in her to blush. 'Yeah?'

'Yeah.'

'Well, lot of good it does me.' She pushed her hair behind an ear, lowered her eyes and waited for him to answer. When he didn't she smiled. 'Do you — uh — want to stay for coffee?' She twisted her knee round a little towards the radiator, opening her leg outwards from the hip. 'Or beer. I've got some in the fridge.'

He looked at her thigh in the jeans. Then he looked at her manicured hand on the radiator. Earlier she'd told him she was a manicurist and did lots of acrylics. She'd said she thought a good set of acrylics was the sexiest thing a woman could get to please a man.

'Thanks, but I'll have to pass.' He got out his keys. 'Don't think of it as a missed opportunity.'

'No?'

'Not at all. Think of it as a lucky escape.'

29

Flea had no idea how the ibogaine trip was going to be. What if she decided to go for a walk or, worse, tried to drive? She had to lock herself down, so they'd decided Kaiser would wait, not where she was sitting — on the sofa in his big, untidy living room — but within earshot: in the kitchen or the study. He'd rolled up the plastic sheeting in the doorway so he could hear her, assembled three electric fires round the sofa to keep the chill away, and now she could hear him shuffling around the other rooms in his tatty slippers.

Taking the ibogaine was like chewing bitter liquorice sticks — a chunk of fibrous root that made her jaw ache and also made her gag. She finished it then sat down on Kaiser's sofa to wait. For a long time she was sipping water and rubbing her tongue across the back of her teeth, trying to take away the fur that had stuck there.

Out of the dirty window the unkempt field where dandelion and bindweed grew was bathed in sunlight. Even in the daytime you couldn't see much from this vantage-point, just the tops of the trees in the Mendip land of neolithic ghosts, medieval cathedrals, legendary caves. Kaiser's rambling garden was so pocked with sinkholes and craters from the old mines that her mother wouldn't let them play out there as children. She'd said there were entrances to shafts that a child could fall down to their death and that she wouldn't put it past Kaiser to have left them open. It was funny, Flea thought, how Jill never realized it would be her, not her kids, who would end up dead at the bottom of a hole.

She sighed and pulled her feet up under her, arranging the dusty old duvet across her legs. She closed her eyes for a while and tried to fix in her mind the position of the bodies in Bushman's Hole. She pictured how Dad might have looked as he started the headfirst descent to the bottom. She'd done a mathematical formula and decided that, fully kitted out as her parents had been, they'd have gone down at about twenty metres a minute. With almost a hundred and fifty metres to go, that slow glide to the bottom of the hole would have taken them eight long minutes. At what point they'd died was anyone's guess.

And then, as she thought of those eight minutes, she realized something she'd never thought of before: that she could see time. You'd never notice it usually, but now it was clear that time was divided up into visible portions if you knew how to look at it, and that things had always been like this, since the very beginning. Some time packages were big and some were small, and each had different colours according to its size: the smallest ones, the ones that represented just enough time to dodge a bullet or a punch, were small and cherry red — time splinters. The ones that were long enough to stop someone choking, or to run after and catch a ball, or to lose control and crash a car were a juicy orange, slightly puffy at the edges. Sleep used pale yellow cubes — eight-hour chunks that got fractured and split open unnaturally when she woke early, and that was why everything felt wrong during the day.

She kept her eyes closed and studied the time packages, and the way they made up her future, stretching out into the distance — lots of little shapes packed together in a long line. There was a noise coming from a distance behind the shapes. *Wah wah wah.* Soft at first, but getting louder. *Wah wah wah.* She twitched her head away because it was a noise she hated as a diver, the sort that could mark the onset of a toxicity overload, but this time it seemed to be outside her head, coming in across the fields through the closed window. *Wah wah wah. Wah wah wah.* She opened her eyes, expecting to see the sound drifting in, but instead she saw that the room had changed beyond recognition.

A crack had formed in the far wall. She stared at it, mesmerized, as it lengthened, shimmering silver as if the entire room was peeling itself. There was a noise as if the centre of the earth was splitting and, just in time, she understood what was happening. She threw her hands into the air as, all at once, the ceiling caved in and rolled sideways. Her ears filled with a racing noise. A heavy, unbearable light dropped hard on her, submerging her, making her cling desperately to the sofa, knowing that if she was washed away nothing could bring her back.

When at last the noise had stopped she lowered her arms cautiously and twisted her head. Nothing was as it had been. Everything had changed. Even the air was different: instead of being clear, it was silver and wavering. Beams of white light rippled through from overhead, silt swirling through them. She knew, just from the feeling of cold and dread, where she was. She was in Boesmansgat. A place for the foolish and the dead. Bushman's Hole.

She tried to wriggle away, but instead of moving backwards into the sofa the water seemed to lift her and roll her over, and before she knew what was happening she was swimming, shooting fast through the cold. She sculled a little with her left hand, turning herself in a small circle because she couldn't orient herself immediately and, to start with, wasn't even sure which way was up. The light rays were there again, but this time they were sharp, like submerged stalagmites, and she didn't dare swim near them, thinking they might cut her. She steadied herself and began to swim slowly, the sweetest, absolute clarity flashing against her face, no bubbles, just the currents streaming around the dry suit. Gin clear. Now she understood what those words meant. Gin. Clear.

She'd swum for some time, going nowhere, knowing now what it felt like to be a fish, when she noticed radiance coming from the right. She brought herself to a halt and turned to it. It was the entrance to a cave, brightly lit, and after a moment's hesitation she swam towards it. As she came within ten metres of it, she saw there were figures inside the cave, lit up like a nativity scene in a church. Three faces in the yellow light,

Dad's, Thom's and Kaiser's. It was a room she was looking at: there were two beds, a chair with a suitcase on it, a print of an orchid on the wall above Dad's head and dusty curtains against the window. She recognized it: the Danielskuil hotel room they'd stayed in the night before the accident.

'Dad?' she said tentatively, her mouth moving slowly. 'Dad?'

The sound came back, louder this time, *wah wah wah*, and, like a film coming off pause and cranking up, the figures in the room began to move. They bent towards each other, talking in low voices, checking their dive gear, and she realized, from the way her feet began to hurt, that this wasn't an hallucination but a memory, that she had been in this room too — somewhere she fitted into this tableau, off to one side, out of the immediate picture, but there anyway, because that night she'd been sitting on a bed with her feet wrapped in bandages, watching the men check the gear.

Kaiser and her father moved aside a little, turning slightly away from Thom, who might have been close enough to overhear their conversation but was so busy repacking the scrubbers on the rebreather units that he didn't pay them any attention. They made it seem casual as they murmured to each other under their breath. It was a private conversation — they were sharing a secret, but Flea could lip-read. She could understand every word they were saying.

Is it strange? Dad said, looking up into Kaiser's face.

Is what strange?

You know. To be back. In Africa.

This is South Africa. Not Nigeria. This isn't the place it happened.

Flea could read every word — it was like having her memory scrubbed clean and bright and replayed at high definition. Every pixel was brilliant in its clarity and the picture stayed quite still, undisturbed by water eddies and silt.

Even so — it must be odd after all these years. Do you think you could come back and live here?

No, Kaiser said, and his face was momentarily sad, old. *You know the answer to that. You know how they tried to show me up — make an example of me.*

The two men continued what they were doing, cleaning masks, checking cylinders, and for a while there was a companionable silence. Dad checked the straps on his buoyancy compensator and, satisfied, put it to one side. Then, empty-handed and finished with his tasks, he glanced over his shoulder to make sure Thom wasn't listening, then leaned forward to Kaiser. *Listen,* he whispered. *This is important.*

Kaiser seemed surprised by the tone. *What? David? What is it?*

Dad leaned closer, and spoke. But this time half of his mouth was obscured and all Flea could make out were the words *down there . . . promise . . . be sure . . . experience . . .*

She stared at him, her heart thumping, but just as she was about to swim nearer, to ask him to repeat what he was saying, something in her peripheral vision made her stop. Moving cautiously because she felt that if her head rocked she'd be sick, she turned towards it.

A long spit of sand lay in the gloom to her right. Slowly, slowly, as her eyes adjusted, shapes began to appear out of the dark. First a skeletal hand, raised up and splayed in the frigid water, the neoprene suit ending at the bony wrist. Then another hand, light lasering eerily between the fingers. Her heart thumped. Another shape was dissolving out of the gloom near the first: the hunched and awful figure of a diver, stiffly jack-knifed, its head buried face down in the silt, the word 'INSPIRATION' stencilled on the cylinders. Two bodies — only ten metres away — she could almost touch them. Her throat tightened as she swam towards them, looking at the terrible positions, knowing she was seeing Mum and Dad.

'No,' she tried to say, but no sound came. She moved her arms back, panicked, trying to cry out. Mum and Dad, in their graves. But before she could cry, another sound started. It was like a wind rushing through a crack in mountains, deafening, and then came a swirl of water and a flash of light, like a door opening, and then, in no time, the bodies were gone and there was silence in her head.

She opened her eyes and lay motionless, registering what she could see. In front of her there was a curtain lit from behind, dirty windows, a flask of coffee on the table, the cupboards on the walls that were always locked. Kaiser's masks, his family's masks, the ones he'd let her play with as a child, looked down at her from what seemed a great distance. There was the noise of a single-engined plane droning overhead and light in her eyes, and she saw how stupid she'd been and that she wasn't in Bushman's Hole, but lying on a sofa in Kaiser's house.

Somewhere she could hear a fly buzzing and Kaiser tapping on the computer keyboard. But when she turned in that direction her head spun and she thought she'd be sick, in spite of the Kwells. So she carefully shifted position and, when she was comfortable, kept very still, trying to focus on the flask. When she was sure her head had stopped spinning she closed her eyes again. Instantly colours bubbled from the corners, like oil on water spreading under her eyelids, pulsing bigger and bigger until they filled her head and ballooned into her nasal passages, suffocating her as if the pressure would make her skull explode, it was so enormous.

She half raised a hand, moving it weakly towards her face, trying to wipe away the colours, making a little noise in her throat, a begging sound, wanting it to stop. Then, just when she thought she couldn't take any more, they popped, like a bubble, leaving nothing. Just cold, clear darkness. It took her a moment or two to realize she was back in the freezing water of Boesmansgat.

'Mum?' She tried to speak but her tongue was heavy. 'Mum?'

She moved her arms in the water, wanting to see her mother's face through the mask, wanting to see her eyes.

'Mum?'

Without warning a face appeared inches from hers. It was partly skeleton, wearing a diver's mask, and round it floated blonde hair and something white and diaphanous — a white shirt billowing like a cloud in the water. Startled, Flea pulled back.

'*Oh, Flea* . . . ' said the voice. '*Is that you, Flea? My baby . . . where are you?*'

'Mum?' She reached out her hands despairingly, opening and closing them in the darkness in case she might feel another human hand in hers. '*Mum*, I'm here. Over here. Mum, *please*, I've been trying for so long. Oh, *Mummy*, I miss you, Mummy, so much.'

In spite of herself, in spite of the fact that she was in the water, trying not to tumble backwards, Flea knew her corporeal self was crying. It wasn't happening down in the cave, but up where her body was lying on Kaiser's sofa. There was wetness on her cheeks.

Silt billowed round the awful ruined face. A wave of nausea overcame her, and Flea tilted her head to compensate. Then the picture stopped seesawing and Mum spoke again: 'Flea. Don't cry.' Her voice was odd — not the same as before. It was soft, low and a little flat. 'Don't cry, Flea.'

'Mum, what were you trying to tell me? What did you mean, 'We went the other way'?'

'Look down, Flea.' She pointed downwards with her skeletal hand. 'Can you see?'

Heart thumping, Flea, sculling her position to keep stable, peered in the direction Mum was pointing. Now she could see that they weren't at the bottom of the hole at all: they were on its gently sloping sides. And there, lit eerily in the gloom, she could see it — the bottom. It must be more than twenty metres further down.

'You didn't get all the way. That's why we couldn't find you.'

'Now listen, Flea. They didn't find us last time, but this time they will. This time they're going to find us . . . '

'This time?'

Flea reached out again, into the silt. She couldn't see her mother any more and that made her panic.

'It's important, Flea, so important. *Don't let them bring us to the surface.* Can you hear me?'

'Mum? *Mum?*' Tears were backing up in her throat. 'Mum? Come back. Please.'

'Don't let them bring us out of the Hole, whatever happens. Leave us. Just leave us.'

'Don't go, Mum. *Mummy . . . '*

But the silt blocked out everything, even the voice, and there was mud in her mouth and dirty water washing through her body and the nausea came back. It sent her spinning round — it was worse than any narcosis or CO_2 overload she'd known, and she had to open her eyes and grip the sofa. Above her the ceiling was whirling out of control, the grubby yellow light-fitting twirling like a centrifuge, the daylight flashing in and out of her eyes, and she could hear a strange noise, a high-pitched whimpering coming from her mouth. She tried to sit up but as she did so she knew she was going to be sick.

'Ohmigod,' she muttered, 'Ohmigod.'

She just managed to get to the bowl Kaiser had put out and hung there, heaving and crying, until it was over and she was back in her body, crouched, a long line of saliva connecting her to the bowl, her mother's voice disappearing, as if into a long tunnel, behind her: *Whatever happens . . . leave us . . .*

30

'The one thing Jack Caffery still hasn't told me is why it's me he wants to see. I'm not a clairvoyant or a mind-reader. I have no magical powers — no eyes like a god's. But I don't think it's police business brought you here.'

'It's not police business. It's my business.'

'And what business is that?'

Caffery rubbed his nose. The day had been weird. That some people would pay to have human blood in their house was beyond him. But with the earthenware bowl being tested at HQ and surveillance on Mabuza, he'd come to the end of what he could do at work. He'd tried going home to sleep, but he couldn't get rid of the feeling that something was watching him, that the shadows around the house were all wrong, so he'd got into the car and come looking for the Walking Man. He hadn't expected to find him so quickly. And he hadn't expected the Walking Man to start so quickly at pulling out the truth.

'Jack Caffery?' The Walking Man was wearing his sheepskin slippers. He had stuffed each of his boots with a piece of cloth and now he tied them inside a plastic carrier-bag and wedged them into a small ditch that ran along the hedgerow. He wiped his hands. 'I'm asking you a question, Jack Caffery. What is your business?'

Caffery looked at the fire, at the way some of

the logs at the bottom had white and red crusts of heat like scabs. 'Someone went,' he said eventually. 'Someone was taken. Out of my life.'

'Your daughter?'

'No, no. Not my daughter. I've got no kids. Never will have.'

'Your woman?'

'No, I left her. Two months ago. Walked out on her.'

'Then who?'

'My brother. This was back in the . . . ' He trailed off. 'It was a long time ago.'

'When you were children?'

'Yeah — it was. It was back in London. We . . . Well, you know how it is.' He held his fingers in the cavity behind his lower jawbone, pressing lightly because he'd learned it was one way to stop himself crying. 'We, uh, we never found him. Everyone knew who'd taken him, but the police, they couldn't get anything to stick.' He swallowed and took his hand from his throat, holding up his thumb to the firelight, turning it round and round. 'On the day he went missing I got a bruise on my thumbnail that wouldn't budge. It should have grown out but it didn't. No one could explain it, not the doctors, no one.' He gave a sad smile. 'I used to look at it, all those years, and think that the day I found my brother my nail would start growing again. But look at it.'

He held it out. The Walking Man straightened and came back, on his slippered feet, to peer at the nail.

'Nothing to see.'

257

'Nearly four years ago. After all that time it suddenly started growing again. The bruise grew out. And with it the feeling went. The feeling for the place it had happened went — just like that. It vanished, as if I'd been told the answer wasn't where I was — in south-east London — but somewhere else.'

'Here?'

'I don't know. The countryside — maybe here, maybe somewhere else.' He dropped his hand and stared at the lights of Bristol, thinking about the east, about Norfolk.

'Something else happened,' the Walking Man said. 'Four years ago something else happened.'

'Maybe.' Caffery shrugged. 'I think I came close to finding him — that's all.'

'Someone died. I think that happened too.' The Walking Man took two or three breaths. 'At the time you lost the connection, I think someone died.'

Caffery nodded. 'Yes,' he said quietly. 'Someone died too.'

'Yes?'

'The one who did it. Penderecki. Ivan Penderecki. He died. Suicide. If you're wondering.'

'I wasn't.' The Walking Man prodded at the fire.

Several minutes went by while Caffery tried to shift this new idea round his head, that maybe Penderecki's death had severed his connection. He'd never asked himself that before. Then the Walking Man spoke again, his voice completely different. 'What,' he said quietly, 'was his name?'

258

Caffery was caught off balance. No one had asked him that in years. They just referred to him as 'your brother', or 'he', as if they thought his name would be too awful to say. 'It was . . . Ewan.'

'Ewan,' said the Walking Man. 'Ewan.'

The way he said the name, gently, as if he was speaking it to a child made Caffery's throat close. He had to press his finger under his jaw again until the feeling passed and he could breathe. He opened a jar of cider, drank a little and pulled his coat collar up round his ears. He gazed at the stars and let himself think, not about Ewan but about Flea at the dockside, cupping someone else's hand in hers and looking up at him, as if she was saying: 'Don't worry, I can take care of this. You go and sit — go and be with yourself for a bit.' For a reason he couldn't explain he wanted to rest on that look in her eyes.

He reached into his pocket for the small brown bag. The crocus bulbs inside were little grainy balls with papery brown skin that slipped off as he touched it. As the Walking Man pulled on his socks, Caffery held out his hand, the bag sitting on his flat palm, the firelight making the dark shapes inside the brown paper glow like coals.

The Walking Man stopped. He stared at the bag for a while. Then, without a word he stood and took it. He pulled out a bulb and held it up to the light, turning it in his blackened fingers.

'The Remembrance.' He examined it reverently, as if it had a message written across its sides. 'When it comes out, the Remembrance, it's a perfect Delft blue. Just a little orange down in the centre, like an egg yolk. Or a star.'

He put the bulb back into the bag and poked his finger around a bit, like a kid counting sweets on a Saturday-morning street corner. Then he folded the top carefully and tucked the bag into the breast pocket of the filthy coat he wore and, as if nothing had happened, went on stoking the fire.

They didn't speak for a few minutes. Caffery drank cider and watched the Walking Man begin his nightly ritual, taking off his clothes and wrapping them, putting them under the sleeping-bag where they wouldn't attract any moisture. At night he wore specially designed sleepwear. It was filthy, but you could tell it was expensive, hi-tech, from one of those extreme-sports suppliers. There was an O_3 logo that Caffery recognized from Flea's dry suit. When he'd finished, the Walking Man pulled on his coat and began to potter around again, feeding the fire for the night.

Caffery knew his time there was almost over. 'Look,' he said, clearing his throat, 'I've given you what you wanted. Now you — it's your turn. You have to tell me what it was like, what you did to Craig Evans.'

'In my time. In my time.'

'You said you'd tell me.'

The Walking Man snorted. 'I said, *in my time*. I need to think about you first.' He threw another log on to the fire, then brushed off his hands. 'Tell me, what do you see when you look into the faces of those girls? Those prostitutes you don't sleep with enough.'

Caffery frowned. He had to pick up his tobacco pouch and roll a cigarette before he answered. 'I don't look,' he said, lighting it. 'I try not to see. I mean, whatever happens, I don't want to see my own reflection.'

'Yes — because if you see it do you know what you're really seeing?'

'No.'

'You're seeing death.'

'Death?'

'Yes. Death. Oh, you've still got a choice. But at the moment the choice you're making is the same as mine.'

'The same *choice*? I'm not making any of the same choices as you.'

The Walking Man smiled and tossed the last log on to the fire. 'Yes, you are. And for now you've chosen death. Yes. That's what you're looking for. You're looking for death.'

Caffery opened his mouth to say something, but the Walking Man's words stopped him. He sat there, his mouth still half open.

The Walking Man laughed at his face. 'I know. A shock, isn't it, when you first turn round and see the bridge you're crossing? A shock to realize you're giving up on life. That what you're really hoping for is death.'

Caffery closed his mouth. 'No. That's wrong. I'm not the same as you.'

'Yes, you are Jack Caffery, Policeman. You're exactly the same as I am. The only difference is that my eyes are open.' He used his filthy thumb

261

and forefinger to open the lids, revealing the reddish tops and bottoms of the eyeballs. He was suddenly monstrous in the firelight, every night monster, every chimera. 'See? I'm not looking the other way. I *know* I'm trying to die. And you?' He laughed. '*You* don't even suspect it yet.'

31

17 May

Once, when Caffery had first started living with Rebecca in his family's three-bedroom terrace house in south-east London, after a particular bastard of an argument, she'd taken his face in her hands and said, in a voice that was tender, not angry: 'Jack, sometimes being with you isn't like being with someone who's still alive. It's like being with someone who's dying.'

For four years he'd kept those words contained somewhere in the back of his head, trying not to forget them but trying harder not to think about them too much, so they got like a memory of her perfume, or a half-remembered tune. Then, of course, along came the Walking Man and jumpstarted the memory.

It had opened something in him. It was as if a new channel had appeared in his head, making the back of his neck ache. Somehow, without understanding how, he knew the Walking Man would point to Keelie and the other girls on City Road and say they were about death, about him hoping for death. And then he'd point directly at Caffery's job. 'And as for that,' he'd say, 'more than anything else *that* is about your death.'

The next morning in his Kingswood office, a cup of coffee and a sandwich from the convenience store on the desk as he opened the orange courier's package that had come overnight from Marilyn, Caffery was thinking about his job, thinking about it as a kind of death. Marilyn had scribbled a note to him on a bit of Met stationery: 'Call if you need any more ADVICE Love M x.'

'Thanks, Marilyn,' he said, with a wry smile. He crumpled up the paper and was about to put it into the bin, then changed his mind. He found Sellotape and taped it to the wall so that Marilyn could do what she'd always wanted to do — monitor him constantly. Then he went back to the package, slowly pulling out the various wallets and bound folders. There was everything in here he could want: photocopied theses on African ritual; a folder of newspaper cuttings about Adam, the boy in the Thames; a list of contacts at universities in the UK and abroad. One, he noticed, was in Bristol. There was also a disk labelled 'Swalcliffe.pdf' in a clear pink cover. An Adobe Acrobat presentation. He slotted it into the computer.

Marilyn, he decided, as the Metropolitan Police logo came up on the screen, had put this together herself. She'd been a HOLMES inputter when they'd worked together and she'd always loved her computers. It was designed as a lecture, with bigger files appended to the presentation through hyperlinks, and that morning, as the sun got higher in the sky, as the Kingswood station came to life around him and people came and went from the shops outside his window, he silently blessed Marilyn for her nerdishness. In two hours he learned more than he'd ever known about a continent that had been a mystery to him for years.

Muti, like she'd said, was a much bigger picture than he'd imagined. It started on the ground with witch doctors 'throwing the bones', casting sacred objects, bones, beans or stones, in a circle to divine the needs of the client. From the witch doctor's divination sprang the remedy, and of these the list was bewildering: there was bushbaby fur for babies who cried too much, chitons to stop your partner cheating on you, pangolin, porcupine fish, aardvark claw. Every part of almost every animal, it seemed, had a place in *muti*.

Caffery tried to read the page to the end, but the words blurred after twenty entries so he went back to the main lecture. When he clicked on it, he knew instantly he'd moved into a darker place: human body parts. The first thing that came up was a picture of a human skull, laid out on a pathologist's table, a measuring tape next to it. He read the text carefully, giving it time to sink in. Most *muti* human body parts were stolen from corpses, but the *muti* from the already dead was weak compared to that from the living: the medicine would be more powerful if the victim was alive when the mutilation happened, the louder the screams the better, and of the living by far the most powerful medicine came from a child. It was all about purity.

He looked away from the screen, suddenly overloaded, his eyes tired. He took time to spoon some sugar into his coffee and watch it make a

265

little island and slowly sink. Vaguely, he remembered hearing that in South Africa six men had been charged with raping a nine-month-old baby, believing that sex with it would cure them of AIDS. The thought made parts of his mind ache.

The next section of the lecture defined the difference between human sacrifice, in which the death of the person was the most important thing and would appease a deity, and *muti* murder, where the aim was the harvest of body parts for use in traditional medicine. *Brains endow the client with knowledge. The breasts and genitals of either sex bestow virility. A nose or eyelid can be used to poison an enemy.* The next slide showed a piece of severed flesh lying on a towel. It wasn't until he read the caption that he understood what he was looking at. *A penis can bring success in horse-racing.*

'Christ,' he muttered, shifting uncomfortably in the chair. He'd have liked a whisky instead of the coffee, but if he let himself have one there'd be another on the heels of the first and before he knew it the day would be in the toilet. He scrolled down, looking for mention of human blood, but there was nothing, so, thinking of his visit to Rochelle's, he searched for the Tokoloshe.

At first he put in the wrong spelling, TOCKALOSH, and the search engine came up with zero. He tried two more spellings, then TOKOLOSHE and this time the computer blinked and whirred and came up with a result. He found the section and had read a short way through when he had the urge to stand and pull

266

the blind down because suddenly he didn't feel comfortable in the office and he didn't like the way he could be seen by anyone on the street.

A Tokoloshe, the Acrobat file told him, was a sprite, a witch's familiar. Left to its own devices it was no more than a nuisance, but if it came under the power of a witch it became a danger, a thing feared and reviled. As Rochelle had said, some believed a bowl of human blood would appease a Tokoloshe, but there were other ways of protecting yourself: a cat, or an image of a cat washing its face, was enough to keep it at bay, or you could cover your skin with grease made from Tokoloshe fat, which you could buy from a witch doctor. Marilyn had scanned in an article about two men in South Africa arrested on an armed robbery. In their car the police had found a human skull with a piece of meat inside it. The robbers had stolen the skull from a grave and the meat was a meal for a Tokoloshe they believed was protecting them.

Caffery clicked on the next slide and the screen filled with a crude drawing of a dwarf-like creature with a lolling tongue, proudly holding its cock up to the viewer. Reading the caption, his chair pulled close to the screen, the sun coming through the slits in the blind and heating his face, coldness crept through Caffery: 'The Tokoloshe's penis is a symbol of his danger and masculinity. Women put their beds on bricks to keep out of his reach. Traditionally a water sprite, he makes his home in a riverbank.'

. . . *a water sprite, he makes his home in a riverbank.* Caffery read it again, his head

267

thumping. He was thinking about the waitress at the Station — about the kid she'd seen exposing himself. And then, inexplicably, he thought about a wisp of shadow in an alleyway, the red of Keelie's lipstick, the sense that a foot had walked across the bonnet of the car. He got to his feet, pulling his jacket off the back of the chair. On screen, the Tokoloshe grinned back at him.

'Fuck off,' he muttered, hitting the button on the monitor rather than closing the file. 'Fuck you.'

It was time to go back and see Rochelle. Time to ask her a few more questions.

★   ★   ★

She was pleased to see him. He could see that right off. In a pink zip-up hooded top, her hair held off her face by a white headband, she looked as if she might have been getting ready for a workout in spite of the full make-up. She put her hands behind her back and leaned her bottom against the wall so her breasts were pushed towards him. 'Hello,' she said. 'Changed your mind about the beer?'

'Can I come in?'

She inclined her head and stood back to let him pass. He went through the kitchen into the living room. The two girls were watching *America's Next Top Model*. They were in exactly the same position as they'd been yesterday. If it wasn't for the fact they'd changed their clothes he'd have thought they'd been there all night. He stepped over their legs and went into the conservatory at the back.

'Can I get you a drink?' said Rochelle, coming in behind him, bending to plump up the cushions. 'I've got a smoothie-maker. Me and the girls had strawberry and peach this morning.'

'That's OK. Just had some coffee.' He reached inside his folder, feeling for the plastic wallet he'd brought. The Dobermann was on the floor in the sun, eyeing at him with vague interest. 'I won't be long.' He found the picture. It had been taken at a Chamber of Commerce event and it showed Mabuza clutching a glass of red wine, talking intently to a councillor. He was wearing a suit and a traditional *mokorotlo* hat over his greying hair. Caffery slid it out of the wallet and held it out to her. 'This guy. Ever seen him before?'

Rochelle glanced at the photograph, then back at Caffery's face. 'Yeah — it's Gift, Kwanele's mate.'

Caffery closed his eyes briefly.

'What?' said Rochelle. 'What've I said?'

'Nothing,' he said, putting the photo back into his jacket. What a fucking idiot he'd been not to ask her yesterday. He put down the folder and sat on the sofa, looking around the room, at the knick-knacks, the little vases and the framed photos of the kids. There was a picture of a cat — a kitten, actually — washing its face in a splash of sunshine.

'Rochelle,' he said, 'do you remember you told me Kwanele was scared of a devil?'

'A devil? Ain't likely to effing forget, am I? The Tokoloshe. Spent his whole time thinking about the bloody thing.'

'Yes,' he said, watching her face. 'The Tokoloshe. And what did he tell you about it?'

'Well, that's just it. He never told me about it exactly. It was Teesh he used to talk to.' She called into the living room, 'Hey, Letitia?'

'Wha'?'

'Come in here a second, beautiful.'

There was a pause, then one of the girls appeared sullenly in the doorway, chin down.

'Wha'?'

'Say hello to Mr Caffery.'

''Lo,' she said.

'Sometimes I think they liked Kwanele more than I did. Didn't you, Teesh, beautiful? Liked Kwanele?'

'Yeah. Suppose.'

'Bought you a Wii, didn't he?'

'Yeah. He was cool.'

'Now, baby,' Rochelle said. 'Remember the Tokoloshe? I want you to tell Mr Caffery about it.'

Letitia peered over her shoulder at the skirting-board behind her — as if that was what really interested her and not Caffery. 'Really short. Lives in the river. Looks black.'

'Speak up.'

'I *said*. I said it's short. It's black. It's deformed. It lives in a river and it's always naked, OK?'

'Letitia,' Caffery said slowly, 'how do you know about it? Did Kwanele talk to you about it?'

'Yea-ah.' She made the one word go up and down so it sounded like a sentence: *Yes, my*

God, didn't you know that? Where've you been all your life, you muppet? 'He only talked about it like all the time.'

'What did he tell you?'

'Just lo-*oads*. It eats people. I seen it once too.'

'Teesh,' Rochelle said warningly, 'Mr Caffery's a policeman. You tell the truth now. Not what Kwanele told you to say.'

Letitia looked at her mother, then at Caffery. 'I did see it,' she said. 'It was like totally weird. Mum just doesn't never believe nothink I ever say.'

'Oh, here we go again.'

Caffery held up his hand to pacify them. 'Letitia, where did you see it?'

'Down by the river. Where Kwanele's warehouse used to be.'

'And did anyone else see it?'

'Just him and me. It was night. He took me there to do some — what d'you call it, Mum?'

'Stocktaking.'

'Stocktaking. And it was late and when we was coming out of the warehouse there's this sound in the bushes, like a bird or something, and there's this thing sort of half bent over. And water running off it. Which makes us both think it was coming out of the river.'

'OK,' Caffery said, his head full of the dwarf in Marilyn's slide presentation, of the pontoon outside the Moat late at night. 'So you're saying Kwanele saw it too?'

'Yeah — and he's like *so* scared. He starts going like this.' She put a hand on her chest and breathed in and out rapidly, hyperventilating. It

271

was creepy, Caffery thought, sitting in the sunlight and watching this little girl acting it out. 'And then he puts his hand over my eyes and makes me get in the car, and he jumps in after me. And we was coming home and he keeps shaking and crying, and speaking African, and saying how he was going to do something about it. I mean, how scary is that?'

'But he knew it was the Tokoloshe?'

'Oh, yeah. He reckoned he was lucky him and his friend had someone who knew what to do about it.'

Caffery sat forward. 'What did he mean by that?'

She shrugged. 'Someone who could get rid of the Tokoloshe — y'know, stop it coming too near him at his work and stuff.'

'Did he say who his friend was?'

'Nah, never said all that much.'

Caffery turned to Rochelle. 'Was this the same time he bought the bowl? The one I took yesterday?'

'Yeah,' she said. 'That's when it all kicked off.'

Caffery put his elbow on the sofa arm and rested his chin on his hand, one finger under the tip of his nose, thinking hard. Someone had helped Kwanele Dlamini. The friend — it had to be Mabuza.

'Letitia,' he said, after a while, 'you're sure you really saw the Tokoloshe?'

''Course I am. Just told you, didn't I?'

'Teesh,' Rochelle hissed. 'Remember? The truth.'

'It *is* the truth, I've told yer.'

'It's what Kwanele told you to say.'

'No,' the little girl insisted, a slow wash of colour coming up her face as she met her mother's eyes. 'It's not what he told me to say. It's what happened. I'm telling you the truth.' She let out a long, impatient breath. 'How comes you never fucking listen to me?'

Before Rochelle could answer Letitia turned on her heels, her fists balled, and went into the sitting room. She said something to her sister, who got up, shooting her mother a pointed look. Then there was the sound of their feet on the stairs and a door banging.

After a few moments Rochelle breathed out. She looked despairingly at Caffery. 'You got kids, Mr Caffery? Any little ones?'

He shook his head. He was thinking about what Letitia had said: *He reckoned he was lucky him and his friend had someone who knew what to do about it.* It was making him think about things he hadn't thought about until now.

'Well,' said Rochelle, 'let me give you some advice. Don't. Don't even think about it.'

★ ★ ★

Outside Rochelle's it was a cool spring day, the acid-green ornamental trees and the tended grass in the development every now and then giving the faintest stir in the breeze. But for Caffery, sitting in the car, his hands resting on the steering-wheel, it might as well have been mid-January. He wasn't thinking about the blossom on the branches or the way the sun was

273

so high in the sky or the slight rise in temperature. He was thinking about circles. About rings.

Criminal behaviour was like a sponge: it sucked others into it. Almost every idiot he'd ever picked up over the years had had a little coterie attached. If you thought about it, it wasn't much different from any other social group. Every ring had a different structure, a different size, a different satellite configuration, but they had one thing in common: they had a leader. Sometimes the group was so loose the MC didn't even realize he was boss. But on the whole, in most rings, the one who was in charge knew exactly what he was doing.

Somewhere, out there in Bristol, someone knew more than was good for them about the African continent. They might be British, they might be African. They certainly knew a little too much about African ritual and belief; they knew very well how deep superstition ran in people; and, more importantly, they knew how much money could be attached to fear. It wouldn't be difficult to pinpoint wealthy Africans living in the country. Nor would it be difficult to hire someone, some poor bastard who'd never have the luxury of normality from all Caffery'd been told, to loop up some ridiculous fucking dildo, grease themselves up and appear to the right person at the right time. Nothing too obvious, a fleeting glimpse. A shadow. Just enough to convince someone superstitious enough they were being stalked by a demon. And then the brains in the operation would go in for the kill,

274

providing the goods to ward off the Tokoloshe, keep it away from the business. Human blood. And for proof that the goods were genuine, a video, real or a clever fake.

Mabuza. Caffery hadn't met him but he remembered his voice — sort of even and measured, a little too educated for comfort. He pulled out his work phone and stabbed in a number. He was going to get Interpol to track down Dlamini and then he'd get the surveillance guys to knock on Mabuza's door. They were going to ask, respectfully, whether he'd consent to the house being searched. And then, also respectfully, they'd offer him a lift to the station. Because Caffery was going to have to do this interview a little earlier than he'd hoped.

The phone clicked through, and he let his eyes wander over to the Nailsea skyline. He was thinking about a human being with dwarf legs: a squat half animal that ran through the streets at human knee height. And he was thinking about African witchcraft, secret rituals being practised behind closed doors. Someone was engineering it, he was sure, but he still had to blink to make sure he was seeing only sky and buildings, because right now, sitting here in the sunshine, he wasn't sure he'd ever get the image of the Tokoloshe out of his mind.

32

On Kaiser's sofa — eighteen hours since the ibogaine trip had begun, Flea came to life again and began to remember who she was and why she was there. She felt as if she'd been to a different planet, as if half of her was still out there somewhere, struggling to find its way back into her body. She sat up gingerly, blinking in the first grey light of morning filtering through the window. After a while she pulled her feet up on to the sofa and slowly, slowly, pulled off her socks.

The problem with her feet had started a few days after the accident, and now it had got to the point that she was so ashamed she wouldn't take her shoes off if anyone was watching. Her feet seemed veined and misshapen, awkwardly crabbed like a monkey's or a lemur's — they made her think of the hand she'd brought to the surface from under the harbour, the brutal way it had been removed from the body. She squeezed the webbed skin experimentally between her thumb and forefinger and, briefly, it seemed to liquefy, to run away leaving her toes free and independent. She stopped moving, trying to keep still, waiting for the drug to stop working. After a while her vision cleared and the skin was back, tethering her toes together. Life was so unpredictable. The things that stayed longest in your mind were always the things you hadn't foreseen.

She pulled on her socks and was about to roll back on the sofa, when something made her stop. Someone was watching her. In the doorway, under the rolled-up plastic sheeting, a figure stood perfectly still.

For a moment it was as if nothing in her body moved, not her heart or her lungs, because she was looking at a creature, a dead creature that should have been lying on the ground, but instead was standing up in the doorway. Its clothing was billowing round it, just like Mum's in Boesmansgat. Its face was a bony mass.

'*Mum?*' she whispered. 'Mum?'

'There now,' the dead animal said, and its voice was not Mum's but Kaiser's. 'Flea?'

There was a pause when she didn't know what to say. Then, in a hoarse voice, she whispered, 'Kaiser?'

The creature moved, turning its face, and as it did, Kaiser materialized from inside it, smiling out from the corpse. Her vision cleared and it was just Kaiser again, dressed in an unfamiliar white shirt, looking very tired. 'Phoebe?' he said, coming into the room. 'How are we feeling?'

She shook her head, not taking her eyes off him.

'Are you all right?'

'Yes. I mean . . . it's still there. The drug — it's still there.' She licked her lips, trying not to think about the death mask. 'I mean you — just now. I thought . . . '

'Yes?' he said slowly, taking a step into the room. She'd forgotten how tall he was. How tall, and how heavy his head was.

'Nothing.' She rubbed her eyes and tucked her feet under her on the sofa. 'It was just the drug.'

He was holding a glass of water and he handed it to her now. He sat down on the sofa next to her, making it bow with his weight. She tried not to look at him. She wanted to say: 'They're not at the bottom.' But she didn't. Instead she sipped the water and kept track of him out of the corner of her eye, thinking of the animal skull.

'I was sick,' she said, after a while. 'You told me I'd be sick.'

'It gets most people like that.'

She looked at the bowl on the floor. 'You cleaned it up for me. I didn't even hear you come in.' She blinked. Everything was familiar, yet strange: the edges on all the objects were hazy and brown, crawling a little as if they were outlined with a column of ants.

'Would you like some more water?'

'I've got a headache,' she said numbly. There was something about his shirt that she thought she should mention, but her head hurt too much. 'A headache.' She wiped her face with her palms. She took some deep breaths. 'Kaiser. Do you — do you remember my feet?'

'No.'

'At Bushman's Hole, I didn't dive because . . . '

'Because you'd cut your feet on some glass. Yes. I remember that.'

'Except,' she murmured, 'except . . . I didn't. I didn't cut them.'

He laughed gently. 'Well, *I* saw blood. I helped you dress them. I pulled a piece of glass out from

278

between your toes. I don't think that was your imagination.'

'No. It *happened*, but it wasn't an accident. Not an accident at all.' She pressed her fingers hard into her temples, wanting her head to stop seesawing. 'I went and found the glass. I got a bottle from the hotel bar and smashed it in the car park. Then I trod on it.'

Kaiser was silent. Not an animal skull. Just Kaiser. 'You know there's something — something *different* about Thom?'

'Different?'

'Yes. We never actually said it but we always knew something was slightly wrong. Poor little sod. But he's OK, you know. As long as he's got instructions, he knows how to follow them. The only thing wrong with him is he's not flexible — he can't think in an emergency.' She pressed her fingers harder into her temples, speaking slowly and clearly: 'He should never — never have been with them. Not on his own that deep. I let him go because . . . ' She shook her head, trying to shake away the guilt, wishing it would lift off her like a skin. 'I was scared, Kaiser. So scared. You don't know what Dad was like. He was . . . We couldn't be weak around him. If we showed fear or weakness it just — just finished him. I didn't want to go into that hole so I trod on the glass.'

It was the first time she'd ever put it into words — the mistake she'd made, the corner she'd turned that meant she would forever be paying the price, forever pulling other people's bodies out of deep water because she couldn't

279

pull up the bodies of the two people she'd allowed to drown. It felt odd to have the words out in the air now. It was as if she was waiting for judgement.

She bent over at the middle, resting her chin on her knees, her hands on her stomach. There was a long silence. It was Kaiser who broke it, speaking in a low voice: 'You know, you are so very much like your father.'

She looked sideways at him. 'Am I?'

'Yes.' He gave a sad smile. 'Oh, yes. So very much like him.'

'Why?'

He laughed and put his arm round her shoulders. 'Oh, I can't answer that. The answer to that question is a long, long road.' His big goat's face creased in a regretful smile. 'That's a road only you can travel.'

33

'When did you last speak to Kwanele Dlamini?'

'Dlamini?'

'Yes. Kwanele Dlamini. Your friend. Remember him?'

Mabuza and Caffery sat opposite each other, another officer in the corner, his arms folded. There was a plate of biscuits on the table and a cup of coffee in front of each man. Polystyrene cups, not china, because this was the custody suite: even though Mabuza wasn't under arrest and even though he was being co-operative, taking a day away from the restaurant and arriving punctually, neatly dressed in a suit and his rimless glasses, the PACE-designated custody suite was a good place to be if things got heated and they needed to make an arrest. It was the polystyrene cup that was giving Mabuza away now. Just the mention of Dlamini had made him lower his eyes and pick nervous halfmoons out of it with his nails.

'Mr Mabuza? I asked you when you last saw Kwanele Dlamini?'

'Dlamini?' Mabuza licked his lips quickly. His head was down and his eyes began a restless flicking back and forth across the table. 'Dlamini was — a long time — a long time ago.'

'A long time? Sorry, help me here. Is that a week? A month? A year?'

'Half a year. Six months.'

'And why haven't you seen him in that time?'

'He's gone home — back to the homeland.'

'South Africa?'

'That's right. We lost touch.'

'I had the impression your friendship with him was closer than that.'

'No. Not close. He was an acquaintance.'

'No forwarding address?'

'No.'

'Only that I want to direct our investigation in the way that'll pay dividends, you know?' Caffery bent his head, trying to look up into the man's eyes, see what was happening there. 'Want to be chasing the right rabbit and not putting pressure on you. A forwarding address would help.'

Mabuza shook his head.

'Or the names of family members. He was from Johannesburg?'

'Yes,' he muttered. 'But that's all I know about him. I met him here. We didn't talk about home.'

Caffery hooked his arm over the back of the chair and looked at the top of Mabuza's head. It was more than the friendship between the two men making him pursue this: earlier that morning Mabuza had signed the forms to allow the police to search his house and in the first two hours the team had come up with a few things he wanted to ask Mabuza about. He looked down at the sheets of paper under his fingers. There was something from the lab there, too: something even more interesting than the team had found at the house.

'You were kind enough to allow us to search your home,' he said, when they'd been sitting in silence for almost a minute. 'We found a few things we liked.'

'I've got nothing to hide,' Mabuza muttered.

'For example, we brought back some carpet fibres. From the front room.' Caffery went slowly, giving each word time to sink in. He'd wanted to be seen taking the fibres legally: the results of the match with the handful Flea had taken would be with him by close of business, so he'd told the search guys to get a sample of the living-room carpet. 'And work it so the missus sees you doing it, if you know what I'm saying.' 'Do you know about fibres?' he asked Mabuza. 'About how they're used in forensics? Say, for example, a person sat on a carpet, or even walked on it, for the shortest time, some of the fibres from that carpet would be transferred on to the person. Did you know that?'

Mabuza was frowning. 'What are you saying? Are you asking me a question?'

Caffery pretended to be considering what he'd said. 'You're right. It's a bit off message, isn't it? Especially with the length of time the labs these days can take to process things. You know, I had to put an express order on those fibres and even then they won't get the results back to me until close of business this afternoon.' He glanced at his watch and shook his head regretfully, as if he was weary of the dumb way the force worked. 'Then again, lucky for me they've been a bit quicker on something else.'

'I beg your pardon.'

He used his forefinger to move the papers around, half frowning as if this was all a great puzzle to him. 'There was a pot at Dlamini's. An earthenware pot. Do you know about it?'

'A pot? What sort of pot?'

'It's about — so big? With a lid? Well, the pot's nothing special, not on its own, but what made me sit up was what the lab found in it.'

Mabuza had opened his mouth to say something. Then he closed it. He looked up at Caffery, then down at the papers on the desk. It lasted only a second or two but something had happened in that instant. Something that made Caffery want to smile.

'Yes,' he said slowly, holding Mabuza's eyes. 'We found blood. Human blood. And this morning they confirmed whose blood it was. Do you want me to tell you whose blood it was — or do you know already?'

Mabuza swallowed. A fine sweat had started on his forehead. 'No,' he said, in a small voice. 'I don't know.'

'It was Ian Mallows's blood.' He tapped the paper with his forefinger. 'You know that name, of course, because he was the poor fucker whose hands ended up under your restaurant. It's here in black and white. Ian Mallows.' He paused for a moment, still smiling. 'And I call that too much of a coincidence.'

Mabuza took out a handkerchief and mopped his brow, shooting glances at the door. Caffery recognized this, the signs of a witness on the point of withdrawing cooperation. The PACE adviser had said this would be a good time to go into rapid-fire formation — if they were going to have to arrest him they'd throw at him all the questions they knew would hit hot spots.

'Mr Mabuza,' Caffery said, 'do you have any feelings about the use of illegal drugs? If one of your staff came to you and admitted they had a heroin problem, what would you say?'

Mabuza blinked. He hadn't expected the swerve. 'Excuse me? If one of my staff had a drugs problem?'

'Yes. How would you react?'

'It's a devil, sir. Drugs are the devil.'

'Is that why you give twenty thousand pounds a year to drugs charities? Or is that just a tax break?' He held up another piece of paper. 'Your bank statements,' he explained. 'The search team found them at the house.'

Mabuza lowered the handkerchief. 'You've been into my financial details?'

'You gave us permission to search the house.'

'I didn't give you permission to do that.'

'You sponsor at least fifty voluntary drugs-counselling groups.' Caffery sat forward. 'It's not negligible what you spend on them. Ian Mallows attended drugs charities. Heroin was his problem. Did you know that?'

'What issue is it to you who I give my money to?'

'You don't maintain your contact with the charities because they're a good source of victims, then? Vulnerable people? People who won't be missed?'

Mabuza pocketed the handkerchief and stood. He was thin and small but there was a fierceness in his face that made him seem momentarily bigger. 'I didn't touch that boy. I don't know how his hands came to be where they were, and I didn't touch him.' He jerked his jacket off the chair and began to pull it on. 'It's time for me to go.'

'Please, please. Sit down. I don't want this going up another level — not while we're all ramped up like this.'

But Mabuza was buttoning his jacket, pulling the sleeves straight with furious movements. 'You've insulted me. It's time for me to go.'

Caffery placed his hands palm down on the table and said very quietly: 'If you try to go, I'll have to arrest you.'

Mabuza stopped, the jacket half buttoned. In the corner the officer was on his feet, ready to make a move. 'I beg your pardon, sir?' Mabuza said. 'What did you say?'

'I said I'll have no choice but to arrest you. Local businessman — sits on the school governors' board I heard? The local hacks would eat that up.'

Mabuza stared. His lips began to look dark blue, as if his blood had stopped circulating.

'Or you can stay — we'll go on doing this nice and quietly, just you cooperating with us. No one need ever know.'

There was a long silence while Mabuza thought about this. Behind him the officer waited, his head on one side. Then Mabuza sank into his chair, his eyes fixed on the table as if he couldn't bear to raise them. When he spoke his voice was subdued. 'You know about my son?'

'No,' Caffery said honestly, opening his hands. 'No, we don't.' He surveyed the top of Mabuza's greying head. 'Why? Has he got a problem, your son? Is he an addict?'

'Was,' Mabuza said. 'He was an addict. He is recovered now, thank you.' He gave a deep sigh, as if his life was sometimes too much to bear. 'When we came to this country it was difficult for him. So difficult. The racism here isn't what we expected. Not from what we were told living in South Africa. It comes from places you never expect — the Caribbeans, Jamaicans, children from St Lucia, Trinidad, the ones my boy is with at school, the ones who look exactly the same as he does. My son, he is a good boy, very quiet. These boys he comes into contact with, they think it means they can bend him. And for a while they did.' Mabuza seemed to drift off for a bit, his head on one side, his face contracting at the memory. 'But someone helped him,' he went on. 'A drugs counsellor. If he hadn't my son would be dead today.'

Caffery didn't speak. His mood was slowly sinking. Yes, something about the son's story sounded a bit overlaid, a bit of a performance, but still the look in the guy's face, in his demeanour, told Caffery that the drugs-charities connection was a blind alley. The bank statements were a coincidence.

He got up, went to the window, and lifted the blind. It was mid-afternoon and schoolchildren were thronging the streets, pushing each other, jostling and laughing. When the search team had come up with the bank statements he'd immediately got two men together. They were out there now, revisiting some of the twenty or so charities on the statement. But now that felt like a bum steer, a waste of manpower, and the carpet fibres might be a better bet. One of the office staff had promised to come straight to the custody suite when they got any results from the lab on them. Maybe that was the thing to do: wait and hit Mabuza with the fibres. Sometimes there was a fax through at four in the afternoon. Another half an hour.

Just as he was about to turn back, the Walking Man's face came into Caffery's head. *You're looking for death, Jack Caffery. You're looking for death.* Caffery dropped the blind and rubbed his eyes, trying to get rid of the image. He turned and looked at Mabuza, who was hunched at the table, picking compulsively at the coffee cup again, little balls of polystyrene clinging electro-statically to his jacket sleeves. He's so nervous, Caffery thought, but what he doesn't realize is that none of this matters. Not really. It doesn't matter what happens or what we do with our lives because we're all dying. I'm dying and you're dying, Mabuza. You'll die and whatever you've done will die with you.

34

10 May

This is a hinterland of horror, a place of unspeakable, unnameable practices. A place where the bodies of missing male children turn up on wasteland near their villages skinned alive, their organs taken from them. A kidney fetches two hundred pounds, a heart four hundred. Your brains or your tackle can make up to four thousand.

'More for a child and more for a white man,' Skinny says. 'Him is more clever, white man. In business him is more successful than us.'

It takes Mossy a long time to accept what he's stumbled into. But slowly, slowly, he maps it out in his head. First, there is this place — it seems like the headquarters of the operation. Mossy has no idea about the exact location. All he can remember is getting out of the car and being led straight through a door, then through another and another. He's got no idea if he's still in Bristol, even. Second, he's worked out there are other people in the city who buy the things Uncle has taken from his victims — people from Africa, says Skinny, who live here and haven't forgotten their homeland beliefs. Third, there are the videos. They are taken by Uncle to record the pain. And this is what Mossy finds most difficult to get out of his head, because Skinny tells him the videos are not for Uncle alone.

Yes, it's true, part of Uncle's tastes are to enjoy seeing pain. But things don't stop there. The videos are a tool, screened as evidence for the customer, proof that the body parts were taken from a live victim because, and this part chills Mossy to the bone, *the louder the screams the stronger the medicine* . . .

'The blood we took from you,' Skinny admits one night. 'Him sell a little at a time. Some him's kept. In the fridge.'

'It's fucking disgusting,' Mossy says thickly. 'Fucking disgusting. What do they do with human blood? You fucking vampires.'

'Only keep it. Keep it to protect from the devils.'

'Devils?'

Skinny nods. His eyes are pinkish in the half-light. 'Uncle, he send a devil to scare everyone.' He gets up from the sofa and crouches next to the grating. He pulls through it a carrier-bag that's been sitting there all afternoon — something Mossy's seen but not really registered. Squatting, he unpacks it. Out come a wig, a pair of boots, and something smooth and shiny. Mossy thinks for a moment it's a limb — an arm, or something. But then Skinny holds it up and he sees what it is. It's made of wood: a long, smooth thing with a top carved to resemble someone's knob.

'What the fuck's that for?' he says, hiking himself up on one elbow. 'You're not bringing that thing near me.'

'No, no,' murmurs Skinny, turning it so that the light falls and slants on it. 'Not for that. It is for scare people, make them think it is the devil. Make them buy the blood.'

Mossy licks his lips and looks at the boots, the wig. 'What? Does he have you go out there wearing it? You strap it on and go out and give them a little show, do you? Is that how it works?'

But Skinny's not looking at Mossy. 'No,' he says eventually. 'Not me.'

'Not you. Then who?'

Again Skinny is silent. Mossy thinks he's lost him, because he's got this distant look on his face. When at last he speaks his voice is sad, reflective. 'My brother.'

'Your brother?' Mossy sits up. 'You never said nothing about your brother. What? Is he here too?'

'Look at me.' Skinny raises a hand and waves it vaguely over his body. 'I am small. My brother, him is small, like me, smaller.' He glances at the cage in the wall, and Mossy gets a moment of creepiness, a feeling that something might suddenly put its face to the bars. 'But him,' he whispers, 'him is made bad. Bad here.' He runs his fingers down his face. 'And here.' He holds his hands to his back. 'Him just made bad. Like a baboon.'

Mossy wants to speak but there's a lump in his throat and he can't get the words out. The word 'baboon', said in such a low whisper, has sent shivers up and down his spine. He's thinking of the feeling he gets sometimes that there's someone else in the place, someone who comes and goes in the night. 'So is he here, your brother?' he manages eventually. 'Here? In this place?' He gestures at the cage. 'Is that where he sleeps?'

Skinny nods. He looks at the cage for a while, then he turns to the grille on the window, at the place that is bent up. Not big enough to let an adult through. But someone else. Someone the size of a child, maybe.

Eventually Mossy clears his throat, tries to shake himself back to reality. 'Things are different here, you know. This is England. The rules aren't the same. Not the way they are back home.'

'I know.'

'You need to realize. What you do, the things you've done, people ain't going to like it. Not a bit.'

'I know, I know,' Skinny says, and his voice is so resigned, so tired, it makes Mossy want to cry. 'And I know that after everyt'ing I do here I go'n' to have to run. Run until the world end.'

35

17 May

The sun crossed the valley slowly. Back at home Flea sat next to the open window under the wisteria, her mother's gardening jacket wrapped round her, and watched the shadows of the trees move across the top lawn. Even though there was still poison in her system — she could feel it in the back of her throat, the way every now and then she caught the world jerking sideways out of the corners of her eyes — her body felt clean and light, as if the drug had stripped away layers she didn't need, leaving her thoughts brightened and uncluttered.

For some reason she kept coming back to one part of the trip: what Dad and Kaiser had been saying in the hotel.

Is it strange to be back in Africa?

This is South Africa, not Nigeria. This isn't the place it happened.

That conversation, she knew, was a memory. Not an hallucination, but a memory she had levered up with the help of the ibogaine. But it had reminded her of another memory: something strange her father had said on the day he had introduced her to Kaiser, something that made her wonder if Dad had been more involved in whatever had happened in Nigeria than he'd ever let on.

It had happened years and years ago, when she and Thom were still little and Kaiser's house on the hill was new, untouched by his interminable tinkering and building, by the way he insisted on burrowing into the hillside like a termite. So she didn't understand why now all she could think about was her parents talking that day in the nineteen eighties as they came up the driveway in the family's Cortina.

'Don't you think it's a kick in the face of science?' David Marley was at the wheel, dressed in a corduroy jacket with a gypsyish spotted scarf tied at his neck. 'What they did to him in Africa? Calling him and the team immoral. I mean, since when has morality had a seat at the dinner table of science?'

Flea could see it all in vivid colour. She remembered sitting in the back seat with Thom, both of them wearing shorts and Start-rite sandals. She remembered looking out of the window at the way the valley plunged from Kaiser's house into nothing. She remembered the house, she even remembered her mother's pink polka-dot blouse. But she couldn't remember anyone saying exactly what had happened to Kaiser in Africa. As if they hadn't dared voice the words.

'Don't you think the university should be had up by the international community for sacking him?'

'Not really,' Jill Marley said. 'If you want my opinion what he did really was immoral. It was outrageous. Inhuman.'

'Inhuman?' David Marley swung the car

294

angrily to a halt in front of the house. He switched the engine off and turned to his wife. 'How can you say that? How can you *say* that? Sometimes I think you're as bad as the rest of them.'

'Oh, darling,' Jill had said, with a shrug. 'I'm sure you don't mean that . . . '

So very typical of Mum, that little shrug — the casual way her shoulders went up. It was always the same: Dad wanting a fight, Mum soothing him, defusing the situation, catching him on his hindlegs so he had nowhere to go, with that little back-down, that little shrug.

There was a crunch of wheels on gravel outside. Back in the present Flea sat up, blinking. A car had pulled up to the front of the house. After a moment or two she got up and went to the window, her thoughts moving slowly, woodenly. She pulled back the curtain, thinking how grainy the material felt in her fingers. Thom was getting out of his battered black car. She stood, a little dreamily, thinking how odd, she'd forgotten he was coming. He'd been right when he said she'd forget.

He got out of the car and came round to the back, stopping briefly to look down the garden, and for a moment she was inside his head, seeing it through his eyes — the trees and the lake, the Bridge of Sighs, the way the terraces wound down and out of sight, disappearing into the tangle of fields. The way it was falling apart.

She went to the back door and opened it. It was warmer outside than in. The sun shone on the black roof of the car.

'Hi.'

'Hi.'

He was dressed a little clumsily, in a worn-out suit and tie, the toes of his shoes a little scuffed. She thought about the way he'd been sitting in her hallucination of the night in the hotel room, with their gear around them: the way Kaiser and her father had turned away from him so they could talk in private. Thom. Always the excluded one.

She took down the Ford Focus keys from the back of the door, still a bit disconnected from her body, as if it wasn't really her hand reaching out to the hook, and handed them to Thom.

'There's a full tank,' she began, then had to stop because there were tears in her eyes.

'Flea?'

She shook her head and put a hand on his arm, fixing her eyes on it, studying it, until she had the tears under control. 'Be careful,' she said, in a small voice. 'Please be careful.'

He put his arms round her, and even though he was slight, not muscular, she felt momentarily enclosed by something — protected. He smelled of soap, something ridiculously floral, like geranium, because he'd never know to wear something manly. 'Don't worry about me. I'm a big boy now.'

She wanted to say, No, you're not. You're still my little brother, but she didn't. She smiled and nodded, and when he'd gone she stood in the doorway for a long time, watching the evening sun moving across the terraces and thinking how different their lives could have been but for a sinkhole in a desert thousands of miles away.

★ ★ ★

During that afternoon in the custody suite there was a moment when Mabuza's anxiety crossed into something more profound. If Caffery had had to describe it he'd have said it was the only moment he truly saw Mabuza afraid. Maybe with all the things they were discussing he had a reason to be afraid, but he only went to that deeper level when the conversation turned to the subject of the Tokoloshe.

'Did Dlamini ever mention any interest in *muti*?' Caffery said. 'Witchcraft? Did he talk about using charms to ward off bad spirits?'

Mabuza didn't move his eyes. But that didn't matter because Caffery had seen him swallow. His hard grey Adam's apple went up and down painfully, and Caffery didn't have to look down to know that his grip on the polystyrene cup was tightening. He knew they were getting close to something.

'No,' Mabuza said quickly. 'No more than anyone else from our country.'

'Do you know where he might have got hold of a vulture's head? Because it's quite a serious thing to have something like that. Vultures are on an endangered-species list.'

'No idea, sir.' His eyes flicked up to the door, then back to Caffery's face. 'Really, no idea.'

'I'm sorry. Did that question make you nervous?'

Mabuza bit his bottom lip. 'You don't know what you're dealing with, sir. It's something you don't understand.'

'Don't I?'

'You're talking about something that is African. Something that belongs to Africa.' He pushed up the sleeve of his shirt and pinched up a chunk of his arm. 'It's in here. In our flesh. And not — ' he jerked his chin at Caffery and the officer in the corner. ' — not in yours. Now, you don't meddle in these things. Don't meddle.'

'That grease on your arms?'

Mabuza blinked. He looked at them as if he was surprised to find them there. Then he tucked them away under the table.

'Don't wipe it off — I know what it is. It's because of the Tokoloshe, isn't it? It's to ward him off.'

At this Mabuza became very still. His eyes seemed to bulge and Caffery thought he was going to jump to his feet again. But he dropped his face, muttering in a low whisper a string of words in a language Caffery didn't recognize. Sweat appeared on his forehead.

Caffery watched in silence, knowing this was something, a species of fear and anxiety, he'd never understand. When he'd asked the CSM if Mabuza's wife had seen him take the fibres, the CSM had said: 'She saw me do it as much as she could see anything. She was acting like she feared for her life if you want the honest truth.' And Mabuza's reaction now was fear. Real fear. Whatever he'd seen on the pontoon outside the restaurant, he'd believed it was real.

'OK,' Caffery said slowly. 'I'll tell you what I think. I think you've seen something you can't explain. Because of that you've paid money — a lot of money — to someone to ward it off. You think you've seen a devil, a *Tokoloshe*, don't you? You think he's threatening your business — and now you'll do anything.'

'Please do not meddle.' Mabuza raised a hand and tugged at his collar. Sweat was coming through his shirt, leaving circular marks on his chest. 'I asked you, do not meddle.'

Caffery tapped his pen down once on the table, giving space in the room for his question to be heard. 'Did you know the superstition that if hands are buried under the entrance to a property they bring in business? Might undo the harm done by the Tokoloshe?'

Mabuza looked up despairingly. There were faint stains round his eyes: tears of fear. 'You should stop this now.'

'*I* know beyond any shadow of a doubt that *you* know exactly how those hands got under your restaurant.' He smiled. 'Now I don't know how I'm going to get you but, trust me, I *will* get you on something. Because you know what you've done is wrong. It couldn't be more wrong for another human being to die for the sake of your business. So I'd say the best thing you can do now is tell me who you paid.'

'I haven't paid anyone for anything. I don't know how those hands got under my restaurant.'

'It must be someone who knows a lot about African traditions, or is getting the information from someone who does. Maybe it's an illegal who's trading his powers for protection and money. Is it someone at work? One of your employees?'

'No. Forgive me, you've asked me this so many times. The answer's no. If you want to know how those hands got under my restaurant you are asking the wrong man.'

Caffery tapped his pen again, thinking about the fear in the guy's face. Half of him almost wanted to believe the bastard. 'Am I? Then who should I be asking?'

He wiped his eyes and swallowed. 'The intellectuals.'

'The intellectuals? What does that mean?'

'The university men. There's a plan against me. I've got enemies. This is a plot to slur my name.'

'Would you like to give me some names? Just something to be going along with.'

'You know, sir ... ' He brought out a handkerchief and mopped his brow. He was still trembling. ' ... I have never had a strong stomach. And what you've found under my restaurant ... This is not a good day for me. Not a good day at all.' He looked up at him with runny eyes. 'How did a hand come to be under my restaurant, sir? Does it mean my business will be finished?'

There was a knock at the door. Caffery got to his feet and opened it. The office manager stood in the doorway, clutching a piece of fax paper he recognized immediately. It was from the lab. He took it and came back to sit down, placing it folded on the table where they could both look

300

at it. He let a few seconds elapse before he spoke.

'Sorry.' He held up the paper. 'This is from the lab. The report on the carpet fibres.' He sat back and opened it, unfolding it slowly, scanning it for the precise line he wanted, knowing he was closing in. 'As I was saying earlier, this morning we . . . '

'What is it?' said Mabuza.

But Caffery had just reached the relevant box. Matches zero. The carpet fibres on Mallows's hands hadn't come from the carpet in Mabuza's house. Caffery lowered the paper and gave the officer in the corner a wry smile. Sometimes you win, sometimes you lose.

'What?' Mabuza repeated, tears gone now, face tense.

Caffery ran his fingers through his hair, letting his nails graze the skin. Suddenly he felt tireder than he had all week. 'Nothing,' he said, standing and kicking the chair under the table. Outside it was getting dark. The officers wouldn't have got round all the drugs charities tonight: they'd have to start again in the morning. Which was a bastard because now the fibres weren't matching he knew the charities was one of the *only* avenues left to them. 'It's nothing at all.'

36

Don't let them bring us up . . .

★ ★ ★

It was late in the day and the shadow of the overhead light was long, reaching almost to the wall when Flea got up and dragged the old leather chair to the computer. Pulling a cardigan round her shoulders she switched on the computer and typed in 'Bushman's Hole'.

At first, after the accident, she had monitored the web all the time. When the inquest and the investigation were over, she became addicted to the chatter in the diving community, the theories about what had gone wrong with *that* dive. It interested all divers, sport and commercial alike: they were afraid and excited by what it might mean. People from Tasmania to Bermuda to the Hebrides, with sig-lines like 'You never have to ask a good diver to go down' from every different time zone, they all hopped in and out of the discussion, adding their experience to the mix. Sometimes Flea would stay up at night silently watching the forums, watching them talk, hoping for a mention of Mum and Dad, hoping it would be more than just technical theories, liking it when they called Mum 'Jill' and Dad 'David', instead of 'the Marleys', winnowing through the chaff for a mention of what they'd been before they were the world's most notorious victims of a cave-diving accident.

Getting into divenet, one of the biggest of the international dive websites, she scrolled down to the Trimix forums — Mum and Dad had been using Trimix to get down to one hundred and fifty metres; a controversial method that always got people talking. Sometimes people talked about Bushman's Hole here, too. Maybe there'd be someone who knew its shape, someone who knew the slope she'd hallucinated.

As soon as she got into the forum she could see there had been more activity than usual. There had been fifty new posts in the last two days — usually the chatroom only attracted five or six a day. Someone must have dived a particularly difficult cave and be getting back-slaps. She didn't want to think of the other possibility: that someone else had lost their life the way her parents had.

She scrolled down. As she did the hairs on her arms stood up. Navigating the mouse to the first thread she clicked again, her heart thudding as the message filled the screen. She read it once, and when she saw it wasn't a mistake she pushed aside the mouse and stared in disbelief at the screen, not seeing, not feeling anything. It was impossible. Impossible.

It took her a few moments to realize the phone was ringing. She picked it up numbly.

'Hello,' said the voice. 'Hello.'

Flea leaned forward and clicked the next message in the thread. On the phone the woman was talking, but Flea wasn't listening — she was glued to the screen, reading the next message and the next. Her heart was thumping so loudly it was making her head hurt.

'Hey, Flea? You there? It's Mandy. Flea?'

Slowly Flea straightened the phone, holding it tight against her ear, her eyes still on the screen. 'Mandy?' she said faintly. 'Yeah. I'm here.'

'You sound odd.'

'No — '

'Out of breath.'

'No — '

'Good. Then can I speak to your brother?'

'My brother?'

'Yes, Flea. Your brother? Thom? Remember him?'

And then it all came back to her. The agreement. Thom and the car.

'Flea? Is he there?'

'Uh, yeah. Of course he's — uh — here.'

'Can I speak to him?'

'No. He's — he's in the garden.'

'He's got his phone switched off.'

'Oh,' Flea said faintly. 'Has he?'

'Yes.' There was a pause. 'Flea, lovey, are you all right?'

'I'm fine.'

'You don't sound it.'

'I am.'

'Then just give Thom a shout, would you?'

'No.'

There was a pause, an intake of breath. Then Mandy said, a little quietly, 'No? Did you say 'no'?'

'I can't. He's . . . ' She looked over her

304

shoulder at the closed curtains. 'He's right at the bottom. All the way down by the lake.'

'By the lake?'

'There's a juniper down there — it's, you know . . . He's giving it a cut for me. I'll . . . I'll ask him to call you when he comes back up.'

And before Mandy could say anything else Flea dropped the phone into the cradle, sank back into the chair, staring at the computer screen, not blinking, the words burning into her eyes. 'Mum,' she murmured, gripping the mouse and inching forward in the chair. '*Mum?*'

★ ★ ★

Ben Crabbick and Andy Pearl were in their twenties and had been diving since childhood. Two health-conscious, extreme-thrill-seeking Australians from the west coast, they had dived almost every cave known to mankind and between them had notched up five hundred Trimix dive hours. Once, in the infamous John's Pocket in Florida, Crabbick had got wedged by his cylinders into a small hole just fifteen metres from the surface. Pearl buddy-breathed him for twenty minutes while they struggled together to free him. Because they were panicking, they were down to their last five bar of air by the time they got to the surface. But even that experience, said Pearl on the divenet forum, was nothing compared to what had just happened in Bushman's Hole.

Pearl was live online from Danielskuil, the town nearest to Bushman's Hole. He was safe and dry with a beer in hand, and now that things had settled he was telling the story to an avid audience, all firing questions at him. 'Me and Crabbick have been mad about Bushman's for years,' he typed. 'It's like the place gives off pheromones, you know, as if all those poor bastards that've died there are attracting the rest of us.' That, he said, could be the only explanation for why other divers insisted on venturing into the treacherous, never-ending watery funnel.

Pearl and Crabbick had raised sponsors in Western Australia for the dive. Pearl wore a Suunto logo on his cylinders, while Crabbick's dry suit had blue and white flashes on the arms and back: the company colours of an Australian broadband provider. Every minute spent at depths of over three hundred metres added hours to their surfacing time, and every second increased the chances of narcosis, so they'd agreed twenty seconds on the bottom, just time enough to photograph each other and their logos, was sufficient to justify the dive. Pearl remained clear-headed enough to stick to the dive plan. Crabbick, the less experienced of the two, wasn't as resilient.

They were at two hundred and fifty metres when Pearl suspected something was wrong with his dive buddy. Crabbick was complaining of a wah-wah sound in his helmet — a sound that to Pearl might mean there was still nitrogen in Crabbick's gas mix and that this was the onset of narcosis. His heart sank. He couldn't let him surface alone with narcosis even though it signalled the failure of the dive. Briefly, he even hated his old friend. But he knew what they had to do.

'Hey,' he said, into his through-water coms mic. 'Let's start for the surface.'

'No,' came the reply in his ear.

'Yes,' Pearl said. It was pitch black down there and he held the torch on Crabbick's chest, not wanting to direct it on to his face and blind him. 'We're going back.'

He shone the submersible torch upwards into the darkness and made a calculation: the first rescue diver would come down to the hundred-metres stage cylinders, the nearest human being, a hundred and fifty metres away, which would take them almost an hour with the right decompression stops. Pearl would lock Crabbick into the shot line and hold him there on the ascent. He hated having to turn back, but he knew he was still physically strong enough to get them both up. If they went now. 'We're aborting, Ben.'

'No. Want to go all the way.' Crabbick was slurring. Another sign of narcosis. His gas mix was definitely wrong. 'No point otherwise.'

'Sorry, Ben, no argument.'

Pearl was turning for the surface when a strong, determined hand gripped his arm. His flashlight rolled up and found Crabbick's masked face there, only a few inches away, the eyes dilated. He was shaking his head. Not speaking, but staring at his friend as if he was a stranger. Pearl wrote on divenet that it was like looking into the eyes of someone possessed. He said that if someone told him there was a devil at the bottom of Bushman's Hole, waiting to swim into the head of any diver who ventured down there, he'd believe them just from the look he'd seen in Crabbick's eyes.

'Ben. Listen to me. It's Andy. Remember me? I'm Andy, and I'm telling you now we're turning back. You always say yes.' He gave Crabbick a slow-motion shake. A move that made his ears tighten and his head spin. 'You always say yes and you always turn back when I say so.'

But this time, instead of speaking, Crabbick disentangled himself and headed towards the bottom. It was as quick as that: one minute he was there, the next he had gone into the darkness and Pearl was left with the image of a flipper moving in his flashlight beam.

'Ben? Ben, you fucker?' he shouted. 'Stop. *Stop.*'

Pearl stayed where he was for twenty seconds or so, his heart thumping, the sound of his breathing getting tighter and tighter in his ears, all the rules he'd learned rattling through his mind. Never dive beyond your own limits to tackle another diver — not even to save their life. It was written in stone. You'll over-exert yourself, forget to check your gas mix and dive computers, and the overwhelming probability is you'll end up with not one, but two deaths. You have to let them go. Pearl knew this — but Crabbick was his best mate. They'd been through high school together and you didn't check out on a friend that easily. His breathing got tighter still. He could almost feel the blood in his arteries, as if thickened by the pressure, struggling through his body. Then he thought that if Crabbick reached the bottom and was still conscious, he could be convinced the journey was a success, and they could turn for the surface.

Pearl might have been right that he could make the bottom and still endure the twelve-hour labour of carrying a friend to the surface. Except that when he got to the bottom he couldn't find Crabbick. He gave himself thirty seconds to look, not a split second longer, and it wasn't nearly enough to find his friend. The floor of the sinkhole was dark and unspeakably lonely, and the shock of finding mud under his feet made Pearl's head spin for the first ten seconds. But even when it had cleared and the nausea lessened, he was still disoriented. His flashbeam wavered over the ghostly desert landscapes, over the long silt dunes, empty as far as the torch would reach. And no sign of Crabbick.

Feeling sick now, his tired heart thudding uncomfortably, he gave the signal on the line that he was coming up.

It was, he wrote on divenet, the worst moment of his life.

37

'The hardest part was keeping him still.' The Walking Man sat with his knees up, cupping a mug of hot cider in his filthy hands. The firelight played across his face, threw shadows up into the trees behind him. 'First I tried tying him to a chair, but that wasn't going to work. I could see that straight away.'

'So what did you do?'

'Tape.'

'Oh, yeah, the tape. I read that in the report. Parcel tape, wasn't it?' Caffery rolled on to one side and rested his head on his hand. 'Handle With Care parcel tape — that bit made it to the media. They loved that detail.'

The Walking Man grunted. 'I didn't choose it for how it would look. It was what was to hand.'

'So you taped him to the chair.'

'But that didn't work either — I couldn't get at him. Then I realized there was an ironing-board in the garage, leaning up against the wall, so I took off the legs and taped him to that. Had to knock him out again, of course.'

'But that worked?'

The Walking Man smiled. 'Oh, yes. That worked. I put it up on the bench and it went perfectly.'

Caffery had found the Walking Man's camp half by accident. It was late. He'd got a PC from Broadbury babysitting Mabuza at his house

— told him it was for his own protection — and had gone straight from the office to one of the girls on City Road.

It hadn't taken long and he'd come away feeling worse rather than better. He kept thinking about what the Walking Man had said: *You're looking for death.* He wondered about that as he drove home while the sun went down, the first stars came out and Bristol faded to an orange haze in his rear-view mirror.

He wasn't consciously looking for the camp, but he knew he didn't want to go home where he'd be alone with nothing for company but late-night TV shows and shadows in the trees, so he drove, heading east, nearly into Wiltshire. He took roads he didn't know and was south of Bath on a small turn-off near the A36 when he noticed a small campfire in some trees just a hundred metres off the road. He stopped the car, got out and walked slowly across a rapeseed field to the wood. Usually the Walking Man would be asleep by now, but not tonight. Tonight he was awake, sitting in the middle of the field, looking over the fire in the direction of the Farleigh Park lake that lay at the bottom of the slope reflecting the moon. At first there seemed something troubled about him — he held up a hand to acknowledge Caffery but he wasn't looking at him. He was scratching his beard ruminatively and staring past him down the hill and across the field to the road where the car was parked. It was only when Caffery told him what he wanted, and handed him another bag of crocus bulbs, that the Walking Man responded. He added another litre of scrumpy to the mulled drink he was brewing in the Kelly kettle, and when they were both settled, with steaming mugs and lit cigarettes, he began to talk.

'When I made the first cut in his nose he bit me.' He held up a grimy hand closed into a fist, and turned it in the firelight. 'Don't know how but he got his head off the ironing-board and bit me. He clamped himself here, round the wrist, like a shark. For a moment I thought it was over.'

Lying on the ground, the cigarette between his teeth, Caffery closed his eyes and tried to picture it: Craig Evans taped to a board, blood pouring down his face. He knew what Evans had looked like before the attack because he'd seen the photos, but by screwing his eyes tight he could replace Evan's face with the one he wanted in his own fantasy. Ivan Penderecki's.

'I punched him in the side of the head and he almost went out again. He let go and that's when I got him by the hair and taped his head to the board. The only part of him you could see was his face, his hands and . . . ' he paused ' . . . his balls and cock. I got those out straight away. Unzipped him and out they came. They were hanging there the whole time — just to, you know, remind me.'

'Then what?' He focused on Penderecki's face in his head. 'What happened next?'

'Then I went back to cutting off his nose.'

'What was it like?'

'Have you ever carved a chicken for Sunday lunch? I used to all the time — before Evans. You know the way it feels when you cut a leg off to put on a plate? The tearing? It was like that.'

Caffery's hands were twitching. His teeth clenched tight, the enamel almost cracking with the pressure. He was seeing it all in his mind's eye: Penderecki screaming, the click and grind of cartilage as the knife went through his nose.

'His eyes were easier than I'd thought. I'd never thought I could dig my thumbs into someone's skull like that, but I did. He passed out again then.'

'And you waited?'

'I waited until he woke up. He was trying to move around — to thrash about — but he couldn't. He kept puking too — every ten minutes or so he'd puke.' There was a moment's silence. Then the Walking Man said, with a smile in his voice, 'But we haven't even got to the best bit yet.'

'No?'

'Oh, no.' And this time he chuckled. Caffery fought the urge to open his eyes. He could believe that if he did he'd find a grinning gnome cackling at him. 'No. The best bit was cutting off his dick. I got more pleasure from that part than anything.'

'Pleasure?'

'Yes, Jack Caffery, Policeman. Pleasure. Because that is what we are here to talk about. The pleasure I got. I am not going to cry about this — I am not ever ever ever going to show repentance, whatever you expect. I am here to tell you that the greatest pleasure I ever got in my life was hacking through that man's balls. I held them in my hands. I pulled them so they were as far out as they could stretch. And I slid the blade across the skin — it went through without me even pushing it — and it snapped back to his body like elastic and there I was, holding his testicles.'

Caffery swallowed. He tried to keep his voice steady. 'And then? What then?'

'And then his penis. I did that slowly. He kept passing out so I had to wait until he woke up each time.'

'What was that like?'

'That was like cutting through a steak. Not difficult. I tilted the board back and put a wooden block on his thighs to rest against. That way I got a better leverage. I had a serrated knife and I used that. The blood soaked into the wooden block.'

For a long time neither man spoke. There was no sound, only the distant rumble of the A36, and occasionally of a car going past on the road. Caffery lay as still as possible, letting the moonlight bathe his eyelids, seeing Penderecki taped down so only his face and groin were visible, the floor and board around him soaked in blood. He'd have done it in the back room, one of those that looked out over the railway cutting because that was the last place Ewan had been seen. He'd have been able to see his own home, the lights on, the places he and Ewan played as kids. Caffery thought, although he wasn't sure, that he would have recorded it on video too, the way the Walking Man had.

'Why did you crucify him?'

'Why did I crucify him?' He gave a hollow

laugh. 'That, Mr Policeman, is between me and him.'

'It's a strange thing to do.'

'Yes,' the Walking Man said calmly. 'And it's a strange thing for a man to rape an eight-year-old child. To rape her four times in three hours and then, when he had finished, to kill her.'

Caffery opened his eyes. The Walking Man sat in the same position, clutching the cider, his eyes fixed on the distant horizon. A taste of metal came into his mouth as he wondered whether the Walking Man could see the death of his only child without closing his eyes. He himself had always been able to see Ewan's death, so why should it be any different for the Walking Man?

'And?' he said, after a minute or two, when he was sure his voice would come out more or less even. 'What then?'

'Then I went and called the ambulance.'

'You were calm on the tape. The prosecution said you were talking as if nothing had happened.'

'That's right.'

'And Evans was screaming in the background.'

'Yes. He was screaming. Do you know what he was screaming? You couldn't hear it on the tape and it never came out in the trial — but do you know who he was screaming for?'

Caffery hesitated. He closed his eyes again and let himself sink deep, deep down inside, feeling a pull somewhere in his chest where he knew truths were. 'I don't know, but I think . . . '

315

'Yes? You think?'

'I think he was asking for his mother.'

In the darkness the Walking Man let out a long breath. 'You're right. He was screaming for his mother.'

38

Night had come. Flea sat in the study staring at the screen, not stirring to switch on the light or close the window. Hours went by as the electronic discussion played itself out, the computer bleeping each time a new message sprang up. Andy Pearl was trying to explain how it felt to get to the first air stop on his line, to scribble a frantic message to the support diver, who didn't have through-water coms, that Crabbick was dead, and to get instead a shake of the head, a gloved hand pointing in the direction of the surface. No, Crabbick wasn't lying at the bottom of the sinkhole. He was alive and clinging to the line several metres above them in the dark.

He had conquered the narcosis. Somehow — and no one was sure what alchemy had choreographed it — he'd hit the bottom, spent seconds there, then started back to the surface. Yes, he was in a poor way, and when at last they got to the top, ten hours later, he had to be pulled out of the water by support divers. He was pale, with broken veins in his eyes and round his nostrils, said Andy Pearl, and his breathing was as if he was trying to blow up an old airbed, laboured and slow, but he was conscious. He was alive. Able to talk for a few seconds before he was taken by the medics to hospital. And what he said to Pearl was what had made Flea's hand crab round the mouse. On the stretcher Crabbick had turned to his dive buddy, reached out a hand and said, in a blood-thickened voice, 'The Marleys. I saw the Marleys stuck on a ledge near the bottom.'

She put her hand to her head, massaging the roots of her hair, trying to picture what Crabbick had seen. She imagined the sound of breathing through cylinders, the solitary torchbeam: imagined a skeletonized hand appearing in the swirling silt below. Mum and Dad, on the slopes of Bushman's Hole. Somewhere, she realized now, she'd been keeping a little light of hope alive: an illogical dream that they might have escaped the accident, that Thom and the support divers and the ibogaine had all been mistaken, that they'd found a way out of Bushman's Hole and had somehow got to safety.

She wanted to type — she wanted to ask questions: *Is Crabbick sure it's the Marleys? Did he take a photograph? Have you any idea of their coordinates? And, most importantly, how near is the ledge to the bottom? Five metres? Ten metres?*

But Pearl wouldn't be able to answer. She could see that from the way he was responding to the questions. Crabbick was still in hospital, unable to talk. *Shall we give the guy a break?* he kept writing on the forum when anyone asked him for more information. *Give him some space to recover — at least let him get his butt out of hospital — then ask him?*

She looked through the posts, trying to work out how long ago it had happened. The first garbled report that they'd been spotted had been two days ago. Two days, this had been sitting in the public domain, and she hadn't known. She hadn't known, yet somehow she'd dreamed Mum warning her about it. *This time they'll find us.*

She rubbed her arms, suddenly feeling cold. It wasn't possible, was it? Uncovering memories — ideas she'd never quite vocalized — yes. But actually speaking to the dead? Wasn't it more likely she'd gone into this site in the last two days and forgotten because of the ibogaine? She forced her mind back through the memory: Kaiser had been using the computer, she remembered him tapping away on it. Had there been a moment when he'd left the house and had she, working from instinct, got up from the sofa, gone to the computer and got into divenet? Kaiser, she thought, as the moon crested the line of cypress trees, Kaiser, what would you say? If I said I'd been talking to the dead, what would you say?

She pulled out the mobile phone and dialled him. He was usually awake at this time of night, pottering around the out-buildings, hammering in nails, and often didn't hear the phone. So she gave him time to make his way back to the house, letting the phone ring thirty times, counting it off in her head, but still he didn't answer. She hung up and went to get Thom's car keys. She'd have to take his car and drive over there. She was putting on her coat when a sentence came back to her.

Thinking they're going to speak to the dead because they inject some shit into their arm . . .

Tig, she thought. How about you? What would you think? As she was pulling on her coat she dialled his number. He answered after six rings. He sounded out of breath, and she pictured him with his mother, slouching in her bedroom, doing her lonely thing with her dreams and the police scanner and Freeview TV.

'Yeah,' he said, swallowing to get his breathing down. 'Yeah, what?'

'Tig.' She zipped up her coat. 'Something weird's happened.'

There was a moment's silence, then he sniffed. 'I'm glad you called,' he said tersely. 'I'm glad because it's what you said you'd do. Always nice to see you doing what you say you're going to do.'

She hesitated, taken aback. Had she promised to call? And then she remembered: the last thing he'd said after Mabuza's was 'Please call', and she'd said, 'Yes, I promise.'

'I've been waiting.' She could hear Tig moving around at the other end of the line, clanking things, as if he was in the kitchen. 'And now you're calling me. It's good, that's what I'm saying, it's respectful of you.'

She finished doing up the zip, feeling beaten. 'I'm sorry.'

'How's your filth boyfriend? Suited and booted and out for a little action?'

'What?'

Tig laughed. 'He likes his laydees very compliant, if you know what I'm talking about.'

'No, I don't know.'

'Ask him how he's settling into the area. Ask

320

him if he needs a tourist guide — take him down City Road and show him around a bit.'

'Tig, please. I called you because I needed you — really needed you. I'm sorry I didn't call earlier but, please, talk to me like a human being. Not in code. Or let's stop talking and do it another day. I'm going out now.'

There was a beat of silence. Then he snorted. 'OK, then,' he said lightly. 'We'll do it another day.' And before she could stop him he'd put the phone down.

She stared at the mobile display, not quite believing he'd hung up on her. Fuck fuck fuck. She flipped up his number and standing in the hallway in her coat composed a text in her laborious text language. It was half complete when the landline on the table leaped to life, making her jump. She dropped her keys into her pocket and picked it up.

'Kaiser?'

'No. It's Mandy. What's going on?'

'Mandy.'

'Yes — Mandy. Look, Flea, I've been trying his phone all night and he's either got it switched off or he's rejecting my calls. I need to talk to him.'

Flea scratched her scalp hard, trying to think. 'Wait a moment.' She put the phone on the desk and went into the hallway. It was pitch black — she hadn't realized it had got so late. 'Thom?' she called into the darkness. 'Thom? Where are you?' She waited, counting to fifty in her head, then went back to the phone. 'Mandy, he's not answering. He must be in the shed or something. I'll get him to — '

'In the shed? It's nearly eleven o'clock — pitch dark out there. What's he doing?'

'I don't know. I'll tell him to call you when he — '

'But you said you'd ask him to call hours ago. Why is he lying to me?'

'He's not lying.'

'Are you sure? Because if he's lying to me I'll kill him.' Flea took a breath to answer but Mandy spoke again. 'I mean it,' she said. 'I'll kill him if he's lying to me.'

Flea stood up straight, looking out into the darkness, at the garden she and Thom had played in as children. Something had snapped in her head. 'You know what, Mandy?' she said, her voice cold. 'You can fuck off and leave him alone. He'll call you when he's ready.'

And she hung up, hands shaking, head racing. She fished the keys out of her pocket and was heading to the door when a car's headlights filled the living room from the front. She went to the side room and pulled back the curtain: the Focus was turning into the driveway, going to the back of the house. Thom. At last.

Feeling weak now, she went to the back door and unlocked it. There were so many things to say to him she didn't know where she would start.

★ ★ ★

At first she didn't realize anything was wrong, even when she saw how fast the car was sweeping down the driveway. Even as she watched him bring it to a halt in a spray of gravel, throw it into gear and reverse it quickly under a spreading juniper, she wasn't thinking about something being wrong with him. She was thinking about what she'd seen on the Web. It was only when he pushed past her, tearing off his coat, going straight into the house and into the toilet, that she understood he was crying.

She stood in the doorway and watched him run the tap, putting his face under it, gulping air, his whole body trembling. From behind her came the sound of another car outside, another pair of headlights sweeping round the side of the house.

'It's the police.' He straightened, took a towel from the shelf and rubbed his eyes with it. 'Police.' He sniffed. 'B-been following me since the A36.'

Flea saw from its headlights that the car had stopped outside the back door. 'The *police*?' she murmured, as if it was a word she'd never heard before. This was so unreal. 'What do they want?'

'Oh, shit,' Thom said. He bundled the towel to his eyes, held it there tight.

'Thom?' Slowly her thoughts were coming back. 'Thom — what's been . . . ?' A horrible thought crossed her mind. She snatched at the towel, got him to lower it. His face was thick and red, his eyes bloodshot, his breath sour. 'Jesus, Thom.' He tried to turn away, ashamed, but she held his wrist so he had to look at her. 'Thom? How many have you had? You *stink* of it. Are you *stupid*?'

'I'm sorry. I'm sorry.' He moved his head

around miserably. 'It's just all gone wrong — all gone so bloody wrong — '

Behind them in the hall the doorbell rang. A dark shape was there, smudged and distorted by the coloured glass. Flea stared blankly at it.

'Please talk to him,' Thom said agitatedly. 'Please, please, Flea, get him to go away. I'll never ask you another favour, I promise.' He grabbed her arm. '*Please*,' he hissed, a note of fear in his voice. 'Make him leave us alone. Quickly.'

In the study the phone was ringing again. Mandy, probably. Outside, the policeman knocked again, then rang. Flea closed her eyes, counted to twenty — trying to bring something calm into her head. She took a breath and pushed her hair behind her ears.

'It's OK,' she said. 'Just go upstairs.'

'I'm so sorry.' He was crying again. 'I really am sorry.'

She turned him towards the stairs, moving him easily because she'd always been so much stronger than he was. 'Go into the back room. Pretend to be asleep.'

The doorbell rang again and the police officer put his hand on to the glass, trying to peer inside. She waited for Thom to climb the stairs, his head hanging, the soles of his cheap shoes muddy and worn as he got higher and higher. Then, heart thudding, she went to the door and opened it.

It was one of the lads from the traffic unit based in her building at Almondsbury. She knew him instantly, sometimes spoke to him at the chocolate machine buying Mars bars. He was square, with a receding hairline that had left a dark V-shape on the top of his head, like a widow's peak. Prody, his name was, or something like it, but they all called him the Motorway Monkey, because he spent his time squaring off to boy-racers on the M5.

'Look,' he said, and she could see he was trying to calm himself by the way he was breathing. Had to keep stopping between words. 'I wouldn't do this, but by the time I'd done a PNC and I knew it was yours, I'd got myself so wound up I had to keep on your tail and — ' He broke off, staring at her incredulously. 'You didn't stop. Why didn't you stop?'

Flea stood quite still, struggling to grab the sense of this. Beyond him she could see the silver Ford Focus, parked hurriedly with its back in the bushes, the light in the cottage porch reflected in its windscreen. The police cruiser stood with its nose a few feet away from the window of the living room, its door open wide. She wondered how much he'd seen of her and Thom.

'I was . . . I was in a hurry.'

'A hurry?'

'Yes — I mean, you know, the old excuse . . . ' She put out her hand to indicate the toilet door open, the light on. 'Really needed — you know. It's no excuse, but . . . '

'You were driving, then? It was you?' He was wiping his forehead. 'I couldn't see from behind — I had an idea it was someone else in there, the way you were throwing it round those bends. Didn't you see me? We could've killed ourselves.'

There were a few moments' silence while he studied her face. There was something twitchy about him and she knew he was angry. She tried to close off her expression, to imagine a veil coming down behind her eyes, hiding the liar in there. She concentrated on the V on his forehead, imagining herself boring a hole into it with her eyes.

'I'm sorry,' he said, 'but I'm going to have to do it by the book.'

'By the book? But I'm — '

'I've started a log now, see. At Control. They've got your index, they've got you down as driving without due care and attention. They're on standby now and if I go back and cancel it after all I've told them it's going to look pretty fucking sus.'

She sighed. She gazed up at the stars, thinking, there is no end to this. 'Shit,' she said, standing back and holding the door open. She unzipped her coat. 'OK. You'd better come in.'

39

Flea stood in the cluttered little kitchen, with the familiar things around her, and tried to quieten her thoughts. There was so much to think about. Why was Kaiser so bloody stupid about answering his phone? *Kaiser*, she thought, *I need to speak to you.*

The kettle was boiling, and she poured the water into the teapot wondering how far Thom had wound Prody up. He was the type of cop who, when he'd decided to 'do it by the book', didn't know where to stop. If he was really pissed off he might even ask for a breathalyser. And there was the ibogaine. The fucking ibogaine. It might play a trick on her and make it come up positive. '*Stupid*,' she hissed. Breathalysers only tested for alcohol, but she didn't know the science, and what if — what if the ibogaine triggered something, a chemical reaction, maybe?

She filled the pot quickly, and moved round the kitchen, finding plates and cups, teaspoons and biscuits in Tupperware containers, trying to behave normally. But by the time the tea was ready and she had put a couple of ginger biscuits on one of her mother's lacy creamware plates, her hands were trembling. The biscuits slid around as she carried them into the living room.

'You really didn't see me?' In the living room Prody had cooled off a bit. His breathing was slower, his face normal in the pool of light from the table lamp at his elbow. 'It's just, you know, I had my lights on all the way from the Freshford traffic lights, and you still didn't see me?'

She put the biscuits and the tea down, sat in the armchair and rested her fingers over her eyes. For a few minutes the only noise was the carriage clock ticking on the mantelpiece. When her heart had slowed she dropped her hands, and forced her voice to stay low, level. 'You know, I think I'm going to have my six-monthly counselling session brought forward. I mean, this is getting crazy.' She looked at him. 'You don't have counselling in Traffic, do you?'

'No, but I know why you lot do. I heard what Thailand was like — all those bodies, all those people you knew you'd never find. I'm not surprised you need to speak to someone.' He finished the biscuit and leaned forward for another, his fluorescent tabard creaking. 'I suppose it's always the kids that are the worst, isn't it? Makes you wonder how the parents deal with it.'

'Yes. That's right.'

'A lot of children in Thailand, were there? A lot of little ones?'

'A fair few.'

'The injuries — on the kids — I bet they were awful. Awful for the parents to see.'

'Yes. They were.' She was quiet for a moment, then she said, 'You know we've pulled some hands out of the harbour recently, don't you?'

'Hands? No. We don't get much filtering through to us, these days.'

'Well, I did. A pair of hands was buried under

one of those restaurants. And for some reason it's got to me — more than anything I've done before. You'd think with all the stuff I've seen, in Thailand and the rest, the kids and things — '

'Yeah, the kids . . . '

'You'd think it'd be easier bringing up a part of a body than the whole thing. Wouldn't you?'

'I would.'

'And so I have to ask myself, why was it this one, these hands, that tipped me over?' She rotated her head, making out she was trying to get a crick from her neck. 'Or maybe it all just built up and now it's coming out. Maybe it's nothing to do with the hands, and everything to do with the last few years. All I know is . . . ' she put a hand on her head ' . . . I've got this pressure in here. And when it comes on sometimes I can't even see my own face in the mirror.' She looked him in the eye, wondering if he was thawing. She thought she saw something in his face relax a little. 'Tell you the truth, you should arrest me. Throw me in overnight. It'd do me good.'

'Know the feeling, Sarge. Just a chance to check out for a day or two — it'd suit us all.' He smiled and she smiled back, feeling a little weight lift off her. She'd cracked him. She was about to lean over and offer him another biscuit when he shifted on the sofa, then pulled out a notepad and the breathalyser from his pocket. She stopped, half sitting forward, fixing her eyes on it.

'Tell you what we'll do.' He tapped his pen on his temple, thinking. 'There are no speeds on the log at Control, but they know I thought you were pissed — OK.' He cleared his throat and glanced at the decanters on the sideboard, the light twinkling in them like Christmas baubles. 'So, why don't we just do this and then it's all out of the way? I mean, you're not acting pissed — and you don't smell it either.'

'That's because I'm not.'

'It's just . . . ' He seemed embarrassed as he switched on the breathalyser, waited for it to run its self-check routine and fitted the mouthpiece. 'I need to rule this out.'

'You're going to make me blow into that?'

'Someone has to.'

'This isn't the custody suite. There're no cameras.'

He smiled again, as if he didn't get her meaning. 'Just so it's out the way. I'm off duty in ten.'

She stared at him, heart pounding. 'You might look stupid cancelling the Control log, but you could breathe in that thing and no one would be any the wiser.'

Prody pretended not to hear her. 'I'm requiring you to provide me with a specimen of breath for a roadside breath test, which I'm empowered to require under — '

'It's OK,' she said, standing up and snatching it from him. 'I know the bloody drill.'

He opened his mouth to protest, his eyes on the breathalyser, but she stood in front of him and breathed steadily into it, keeping her eyes on him, counting in her head up to five until the unit made a little click and beeped twice. She took it out of her mouth and looked at the LCD screen. 'ANALYSING', it said.

'There,' she said tightly, handing it back to him and sitting on the sofa. She watched him study the gauge, hating him. A few seconds passed and the machine bleeped. His expression didn't change. He leaned across the table and showed her the readout.

'ZERO', it said.

She gave a small smile. She'd have liked to say something. She'd have liked to say, 'It serves you right, you shit-for-brains bastard.' But she didn't. Best not to lose it with the traffic guys, motorway monkeys. Really best not. Instead she waited for him to finish his pocket book, then got up and held the door for him, politely extending her hand to lead him out.

★ ★ ★

Ten minutes had gone past and Caffery's body was so clenched and tense it had started to ache. He opened his eyes and, moving stiffly, sat up a little. He had to rub his eyes they'd been closed for so long. The moon had moved in the sky, but the Walking Man was sitting exactly where he'd been, on a rolled-up chunk of foam, staring vacantly into the fire as if he'd forgotten anyone else was there.

'I've been thinking.' Caffery cleared his throat. 'You know you told me I was looking for death?'

The Walking Man didn't nod or respond so he got painfully to his feet. He could feel the cold in his bones and now he remembered how tired he was. He looked down at the Walking Man, who still hadn't made a sign that he'd heard. He took his keys out of his pocket and jangled them a little, waiting for a response. The Walking Man wiped his eyes, as if tears had been there, but his face remained the same — stony and distant, as if he was off somewhere, fighting a war in a different universe.

'What did that mean?' Caffery asked, in a quieter voice. He stood next to the man. 'I can't get it out of my head — that I'm looking for death. What did that mean? You said you were the same, that you were looking for death.'

The Walking Man didn't move. He sat, the cup still in his hands, his dark, intelligent eyes reflecting the dying flames.

Caffery bent to place his own mug next to the fire. He had straightened and turned to go when a hand grabbed his ankle. He twisted, surprised, and there was the Walking Man splayed out on the ground like a snake, his face turned up to Caffery's, the sinews in his neck taut and shadowed, the moonlight glinting in his eyes.

'Death and I are best friends,' he hissed. 'I know death better than I know anything.'

'*What?*'

'Can't you see it in my eyes? Can you see how well acquainted I am with death?'

'Hey.' Caffery moved his leg, not liking the vice-like grip. He could feel the blackened nails digging into his skin. 'Let go now.'

But the Walking Man wasn't listening. He dug in his nails harder. 'I see death everywhere I go. I am the rod that attracts death. I bring it to me.

I saw it tonight — over there.' He nodded in the direction of the road beyond the field. 'I saw death tonight — I looked it in the eye before you came. I was that close. And from that I know it will be my constant companion.'

Caffery wrenched his foot free and stood above the Walking Man, breathing hard, staring at his face, at the wild hair, the night sky reflected in his eyes. 'What is this bullshit? What shite've you started spouting now?'

The Walking Man rolled back his head and laughed, as if he'd never heard anything so funny. He got on to his knees and pushed himself to his feet, laughing even harder. 'Goodnight,' he said, holding up a hand. 'Goodnight, PO-LICE-MAN. Have a good night.'

And he turned away, pulled his sleeping-bag out from a water-proof bag, and began to get ready for the night. Caffery watched him for a minute or two, then headed wearily back across the field to the car.

* * *

There was a light on in the Oscars' — in one of the windows Katherine Oscar liked to use when she was watching the Marleys. Flea noticed it the moment she opened the door to let PC Prody out. She noticed a shape there too — something that might have been the curtain slightly out of kilter, but might have been a person. She ran through the possibilities of what Katherine had seen: Thom coming through in the car maybe, Prody at the door. She thought

333

about it for a few seconds and then, because she would never allow the Oscars to upset her again, she put it out of her mind and forced a smile at Prody. 'Goodbye,' she said calmly. 'Goodnight.'

She held the door for him, but he seemed reluctant to leave. He took a step on to the gravel drive and looked up at the stars. Then he took in the lawns sweeping down to the lake, the row of pollarded poplars lining the garden and the steps leading down. She waited for him to say it. To say that she'd done well for herself, a twenty-nine-year-old on a sergeant's salary, done well to have a spread like this. But he didn't.

'I didn't hear about the hands,' he said instead. 'I admit. But I did hear about the other thing.'

'What?'

'The car-jacker. Last year.'

'Oh,' she said. 'That.'

'Yeah. That. And, for what it's worth, I thought you got a raw deal. I mean, you were only trying to help.'

'You like your gossip, do you? Over in Traffic?'

He leaned his head back a little and scratched the underside of his chin. 'You know what they said in Traffic? In Traffic, they said you were on your way to joining the suits.'

She looked at him stonily. 'Why would they say that?'

'Because around these parts CID have got their heads up their arses, and what they need is people who think outside the box. You know,

334

laterally. People like you — thinking about the car that guy took and about why he took it.'

Flea stared at him, not answering. It took PC Prody a moment or two to see from her face that the conversation was over. He gave a shy smile, took his keys out of his pocket and half turned towards the car. Then something seemed to change his mind.

'Just one last thing,' he said. 'You had your reasons for running away from me — but you need to be careful along there, the A36. Been three RTAs last month — remember that little girl thrown through a windscreen? No seat-belt. Did the last twenty feet on her face.' He shrugged and looked up at the cottage, then down, past the cooling Ford Focus, to where the lake glinted silver and black. 'Yes,' he said. 'If you ask me she was lucky it killed her. Wouldn't want the parents to see her like that.'

He got into his cruiser, touched his forehead, a mock-salute, and started the engine.

Flea watched him pull away. When his headlights had faded it was just her, the night and the shadow of an owl swooping past the distant city, by turns blotting out the church spires, the abbey, the hills beyond. She felt a cool presence envelop her, starting in her middle and moving up to her head, wrapping her like a second skin. She kept still, knowing, without understanding how, that Mum was touching her, telling her it was all right. Kaiser could wait until the morning. For now, deal with Thom.

She let a few minutes go by, breathing slowly, until the presence had melted and passed away, and the night was just the night again. The owl swooped away into the trees and disappeared into silence. She turned to go back into the house, registering, but not caring, that the light in the Oscars' window had been switched off.

40

18 May

It was ten o'clock in the morning, very sunny, and Jack Caffery was thinking about redemption. Last night, after the Walking Man, he'd gone home and lain awake thinking about Craig Evans — crucified, strapped to an ironing-board — and about Penderecki, about the ache he still got knowing that the overweight old Polish guy had cheated justice twice — once by getting away with Ewan's murder and then by taking his own life. Caffery had found him hanging from a ceiling surrounded by flies, barbiturates and his own shit. The guy who'd killed Ewan had never been brought to the same balance Craig Evans had been. And now it was morning something else that the Walking Man had said came back to Caffery as he stood in the sun-blistered car park of the Mangotsfield community hall. *Don't try to make me believe about redemption*, he'd said. *You must not try to make me believe in redemption.*

He'd come back to those words today because he'd spent the morning finishing off interviews with the trustees of the remaining drugs charities and now he found himself at one of the last on the list of Mabuza's beneficiaries: Tommy Baines, the chief trustee of the User Friendly charity. He looked up at the church hall, the mullions and ornate cornicing work casting sharp shadows. The analysis of Mabuza's bank account linked with the list the Bag Man had given them showed that every one of the eighteen drugs groups BM had mentioned as a place Mossy might have gone was a beneficiary of Mabuza. Some got more money per annum, some less, but the South African had contact with all of them. But for some reason Caffery's head was twitching more about Baines's charity than any of the others.

He pushed open the front door and went into the cool, his footsteps muffled on the navy industrial cord carpet. 'Tig', Baines called himself. Caffery remembered that as well because it had irritated him, the nickname, and he found that when he thought about 'Tig' he got a feeling he couldn't put a finger on. He wondered if it was a kind of residual anger, a pissed-offness that Penderecki had got away with it, that people like him and Tig always seemed to get a second chance. And then he thought, as he rounded the corner to the office, even though it was petty, the one small thing he *could* do was to make life uncomfortable for 'Tig'.

'You again?' Baines said, looking up from the photocopier as Caffery entered the room. There were two older women in the office, in nondescript sludgy-coloured dresses, pottering around holding sheets of paper. Next to them Tig was a total contrast, standing in his vaguely aggressive way, wearing a Duke Nukem vest, camouflage trousers and Dr Martens. 'I've got a

338

session at eleven and they start arriving before that so whatever it is make it quick.'

Caffery gave a small laugh. This was exactly the way he'd expected Tommy Baines to react. 'I'd like to talk to you,' he said, 'somewhere quiet.'

Tig looked over his shoulder at the two women. 'We can use the hall,' he said, jamming a palm on to the photocopier stop button. 'No one in there yet.'

They stood in front of a board covered with notices about Pilates, children's cooking courses and hall-hire tariff charts. Tig's arms were crossed tightly, like a bouncer's, a vein in one of his arms standing blue and hard-edged as if he'd been pumping just before Caffery had arrived. But Caffery was taller and he took advantage of that. He stood with his hands in his trouser pockets, his head forward a little, making sure Tig was aware that he had to bend a little to look into his face.

'Mabuza,' he said. No preamble. Better this way — just give him the name, and check out the response. 'Gift Mabuza.'

'Mabuza?' Tig frowned, trying to act surprised, but Caffery could see he wasn't. Not at all surprised to hear that name. 'Yeah, of course I know him. What about him?'

'How do you know him?'

'He's a benefactor of the charity.'

'He gave you money.'

Tig didn't answer at first. He didn't back away but took his time eyeing Caffery, making sure he knew it was happening. Classic aggressive behaviour, Caffery thought, but go ahead, take your time, if it makes you feel better.

'He gave me a one-off donation for the charity. That's all.'

'Why do you think he did that?'

'He's done it to all of us.' He turned away and began to study the board, pulling notices off and reordering others. Another classic tactic, Caffery thought. Just show me how disinterested you are. 'If this is something to do with that photo you gave me, you're making connections where there aren't any.'

'Am I?'

'Yeah.' Tig screwed up a couple of out-of-date notices and chucked them into a bin, moving casually so that Caffery would know he wasn't intimidated. 'Mabuza's son was an addict — did you know that? He's recovering now, thanks to someone a bit like me. Where I come from that makes the money straightforward. He has a thank-you to say.'

'But not to you. It wasn't you helped get his boy off the gear, was it?'

'No. But he knows how to spread it around.'

'So he's got other thank-yous to say? Do you know to who else?'

Tig shook his head. 'Nah. Nah — see, this is where I can't help. I really can't. I can't be talking to the police about him behind his back.'

'Why not?'

'There's nothing to tell. Even if I wanted to, there would be FA to say.' He turned from the noticeboard and held Caffery's eyes. 'Fuck All.'

'And what happens if I move the goalposts?

340

What happens if I tell you he might be involved in a killing? The mutilation we were talking about? Ian Mallows — not even out of his teens. What do you say then?'

The word 'killing' got Tig. He blinked once or twice and swallowed. 'You know, it's just occurred to me this conversation is over.'

'I don't think so. You've got more to tell me.'

Tig turned back to the board and began fiercely jamming in drawing-pins, turning them with his thumb as if they'd fall out without his help. But Caffery could see the effect on him. He could see colour starting in a band on the top of the man's shaved head and spreading down the back of his scalp, finding a spidery network of veins on his neck and going down under his T-shirt. Sometimes it got people like that, when they heard words like 'killing'. It was then that some realized, for the first time, how serious things were.

'Like I said, I think you've got more to tell me.' He waited, but Tig didn't answer. He went on with the drawing-pins, working furiously as if his life depended on it. 'What? Nothing else? Even when I remind you of the way they cut off his hands? When he was still alive?' But still Tig didn't answer. Caffery got his card out of his pocket and stepped forward, used a pin to fasten it to the board. 'There.' He tapped it. 'That's for if you remember anything.' He considered the side of Tig's face, then walked away, swinging his keys on his forefinger.

He was at the door when Tig spoke, so low that at first Caffery thought he'd imagined it. He

341

turned. Tig still had his back to him, but he'd stopped the furious jamming in of pins, and was standing with one hand resting at the top of the board, the other pressed into his side, his head down like a runner recovering from a stitch. As if he'd surrendered.

'What did you say?' Caffery walked back across the hall, his feet squeaking on the laminate floor.

'TIDARA.' Tig said it quickly, as if that would excuse him spilling the beans. 'The name of the clinic.'

'Clinic? What clinic?'

'The place he gives money to. It's the only place he won't talk about and I don't know why.'

'TIDARA? Where is it?'

'I don't know anything about it, just the name. TIDARA. But you didn't hear that from me.' He raised his head cautiously. 'Not from me — OK?'

In spite of the bad state this guy was in, in spite of the way he was trying to help even though he didn't want to, it was difficult to summon up any liking for him, Caffery thought. He nodded, then came back and unpinned his business card from the board and put it into his pocket, patting it to show it was safe.

'You never even spoke to me. I was never here. Never set foot in here. And . . . ' He tipped back on his heels and looked at the door, at the empty hall. No one was watching them.

'And?'

'And I never said thank you. OK. That bit never happened either.'

* * *

342

He found TIDARA through a directory search and drove the ten miles out of Bristol to a tree-surrounded complex near Glastonbury, with laminated-glass walls and water flowing discreetly across flat white pebbles. Specialists of every description had clinics here — aromatherapists, acupuncturists, chiropractors. TIDARA occupied a light-filled building, surrounded by green bamboo and reached along wooden walkways that spanned the running water. The reception area resembled the entrance to a swanky spa, with two girls in matching cream waffle yukatas smiling up at him from the desk.

TIDARA had been open for ten months and its director — Tay Peters, a coolly attractive Malaysian in her forties, dressed in cream linen and expensive sandals — was relaxed and courteous as she showed him into her office. She poured two tall glasses of juice and pushed one towards him.

'Acai,' she said. 'From Brazil. Twice the antioxidants of blueberries.'

Caffery put his finger into the lip of the glass and tipped it towards him, inspecting the liquid. 'Thank you,' he said, pushing the glass to the side. He picked up his folder and pulled out a file. 'And thank you for seeing me so quickly.'

She held up her glass to him and smiled. 'You're very welcome.'

He took out his notebook, loosening his tie and getting comfortable. He didn't really need the notebook — used it as a prop, a way of giving himself room to think. 'I wanted to know about your funding.'

She raised her eyebrows and lowered the glass. 'Our funding?'

'It sounds like I'm going round the houses, doesn't it? But bear with me because I am heading somewhere. You've been open — what? Ten months? And you started from scratch?'

'I did. I had some seed money from my husband, but the rest of it was my own work — you know, business plans, executive summaries, a mail-shot, then interviews, presentations, et cetera, et cetera. It was all me — on my own.'

'And your investors?'

'All private, no public money. Some are venture capitalists, but I've got my angels, you know, my private investors, and even some philanthropists giving me donations. Philanthropists because of what we do here.'

'You get people off drugs?'

'Yes, but not in the usual way.' Tay opened a drawer in her desk and pulled out a leaflet. On rough, unbleached paper, the word 'TIDARA' was embossed in pale grey. 'We use all natural products. This,' she opened the first page, 'is the Tabernanthe iboga root.' Her manicured finger rested on an illustration of a gnarled root, coiled like a basket. Above it were two or three leaves. 'We create an alkaloid from it we call ibogaine. It's a psychoactive drug, used ritually by the Bwiti tribe in Cameroon. It reduces the craving for heroin and crack cocaine, helps the user understand his or her motives for taking the drugs and, more importantly, reduces the

344

symptoms of withdrawal.'

Caffery studied the picture, thinking: Ibogaine. *Ibogaine.*

'The withdrawal symptoms are the reason most people come to us. The other two effects are sort of side benefits — a happy coincidence, if you like. And all completely legal. Please.' She closed the leaflet and passed it to him. 'Keep it.'

He took it and flipped through it. 'I'll pass it on to someone in Community Safety — I think they keep a list of organizations.' He put it into his pocket. 'There's a name I want to give you. You might know him as one of your philanthropists.'

She shrugged. 'I've got nothing to hide. All my donors are extremely high-class individuals.'

'Is the name Gift Mabuza familiar?'

'Yes.'

'Can you tell me about him?'

'He gives a lot of money to charities. He's known in the industry — if you can call this an industry.'

'And you? Did he give you a lot of money?'

She smiled. 'No. He didn't give us any.'

'I'm sorry?'

'He didn't give us any. In fact, he didn't approach us and we didn't approach him.'

'But you know him?'

She laughed. She had the whitest, most even teeth he had ever seen. 'It's a small world but not that small. I've never met Mr Mabuza. I know him by reputation but I've never seen him face to face.'

'Or had any business dealings with him?'

'Or had business dealings.'

'Are you sure?'

She stood up, went to a filing cabinet and brought out a manilla folder stamped with the name of a firm of accountants. 'Here.' She pulled out a bound report and placed it on the table. 'The details of my investors.'

Caffery studied the details, scratching his forehead distractedly. 'TIDARA,' he said. 'Is that a name of something?'

'Tabernanthe Iboga Detoxification and Rehabilitation Association.'

'And are there any others called that?'

'I sincerely hope not. We're a registered company.'

'No other branches?'

'Just us. Why?'

The woman's cool was making him feel inefficient, like Columbo in a creased raincoat. He pulled out the photo of Mossy and pushed it in front of her. She took a pair of reading glasses from a slim ivory case and perched them on her nose. He kept his thumb on the corner, and was ready to pull it back, but she frowned and rested her forefinger on the other side and drew it closer.

'Ring any bells?'

She was silent, studying Mossy. Then she went to the door. 'Chloë,' she said, to one of the receptionists, 'would you?'

There was the sound of a chair being pushed back, then the taller of the two girls, her black hair tied in a neat ponytail at the nape of her neck, came into the doorway. Tay handed her the photo. 'I was thinking about last week,' she said, 'when we were waiting for that delivery — remember?'

The girl studied the photo. 'It could be.' She held the photo at arm's length, considering it with her head on one side, nibbling at her thumbnail. 'Yeah — I mean,' she looked at Caffery, 'he was only here for a second or two, but it could be. Why? What's he done?'

Caffery came to stand in the doorway with the two women. Outside, the sun slanted through the trees in white stripes, filling the reception area with light. 'What happened when he was here?'

'Not much. He came in, asked how much treatment would cost. I only remember because, to be honest, it's not usually his type here. Can't afford it, and people don't just wander in off the streets. We're not a drop-in centre.'

'How much is the treatment?'

'Depends. If you have a full medical with us it can be up to seventeen hundred pounds. But his type, he could probably get the medical done at his GP's if he was clever and said the right things. Anyway, I told him how much and he goes, 'OK, see ya', and that was it — he was gone.'

'On his own, was he?'

'Yeah — I mean, he came in on his own, but he, you know, had his mate waiting outside for him.'

'His mate?'

'Yeah. He went out and must've told him how much it was, because the other guy got straight

347

on the phone and was telling someone.' She gestured at the front to where a varnished tree-trunk had been carved into a bench and set into the concrete just outside the glass doors. 'They were right there. And when they stopped talking on the phone the two of them just sat, really quiet, not even looking at each other. I got the feeling they were upset, as if they were sort of scared to speak to each other because everything was awful. But there you go,' she said. 'A lot of people are like that round here.'

Caffery stared at the bench in the dappled light. 'What was he like?' he said. 'The friend? Did you speak to him?'

'He stayed outside. Never come in.'

'Do you remember what he looked like?'

'Not really.'

'Nothing? Was he white? Black?'

'Oh, black,' she said, as if that much was obvious. 'But I don't remember what he actually *looked* like.'

'Was he old?' She had pushed a finger into her mouth and was sucking it thoughtfully, trying to remember. She wasn't nearly as sophisticated as he'd thought at first — he could see the places her lip-liner had gone wrong. 'Young?'

'I really don't know.'

'Tall?'

'He was sitting down.'

'What was he wearing? What was his hair like? Did he have anything unusual about him? Anything at all?'

'I think he might have been wearing a white shirt,' she said. 'Maybe a jacket over it. I'm not sure. I wasn't paying attention.'

'OK,' he said eventually, a little vague because he was trying to think too. Even if Tay thought Mabuza hadn't got a connection here she was wrong. There was a connection, but maybe she wasn't aware of it.

'OK.' He patted his pockets. 'I need to make a phone call. I'm going to sit outside for a minute or two.'

'Please,' Tay extended a hand to the door, the creamy cuff riding up her slim arm, 'I'll put your juice in the fridge.'

Outside it was warm. The world was getting hotter and who knew what parts of this country would still be above water in fifty years' time? The trees stood, as they must have for decades, on the south side of the slope, native deciduous trees and small, Oriental saplings lining the path, keeping the entrance to TIDARA shady. He looked back into the reception area. Chloë and Tay had their backs to him, both bending over paperwork. He went behind the bench, half sat on its hard back where he was out of sight, and pulled his tobacco pouch from his pocket. He had lied about the call. He needed a smoke. And to think.

It was the character in the white shirt and jacket he was interested in. He lit the cigarette and filled his lungs, letting the poison touch his body in all the places he knew it shouldn't. Someone had been sitting on this bench next to Mossy on maybe the last day he was seen alive. Pretty fucking interesting in its way. He exhaled, letting the smoke make a snake trail, up, up into the pine needles, curling subtly around the hand-like ginkgo leaves and heading up into the blue.

Something in the trees moved. He caught it out of the corner of his eye, but when he turned there was nothing, just a few frayed shadows dancing across last year's leaves on the ground. He stared hard at the tree-trunks, trying to decide if it had been an animal or a branch moving, or just something scampering around on the inside of his brain. There was something creepy about this part of the world anyway. The land he was sitting on had once been under water. Until the seventeenth century Glaston-bury Tor had been an island. But then had come the drainage of the Somerset Levels, and Glastonbury had spread as a town with its reputation as a centre for witchcraft. It was funny, he thought, it didn't matter which country or culture you came from, somewhere superstition and witchcraft had a hold. Tay had said the ibogaine was used by an African tribe. Used ritually, she had said. Ritually . . .

He pulled the TIDARA pamphlet out of his pocket. Clenching the cigarette in his teeth, he fished inside his breast pocket for a pen. With the pamphlet folded on his knee he drew a hard, deep outline round the picture of the plant root. Tabernanthe iboga root: ibogaine. He'd never heard of it until today. But somehow it was connected to what had happened to Mossy. And maybe that connection was witchcraft.

He put away the pen and tucked the pamphlet into his pocket. He was bending to crush the cigarette against the bench — not in the bark underfoot because he could picture the reaction from Tay Peters — when something above the front door arrested his eye. A small circle of glass above the front door. He smiled. An ironic, relieved smile.

Thank God, he thought, shredding the cigarette with his nails and sprinkling it in the bark mulch. Thank God for the humble CCTV camera.

41

18 May

When Flea woke, the sun was high above Solsbury Hill, quivering hot and orange at the crest of a towering cloudbank. The air was humid and oppressive, making her head thud. She'd had only five hours' sleep. Last night when she'd gone upstairs to speak to Thom she'd found he was gone. Vanished. His beat-up car had gone too — he must have sneaked out of the cottage, taken the handbrake off and rolled it down the hill. The little sod, being quiet so Prody wouldn't hear. She'd spent an hour calling his phone, and by the time she'd given up, accepted he wasn't going to answer, her head was aching so hard that she hadn't wanted to go to Kaiser's, just to swallow paracetamol and sleep. But when she woke the headache was still there, and so was everything else: the unsettling sense that the ibogaine really had let her communicate with the dead, just as Kaiser had said. She had to see him — ask if he really believed it was possible.

There was a message on her mobile: the team didn't want to bother her on her day off, but she should know they were going to be working near the Wiltshire border today where a celebrity had gone missing without trace. Misty Kitson, the very pretty estranged wife of a premier-league footballer had wandered away from a private rehab centre some time after three the previous afternoon. The POLSA officer had set search parameters, super-imposing Blue8 software over the local Ordnance Survey map, and the first thing he'd noticed, two miles away from the rehab centre, was a large man-made lake. That was enough for the Underwater Search Unit to be called in. It might turn into one of the sexiest, highest profile cases the unit would ever deal with, but Flea wasn't interested in missing celebrities. Let the team handle it. She had a question for Kaiser. She deleted the message, showered and dressed quickly, got into the car and, by nine thirty, was heading in the direction of the Mendips.

But fate wasn't going to let her get away with it that easily. She was halfway down the M5 when the phone on her dashboard rang. She recognized the unit mobile number and for a moment thought about not answering. Then, muttering, 'Fuck fuck fuck,' she hit the answer button. It was one of the unit PCs.

'What d'you want? I'm on annual. I've told you.'

He cleared his throat. 'I know, Sarge, but I really think you ought to come down. It's important.'

'No way. Just 'cause she's a celebrity doesn't make her more important than anyone else. You can deal with it.'

'It's not about her, Sarge.'

'Not her? Then who?'

353

There was a pause. 'It's Dundas, Sarge.'

'*Dundas?*' Dundas was supervising the dive today — he'd never let her down before.

'Sorry, Sarge,' said the PC. 'He's not talking to us. Think you'd better come over, that's all.'

And so, swearing under her breath all the way, she reversed her route, coming back up the M5, then the M4 until she was at the search site. Avon and Somerset had picked the case up because the rehab centre, Farleigh Wood Hall, stood deep in the countryside a little to the west of the leafy Wiltshire border. As she arrived, driving slowly past the gate, she could see that the old Palladian building was already heaving with reporters. The rehab centre had brought in a private security firm to deal with them — men in Secret Service headsets and sunglasses wandered the grounds, glaring through the wrought-iron gates at the press.

She continued down the road for almost two miles, parking next to a hedge. She jammed her feet into her trainers, the laces undone, and set off across the field towards the little kissing gate at the head of the path, flashing her warrant card to the PC at the site entrance.

Down in the valley the lake was surrounded by staff equipment and cars, the unit's Mercedes van in the middle. No one was in the water but she could tell, from the centrally placed orange buoy, that Dundas had chosen a circular sector search pattern, exactly the pattern she'd have chosen herself with a lake like this: it was round and small enough for a single diver, and although it had weeds it was motionless enough to allow some visibility. But, and this knowledge came to her naturally, the lake didn't contain Misty Kitson's body. No doubt about it. Wherever Misty Kitson was found — sleeping on someone's sofa in a Chelsea pad, or being papped leaving Heathrow for the Caribbean — it certainly wouldn't be in the lake.

She went through the kissing gate and continued down the path between a rapeseed field and a meadow, searching the figures for Dundas. One of her team was talking to a guy in a suit — she recognized him as a chief inspector from E District. A DCI, not because finding Misty Kitson would be more difficult than finding another misper, but because the press would be all over them and they needed the highest rank possible. As she got close the PC caught sight of her. He broke off, but instead of starting towards her, pointed silently up the hill. She looked to where the field rose in a series of undulating bumps, ending in a small line of trees at the top.

Just visible against the trees the small figure was instantly recognizable from his red hat. He was walking away from the lake, and there was something oddly sad about the way in which he was moving. She hesitated, then started up the hill.

'Rich?' she called, as she got closer. 'Rich?'

She saw him hesitate, then turn to her. She slowed, shocked by the expression on his face. 'Shit,' she muttered, hurrying up the hill, her trainers slapping. 'Rich? What is it?'

He shook his head as he took a deep breath.

'What?'

He looked more ill than she'd ever seen him, and just as she reached out to touch him he sat down on the grass with a thud, as if he was faint.

'Rich.' She crouched next to him, her arms round his shoulders. 'My God, what's happened?'

'It's Jonah,' he said at last. 'I just got a phone call from Faith.'

'Oh, Christ.' Flea patted his back. If there was one thorn in Dundas's side it was his useless sodding son. Always in trouble, always bringing problems to his doorstep. Everyone was fed up with him, including Dundas, who had got to the point of refusing to get involved or bail him out. He'd learned to let Jonah's problems wash over him. But something was different here. 'What's he done this time?'

'That's just it. It's not 'this time'. It's not like the others.' Dundas raised his eyes to her and from their red rims she could see he was scared. 'He's gone.'

'Gone? Gone where?'

'Faith gave a party for some friends last night. Jonah was supposed to turn up, but he never did.'

Flea tipped forward on to her knees and rubbed her legs, feeling awkward. She didn't want to say it, when Dundas was looking so awful, but drug addicts, especially those who were on the game to pay for their habit, well, they weren't the most reliable people. She looked down the hill at the sunlight reflecting off the top of her car. She had to get to Kaiser's.

'I know what you're thinking,' he said. 'You're thinking that people like him don't turn up to things all the time. And you're right — he's a waster and a piece of shit and not fit for Faith to wipe her feet on and, yes, he's done some terrible things, but when it comes to family he always, *always*, keeps his promises.'

Flea stopped rubbing her legs. She always believed Dundas. He had more integrity than anyone else she knew. If he said his son could be relied on, it was true. 'OK,' she said. 'Tell me what happened.'

'He owed Faith money. Nothing new there, she's soft as shit with him, he always owes her money, but he said he was going to pay her back this morning. He said he had a job that was different, that would pay back everything he owed.'

'What sort of job?'

'I don't think it was just another trick.' Dundas swallowed. He was an old copper. He knew the language of prostitution but it had taken him years to get used to using it for his son. 'If it was just another trick he was turning it must have been a spectacular one. He owes Faith nearly eight hundred quid, and you don't make that sort of money in Knowle West. And he'd've called if he was going to be late. He had his phone with him. She's been ringing him all morning but it's switched off. He'd've called if . . . ' He let the word carry across the grass. 'If he could.'

They sat without speaking, looking out at the sky, at the long field leading away from them and

357

the lake nestling in the grass like a silver coin. About five feet to their right there was a blackened area where someone had made a fire, recent because the smell lingered. No bottles or rubbish, so kids maybe, or someone on the run. There was a tramp in this area, an ex-con the public had monikered the Walking Man, and it made her think about all the people in the world who would have no one to notice if they vanished tomorrow. Lost souls. She turned to Dundas and hugged him. 'Don't worry. It'll be OK.'

'No,' he said. 'I don't think so. I don't think it will be OK.'

She stood up and gazed at him, at his big old face, at the way the skin on his neck was red and mottled, permanently sunburned from years of diving. She knew there was no replacing Dad, no such thing as a replacement father, but now she felt so tender towards Dundas she had to fight an overwhelming impulse to hug him again. 'Rich?' she said. 'We're going to do our best.'

'Yes,' he muttered thickly. 'Yes. Thank you.' There was a long pause, while he seemed to squirm a bit, as if something was coiling through his stomach. 'Thank you.'

42

11 May

Everything Mossy finds out about Skinny's brother is creepy. He never sees the little bastard but he knows he's there — he's seen his fucked-up shadow on the wall. He's smelled him, and heard him. But there's worse: from everything Skinny's said about the way he acts, the things he does, Mossy's come to the conclusion that the brother's deformity doesn't stop at his baboon body: it's got into his brain too.

It's Mossy's opinion that Skinny has the exact right attitude about the fucked-up business they're in: there's money in human parts. It's taken Mossy a long time to accept it, but now he understands it's the way Skinny has to survive. But his brother has totally the *wrong* attitude. The brother — and sometimes just thinking about it makes Mossy feel cold in the head — actually believes in the *muti*. He's never asked if the brother has actually swallowed human blood — or if he's eaten pieces of the skin the two of them trafficked — but he's made guesses.

Because the brother believes the *muti* can do more than just cure him. He thinks it can do more than just straighten his spine and unlatch his baboon hands. He thinks it can influence others around him. In the times he's out of the flat, doing whatever weird thing he does out there, the brother has fallen in love. Never slept with her, only seen her at a distance, but it's love. She's a street girl, one of the City Road girls, called Keelie. Mossy knows too well that, of all the bad people in the world you can fall in love with, a street person is the worst — but the brother's got it into his head, Skinny says, that the *muti* is going to work here, too. It'll stop the girlfriend shagging other men for money.

Skinny doesn't talk much about it. He tries to pretend it's not happening, but then something forces him to go past all that. One day something starts him sweating.

It must be the third or fourth day, Mossy's almost sure he's been here three days, and it starts with shouting. He sits up on the sofa and peers into the darkness. The noise seems to be coming from somewhere beyond the gate, maybe from somewhere nearer the cage, and from the echoes he gets a sense of what this place is like, of the labyrinth of rooms. There's the noise of something being thrown against the wall, more shouts, then silence. He waits what seems for ever. Then, just as he's lying back on the sofa, suddenly people are in the corridor jostling, adrenalin and violence in the air, Uncle, maybe someone else. The gate is opened and Skinny is pushed inside. When Uncle has gone and the corridor is dark Mossy leans over and hisses, '*What?* What is it?'

There's a moment of silence, then Skinny

skulks over, sits on the threadbare sofa, wraps his arms round his shoulders and gives him this look that says everything's gone wrong.

'What?'

Skinny shakes his head and his eyes turn away, staring at the barred cage. It's back to the nightmare, then.

'Your brother,' Mossy says. 'It's your brother?'

Skinny nods miserably and wipes his nose with the back of his hand.

'What then? What the fuck's he done now?'

He swallows hard as if there's a lump in his throat.

'What?'

Skinny puts his hand to his mouth, taps it a couple of times with his thumb. At first Mossy thinks he's doing it to stop himself crying, but then he sees it's a gesture. Skinny does it again and he understands.

'Drinking?'

He nods.

'He's drunk? Uncle caught him?'

Skinny screws up his face and rubs his fingers hard into his arms. The look on his face is making Mossy's skin crawl.

'What's he been drinking?'

And still Skinny can't answer. Mossy knows for sure now that something the brother has done has really chucked the shit at the fan. He can tell from Skinny's face and from the noises out there that Uncle has caught the freak doing something, drinking something he shouldn't. He's getting the words and the ideas straight in his head, and he's about to say it all, when the

361

whole thing dawns on him. It's like having a snake go fast through his belly.

'*Shit*,' he says faintly. '*You're fucking joking. You're fucking joking.*'

He gets up slowly, in a daze, because he can't sit here waiting for Jonah a minute longer. This is all too screwed up. He goes to the gate and rattles it.

'Hey,' he shouts into the little corridor, with the bare light fitting. 'Let me out.' There is silence out there now. The banging and shouting have stopped. He shakes the gate a little harder and the noise echoes through the building. 'Hey!' he yells. 'Come and let me out! I've had enough of you bunch of fucking freaks.'

'Don't,' Skinny says, from the sofa. 'Don't. You go make him angry.'

But Mossy doesn't care. He's trying to shake the gate out of its moorings. 'Let me out.' His voice is rising, louder and louder. 'Let me out, you shithead. Let me out.'

He's trembling because if there's one thing he knows it's that he's not staying in a place with an animal, because that's what Skinny's brother must be, to do what he's done. Drink his blood. There's no need to spell it out. The weird fucker has been into the fridge and drunk the blood, and now there is nothing Mossy won't risk to get out of this place into the sunlight.

'*Come and let me the fuck out!*' he screams, throwing himself at the gate. '*Let me out!*'

★ ★ ★

He's been yelling and rattling the gate for ever when from the darkness at the end of the corridor there's a sound.

At first Mossy doesn't notice it, but then he sees a crack of light and his voice dies. There's the sound of nails being pulled from wood. He freezes when a head appears as if from the wall, and suddenly in the corridor Uncle's coming towards him. He's dressed in a blue shirt and pale trousers and this is the closest Mossy has ever got to him. He's wearing black gloves, but the thing that really scares Mossy is that he can see why his head always looks so big. He's wearing a rubber S&M mask zipped over his face.

Mossy lets go of the gate and backs away across the room. Skinny has curled up in the corner.

'What?' Mossy yells at him. 'What're you looking like that for? What the fuck's he going to — '

But the lock rattles, the gate opens and, before Mossy can do anything, Uncle is in the room. It all happens so quickly that afterwards Mossy won't remember much. He won't remember whether Skinny helped or what happened, because all he knows is that one minute he's running towards the bathroom and the next he's been thrown back on to the sofa, all the air coming out of his lungs, and someone's on top of him. It's like being picked up by a bull because Uncle is fast and sinewy, and so pissed off you'd think he could rip the walls apart with his bare hands.

Mossy tries to struggle, but he's winded. He lies on the sofa, gulping air, trying to see, trying to scream. Someone straddles him — he can't see who because there's something across his eyes but he guesses it must be Uncle from the strength. His weight drops on to Mossy's chest and squeezes the air out. He can feel it — feel the sides of his lungs pressing together, and he knows he's gone from alive to nearly dead in a few short seconds.

He can hear sounds coming from his own throat, strangled sounds, as he tries to suck in air, and above him the sound of Uncle breathing in the mask: hard and scratchy, like a horse. Then someone has grabbed his arm and although he tries to squirm away he can't. There's a cold, familiar feeling on his arm, a puncture. He tries to pull away but the needle is in and almost instantly, much faster than a hit of scag, his head goes silver, there's a long rush of energy up through his body, a sense of voices gathering in his head and then it's over. His head slumps back and he lies there, making weak movements with his arm as the rest of the liquid is forced into his shattered vein.

Afterwards there is silence, while maybe Skinny and Uncle wait to see what he will do. Then, with a grunt, Uncle climbs off him. Mossy doesn't try to get up. He doesn't care any more. He lies on his back with his arm hanging limp over the side, fingers on the floor, and lets his eyes roam across the ceiling. He can see cities and mountains up there. He can see stars and clouds. He is floating, he is flying, and nothing else matters. It doesn't matter that somewhere in the corner of the room Uncle is plugging a piece of equipment into the wall. It doesn't matter when he hears the power saw start up. All that matters is staying in that flying feeling. The feeling that makes him believe he can reach the stars if he only wishes it enough.

43

18 May

'It's for the insurance,' Tay said, as she crouched behind the reception desk and ran her manicured nails across the DVD cases neatly lined up and labelled. 'I get a big break on my premiums by having the place covered. I mean, some of the people we get in here are in very distressed states and you never know.'

'Yeah,' Chloë echoed. 'You never know.'

Caffery watched from a few paces away, wanting to avoid the withering look he was sure he'd get if Tay smelled the tobacco on him. 'You mentioned something earlier, Tay,' he said, as she examined each label, pulling one or two out and piling them on the counter. 'You said ibogaine was used in a ritual.'

'The Bwiti tribe.' She pushed her glasses up her nose and crouched again to check the remaining disks. 'They use it to get in touch with their ancestors.'

'A sort of shamanic ritual?'

She glanced up at him.

'A shaman,' he explained. 'Like a witch doctor.'

'I don't really understand that side of it. My interest is the biochemical aspect, not the anthropological.'

'Do you know if it's used any other way, in other types of African magic? Maybe as a remedy?'

She shook her head and straightened up, putting three more disks on top of the pile. She fished a brown-paper bag out from under the desk and put it down next to them. 'It's not really my thing, Mr Caffery. We've had an academic here who was interested in our work. He'd be able to tell you. I cooperated with him — for the publicity's sake — but I didn't get involved because it was in the early days when I was doing the preliminary treatments.'

'He came and observed,' Chloë said importantly. 'You know, for his research.'

'And what did he do with it all?'

'Told us he was trying to get it published. I mean, that's what they do, isn't it? These academics?' Tay leaned across Chloë and clicked her way into a database. The printer under the counter whirred into life. 'We use his home address because he hardly ever goes into the university.' Paper shot into her hand and she passed it to him with a smile. 'He's very accommodating, will talk about ibogaine and ritual use *ad infinitum*.'

Caffery took the paper and looked at the name. 'Kaiser Nduka,' he murmured. A German-sounding first name and an African-sounding surname. He'd seen it before — it had been on Marilyn's list of consultants. She'd highlighted it because he was so local. 'Right,' he said, sliding the DVDs off the counter and into the paper bag. 'I'm taking these up to the multimedia unit at HQ to get them analysed — and then I might stop by and speak to Mr Nduka.'

'Say hi to him from us.' Chloë waved with her fingertips.

'Yes,' said Tay, holding the door for him. She gave Caffery that cool, slightly contemptuous smile again. For a moment he thought she was going to sniff, wrinkle her nose at the smell of cigarettes, but she didn't. She inclined her head as he left. 'Please do. Please send him our regards.'

★ ★ ★

Misty Kitson might have been a drug addict, like Jonah, but she was pretty and a famous one. And this made the difference. Flea and Dundas both knew that although he was a police officer's son Jonah was still a whore, and his disappearance would be swept under the carpet. They called the duty inspector at Trinity Road, the nearest police station to Faith's flat, and got him to start a missing-persons report. But there was something unconvincing about the way he promised to prioritize, and Flea decided she needed to speak to someone she knew personally.

Caffery. She had the strangest feeling he was the sort who'd stick his neck out for someone like Jonah. She didn't know why, but she thought he was the only person who wouldn't stop until he'd found him. But he wasn't at Kingswood — the staff gave her his mobile number but it was switched off — and it took some digging to find someone who said they'd heard Caffery was heading to HQ to go through some CCTV footage with the multimedia unit and she might catch him there. Portishead was en route to Kaiser's anyway, so once she'd got the team sorted and a new supervisor on duty, once Dundas had left to drive to Faith's, Flea went back to her car parked on the road.

She'd got the door closed and the key was in the ignition when a short man with stocky legs and an intense look in his eyes appeared at the window, tapping on the glass. She turned on the ignition and opened the window. 'Are you Sergeant Marley?'

'What can I do for you?'

'I'm the POLSA.'

The police search adviser — the person who'd have set the parameters and put her team in the water in the first place. She'd never seen him before. His stripes told her he was a constable. 'Yeah, well,' she said flatly, pulling on her seat-belt. 'I'm on annual, so speak to someone else in the team.'

'I would, but something's going on with your team today. For a minute there I thought they were going to stop searching altogether.'

'We had a staffing problem,' she said, 'but we've put another officer in as supervisor and he's got everything in hand. We've lost an hour tops. OK?'

She pressed the button to close the window, but the POLSA put his hand on the top of the glass, stopping her.

'I'd like an extra person in there now,' he said. 'I'd be happier with that — if you could get someone in there. It might even cross your mind to cancel your day off for a case this important.'

A tic was starting in her eye. 'No,' she said. 'It won't cross my mind. The team you've got there is perfectly capable of doing the job.' She raised her eyes to his face, to the bulbous nose, to the first sprinkle of burst capillaries on his cheeks, and then something in her slipped a little. It was to do with his face, with the way he had his hand on her window, and it was to do with a million other things. Something inside her just slipped off a hook. 'Tell you what, let's speak the truth here, save both of us some time, shall we?'

'The truth?'

'Yes,' she said, knowing she should stop, but enjoying the way the words were coming clear and clean. 'We both know you're not going to find her in there.'

'Do we?'

'Yes,' she said. 'We do.'

His eyes were a washed-out blue, the rims red. 'It's funny, because if your unit hasn't even finished searching the lake yet, I don't see how you can be sure where she is. What makes you an expert on knowing where a body's going to end up?'

Years of training? she thought. Years of knowing what water does? Oh, and a bit of premonition too — a little skill I didn't know I had until yesterday.

'You're not trained on search parameters,' he said. 'I mean, let's face it, you're just a — '

'A diver? Just a diver. Is that what you were going to say?'

'There are established profiles for people in Kitson's condition. Nine times out of ten someone who wanders off from a clinic, like she has, will be found trying to score in the nearest town or climbing on the next bus out. But if they've topped themselves the body'll be within a two mile radius of the clinic.'

For a moment or two Flea was silent. Then she looked down at the hand still resting on the window. 'New, are you?' she said. 'I've not seen you before.'

'I've just completed my training. Yes.'

'And what part of learning to find a bomb taught you how to find a body?'

'Our training is more than just for improvised explosive devices, you know.'

'I know. After the IEDs you sit up in North Wales for a couple of days, learning how to read a few profiles. You know how to use an electronic map, but you don't know how to — ' She pictured Prody on her doorstep last night, the light on his face. 'You don't know how to *think outside the box.*'

The POLSA straightened up. She could see up his nostrils, the little hairs and the red folds of skin up there — as if he had a cold and had been blowing his nose over and over. 'Well,' he said, with a sarcastic sniff, 'how about you teach me how to 'think outside the box'? Tell me how you know there's no body in that lake.'

Flea sighed, turning on the ignition and taking off the hand-brake. 'Because,' she said patiently, 'she's a beautiful girl. A famous girl. And when famous beautiful girls kill themselves they make

371

sure they leave a good-looking corpse. And that means not drowning themselves. And especially not drowning themselves in a shitty old lake like this one. Get it?'

And without waiting for a reply, knowing the constable was going to run straight back to the DCI and tell tales, knowing that she should have stopped her mouth and her head slipping away from her like that, she put the car into gear and drove away, leaving the POLSA standing in a cloud of dust, fury on his face.

44

At HQ Flea saw Caffery's tatty car straight away. It stood at the edge of the car park, looking a little obstinate in the way it was so separate from the shiny Mondeos and BMWs.

She pulled in next to it, switched off the engine and sat for a moment or two, looking at her hands resting on the steering-wheel, her fingernails a little pale. She had an image of a line being stretched very tight. Her body felt empty, her head light. If she didn't get to Kaiser's soon she thought something would crack open inside her.

A familiar figure was coming out of the glass atrium. Caffery's jacket was open, his hands in his pockets, his stomach lean and hard against the white shirt. By the way he'd stopped at the head of the pathway and was looking from left to right across the neat lawns and fountains, she could tell he was preoccupied, as if he'd forgotten what he should be doing with himself, as if he'd like to get into his car but thought he might have left something behind in the building. She wondered what she was doing there. Was it really that she thought he'd take her seriously about Jonah? To start on a wild-goose chase like this, a person would have to be either crazy or know at first hand the agony of someone close going missing. Stupid to think he'd listen. And maybe, she thought, pissed off with herself now, that wasn't the real reason she'd chosen him anyway.

But just as she was about to start the car and leave, to head down to Trinity Road to speak to the inspector there, Caffery saw her. He didn't speak or change his expression but she knew it from the way he became very still, his shoulders back, his face pointing in her direction.

She waited for him to cross the grass, then took off her sun-glasses and got out of the car.

'Hi,' he said.

She gave him a bleak smile. 'You were in the multimedia unit?'

'Had some footage to run through, but turns out it isn't something that happens overnight. I'm in their way, hanging over their shoulders.' He paused. 'What are you doing today?' he said. 'I'm going out of town to the countryside.'

'Out of town?'

'It's work,' he said. 'Nothing else. Just thought you might like the drive.'

'No,' she said. 'I mean I'm going to — I've got to see a fr — Someone I've got to see.'

He was looking at her in a thoughtful way, as if something about her made him curious or amused. A tiny shard of sky was reflected in his iris that made her want to close her eyes. It made an ache start in her lower belly that she hated. 'Why are you here?' he said. 'You look like you came to tell me something.'

'I need your help. I wouldn't ask if there was anywhere else I could go.'

'OK,' he said cautiously.

374

'Richard Dundas — you met him, he's in my team.'

'Yes. I remember.'

'His lad's gone missing. Jonah. Told his mother he had a job that was going to pay a lot of money. Went out and she never saw him again.'

'A job? What sort of job?'

She sighed, scratching her head distractedly. 'He's a hooker. That's why I came to you. If I just send this through the duty inspector at Trinity Road it'll never be taken seriously. He's on the game, he's a user. He's a mess.'

'And it's not the first time he's disappeared?'

'No — it *is* the first time. That's the problem. I know Dundas and if he says something's wrong then something's wrong. I came to you because I thought . . . ' Her stomach clenched. 'Because you seem like someone who'd do something about it.'

Caffery was looking at her mouth, as if he was considering the words that had just come out of it. He seemed about to say something, then apparently changed his mind. He stared up at the sky, as if he was thinking about the weather, maybe, or trying to catch a scent on the air. He was silent for such a long time she wondered if he'd forgotten she was there. When at last he turned his eyes back to her she saw instantly that everything had changed.

'What?' she said. 'What is it?'

'I'll do it. I'll do it now.'

He pulled out his keys, seemed again about to say something, then nodded, almost to himself, and walked away from her, one hand raised briefly to say goodbye. He got into the car and drove out into the lane, past Security, leaving her in the sun, wondering if it had really been that simple, if he'd meant what he said or if he'd have forgotten about it by the time he reached the main road.

45

Mossy lies on his back, tears running down his face. The room is still now. At last it has stopped its rolling, its thumping like a giant heart, and he's grateful at least for that. He takes a few breaths. It's daytime and on the other side of the grille, very close, a car's just pulled up. Maybe it's the others coming back because the place has been empty for hours. They've left him here with the locked gate, Will Smith looking at him impassively over his rocket-launcher and Brad Pitt frowning, the sun glinting off his breastplate.

It's the first time in what seems like a lifetime that the pain has gone down to a level where he can concentrate, to think about his situation. He's no idea how long it's been since Uncle took his hands. Lately time's been slipping all over the place, he's been in a fever, he knows that, and somewhere in the fever he's lost track of who he is and where he's located in the world. He closes his eyes and tries to think his way back, but all he can remember are the first few hours when he came round from the drug.

It was like being hurtled into a white wall, or taken into space and set spinning with no sense of up or down. It was a pain like nothing he'd experienced, worse than the agonies, worse than the ulceration he'd had on his leg at Christmas. He lay on the sofa and howled, his arms clamped between his legs, the inside seam of his jeans pressed hard on the wounds as if that might stop the agony. He didn't dare look at what they'd done to him.

Skinny sat with him, trying to keep him calm, giving him a hit regularly, using his hard little fingers deftly and pushing the needle gently through the skin, always taking time to find a place that wasn't already broken. It was only on the second day, when he'd screamed just about all he could, that Mossy got up the courage to look. He waited until Skinny had given him a hit and, gulping hard because he thought he'd puke, he did it. He looked at the place his hands had been. He held his arms up. His head went dead for a moment, wouldn't move, and all he could do was stare. His first thought, when it came, was ridiculous and surreal: it was how short his arms were. Someone had wrapped the stumps in bandages, the sort you could get from a first-aid kit. They were thick and crusty with blood and fluids and had been taped secure with lots of ordinary Elastoplast, all with black gum round the peeling edges. Shaking so hard his teeth were chattering, he laid the stumps on his thighs and stared at them for a long, long time thinking how fucking *short* his arms were. He kept coming back to that — that his arms were tiny. He wondered how he'd never thought to notice this — or to notice how big or small his hands were.

And then it hit him, a dead weight slamming him in the chest. He'd seen them every day of his life but he couldn't remember what his hands were like. He'd never see them again. His own fucking hands and he'd never look at them again. He dropped his head back on the sofa.

'*You fucking bastards,*' he screamed. '*Give me back my hands.*' Tears rolled down his cheeks. Skinny crawled across the floor and knelt next to him, stroking his forehead, but there was a howling hole of sadness at Mossy's centre that couldn't be smoothed away. 'My hands. *My* hands. Mine. They're *my fucking hands.*'

And it is this he keeps coming back to. *They are my fucking hands.* Over the last few days, while the pain has lessened, while Skinny has changed the dressings in the best way he knows how, Mossy's just kept up the rage that someone's dared to take something of his own away from him, that if he could just *see* them he'd be able to do something about it, reverse it maybe. He is more jealous of his hands than of anything he's ever owned. There's no boyfriend, no gear, nothing he could ever have felt this way about. They are something no one could replace — something his parents gave him, and this thought makes him cry even more. That his parents gave him something precious. He hasn't given a toss about his parents for years, but now he can't stop thinking of their sadness if they find out his hands have been taken from him. His capacity to feel something about Mum and Dad makes him wonder how he ever ended up a scag-fag like this.

A smell has started to come from the wounds. Three days ago, when he was trying to turn over on the sofa, he felt something inside the bandages on his left stump give with an unzippering sound that made him want to puke.

A thick, milky fluid leaked into the bandages. Within a few hours the fever set in and Mossy was taken away again to another world, a world of pain where his body was nothing more than a giant pulse. For days he sweated and thrashed on the sofa, getting brief moments of clarity, the Men in Black staring down at him. Sometimes the poster read, *Protecting Scum From the World* and sometimes it read, *Get the Fuck Out of the Universe, Mallows, YOU Scum*. Whenever the world stopped turning, he screamed about his hands, rolling sideways on the sofa and yelling into the dark grille, *Give me back my fucking hands, you cunts.*

And now his strength is gone. His body has given up and all he can do is lie there, breathing weakly, and listen to the empty building creaking around him. It's easy to pretend that none of this has happened, that he never went to that counselling session, that he never met Skinny, and thinking about what it was like before it all went wrong makes his heart feel like it's cracking. Now that he's thinking straight he knows the truth. There's no going back. He's going to die here. He lets the voices come into his head, lets the few weak rays of sunlight come into his eyes and he knows it's the last sunshine he'll see.

And then, outside, behind the grille where the sunlight is and trees are green, the car's engine cuts and a door slams.

46

The interior of the Ford smelled stale, so Flea wound down the window as she drove to Kaiser's. It didn't take long. In less than half an hour the Mendips had her, with their dense forests and unexpected ravines, and she remembered how lonely the world could be. She came slowly up the drive, parked in the gravel bay, cut the engine and wound down the window. The sun was nearly at its zenith, with clouds flitting across it, the ground parched, the house uncared-for. A cat, asleep in the shade of a water butt, blinked and raised its head sleepily, but apart from that nothing moved. She looked up at the boarded-up windows, the curtains closed in all the others, and thought about the times she'd been here as a child. She tried to remember whether Kaiser's place had always seemed sinister or whether that feeling was new.

After a while, when no one came, she got out of the car and slammed the door. The noise echoed round the empty field and she hesitated, wondering if Kaiser had heard it inside. But when he didn't appear she took off her sunglasses and, stopping once or twice to pat one of the legion of dusty cats that came out of the weeds and rusting old machinery and butted her calves, went to the front porch and peered inside the plastic sheeting. When she couldn't hear anything she went round the side of the house.

The back door was unlocked and Kaiser's car was there, the rusty old Beetle, but there was no sign of him, neither in the outbuildings nor in the greenhouses. She went into the kitchen and stood there.

The plastic sheeting leading from there to the hallway was flapping very gently into the room as if a window was open somewhere. There was a half-eaten sandwich on the table — a few flies buzzing round it — three halves of avocado on a wooden block, their cut stones leaking a thick, blood-like liquid, and everywhere else the usual chaos of Kaiser's life, piles of *National Geographic* on the sideboard, a guinea pig staring at her, huddled on the floor of a cage on the table. She took off its water bottle and refilled it, wedged it between the bars and watched the little animal fasten its pink mouth round the nozzle, sucking noisily. Then she picked up the board and shovelled the avocados, with their leaking hearts, into the bin.

In the living room there was a plate with a paper napkin and crumbs on it, and in the centre a lawnmower engine in pieces lay on newspaper. Flea shook the mouse on the computer at the desk, but the screen was dead so she went to sit on the sofa where she'd spent Saturday and tried to remember lying there for eighteen hours. She pressed her hands into the sofa, peering down at it, as if she might get a flashback from its fabric. She tried to recall getting up and going to the computer, but all she could think about were the hallucinations: her parents' skeletonized bodies in the swirling waters of Bushman's Hole.

And her mother saying, *This time they're going to find us* . . .

She sat back, her arms folded. Arranged across the walls were the locked cabinets, the ones Mum used to say Kaiser kept his drugs in. Beyond that was the doorway where he'd stood yesterday, in his white shirt, his face in ruins. She thought of a picture she'd seen in his witchcraft book, the one in Dad's study. It showed a shaman dressed in a beaded shift, on his headdress a goat's skull, the eyes picked out with silver foil. She massaged her arms, and glanced over her shoulder, feeling momentarily cold, as if a draught had come in from the window behind her. Kaiser's African masks stared back at her. She'd seen them a million times. No reason to feel strange. Just that everything was weird now, with the way she'd spoken to the dead, the way she'd known her parents would be found.

She went into the hallway and called up the stairs. 'Kaiser? Are you there?'

No answer. She looked down the hallway, at the tattered walls, the paper hanging off in strips, the metal stepladder with a discarded plasterer's float tipped on its side. For all Kaiser's labours this house didn't get any more like a home. She understood why Mum and Thom were uncomfortable here — with the draught coming down the hall they'd never wanted to go further in.

She wondered if she should search the other rooms, check Kaiser wasn't lying somewhere with a broken leg, or the victim of a stroke maybe, and then, when there was absolute silence, just the distant clack-clack-clack of a loose window moving in the wind, she went back into the living room.

A red standby light shone on the television set and the videoplayer was whirring, the green numbers clicking by. She watched the numbers, she let her thoughts roll, and then, because she'd never known Kaiser watch videos before — in fact, she'd never known him watch television — she got the remote control and idly switched on the TV. It crackled reluctantly, then burst into life.

The sound was down, but before she could reach out for the remote control to turn it up an image came up on the screen. Shot in the slightly brown-stained colour of old film, it showed a man lying on a bed. What he was doing made her grip the remote tightly.

He was young, black and very thin. There were sweat stains on the plain khaki shirt he wore and his face and body were contorted with pain, his torso sprung up in the air like a bow, his jaw clenched. She couldn't see where the pain was coming from but it was real: sweat ran down his face. He stayed in that position, his face locked in agony, his body distorted, for about five seconds. Then something changed. The tension in him went. His eyes flew open as if he'd come back to consciousness. There was a breathless pause in which he remained bent up, away from the bed, eyes flicking backwards and forwards, unable to believe the pain had stopped. Then, in one shudder, he collapsed into a foetal shape, holding his knees. The screen flickered, then went blank.

Flea stared disbelievingly at the screen, not sure of what she had seen. She kept as still as she could for as long as she could, and then, when she couldn't think what else to do, she got up and ejected the videotape, dropping it on the little table, pulling her hand away as if she'd been burned. Her heart was thudding. Torture. That was what she'd watched. *Torture*. What the hell was Kaiser doing with a tape of torture in his house?

A noise from behind made her spin round, her mouth dry. Kaiser was in the doorway. He was wearing the same grass-stained white shirt as yesterday and was holding a pair of long-handled shears.

'Kaiser?' she said, her voice slow and suspicious. 'Kaiser — I don't get it . . .'

He didn't answer. Instead he gave a sad smile. It was the sort of smile that said he'd always hoped the world would never have brought him to this moment. It was the sort of smile that said this was one of those nasty necessities in life.

'Phoebe,' he said slowly. 'Phoebe. I think it's time we had a talk.'

47

The sound of the car door slamming makes Mossy come to a little. He opens his eyes and blinks, turning his head painfully to one side. He uses his upper arms to rub his eyes, trying to clear his vision, wondering why he's suddenly alert. It isn't unusual to hear cars outside. But there's something in the sound of this one that's different. As if it's got a purpose that's connected directly with him. Maybe it's the Peugeot.

He cranks his head back so he can see the gate, expecting light to flood in, to see Skinny. And there *is* something in the corridor, but it isn't Skinny. Mossy's heart starts to beat hard and monotonously, a trickle of fear coming cold in his veins. He's sure he can see it — something moving out there in the dark — something small, close to the ground. Something that might have been a trick of the light, but might also have been a shape moving fast. A shape with eyes.

'Hey?' he whispers. 'Who's there?'

Silence. But — he feels cold as the thought comes to him — he knows who it is. The brother. The one who took the bottle of blood out of the fridge and drank it. So he hasn't been alone all this time after all. The brother's been there all along. His heart goes even faster. Somehow he's sure the smell of his stumps will bring the brother in, make him sniff around.

'You fucker,' he hisses, his head seesawing

sickeningly, making him want to puke and cry at the same time. 'You try anything, you fucker, and I'll have you.'

The dark shape seems to hear him. There's a moment when it looks more like a shadow than ever, as if it might run straight up the wall, but then a tension comes into it, as if it's listening.

Jabbing his elbows into the arms of the sofa, Mossy struggles into a half-sitting position, head wobbling, teeth chattering. 'You arsehole,' he mutters. 'I'm ready for you.'

The shape reacts quickly to this. It coils itself into a ball. There's another pause, while Mossy hardly breathes, trying to get his body ready to fight. He raises his head and bares his teeth, ready to take a chunk out of the little bastard if he comes near. But nothing happens. The shape doesn't come towards him. Instead, after a moment or two, it slips silently away, leaving him staring at the space it left, his head pounding.

Mossy stays there for a long time, his eyes locked on the gate, his body tense, breathing hard. He wishes Skinny would hurry. If that was him in the car he wishes to Christ he'd come straight through. He fights the nausea he got from sitting up, wishing the little African was here, until at last he gives up and something pink and familiar and dark, like the insides of mouths and wounds, swims up inside his eyes and takes him back down.

48

In spite of all his instincts, he'd decided not to go to Kaiser Nduka's. For a moment, standing in the car park looking at Flea, Caffery'd had the feeling he was balanced on an edge, that a breath of air could send him one way or the other: to help her, or to keep going on his usual pattern of following the job regardless. In the old days he wouldn't have been swayed by what a woman said, so what did it tell him that with Flea he'd fallen effortlessly on to her side of the fence? He'd made a solemn promise to investigate the disappearance of a scag-head who was too busy whoring himself to turn up for one lousy meeting with his mother. Still, it had been a promise, and the choice he'd made — of doing something to help Flea — well, he had a feeling the Walking Man would say something about it. In fact, he had the weirdest feeling the Walking Man would approve.

And now here he was, looking at the bedroom in Jonah Dundas's tiny flat. It was small, just enough space for the single mattress and a large milk crate containing some balled-up T-shirts and a pair of trainers. The top pane of the metal-framed windows had been smashed through and carrier-bags from a supermarket — Eezy Pocket — had been taped over the hole. They sucked and blew, in and out, as the air currents fifteen storeys up moved and buffeted the building.

Faith Dundas and her ex-husband Rich were in the doorway, trying to see the room through Caffery's eyes, hoping he would pick up a clue they'd missed. Faith was an unremarkable woman, dressed in a plain navy blue skirt and a pink sweater, neat low-heel pumps on her feet. Her hair was greying, scraped back in a bun, and she didn't look like the mother of a drug addict, except that her eyes were swollen from crying. It made her look as if she'd been punched in the face. This was the thing with the parents of addicts, Caffery thought: either they kicked the kids out and let them take their chances in the world, or they became cuckoo parents, killing themselves to keep up with the child that took more than its fair share of everything.

'Did he say where he was going last night?' Caffery asked, with his back to the window. 'Anything at all?'

'No,' Faith said, in a muffled voice. She had a tissue pressed to her mouth and it was hard to decipher what she was saying. 'All he said was he had a job. A special job. I've been thinking about it and thinking about it, but I can't remember anything else.' Tears rolled down her face. 'I didn't pay him much attention. I thought I'd heard it all before and I just . . . ' Her voice trailed off into low sobs.

'What did he mean, 'a special job'?'

She shook her head, more tears squeezing out of her eyes. Caffery raised his eyebrows questioningly at her ex-husband.

Dundas cleared his throat, squaring his shoulders. 'He was . . . I don't know. Going to make a lot of money.'

'How much is a lot?'

'One thousand eight hundred pounds.' He looked sideways at his wife. 'That's what he told her anyway.'

'One thousand eight hundred . . . ' Caffery shook his head. 'Nearly two K? What sort of job was he going to do?'

'I don't know.'

'I mean, that's one hell of a night's work,' Caffery said. 'You've got to agree — it's one hell of a good night.'

'I wasn't there.' He glanced down at the top of his ex-wife's head. 'Maybe if I was there I'd've . . . ' His big face tightened, as if he was going to cry. 'I'm sorry,' he said, putting a finger on the end of his nose and closing his eyes as if that might calm him. 'It's hard to say what he was going to do when I wasn't even there.'

Caffery picked up a T-shirt. It was balled tight, glued together by something white and crusty. He didn't want to think about what it was, so he dropped it and brushed off his hands. He eyed the pathetic mattress with its rucked nylon sheets and lumpy pillow. He told himself he'd been right not to have children with Rebecca. That he'd never have to be in Faith's position, in tears over the loss of someone who'd sucked him dry the way Jonah had his mother.

'He's sold his belongings, hasn't he?'

Faith stopped crying. She held her breath for a moment, then said, 'Yes. I believe he has.'

'Things you bought him?'

She nodded again.

'To keep his habit going?'

'I think . . . I think maybe.'

Dundas pulled her closer. He looked directly into Caffery's eyes, a hint of anger there. Trying to protect his ex-wife from herself. 'He'd been telling his mother he'd found a way to pull out of his addiction.'

'I see.'

'It might have been the truth.'

Caffery nodded neutrally. 'It might.'

'He said he'd made up his mind. He was going to clear his debts and use the rest to get off the gear.'

'And I suppose she gave him the money.'

'Not this time. This time she said no.'

Faith looked up at her husband, her chest in the marshmallow-pink sweater heaving. 'And now look.' She sobbed. 'Now look.' She buried her face in his chest, her voice rising higher and higher. 'And now look what's happened. Now they're going to cut off his hands, like they did to that other poor boy, and if they take his hands, if they do what they did to the other one, then I'll have to die too. Do you hear me? *I'll have to die too.*'

At these words Dundas went very still. He lifted his eyes and met Caffery's. He didn't say a word, but it was the kind of look that said paragraphs. Whole pages. They both knew what the other was thinking.

'Uh . . . Faith?' Caffery said. 'Why do you — what makes you think that's going to happen? What you said about his hands. What made you say that?'

'He's been here,' she whispered. 'Here in this flat. He used to come here sometimes. Jonah told me.'

'Who's been here?'

'Him. That poor lad.'

'*Mallows?*' Caffery glanced at Dundas and saw the words had come at him with a thump too. His face was grey, blue-veined. 'Faith?' he said. 'You're telling us Jonah knew Ian Mallows?'

'They were good friends.'

Caffery's thoughts moved very slowly, slowly but clearly — Jonah and Mossy. Jonah and Mossy. He put his face near to the window, staring past trickles of condensation trapped in the double-glazing. The brown lawns and parking spaces two hundred feet down looked as if they belonged to a different world, the people just specks of colour. In his head was BM's voice: *He said people were going to get hurt. I remember him saying it now — said, 'There are some sickos out there, BM, and I don't know who they'd go out and hurt if it wasn't for people like me, stupid fuckers who give it up without a fight.'*

★ ★ ★

In the end there was something about the fear and misery in Jonah's flat that Caffery couldn't bear. He called a family-liaison officer for the Dundases and when she arrived he made his excuses, rode the eighteen flights down in the lift and sat locked in the car to make the rest of the calls. He spoke to the inspector at Trinity Road, then to his SIO, and within half an hour he had door-to-door teams organized, bringing in half of the team that were out interviewing the drugs charities. When he'd done that he tried calling Flea's unit phone even though he knew she wouldn't answer. The acting sergeant was understanding, gave him Flea's private number, but the call was diverted straight into her voicemail. He didn't know what to say, so he hung up.

He sat for a while, watching a gang of hoodies glowering at him from the tower lobby — they could smell cop faster than they could spit, these kids — and he wondered about the money Jonah thought he was going to make. Eighteen hundred quid. Just a tad more than TIDARA were charging addicts to get clean. The pamphlet sat on the passenger seat and he picked it up, looking at the gnarled root, with his biro markings round it. He pulled out the phone again and called the multimedia unit in Portishead to tell them that when they'd found the CCTV footage of Mossy they needed to send a still of the guy in the white shirt to his phone. Then he switched the car engine on and slowly, slowly, let it ease out of the estate.

He was thinking about ibogaine again. Ibogaine and Kaiser Nduka, who knew all there was to know about how it was used in religious ritual. His address was in the Mendips, not far away: just one exit along the M4. Not far. The team could pick up here — he'd have time to get there and back. And, anyway, he had an itch that Nduka was important to the investigation.

Nduka lived in a part of north Somerset that had a look of France, with derelict stone buildings and wooded lanes that wound up and down the sides of hills.

Caffery drove slowly through clouds of midges, stopping once for a string of riding-school horses to trail past. The entrance to the driveway was easy to find, an oval wooden sign tucked into the hedgerow, the words 'Dear Holme' carved into it — a relic from when the place was built, by the look of it. From the road the going got rougher. The driveway rose steeply and was unkempt, with ruts and potholes and overhanging cowslips that brushed the car and left pollen traces on the windscreen. He felt as if he was coming through a jungle, as if he was venturing off the map, and when he looked at his phone display he wasn't surprised to see the signal icon shrink then be replaced by a crossed-out phone.

'Shit,' Caffery muttered. He shoved the phone into his breast pocket and drove on, losing all sense of direction until suddenly the overhanging plants and trees cleared, he passed a little area of overgrown grass, and the drive opened out. He was about a hundred yards from a ramshackle nineteen-fifties house, perched on the edge of a sweeping valley and surrounded by tumbledown outhouses. There were weeds in the asphalt, panes of glass — maybe dismantled greenhouses — piled up on the verge, and boards over some of the lower windows. It was deserted and forgotten-looking, but it wasn't the house that was making his heart thud. It was what was parked with its nose facing the front door.

A silver Ford Focus.

The number plate started 'Y9'. Flea's plate began with 'Y9' — he'd noticed that this morning in the car park at HQ. It wasn't much of a coincidence — there'd be hundreds of Y-reg silver Ford Focuses in the area. It was other things he'd noticed in the car park that bothered him more about this car: the tiny piece of material poking out of the closed boot as if she'd carelessly shut it on something, and the navy force holdall on the backshelf. Those couldn't be coincidence too.

Turning to the house, Caffery couldn't say why, but he had an image of things happening out here that couldn't be explained — of people doing brutal dances in the dark. Kaiser was one of the country's leading experts on witchcraft. He had a connection with TIDARA. Something cold trickled through his veins. What had Mabuza said? That the intellectuals were trying to set him up?

He slowed the car, letting it creep forward. Going quietly, taking care not to do anything quickly that might alert anyone inside the house, he turned off the drive into the grass, making a U-turn so the car was facing towards the road. He killed the engine and got out, closing the door with a quiet click. He didn't like places like this, desolate and uncared-for: they reminded him of a place he had been to once in Norfolk, a place where he'd once thought he might find clues about Ewan.

He stepped into the grass and approached

slowly. There were no sounds, only the click-click-click of his car engine cooling behind him. A cat lying in the shade of a water butt opened its eyes and regarded him contemplatively. He got to the side of the house and stood in the shadow, the heat in the brick radiating against his back, feeling idiotic, creeping about like the SAS. He took off his jacket and draped it over the handle of a rusting garden roller, wiped his forehead with his sleeve and began to count. When he got to ten he'd walk to the front door and ring the bell, be official, say he wanted to talk about work. He'd laugh about it, stop tilting at windmills.

And that's exactly what he would have done if, by the time he'd counted to five, someone inside the house, someone only on the other side of the wall, hadn't begun to scream.

49

He'd been in the job long enough to know when to follow his training and when not to. He knew this was a time when he should follow everything he'd been taught and put in a call to Control, but the red light on the radio was blinking, telling him it was out of range too. He wasn't going to drive back down into signal range so he did the exact opposite of what he should have done. He kept going.

About four feet away from him, resting against one of the piles of glass, was a wooden handle. It had belonged to a pickaxe or a shovel and it was exactly the right size and weight. He snatched it up and backed into the lee of the house, standing with the handle out, his arms trembling. The screaming stopped and he edged forward to the nearest window, straining to hear what was happening. Then he squatted and crab-walked his way under the ledge, straightened and went to the corner of the house, put his back to the wall as if he was in a western shoot-out, and peered round it.

A cloud had gone across the sun and the front of the house was in shadow, the greying pebbledash pocked in places as if it had taken shrapnel. The cat was still sitting there, washing its face, as if nothing was happening. About ten feet past it, what must have been the front porch was shrouded in plastic sheeting. Bricks had been piled on top to hold it in place. Caffery edged towards it, breathing hard, the wooden handle held out in front of him.

He got to the porch and lifted the edge of the sheeting tentatively. From here he could see there was no front door. Instead the gap had been clumsily covered with blue membrane, the manufacturer's logo printed on it in white. Carefully, trying not to make any noise, he ducked under the plastic sheet and stepped inside, pressing a finger to the plastic membrane. It gave a little. He wiped away the cobwebs from his face and hair, and stood close to it, holding his breath. The screaming had stopped: he couldn't hear a thing, not a sound or a movement. A voice in the back of his head told him to back off, *back off, idiot* . . . but instead he got out his car keys and used the little Swiss Army knife on the fob to make a hole in the blue plastic.

As the knife went in he stopped, thinking what it might look like from inside — a bulge and then the little nose of the knife poking through, glinting maybe. His heart was thudding and he could feel sweat run from his armpits, making his sides and back itch. He counted to ten, then, when no one came running out at him, he slid the knife cleanly down the membrane making a long, straight slit. He stepped back, shocked by the noise, breathing hard.

After a minute or so when there was still nothing from inside, he crouched next to the slit and pushed one finger in, pulling it aside so he could see a few yards into the dim interior and listen. There was a smell of neglect and decay, a smell of raw concrete and stagnant water, and a lazy flapping, like slow wings beating somewhere in the darkness. Nothing else except the eerie silence.

He used the wooden handle to push into the gap and moved aside the sheeting, feeling the cooler air inside shift across his skin. Carefully he put one foot through, and then, with a quick sideways twist, followed it inside, dropping into a crouch. He held his breath and listened again. It was a moment or two before his eyes were used to the dark, but when they were he saw what had caused the flapping noise: every doorway leading away from this area was covered with white plastic sheeting, taped at the top with slits at the sides, lifting and rippling on unseen currents. With the deathly hush and stale air he couldn't help thinking of mortuaries.

Slowly he went to the first piece of sheeting and looked through into what had once been a utility area. The washing-machine was still in the corner, but it hadn't been used recently. Boxes of books were piled up in front of it, and the ironing-board was draped with filthy tea-towels. He moved to the next sheet and found he was looking into a kitchen — left-over food on the table, magazines piled everywhere, a guinea pig staring beadily at him from a cage on the work surface. He was about to go through the next sheet when, from the other side, the screaming started again.

50

Run until the world ends . . . Run until the world ends . . .

As he lies on the sofa, his eyes moving under the lids, Skinny's words make patterns in Mossy's head, repeating themselves in long, feverish strings. *Run until the world ends . . .*

He's too submerged in his thoughts to notice the shadow return in the corridor. It hovers there, yellowing eyes watching him thoughtfully, and it might have stayed there if it hadn't been for a door opening. The shadow scuttles away just as light floods into the corridor. There's the sound of another door closing and, in the background, low, vicious voices.

Mossy opens his heavy eyes. His head is thick but he can see people out there — not just one or two but more. He can see shadows on the wall, can hear the muttered threats. Someone raises a hand and there's a scuffle. There's a noise too. It starts as a hoarse sob, then stretches into a long drawn-out cry, so high and thin it might be a girl screaming.

'Keep the noise down,' someone hisses. 'Keep the fucking noise down.'

Something heavy and clumsy falls on the floor and immediately the screaming stops.

Mossy's awake now. He sits upright, staring at the gate. He can't see anything from this angle: whatever's happening is happening out of sight, but too far down the corridor to see. From the sounds he can guess. Whoever was screaming has stopped because they've been thrown down, maybe knocked out. There's a gagging sound, then a noise like water being poured on the floor or someone throwing up. Then silence.

Mossy stays where he is, his heart leaping in his chest, wanting to cry. He prays that it's Jonah he can hear, arrived at last. He wants it so much that he knows he's not going to welcome him, be humble. He'll yell at him and strangle him, because the bastard needs to know that it's too late now, and that whatever happens next, whatever he'll go through, whatever sacrifices he'll make, none of it'll matter. None of it will matter because he's *too fucking late*.

★ ★ ★

Caffery came through the sheeting into the living room fast, the wooden bar behind him, his hand over his breast pocket where his warrant-card holder was, neat and efficient. He might have appeared calm, but the aggression was there, more than it had ever been. He scanned the room: the standard 360-degree sweep. He'd come in behind a large sofa that faced a TV on the far wall where a grainy black-and-white image played — a young man dressed in a khaki shirt squirming and turning on a bed, his screams filling the air. On the sofa a man's big carved face, a halo of greying curly hair, was turned to him.

'Kaiser Nduka?' he shouted, above the

screams. 'Are you Kaiser Nduka?'

'Who are you?'

Caffery flicked out his warrant card, holding it out to him, still ready to bring down the wooden handle if the weird fucker did anything. Flea wasn't in the room. An engine was in pieces on the floor and a pair of gardening shears on the table. He monitored the shears out of the corner of his eye while Nduka inspected the card, his big nose twitching as if he could smell it. Then he sat back resignedly on the sofa. 'I see,' he mouthed. His face was calm, almost mournful, as if it was a terrible shame it had worked out like this. 'I understand.'

Caffery stepped carefully round the sofa past the engine. Mounted on the wall ahead was a cupboard, the doors open to reveal row after row of videotapes, about forty lined up, all bearing a white label. He snatched up the remote control from the table and turned down the volume. The sudden quiet in the room was almost as shocking as the screaming. On screen the man on the bed continued convulsing silently, his arms going up and down like a marionette's. He'd wet himself, Caffery saw. A dark stain was spreading across the sheet.

'OK,' Caffery said. 'What the fuck's that all about?'

Nduka shrugged pointedly, as if he was weary of the way the police behaved but knew he had to go along with it. 'An experiment.'

'An *experiment*?' Caffery's fingers on the wooden handle were sweating. 'You weird fuck. You made that video for your clients, didn't you?

402

To let them know how genuine the goods are.'

Nduka passed a sinewy, elongated hand across his forehead. 'I don't know what you're talking about.'

'You gave it to your punters.'

'I'm sorry?'

'I said.' He gritted his teeth, pointing a finger at him. 'I said is *this*, are *those* — ' He gestured at the banks of videos in the cupboard. 'Are they the videos you give to your punters?'

'They're very old.'

'I don't care how fucking old they are. That wasn't the question. The question is, are these the ones you give to your clients?'

'The young man consented to what was done to him. He allowed it to happen. But maybe human consent means nothing to you. And while I appreciate your being here, if you want to arrest me then arrest me for *that*.' He raised a hand to indicate the outhouses. 'For the magic mushrooms I'm growing there, with the marijuana, the skunk weed and all the other things. In fact, do you know I'd rather welcome that? The publicity might stop the university harassing me about my research assessment quotas. You should arrest me for that and not for — '

'Shut up,' Caffery said coldly. 'Just shut up.'

Nduka gave him a serene, almost pleasant smile, as if they were having a nice cup of tea on a sunny afternoon. And, very calmly, he stood and reached sideways for the shears.

'No you fucking don't.' Caffery hefted the handle and slipped round the side of the coffee-table, skidding in his work shoes but getting there just in time to knock the shears off the table. They fell with a loud clatter, spinning and clattering across the floor, making both men take a step back, surprised at how quickly this had become violent.

Nduka lifted his arms into the air, as if he'd never intended going near the shears. He took a breath, walked back a few tottering paces, and stood in the middle of the room, wiping his hands on his shirt as if he was confused and the solution would be to get his hands clean.

'Move,' Caffery said. 'Back — back to the sofa. That's it.'

'Of course,' Nduka said, blinking a little. He sat, his long legs jack-knifed almost to his chest, his arms half folded round himself. 'Of course.'

'And stay there.' Caffery jabbed a finger at him. 'Right there.' He held the finger for a few more moments, until he was sure Nduka wasn't going to move. Then he went to one of the curtains and flipped it aside. Flea's car was sitting outside in the sun. 'That's Sergeant Marley's car out there.'

'Whose car?'

'Sergeant Marley. You know who I'm talking about.'

'Phoebe, you mean?'

'What's she doing here?'

'She came to see me.'

'About what?'

'A personal matter.'

Caffery dropped the curtain. 'A *personal* matter? What? Now you're telling me she's a fucking friend of yours?'

Nduka didn't answer. He just went on looking at Caffery with his deep brown eyes, something almost amused in his face.

Caffery felt the blood rush to his head. 'What have you done with her, then?' His voice was calm even though sweat was running down his back. 'Where is she?'

'Oh, she's . . . ' Nduka rubbed his forehead. 'Yes, she's busy.' His hand half covered his face, but not enough to stop Caffery seeing that his eyes had flickered in the direction of the hall.

'The hall?' he said, pushing himself away from the window. 'Is that where I need to go?'

Nduka didn't answer. He kept his hand where it was, half covering his eyes.

'Yes,' Caffery said. 'In the hall.' He went back to the doorway, flipped back the sheeting and peered into the darkness. 'What's down there?'

Nduka dropped his hand. 'My house. It's not very beautiful, I grant you, but it's my house.'

'Show me, then.' Caffery beckoned to him. 'Come on, shithole, show me.'

As if his back was paining him, Nduka got up and came forward slowly, placing one foot carefully in front of the other, as if this was a dance he was performing. At the door he threw Caffery a sideways glance with arched eyebrows.

'You first,' Caffery said, keeping his back to the wall, clutching the wooden handle in both hands. 'I'm not letting you walk behind me.'

With a mournful expression Nduka moved past him and began to walk into the gloom on his long, stiff legs. Caffery dropped the plastic

405

sheeting and followed a few steps back, still holding the wooden handle, ready to use it. It was difficult to see but the hallway was carpeted in something old and threadbare, something paint-splattered. DIY warehouse architraves had been clumsily glued into the gaps between wall and ceiling, and the wallpaper had been half removed, then abandoned. There was a cold stale draught coming through here that made the hairs on the back of Caffery's neck stand up.

'The videos were done when I was at university,' Nduka said, from the gloom ahead.

'Shut the fuck up about the videos.'

'They volunteered. All the young people volunteered.'

'I said shut up. Tell me what you've done with her.'

Nduka stopped. He pointed to the end of the corridor where another door was covered with plastic, something on the other side giving it a blue, ethereal light, almost like in a hospital. For a moment neither man moved. Caffery's heart was beating faster, but he approached, holding the handle in front of him. He took a deep breath, pushed aside the sheeting and found himself in a large conservatory, sunshine slanting through dusty windows. It was unpainted and smelled of turps and solvent. It was empty.

He turned to Nduka. 'She's not fucking here.'

'Oh, she is,' he said unconcernedly. On their right, painted pale blue, a door led back into the house. He nodded to it. 'I put her in there.'

From his mental map of the house Caffery knew it would lead into the side of the kitchen.

He took an automatic step towards it, then stopped, his chest constricting. Suddenly he was back seven years at a small bungalow in the back-waters of Kent. He was back to a psychopath who had told him where a woman could be found, a psycho who'd enjoyed letting Caffery go and find her and discover all that had been done to her. It wasn't anything to do with the door, it was Nduka's calm that made him think of it. That, and maybe the location — a deserted house with only trees and sky for company.

He clenched his fists, held them, then released them. Did it once again. Then he looked sideways at Nduka. 'You open it,' he said, feeling something under his sternum squirm. 'Go on. You open it.'

Nduka pressed a finger against his temple. 'Well,' he said, 'if I must.'

He stepped forward and pushed the door inwards. Beyond it there was a small well-lit room, books stacked floor to ceiling, a reading light hung low. There wasn't much space in there with the desks and the huge box files crammed with paper, but in the centre Flea sat, in a black sweatshirt, her hair in a ponytail. On her lap was a pile of papers. As the door opened she turned her eyes, seeming surprised.

'You?' she said, blinking at him. 'What are *you* doing here?'

Caffery didn't answer. He didn't care, he told himself. He didn't give a shit about her. He said it to himself slowly in his brain, his eyes closed, the sun filtering through his eyelids: *You don't care if she lives or if she dies.*

51

He was the last person she'd expected to see: Caffery standing in Kaiser's conservatory in his shirt, dust on his sleeves, clutching something that might have been a pitchfork handle. One moment she'd been sitting there, going through the thirty-year-old paperwork Kaiser had given her, a slow feeling of dread as she read, knowing that this was connected somehow to her father, and the next moment the room was flooded with air and light.

'Kaiser?' she asked, but his face was blank, as if something awful had happened between the two of them. There was no expression on Caffery's face either, just his watery eyes on hers, emotions working their way through him. For a moment she thought he looked sad. Then she got the impression that it wasn't sadness but anger, that he was about to hit her. Lastly came something cold creeping into his face, as if the only thing he felt for her was contempt. He took his hand off the door and turned away into the conservatory.

'What are you doing here?' she repeated, putting down the stack of papers and getting to her feet. 'How did you get here?'

'Fucking hell,' he muttered. 'I'll never get used to this, the way people lie to each other.'

'What?' she said. She followed him into the bright daylight. 'What does that mean?'

But he wasn't listening. He threw the pitchfork handle on to the floor — it spun away, hitting the wall — then grabbed Kaiser's arm. Before she knew what was happening he'd pushed him roughly back into the little room. Kaiser didn't resist, just allowed himself to be manhandled, not objecting when Caffery closed the door and turned the key.

'Hey,' she said, reaching out to grab his hands. 'What do you think you're doing?'

He snatched away his hand and pocketed the key. 'Shut up. Or you can go in there with him.' He headed back to the corridor.

She paused — not believing this was happening — then caught up with him. 'You're supposed to be looking for Jonah. You promised. What're you doing here?'

He didn't answer. Instead he went into the kitchen and began to open the cupboards, pulling things out, crouching to look inside. 'What?' She stopped in the doorway and watched him. 'What're you looking for?'

He ignored her, straightened and opened the utility-room door, roughly pulling aside boxes and bin-liners. 'I said, what are you looking for?'

'For Mallows's body.' He pushed past her, going back into the hall. 'Remember? The one who got his hands cut off.'

She stared at him as he mounted the stairs two at a time. At first the name Mallows didn't make any sense. Then the daze broke. '*Mallows?*' she said, following him. She caught up with him on the landing where he was opening doors, pulling aside curtains, delving into wardrobes.

'What the hell makes you think he's here?'

He went into the bathroom, kicking at the bath panelling, looking into the airing cupboard. 'Your mate downstairs is a little too close to the last place Mallows was seen alive. And you know about the videos he's got, apparently. Strange that, a serving police officer knowing about videos of people being tortured.'

'The videos?' She licked her dry lips. 'Yes, yes, I do. But they're . . . '

'Torture. They're videos of someone being tortured.'

'But not Mallows.'

'Are you sure?' He went into the next bedroom, picking his way through the piles of clothes and books. He checked under the bed, then threw open the wardrobe door. 'You're telling me one of those in that bookcase of his doesn't show Mallows having his hands taken off, having his blood taken? Is that what you're saying?'

'They're old films. They happened in the eighties.'

'That's what he *says*.'

Flea came into the room and closed the door behind her. She didn't like it being open, with the echoey rooms downstairs, the row after row of videos beneath and Kaiser locked in the study. She went to the bed, sat heavily on it and massaged her temples, thinking about Mum saying, 'If you want my opinion what he did really was immoral. It was outrageous.'

Caffery was staring at her. A bead of sweat rolled down his forehead. 'Well?'

410

'Oh, Christ,' she whispered, rubbing her arms because goosebumps had come up on them. 'I don't know. He's my father's friend, and I always knew he did something wrong years ago, I just never knew how really, *really* fucking wrong it was. I haven't worked it all out yet, but he was . . . ' She trailed off, not liking the words. 'I've seen eight of the videos — they're all the same. Electrodes. That's what he was using. It was an experiment.'

'An *experiment*?'

'I know. All done in the name of science.' She pushed her fingers into her temples, as if that would get rid of the pressure. 'Things must have been different then, and it wasn't here, it was in Nigeria, in Ibadon — and, you know, maybe the ethics were different because nobody stopped him. Not until the very end. The, uh, the people you saw — '

'I only saw one.'

'There are more, lots more, but they consented. I've seen the consent forms — that's what I was going through when you came in. They were mostly research students. The others came off the streets, did it for money.' She paused because something had just hit her. Thom's night terrors. He'd always been convinced Kaiser used to hunt people in the streets at night. She felt cold. Maybe Thom had always known the truth. Or suspected it. What she'd said to Caffery was true. The videos could be explained away — sinister, but not as sinister as he was thinking. But on a deep level, in a low part of her stomach, she knew they were sinister

411

because they said something about Dad she didn't want to think about.

She wiped her forehead, trying to keep her face composed. 'So — you see what I mean? Nothing to do with Mallows.'

Caffery took a weary breath. He looked as if he hadn't slept in years. 'I should at least lodge a report at Weston and get a section eight warrant raised.'

'Technically,' she muttered. 'Yes, you should.'

'Except I can't nick him here in the UK. Unless he was a public official in Nigeria at the time. Which I take it he wasn't?'

'No.'

'In that case it's over to — '

'Interpol,' she said. 'I know — I've already thought about it.'

He held her eyes a little longer. Then he let go of the door and pulled at his tie until it was loose enough to lift over his head. 'Come on,' he said, as he thrust it into his breast pocket. 'We'll cross that bridge when we come to it. Right now I've got something else I want to talk to the old bastard about.'

★ ★ ★

'Secondary attention. The 'path of the heart'. A place, a crevice in our consciousness we sometimes stumble into — the place of enlightenment.'

Kaiser talked quietly as he allowed Caffery to lead him back down the corridor, his oversized trousers hanging half off his skinny frame. Flea followed a few paces behind, wishing she could stop him talking. She didn't want to hear what he might have to say about Dad and the videos.

'The Christian Church,' he went on, 'tries to pretend it doesn't exist. But other religions aren't so coy — the ancient religions, I mean, the ones born out of passion and intelligence, an understanding of the earth and the way the seasons move, not the ones spread and imposed through politics and imperialism.'

'What were you doing at that clinic?' Caffery said, propelling him into the living room.

Kaiser settled down on the sofa and, as if he hadn't heard the question, continued, 'The ancient religions understand that there is a place we rarely have access to that is the place of true enlightenment. It is a difficult, *very* difficult, place to access. To study.'

'Kaiser . . . ' Flea said. She was facing him with her back to the open cupboard: the cupboard she'd believed all her life had contained drugs, her fists held clenched behind her back. 'Answer the question, Kaiser.'

'It exists in all of us. Every one of us can find it, but only a few ever do. Except, of course, when we die. For the few seconds before we die our neural pathways are programmed to close down in such a way that they allow us the briefest entry to that place — the place I am drawn to.'

Caffery picked up the pair of gardening shears from the floor and set them at the back of the room. Then he crossed his arms and leaned against the window. In one hand he was holding

413

a bundle of papers: the consent forms Flea had dropped on to the floor. 'I asked you what you were doing at the clinic. Can you answer that question?'

'Ah, yes, but I am trying to explain why I was forced to use *pain* as the nearest approximation to death. Some believe another route exists through certain hallucinogens. For example, Phoebe's father — '

'*Kaiser!*' she said abruptly, startling him. '*Answer the question.*'

Kaiser looked at her, shocked. 'What question?'

'My question.' Caffery moved away from the window and pulled out a chair from the dusty dining-table. He set it in front of the sofa and sat, hunched over with his elbows on his knees, scowling at Kaiser. 'My question was, what's your involvement with TIDARA?'

'TIDARA?'

'In Glastonbury. It's the last place Ian Mallows was seen alive.'

'Ian Mallows?'

'Don't pretend you don't know who I'm talking about.'

Kaiser blinked. He looked at Flea for interpretation. She held his eyes. Kaiser: one of the only friends she'd thought she had. And now it was all upside-down. She had to struggle to keep her voice in control.

'I'd know if he was lying,' she muttered. 'He doesn't know anything.'

Caffery sighed. He cast the consent forms on to the table and sat back, putting his hands

414

behind his head and stretching a little, as if he'd come in from a hard day and was relaxing. But it was an act. She could see that he was shaking, as if the adrenalin from earlier was still in his system. 'They told me you'd been observing their work.'

'Ah, yes.' Kaiser took a handkerchief from his pocket and wiped his forehead. 'It was part of a body of research I was doing. The results will be published in the *British Journal of Psychology* this September. The use of ibogaine in withdrawal from the opiates.'

'So tell me about it. Tell me about ibogaine.'

Standing behind Caffery, Flea gave Kaiser a fierce look. The last thing she needed was Caffery knowing she'd taken it. Kaiser gestured to the books on the shelves. 'If I may?' he said. 'I have some literature.'

'Go on, then.'

Kaiser got up stiffly and went to the shelves, hauling books down and piling them in front of Caffery. He propped broken glasses on the end of his nose and sat down, leafing through the books, holding out photos of tribal dances, fetishes and masks for Caffery to look at. 'Ibogaine is from the Bwiti tribe. It is used to dislodge memories from the mind.'

Flea came to the sofa and sat on the arm. She wanted to be ready to stop Kaiser if he went too far. But Caffery spoke: 'Is it used in black magic? In African witchcraft?'

'*African witchcraft?*' Kaiser peered over his glasses as if Caffery was a mystery. 'I'm not sure which of those two words is the most ignorant and patronizing. To describe a deep-seated cultural belief as 'witchcraft' or to apply the universal label 'African' instead of using the name of a tribe or, at the very least, a country. Even if the concept of a country is a colonialist construct, it's better than giving them all one title — 'African'. Tell me, do you recall the case of that poor child's torso in the Thames?'

'I know what you're talking about, yes.'

'The way it was handled by the police — another astonishing Western misconception of how the African continent works. The child's genitals weren't removed, if I remember correctly?'

'That's right.'

'So even before your people conducted the tests I could have told them that South Africa *muti* was the wrong place to look for his killers. In South African *muti* he would have had his genitals removed — it would have been the first thing. And yet how strange it was that although the child came from Nigeria your police gravitated to South Africa. That they talked to Nelson Mandela. One asks oneself what Nelson Mandela has to do with a small Nigerian child. So when you say 'African witchcraft' you're conveniently forgetting you're not only talking about a deeply rooted faith but about the beliefs of forty-seven different countries and countless different tribes. Medicine and mystic belief vary enormously from region to region.'

Caffery had opened his mouth to speak, but something in Kaiser's last sentence seemed to strike him. He was silent, thinking about it, then he frowned. 'You can be specific about what area a belief or superstition comes from?'

'Fairly specific — fairly.'

Caffery studied him thoughtfully. 'Have you heard of the Tokoloshe?' he asked.

'The what?' Flea said.

'The Tokoloshe,' Kaiser said. 'People say he's the result of a mating between a human female and a baboon and, indeed, one does occasionally hear anecdotal evidence of women trying to conceive a Tokoloshe.'

Caffery raised an eyebrow. Kaiser smiled. 'Yes — it shows the belief and respect some people invest in him, doesn't it? Of course, left to his own devices the Tokoloshe is hardly a danger, only a nuisance. But he's a witch's familiar and it's *then*, when he's under the influence of a witch, you need to have regard for the Tokoloshe. *That*'s when you need to take special precautions.' Kaiser held up a book. 'This man claimed his truck had run over a Tokoloshe on a Drakensburg highway. A fake, naturally, but can you see how clever it was — you can understand why people were taken in.'

When Caffery took the book she could tell from his eyes that he was looking at something monstrous. She could half see its reflection, but more clearly she could see the effect it had on him.

'Can I look?'

He held out the book for her to see. The photo showed a man in rolled-up shirtsleeves holding up a small dried-out corpse, flattened into a round, blackish pancake the way rabbits and badgers were flattened on the local Somerset roads. The black arms were out to the sides like an angel's, the squashed head turned sideways, mouth open. She felt a finger of unease work its way up her back as she stared at this strange, twisted corpse.

'An ex-colleague in Nigeria got hold of the cadaver,' Kaiser said. 'In fact, he paid for it, almost three thousand rand I'm told, because the man drove a hard bargain. It turned out to be a baboon with a human skull grafted on to it, both burned then left out in the sun. I think there was a police inquiry, but they never found out whose head it was. One assumes it was retrieved from some unfortunate's grave.'

'And this was in South Africa?'

'Yes.'

'Is Tokoloshe specific to South Africa?'

'Water sprites like him crop up all over the continent with different names — the crocodile god, for example. But in South Africa and up into parts of Malawi, Mozambique and Zimbabwe he's the Tokoloshe.'

'What about the tradition of offering him a bowl of human blood?'

'Human blood? Yes — off the top of my head I'd guess that tradition comes from Natal or Gauteng, not from the Cape.'

Caffery grunted. 'Thank you.' He closed the book and got to his feet, holding out his mobile phone to Kaiser, showing him the screen. 'Anywhere round here I can get a signal?'

'There's a mast in the north of the valley. I don't use a portable phone but I'm told one can

418

get reception from the back of the house. Go through the conservatory.'

Caffery left the room, and Kaiser — suddenly seeming a little lost — sat back, deflated. Neither spoke for a while. She stared at him, the droopy brown eyes, the huge head and the thought of the way he'd appeared to her in the dooway: an animal skull in a white shirt. She'd always thought she and Kaiser were close — now she wondered whether she knew him at all.

'The videos,' she said eventually. 'Dad knew about them, didn't he?'

Kaiser sighed. He inclined his head, nodding almost imperceptibly. 'I can't lie to you, Phoebe. Yes, he knew.'

'He was involved in the experiment, wasn't he? I heard you talking about it the night before the accident.'

'This is something we shouldn't be discussing. David is gone now. He can't explain it to you because he hasn't got a voice any more.'

'No,' she said bitterly. 'No, he hasn't.'

Kaiser shifted in the chair. 'Well? Is that what you came here for?'

She didn't answer. She didn't want to tell him about Mum and Dad's bodies being found, or ask him how she'd known it would happen; she didn't want to talk about ibogaine or whether she'd been on the computer during the trip. No, she decided. I won't tell you anything. You said once that there are roads I have to travel alone, and you're right. This road is a long one, and at the moment I don't trust you to walk it with me. She closed the book, shutting away the picture of

419

the awful dead Tokoloshe.

'Phoebe?' Kaiser said, but she stood up and left the room, going down the corridor, into the conservatory to find Caffery.

He was standing in profile with the phone to his ear, looking out at the valley. He ended his call and turned. 'What?' he mouthed through the glass. 'What is it?'

She opened the conservatory door, stepping out into the sunshine. There was the smell of mould, grass clippings and distant cows. She saw he was still shaking, just a little.

'Are you OK?'

He nodded.

'What is it?'

'Nothing.'

'Nothing?'

'I thought you were in trouble, OK? Back then, when you were in that study. I was wrong, but it doesn't change the way I thought I was going to come in and find you — '

'Yes?'

He bit his lip and shot her a sideways glance. Although the side of his face nearest her was in shadow there was enough light for her to see him clearly — and she couldn't help staring. His tight, slightly feral face was tired and defeated. 'Not now,' he said turning back to the horizon. 'Not now.'

She blinked, tried not to stare. 'Is that all? Is that the problem?'

He shook his head, and now she saw there was something else on his mind.

'What? What is it?'

'Jonah.'

'Oh, Christ,' she said flatly. 'What?'

'Something his family didn't mention before — something that turns it all round, that makes me scared for him,' Caffery said.

'Makes you scared?' she whispered, a soft *whump* of panic under her solar plexus, as if someone had punched her there. 'What? What didn't they mention?'

'Mallows. He and Dundas's lad — '

'Oh, shit.' Flea felt as if something was falling inside her. Suddenly she saw it: the same habit, the same background. Of course — of course. They must have known each other. 'Shit. I know what you're going to tell me. Shit, oh, shit.'

Caffery pocketed his phone, took out his keys and headed away from her, back round the side of the house. She followed at a trot, drawing level with him at the front of the house. He was picking up his jacket from a rusting garden roller. He glanced at her. 'It's OK. You go back to Kaiser.'

'What are you doing?'

'I'm going to work.' He put on the jacket and went towards his car.

'No.' She kept pace with him, walking fast alongside him. 'Wait.'

'I'll call you as soon as I have anything.' He got into the car and slammed the door. The keys were in the ignition and he'd started the engine when she ran to the front and put her hands on the bonnet.

He rolled down his window. 'I'm sorry?' he said. 'You're in my way.'

'Yes,' she said. 'Yes, that's right.'

'And you're going to stop me leaving.'

'I want you to wait. Let me get my keys so I can come with you.'

'Movie stuff, you mean?'

'Movie stuff.' She pointed at him, an index finger like a gun, trained on his forehead. 'Now, you.' She jabbed the finger at him. 'You don't go anywhere. You wait there while I get my keys.'

52

Flea followed Caffery in his beat-up car. He drove it fast through the country lanes, brushing through the lush hedgerows, as the smells of horses and pollen came through her window. She had to concentrate to keep up. Along the A38 to the city and into the side roads near the Easton area, through neighbourhoods with graffitied walls where men sat outside newspaper shops playing chess on trestle tables, under flyovers and past warehouses, until at last Caffery slowed, checking out of the window and eventually stopping at the corner of a residential road.

She parked her car, locked it and went to him, opening the door and getting into the passenger seat. 'What're we doing here?' she said. Across the road a church, a bookie's and a supermarket were squeezed into one block.

'The supermarket,' he said.

She leaned forward and peered at it. 'Eezy Pocket,' said the red and yellow sign. There were grilles on the windows, a newspaper hoarding with local headlines at the entrance, and one or two kids hanging around outside, looking shiftily up and down the street as if they were waiting for someone. 'What about it?'

'I don't know.' Caffery tapped the steering-wheel thoughtfully. There was a long silence. His shirt was very white against his skin, his dark hair clean but half wild. And she noticed he'd got back that look — the one that made her think he was working hard to hold something in.

Just when she was about to say it — *Christ, I know how you feel* — he held up his mobile phone. There was a picture on the screen of a small, ratty-looking black guy with a slopy head wearing a white shirt and a tatty brown corduroy jacket.

'The multimedia unit scanned it from the CCTV footage at TIDARA. He was with Mossy the last time he was seen alive.'

'Do you know who he is?'

'Nope. Never seen him before.' He put away the phone and shifted a little in the seat. 'Something else you didn't know,' he said, 'is what I found at a mate of Mabuza's. Guy called Kwanele Dlamini had a bowl of blood in his living room.'

'Nice.'

'Yeah — turned out to be human.'

'Even nicer.'

'Turned out, in fact, to belong to Mossy.'

Flea sucked in a breath. Jonah's face came to her. She'd met him only once, at a Christmas party at Dundas's place. He'd shown her his PlayStation and told her that one day he wanted to write video games. Of course, she hadn't had a clue what was in his future.

Caffery turned his eyes to hers. 'Remember Kaiser said something — he said giving a Tokoloshe blood, that it's a superstition from the East.'

'You were listening to him, then?'

He gave a wry smile. 'I called someone in

424

Immigration — they've got an officer attached to Operation Atrium, nice guy. Helpful. He gave me the heads up on Mabuza and Dlamini's status last week.' Caffery patted his pockets, took out a tobacco pouch and put it on the dashboard. 'But I wanted to know more about them — '

'Like what?'

'Like did Immigration know if they were from the east of the country? Where the Zulu tribes are.'

'Because of the thing with the blood?'

'Because of the thing with the blood. Only problem with that is he can't answer me — not straight off — so he says he's going to ask around. But then he mentions that most black South Africans who come from Zulu territory to Bristol sooner or later end up right over there.' He dug a finger in the direction of the supermarket. 'The guy who owns it is from a Durban slum. He's been running rings round Immigration for years, and his place is where people go when they first hit the streets round here. He does the lot — gets them work, gets them drugs, gets them boyfriends or girlfriends, depending on what they want, the works. Immigration would like nothing better than to get something on him, so they were well up for me having a look.'

Caffery broke off as a group of schoolkids ambled past, boys of about ten years old, socks gathered round skinny ankles, schoolbags dragging along the floor. Some bent to peer into the car, one grinned at Caffery, threw him the West-Side salute, then strolled off, casual and already as slink-hipped as the older boys.

'That's the Hopewell estate where Jonah lives,' Caffery said, when they'd gone. He put a finger on the windscreen to indicate the high-rise looming above them a few streets away. 'Not that far, but I can guarantee there are at least twenty of these convenience stores between here and there — so why did he come to this place?'

'How do you know he did?'

'Bags. In his bedroom. Unless it's a chain, which it doesn't look like. So he must have been here. And that means someone here knows him, and *that* means — '

He was staring at something. Flea followed the direction of his eyes. The boys had crossed the road, passed the supermarket and some parked cars, and were turning into a side-street.

'What?' she said. Caffery's eyes had narrowed, and she could see from the way his jaw had hardened that he was clenching his teeth. 'What is it?'

He unclicked his seat-belt, opened the door and swung out on to the pavement. 'There's always someone in a place like this who knows everything. And,' he said, bending to give her a smile, 'I know just who that someone is.'

★ ★ ★

He got out his warrant card, took off his jacket and threw it on to the back seat. Ignoring Flea's puzzled frown, he closed the door and crossed the road to the supermarket. The car he was interested in, a blue Nissan, was parked about

426

twenty feet along next to a postbox, the driver — a fat guy in an England T-shirt — sitting kerbside with his window open.

Caffery approached obliquely, going casually but keeping himself tucked into the sides of the cars behind so the driver wouldn't notice until he was on top of him. Then he opened the car door and, before the driver could do anything, grabbed the keys from the ignition, pocketed them and slammed the door.

'Hey — what the fuck do you think you're — ?'

The driver scrabbled with the door, opening it as Caffery crossed in front of the car and jumped into the passenger seat. The driver followed him round, as fast as his weight would allow, his chunky arms pumping him along.

'Hey,' he said, tugging futilely at the passenger door. 'Get out, you cunt. Get out of my car.' He hammered on the window. 'Get out or I'll get the fucking police on you.'

In the car Caffery took the warrant card from his trouser pocket and slapped it, face out, against the glass. The driver stopped mid-sentence. He didn't have to get close to know what the card was — Caffery knew he'd have seen one enough times. He stopped hammering. His shoulders drooped in defeat and he rested his hands on the car roof. He turned and looked around the street, as if he was thinking of running. Then, as if he'd thought better of it, he trudged wearily to the front of the car and got in, not speaking.

There was a bad smell in the car, of sweat and food and old clothes. When the man got in, the car creaked and shifted — it took him some time to get comfortable in the small seat, and by the time he had settled the sweat was running down his face.

'Well?' he said. 'You can't get me on anything. I'm not on a warning or probation or anything. I'm clean. I can sit where I want when I want.'

Caffery didn't answer. The gang of schoolkids were trailing away in the distance. He knew it was them the man was trying not to look at. He knew it because he'd got the measure of this guy just from watching him across the road. Maybe it was his curse to recognize a paedophile from a hundred yards. When he didn't answer the man sighed and sat back, crossing his arms. He was wearing shorts, and his fat, sparsely haired legs were jammed up against the steering-wheel.

'The thing is, I keep telling you guys, we're all the same. On the inside, us men are the same — in our thoughts, in our . . . ' he nodded in the direction of the schoolboys ' . . . in our *desires*.'

Caffery clenched his teeth.

'The only difference,' said the man, smiling, 'is that I've got the courage to be free. To express myself. And you haven't.'

Caffery took a long, deep breath. Then, when the driver had been silent for some time he turned in his seat and, in one unbroken move, cannoned his fist into his face. The guy's head collided with the seat-belt mooring, his mouth flew open, saliva shot out. He ricocheted back in the seat, both hands clutching his cheek. A line of blood was coming from his nose and tears were in his eyes.

428

'Whad'd you do that for?' he said thickly, holding his hand under his nose to catch the blood. 'I know my rights. You're not allowed to do that.'

'And I'm not allowed to do this either.' Caffery took hold of the guy's football shirt and twisted it so tight that the neck dug into the rolls of fat, making his face bulge.

'Get off — get off . . . ' He scratched uselessly at Caffery's hands. 'Get off.'

'Who are you waiting for, dog turd?'

'No one.'

'Don't tell me that.' Caffery tightened his grip. 'You're waiting for someone.'

'No — no, I'm not.'

Caffery threw him back against the seat, got out of the car and came round to the driver's side. He had a flash frame of Flea, out of the car on the other side of the road, sunglasses off, watching intently. Then he was opening the door and heaving the man out.

'Get out, slob,' he muttered, struggling with the weight. 'Get the fuck out.'

The driver plopped on to the street, like a cork coming out of a bottle, falling on to all fours, whimpering, blood dribbling from his face.

'You can't do this to me — you can't.'

Caffery put a hand on the back of the man's head and pushed him down so his face was jammed between the postbox and the car's back wheel. He couldn't get Penderecki's face out of his head. There was a dried piece of dog shit on the kerb next to the guy's mouth and, still thinking of Penderecki, Caffery forced his face a little nearer, half wanting to make him eat it.

'Please stop.'

Caffery leaned his shoulder against the car and knelt on the guy's back. A voice in the back of his head was reminding him, *This is how suspects die. This is how they die in detention. Suffocated. The coroner will find cracked ribs, bruises consistent with the victim being knelt on. They die from not having the strength to lift their ribs and let air into their lungs.* And then the voice said: *It's what you should have done to Penderecki.*

'This can kill you,' he hissed into the man's ear. 'What I'm doing will kill you — fat though you are. If I stay here long enough you'll die. OK?'

'Please, please don't. *Please* . . . ' He was crying now. He couldn't sob because Caffery was too heavy, but tears were rolling out of his eyes and mingling with the sweat. 'Please.'

'Tell me, you fucker, or we'll be here until you *die.*'

The man screwed up his eyes. He put his hands on to the ground and tried to lift his weight off the pavement to suck in a breath. 'OK,' he sputtered. 'Get off me and I'll tell you.'

Caffery slapped one hand against the car and got to his feet. The driver struggled on to his back, breathing hard, his face pressed against the grimy postbox.

'There are a few . . . people,' he panted, 'a few people who come here.'

'All on the game or do you like to be the one who converts them?'

430

'No.' He swallowed. 'No. They're all professionals.'

'And black? You like them black? Is that what your record will show? Young and black?'

He nodded miserably, a line of spittle hanging from his mouth.

'What?' Caffery put both hands on the car so he was stretched over the driver. He could sense one or two people watching him from outside the supermarket, but he didn't look up. 'What did you say?'

'I said yes.'

Caffery felt in his pocket for his mobile, pulled up the picture the multimedia unit had sent him and thrust it into the guy's face. 'This one. Fucked him too, have you?'

He glanced at the picture and away. 'Yeah,' he muttered. 'He's one of them.'

'Name?'

'Changes. Jim, Paul, John, whatever he feels. There's something wrong with him. He's not really twelve, he just looks it . . . Really he's eighteen — I swear. He's got a condition that makes him smaller . . .'

Caffery remembered a boy in London, a twelve-year-old, who used to advertise saying, 'I am an eighteen-year-old who had an accident that has left me looking just eleven years old.' Designed for all the old nonces who wanted to get away with their dirty child-rape habits. 'I've heard that story before, you piece of shit.'

'It's true.' The man stared at him. 'It's true. Ask anyone. Any of the ones who hang out here, they all know him. He dressed for me like a schoolkid, but he isn't, really. I swear he isn't. I don't do that any more — you know, with the kids.'

'Sure you don't.'

'Don't tell him I was the one who told you. I think he's got — friends. Family.' He wiped his nose, gulping down tears. 'Please don't tell him I told you.'

Caffery raised his head. Outside the supermarket three kids in board clothes were staring at him. When he met their eyes they turned away, pulling up their hoodies. 'So,' he said, 'when's he coming? Today?'

'Maybe.' He sniffled. 'Sometimes he comes at lunchtime, but if not him there'll be others.' He wiped the tears out of his eyes. 'Please don't say I told you. I don't want to upset anyone.'

'If you don't want to upset anyone, then stop fucking little boys,' Caffery said. He put his hands in the small of his back and flexed his shoulders, letting them click so his tense muscles would release.

'All right,' he said, helping the man to his feet. He opened the car door and shoved him towards it. 'Wait there. Don't move. Any of your other boyfriends come along you send them on their way, even if you and your sad little hard-on have to sit there all day. When *he* comes, act like nothing's happened. Get him in the car — I'll do the rest.'

'What about my keys? What am I going to do without my car keys?'

'Jesus Christ. I'm telling you to help me because you're a piece of shit and you owe something to society. Not because I've turned

432

into the archangel fucking Gabriel. Now. Get. In. The. Sodding. Car.'

★ ★ ★

Caffery was sweating when he came back. 'It's a waiting game now,' he said, grabbing the tobacco pouch and beginning to roll up. 'The clue we're looking for will walk right up to that car in about ten minutes.' He licked the paper and lit the cigarette.

Flea watched him smoke. She could feel the last two days tugging her down and she had an overwhelming urge to cry or sleep, she couldn't tell which. Next to her Caffery smoked the whole of the cigarette, watching the blue Nissan in silence. Then he crushed the butt in the ashtray, rolled up the pouch, put it on the dashboard and said, in a level voice, 'When I was eight my brother disappeared.'

'I'm sorry?' she said numbly.

'My brother went missing,' he said calmly, as if he was telling her what he'd had for breakfast. 'I was with him when it happened. We had . . . There was a fight, and he left, walked out the bottom of our garden into a railway cutting. It wasn't dangerous because we'd been there a million times. Except this time . . . ' For a moment it was as if he'd forgotten he was speaking. 'Except this time he didn't come back. There was a convicted paedophile lived on the other side of the railway. We didn't call them that then — called them child-molesters, kiddy-diddlers. Everyone knew it was him, but no one

433

could prove it. That was thirty years ago and I still don't know where my brother is.'

She stared at him, her heart thudding. He'd heard. He knew what had happened to Mum and Dad — someone in the force must have told him how her life had been changed by the accident, that she'd never get her life back. She took a breath. 'Why are you telling me this?' she said, her voice small. 'Why?'

'Because you want to know why I half killed that guy just then. See, I walk around with this fucking great weight of guilt on me about what happened to my brother because when something like that happens — to the wrong son, that's how my parents saw it — when it happens you never get past the guilt. And it comes out in ways I'm (a) not proud of and (b) could get me shafted big-time.' He jerked his head at the blue Nissan — the driver had pulled down the rear-view mirror and was inspecting the damage to his face. 'He's a nonce.' He gave a pained smile. 'My nonce radar, if you want to call it that, is tighter engineered than most people's.'

She couldn't answer. She went on looking at him for a few more moments, and then, when she couldn't bear it any longer, turned away and stared out of the passenger window, her mouth open a little because she was breathing fast.

'It's OK,' he said behind her. 'I'm not asking you to forgive me. You can go ahead and report me. I don't much care any more.'

Behind her Flea heard the creak of leather as he moved in his seat, the rattle of his keys, and then she felt his hand on her shoulder.

434

'I'm sorry,' he said quietly. 'I didn't mean to put you in that position. I really didn't mean to.'

She couldn't move. All she could think about was his hand on her back. Then, just when it seemed they'd be there for ever, in that car on the dusty urban street, listening to one another's breathing, something inside her unlocked. Her mouth opened and words came out.

'If you cut your own arm off it wouldn't be enough. That's what it's like, isn't it? The only way you could make amends would be to die yourself — to die more horribly and in more pain and fear. It's the only way.' She turned to him, her face hot. 'You wish over and over again that it could have been you — you would die their death a million times over rather than feel one more second of that guilt.'

Caffery pulled his hand away, his skin suddenly grey, as if all the late nights and worry had caught up with him in one hit.

'My parents,' she said. 'A few people in the force know, but they'd never talk about it. Two years ago, and I still haven't got their bodies back. Not like with you — I know *where* they are, exactly where. Everyone knows. It's just that no one can get them back.'

She stopped speaking as suddenly as she'd started, shocked by the amount she'd said. His eyes were focused on her, his pupils narrowed to pinpoints. For a long time he didn't say anything. Then he half lifted his hand and, for a split second, she almost thought he was going to hit her. But he didn't. He lowered his hand, dropped it on to the steering-wheel and turned wearily to look out of the window. There was a long silence while she tried to find the right thing to say. Then, as she was about to speak, something happened that made it all too late. A small figure dressed in a strangely oversized brown jacket and rolled-up jeans walked straight in front of the car, going in the direction of the supermarket.

And that, of course, was when it kicked off.

53

Caffery swivelled in his seat to stare at the guy. 'Fuck,' he murmured. 'I think that's him.'

'What?'

'The one on my phone.'

The figure was heading towards the blue Nissan. He stopped at the bin, dipping his head briefly, then carrying on his way, stopping at the Nissan and using a thin hand to knock on the window. A thought came to Flea: I know him. Where do I know him from? But then Caffery was out of his seat, rolling up his sleeves, and everything started happening so fast she forgot it.

From the Nissan came a bellow, primeval-sounding: '*Police!*' It was the driver yelling, waving his hand out of the window. '*Get out of here! The police!*' Then two things happened at once: the small figure in the oversized jacket ran clumsily back in the direction he'd come while Caffery hit the roof of the car — like a declaration of intent — and sprinted after him.

Flea was trained for all of this, but everything drained out of her head instantly. Caffery was rounding the corner out of sight and she didn't know these streets. She fumbled for her phone, dropped it, picked it up and realized the back had cracked — the SIM card and the battery were hanging out. She threw herself on to the driver's seat, groping under the steering-wheel, saw the keys weren't there and wrenched herself back the opposite way, clutching the phone and battery in one hand, fumbling her keys with the other.

She rolled out of the car, raced back to the Focus and jumped in. The car leaped forward, almost into the path of a delivery truck. She braked, clutching the wheel and swearing while the truck drove leisurely past, then raced the car across the road to the opposite side, taking the left-hand turning.

The street stretched ahead of her, one of those Victorian terraces that made her think of the north, red-brick and featureless. She let the car idle, not knowing which way to go. Caffery and the little guy might have been anywhere. And then she saw them, about a hundred yards down, bursting out from the line of parked cars, first the figure in the ridiculous jacket, then Caffery, his white shirt like a flag. She pushed the car forward, drawing level with them as they skidded sideways into an alley.

She reached over and pulled out her A-Z of Bristol, fumbled furiously to the index, then ran her finger down to Hopewell. Behind her a car was hooting, wanting to get by, but she ignored it. Jamming the book between her knees, flicking through to the page, she spread it on her lap. She saw where they were, and that the alleyway ended on the Hopewell estate. The driver behind her wound down his window and was screaming something about why was it always women who fucked with the rules of the road, and what was she doing? Putting in a Tampax? She gave him

438

the finger and flung the car into gear.

The back-streets were narrow, only room for one car in one direction at any time, but she wove and spun the Ford through the warren in less than a minute, and came out braking hard on a wide street with grass verges at either side and wire-enclosed saplings planted at intervals. She was at the entrance to the Hopewell estate, and from her calculations the road to her right led down to the alley. She opened the window and sat forward, heart racing.

At first she thought she'd missed them. But then she heard footsteps racing towards her. The little man in the jacket burst out of the street, straight past her — she glimpsed thin limbs and a drawn face — then he was out on to the scrappy square of grass, racing across it, the shadows of the tower blocks flick-flacking across the crown of his head. She unsnapped her seat-belt and started to get out of the car, because there was no Caffery behind him and she'd been sure he'd be on the guy's heels. But then, just as she was about to take off, he appeared, walking now, his finger to his mouth when he saw her, waving her back into the car. She sank into her seat, keeping her feet on the pavement but pulling the door half closed against her calves as he walked past.

She watched him, mind twitching, eyes darting around, taking it all in. She didn't know the roads to the east, where the supermarket was, but she knew this estate. It was arranged around six behemoth tower blocks interconnected with figure-of-eight cast-concrete walkways, surrounded by triangles of grass. She could picture it from above, like a town-planner's model. And from the way the little guy was running, she guessed he was heading to the North West Tower, the notorious drug-trading tower. She waited a moment, her heart thudding against her ribcage. Then, the moment Caffery disappeared in the lee of the South West Tower, she swung back into the car and fired it up, steering round the little car parks and rubbish depots.

She was taking a risk — they could have gone in any direction — and when she shot out almost at the foot of the North West Tower she thought her gamble had backfired. The place was deserted, just the empty entrance to the estate covered with flypostings and graffiti, a row of recycling bins with filthy carrier-bags bulging from their mouths. Not a soul.

And then, like a burst of light on her retina — how come she hadn't seen him before? Caffery was standing about ten yards away, staring at her.

She threw open the door and jumped out. 'Jesus Christ! What is — '

He held up one hand to her, warning her to be silent. But the other arm was extended in the opposite direction, the fingers arranged in a neat point, telling her to look that way. And when she saw what he was pointing at, it was like having something dark and nasty go through her, because now she knew where she'd seen the guy in the jacket before. She'd seen him here. In exactly the place Caffery was standing now. It had been brief, only a moment's glimpse, but she remembered it clearly because it had been only a couple of days ago that he'd briefly walked past her. She looked again at the door Caffery was pointing to.

And suddenly nothing, *nothing*, was as it should be.

54

The door was blue, pale blue, the number eleven on it in mirrored stick-on letters and the guy in the jacket had disappeared through it. Caffery stood looking at it, his jacket pushed back, catching his breath from the run. An ordinary enough door — sad-looking net curtains in the window the dingy colour of used teabags from years of grease and neglect — and intuition told him this was the place where Mossy had been cut into pieces. God only knew what it was going to be like inside.

He went round the base of the tower to make sure there wasn't a back way out, but it was built as a square, with the lift shaft tacked on at the side. On the other side of the tower there were more front doors — no rear ones. He waited, looking at them, at the boarded-up windows, getting his breath back, and suddenly knew where he was — back on the Hopewell estate, just come at it from a different angle. Jonah's tower was the one in the far distance. He couldn't see them but there'd be about twenty coppers crawling up and down its stairwells right now. On this tower most of the bottom-floor windows were boarded. He watched those windows carefully, so silent in the midday heat. A little trickle of sweat broke from between his shoulder-blades and ran down his spine. He went back to the other side. And now, for the first time, he saw there was something wrong with Flea.

'Number eleven,' she murmured. 'It's number eleven.'

'Yeah,' he said. 'What about it?'

She tilted her head, then walked back a few yards, beckoning him. He followed, going nearer the cars until they couldn't be seen from the flat. He had to bend slightly to hear what she was saying.

'I know who lives here,' she whispered. 'I mean, he's a friend of mine.'

'Oh, great. Fucking great.'

'Yeah — and you. You — you know him too. Tommy Baines. Tig. The guy at the drug centre in Mangotsfield. The one with the eye.'

Caffery was trying to work this out in his head. 'The one with the — ' He broke off. 'How the hell do you know him?'

She closed her eyes briefly, her face pale as if she couldn't believe this was happening. 'I've — oh, Christ, I've known him for ages, OK? But I've seen him recently too. He told me you'd questioned him.'

'Fucking magnificent. It really helps matters when people around you can't keep their mouths buttoned and when — '

'Wait a second,' she muttered, her face clouding. 'Just because someone's gone into his flat doesn't mean he's got anything to hide so don't get arsey with me. I mean, it could be nothing — it could just be that . . . ' A thought stopped her in her tracks. She closed her mouth abruptly, and her eyes went up a bit, as if she was focusing on a place in the sky. 'Oh, shit,' she said. She rapped her knuckles on her forehead. 'Shit and double shit.'

'What?'

'That's me royally fucked.'

'What?'

She sighed, dropped her hand and walked across the sun-baked Tarmac to her car. He watched her throw open the door and haul out her holdall, then rummage through it. She straightened up, then slid something that looked like a holstered knife, a dive knife, maybe, into the back of her trousers. Then she shut the door and was coming back, holding two Kevlar body-armour vests, one kitted out, the other with empty pockets. She stopped in front of him. 'The day we found the hand in the harbour?'

'Yes?'

'I got a text on my phone from him. From Tig.' She pushed the kitted-out vest towards Caffery. 'He wanted to see me. Hadn't spoken to him for ages, then suddenly he's in touch again. And when I came over he dug a bit, tried to get me to tell him what was happening with the case.' She made a face. 'There,' she said. 'I'm an idiot. Probably lose my job now, won't I?'

There was a short silence. Caffery was remembering the physical sensation he'd got around Tig, the one that had made him itch to thump him. It was coming back to him now.

'OK,' he said, ignoring the kitted vest and reaching for the empty one. 'Let's not jump to conclusions. Like you said, just because some-one's run into his flat doesn't mean anything. Let's check it out before we jump. OK?'

*   *   *

When they both had their vests on Flea pushed her hair off her face, stood up straight and stiff and knocked loudly on the door.

There was silence. She stood on tiptoe and tried to peer through the little glazed section. 'Tig?' she yelled, banging hard on the wood with the flat of her hand. 'Tig! Are you in there? It's me.'

From the other side of the door came the sound of whispers, of people moving around quickly. A door slammed.

'Tig? Just a quick word.'

More noise. A long silence. Then another door opening and suddenly, on the other side a hand pulled back the curtain. There was a shuffling noise, then a face appeared at the grimy glass.

'Mrs Baines.' Flea put her hand on the glass. 'It's me. Are you all right? Can I come in?'

The woman stared as if she didn't recognize her.

'It's me. Can I come in?'

There was a sound of latches being unfas-tened, then a frail woman in a tattered housecoat opened the door. 'I don't know where he is, lovey. He's off somewhere with the blacks again.'

Caffery peered into the dingy hallway. Inside, the flat was a mess — piles of newspapers everywhere, all sorted out and organized into separate carrier-bags. Written in felt-tip above each pile were dates: 1999–2006. There was a smell of tomato soup and something else — something he couldn't put his finger on. All the doors leading from the hallway were closed.

Tightening the side fastening on the body armour, he stepped inside. 'You on your own, my love?'

'Yes, yes. Always left on me own.'

Caffery opened a door. A kitchen, small and cluttered with washing-up in the sink. No one in it. 'It's just we know there are some people living here.'

'Do you, dear?' She seemed unconcerned as Flea went into the living room, checking behind the sofa, the curtains. 'Well, you'll have to ask my son about that.'

Caffery opened another door and then another. 'Is he here?'

'Oh, no. Not properly here. Not in the way you'd think.'

'What does that mean?'

She gave a toothless grin. 'Lord knows. I'm a bit doo-lally. That's what they keep telling me — that I'm not all there.' She tapped her head. 'Not what I used to be.'

'Look, Mrs Baines, is your son here or not?'

'Oh, no. Of course he ain't.'

Caffery looked at the darting eyes, at the soiled quilted housecoat and the thinning hair. He had a mother somewhere; as far as he knew she was still alive. She'd given up on him when Ewan had gone missing, and thirty years later he'd even stopped wondering where she was.

'Got your scanner on, have you?' Flea asked.

'Me scanner? Oh, no, gone orf it — watching the telly now.'

'All right if I have a look at it?' Caffery said.

She waved her hand, as if she was dismissing them. 'Oh, do what you want. See if I care.'

He went into her bedroom, with its unmade bed, its closed curtains, four or five mugs crammed on the bedside table. It was small and it didn't take him long to work out there was no one in it. He looked at the scanner. Like she said, it was switched off. There was a cold feeling in the room, as if stale air was being pumped in from somewhere. He went back into the hallway and found her scowling at him, holding up a finger as if she was warning him. 'You'll have to get the police in anyway,' she said. 'To stop what he's up to.' She smiled. 'That's all I'm saying.'

Caffery glanced at Flea. She was standing just inside the living-room door, frowning at Mrs Baines. 'What does that mean, Mrs Baines? Stop what he's up to?'

'What I said. That the police'll need to come to sort it out, I shouldn't wonder. With him letting the blacks run over the place all the time and what they get up to together. But don't worry about me. Don't you worry about me.' She tapped the side of her head and limped back inside her bedroom, closing the door firmly. There was a pause, then the sound of the television. Flea turned to the door, as if to follow her, then seemed to change her mind. Instead she turned to the one door they hadn't tried.

'His room,' she muttered. 'I've never been in there.'

'Still got that knife in your knickers?' Caffery asked.

'You saw it?'

He didn't answer. He pressed his back against the wall and lifted his foot, putting just enough pressure on the latch to open it. It swung wide and they found themselves looking into a darkened box room, a tatty blue bedspread hung over the window. There was a wardrobe against the far wall, a computer desk in the corner, and a teenager's metal bunk bed taking up most of the space. Keeping his back to the wall Caffery reached inside and clicked on a light.

'Empty?'

She darted her head in, then out again, nodding. 'Empty.'

He swivelled through the doorway and into the room, went to the wardrobe and opened it. There was a line of clothes hanging up; no one was inside it. Caffery glanced under the bed and pulled back the duvet. The window was closed. No one had come through here. It was as if the skinny guy in the jacket had vanished into thin air.

He was trying to work out what he'd missed in the flat when he realized Flea wasn't moving. She was still standing in the doorway, staring at the walls. He followed her eyeline and saw why she was being so quiet.

The walls were papered in hardcore gay S&M. One bore posters from Deviant, the S&M club in Old Market, boasting its equipment of '2 slings,

448

2 crosses, 2 doggy tables . . . ' Another wall showed a series of pictures of a man in a see-through plastic tunic, his penis in a leather ring, blood pouring from the wounds on his body and congealing under the plastic like packed meat. In the first two pictures he was being forced to lick the feet of a fully dressed businessman. In the last he was being held face down in a toilet.

'Whoa.' Caffery whistled. 'Heavy-duty shit.'

He went to the last wall, which was covered with a single blown-up photo, real or mocked-up, it was difficult to tell. It showed a shaven-headed man in a leather apron biting off the nipple of a man wearing only black Dr Martens and a white studded dog collar. Stapled to it at waist height were ten photographic A4s. Caffery bent down to them and saw something that would convict Baines in a second. The photographs showed everything that had happened in the North West Tower on the Hopewell estate. They showed a small black guy in a tribal outfit, a red tabard, his hair beaded and white paint smeared on his cheeks. It was the guy in the jacket, pictured in different poses: one showed him performing a ritual dance wearing the robes of a witch doctor, baring his teeth at the camera lens, but the others showed him standing next to a half-naked man on a sofa — Caffery guessed it was Ian Mallows — and inserting a cannula into his arm, letting the blood drain off into a large plastic jug. And the next one — Caffery had to pinch his nose to stop stomach acid coming into the back of his throat — showed the witch doctor crouched next to a body, holding a knife to the raw, bloodied stumps where hands had once been.

He swallowed hard and steeled himself to look closely at this picture. There were things to avoid: Mallows's pale body — he was assuming it was Mallows — the blood that had fountained up the whitened arms, the eyes rolled back. He had to concentrate to block these things because something else was more wrong than all of the obvious wrong. There was only one unreal thing in the photograph, and that was the face of the witch doctor.

He squinted at those eyes and saw something he recognized: a blankness, a lie. There was something about the posture — the knife held up for the camera, the face too posed — that made him think of holiday snaps. It came to him quite fast: *It's not you who did the cutting, is it? You're just the act.* He didn't have to form the question, *So if not you then who?*, because he knew the answer. He knew the person who had done the cutting.

Shit, he thought. There's no giving you the benefit of the doubt, Tig, mate. You're never going to be redeemed. You steered me wrong, sending me to TIDARA. And then, in a flash, he understood why.

'Baines,' he said. Flea was standing behind him, her face white. 'Did he know Kaiser? Through you?'

'I'm sorry?'

'I said, did Baines know Kaiser.'

'No,' she said faintly. 'No — I mean — ' She

450

glanced at him. 'Yes — he knew of him.'

'About him and ibogaine?'

Her tongue darted out and she licked her lips. 'Probably. Why?'

He sighed. 'Nothing. Ever get the feeling you've been led by the bollocks?'

Flea came up beside him, still staring at the photos. She held up her hand towards them, her hand hovering, not quite touching them, copper's instinct not to touch, but he knew she wanted to.

'Christ,' she breathed. 'Who is he?'

'I don't know, but probably our friend in the jacket. And if I had to lay bets on it I'd say that's Mallows on the sofa.'

'Oh, fuck,' she muttered thickly. 'It's true, then.' She sat down at the little computer table, propping her face in her hands.

He turned away from the photographs, wanting to touch her, to rest his hand on her hair, knowing that he couldn't. 'Tell me.'

'Nothing,' she said. 'Except . . . '

'Yeah?'

'Except that when I went to see Mabuza I was so sure he knew I was job.'

'How come?'

Something guarded crossed her eyes. 'Nothing — just I had a feeling he'd been warned. The place was covered with crucifixes, as if he was trying to show he ran a good Christian household. And . . . '

'And?' Caffery said, eyes on the photographs.

'He's gay,' she said quietly. 'Tig. Very gay.'

'Gay as nails,' he said, 'by the looks of things. Didn't you know?'

451

'Yes, I knew,' she said, in a monotone. 'I always knew. He let me doubt it, but now I think he was trying to open me up, get me to feed him information about the case.'

'Which he'd feed back to Mabuza. I knew someone was emceeing the fucking thing, just didn't think it'd be some white gay boy.'

Flea was still staring at the walls. 'But that's Tig for you — most of his clients are black, Asian. He's street, you know. He's one of them. For a while Atrium even liked him for a snout.'

Caffery examined the small bookshelf above Flea's head. Lined up was a row of MPF diskettes. One had the word 'Magic' scrawled across it in crude writing. The next two had the name 'Mabuza' printed in Magic Marker.

Caffery had his hands on the little MPF diskette when something stopped him. It made him feel cold and still all at once. It made him turn to Flea. They didn't need to speak — both knew what the other was thinking. They were thinking that they had just heard what sounded like someone, quite nearby, pushing over a large piece of furniture.

★ ★ ★

'Where was it from?' Caffery whispered. He stood above her, hand out, the dust and sweat from the chase through the streets engrained on the underside of his shirt sleeve. 'Where did it come from?'

'I dunno,' Flea murmured. It wasn't coming from the flat . . . not exactly. It was coming from the back of the room where another flat would be.

She turned very slowly and looked at the bed, the cupboard. She was picturing Tig's mum last week, muttering to herself in the kitchen. *Stop the blacks coming through the walls. Stop them putting their faces through the walls.*

'The walls,' she whispered.

'The *walls*?'

'Check them.'

He gave her a strange look, but went to the wall anyway, sweeping his hands along it, feeling for anomalies, his expression saying he was humouring her. He pulled the bedspread away from the window, searching for an airbrick maybe, or a hole he hadn't noticed, while Flea got down on the dirty, gritty carpet to scan the wall under the bed. Nothing. It was only when Caffery went back to the wardrobe and opened it, kicking aside the junk on the floor, that she saw him react. She saw him half turn away, then stop.

'What?' She got up, came to stand next to him and saw what he was looking at. The back of the wardrobe wasn't plastered. A piece of plywood was propped upright behind the hanging clothes. He dropped to a squat and looped his fingers behind it, then pulled it away from the wall, setting loose a cloud of plaster dust. Immediately they could smell mould and ammonia.

'OK,' he muttered, dusting off his hands. 'I think we've found him.'

Behind the plasterboard a hole about five feet tall and three wide had been knocked into the wall. Plaster dust covered the floor, and a piece of ragged wallpaper hung in shreds. They bent their heads and peered through into a small corridor, with ruined walls, electric leads hanging from the ceiling. Light filtered from an opening to their left, blocked by a padlocked iron gate. Somewhere inside water dripped. Beyond the gate they could see the beginnings of another room. Only the floor was visible, threadbare bits of carpet glued to the flaking underlay, a newspaper lying folded with the sports page face up. But in front of them the corridor extended into darkness.

Caffery crawled through the opening, giving the gate to the left an experimental push with his foot. He checked the padlock — fastened — dropped it and turned the other way, into the darkness. 'That's what he's done, the little shit. Dug his way into another flat.'

'Jesus.' Flea shivered. The air was damp, stagnant, like a long-closed cave and now, as she imagined a rats' nest of corridors, a maze, her heart wouldn't stop thumping. Quickly she ran her hands along the walls at shoulder height, sweeping for a light switch. Nothing. Just the daylight from the left and ahead the darkness. 'He must have — '

A shuffling noise was coming from the dark ahead. She leaned forward, trying to see into the room, her eyes pricking with fear. She could see a red light flashing on and off in there — not big, no more than a pinpoint — the size of a human iris. Something electronic, maybe. The sound came again and beads of sweat broke out in her armpits.

454

'Fuck it,' she muttered, stepping back into the bedroom, fumbling for her airwaves radio. She hit the emergency button and blocked out all other traffic. 'Bravo Control, bravo Control,' she hissed. 'Location is Hopewell estate, North West Tower, status zero, urgent assistance required. Suggest any attending units bring support unit bags and method-of-entry tools. And, uh . . . ' She squinted down the corridor, which seemed to stretch right into the centre of the building. It made her blood run cold to think of it — Tig burrowing into the walls of his flat like a fucking termite. 'Yeah, tell them to contain the building from all sides. It's Sitexed so bring a Scott pack too.'

She signed off and turned to Caffery, who was standing in the opening, his back to the wall. Beyond him the red light was flashing on and off, illuminating the edge of his face. He was shaking his head.

'What is it?' she mouthed.

'You're going to wait for them?' he whispered.

'Yes.' She shifted the vest so that it rested on her pelvic bones and her breasts were more comfortable. 'Risk assessment,' she murmured. 'I've done one, and that's my decision.'

'And how far into the fucking building do you think he's gone?'

She knew what Caffery was saying. She knew where he was going with this. 'I don't care how far he's gone.'

'But you care if he's getting out the other fucking side,' he hissed.

'I care about doing my job and about me

455

coming out the other side. It's basic training, one oh one — no light, we don't know what's in there and I'm not putting my life at risk. You might be in a hurry to die, but I'm not.'

With her last sentence the light reflected in Caffery's eyes became a little harder. He opened his mouth to say something, but seemed to change his mind. He looked back down the corridor, then at her, and for a moment she thought he was going in on his own. But he didn't. Instead he took a step back into the room and reached for her. For the second time that day she flinched, as if he was about to hurt her. But he was reaching to unsnap a holder on her body armour, to pull out the grey canister of CS gas. Then he put his lips very close to her ear. The hairs across her neck were stirred by his breath. 'Now that,' he whispered, 'is the biggest lie I've ever heard come out of another human being's mouth.'

Flea went very still. She watched him step away from her into the corridor, the eerie on-off, on-off of the red light in the dark room sparking round his outline. She could feel the small muscles in her jaw moving as she pictured Bushman's Hole, remembered letting Thom go down. She thought about the dark water, of what he was thinking when he saw Mum and Dad heading into the blackness, and a sensation like air rushed through her, like something rising up from inside her and cracking. She slammed the mobile into the Velcro fastening on the vest and caught up with Caffery in the corridor, laying a hand on his shoulder.

'Listen,' she hissed, narrowing her eyes, straining to see into the dark room ahead. 'The gas. Only use it if you have to — this place is too enclosed. You use it and we'll all get some of it and then we really will be waiting for the cavalry.' She ran her left hand across the pockets, checking everything was there — the Quikcuffs, the radio. She yanked the knife from inside the back of her trousers and handed it to him. 'They'll be expecting us at head or chest height. So we go in low.'

She pushed past him and dropped to a squat in the doorway, side on. Caffery was close behind her. She heard him drop too, then the in and out of his breath near her neck, but in front there was only silence — the shuffling had stopped. She tried to stretch her eyes into the room, her head automatically reeling off everything she was supposed to think about — the shape of the room, the position of the target, what her objective was — knowing that none of it would make any sense, that here her training counted for nothing.

'You go left, I'll go right. On three.' She unsnapped the ASP — the heavy, neoprene-covered expandable steel tube — and squeezed it, the weight in her hand reassuring. Keep it unracked for now. It was just as effective and wouldn't get in the way at ground height. 'One, two, three.'

She went into the room in an undignified scramble, half rolling, half crab-running, one hand in front of her face. About four feet inside, her trainers slid on something, sending her skidding forward. Her knee made contact with a hard edge and she felt something brush her face as her elbow slammed into the floor. The tumble stopped. She'd hit a wall, was lying on her side with her back against it, her heart hammering in her chest. She took a moment or two to get her breath back then, with an effort, manoeuvred herself on to her side, pushing herself up.

'Stop.' Caffery's voice came from somewhere in the darkness. 'I can see something. Don't move until I find the fucking light.'

She froze, on her knees, her elbows locked under her, her hair hanging round her face.

'I mean it. Don't stand up.'

Trembling, sweat running down her arms, she listened to him moving around in the darkness. There was a smell here — something familiar, coppery and dead — and when she turned back towards the entrance something about the light, the way it was chopped short, gave her the weird idea that she was enclosed — that somehow she'd rolled under something. There was a sound too, it dawned on her. A sound, under and above the noise Caffery was making finding a light switch. A dripping, thick and unpleasant.

'What's going on?' she hissed. She didn't want to think too hard about that dripping sound. 'What're you doing?'

There was a silence. Then Caffery released his breath and everything was flooded with bluish-white light. Flea blinked, her brain taking a moment to make sense of the shapes and

458

colours, and when it did it was as if all the air had been knocked out of her. She began to pant, low and hard.

'Oh, fuck,' she heard Caffery say. 'Fuck fuck fuck.'

55

The good thing about not having much to live for, was that you stopped caring.

It had crept up easily on Caffery, this resilience to all that was wrong in the world, until it was as natural as opening his eyes in the morning and yawning when he was tired. So it was strange that day on the Hopewell estate, scrabbling along the walls trying to find a light, tearing his hands on exposed plaster and brickwork, to feel a moment's trepidation, a brief pulse of unease just before he put on the light. It lasted only a few seconds. Then he'd found the switch, the room was illuminated, and he saw what they'd been sharing the darkness with.

The room was about as big as Baines's bedroom, but from the patterned lino on the floor and the marks round the walls where cabinets might have stood, he guessed it had once been a kitchen. The wallpaper had been pink-striped before the mould and the bad air had eaten into it and it contained only two pieces of furniture: a sofa to his left and a table, which was pushed up against the wall, with Flea under it.

He got a snapshot of her — of the way she didn't really understand what was happening. She was kneeling frozen and shocked, blood on her arms and on her T-shirt, her hands planted on the ground, eyes swivelled to him, waiting for him to tell her what to do. She couldn't see what lay on the table above her. A body, on its back: bare-chested, jeans, a leather belt securing it at the waist.

Caffery knew who it was. Even without stepping forward, he knew it was Jonah. And that he hadn't been dead long. The blood pooling under the table hadn't begun to congeal. It was still dribbling slightly out of the hacked-out hole in his neck, dripping into a plastic measuring jug under the table and spilling over the top on to the floor. Once Tig had made the first cut into Jonah's neck there was only one way it was going to end. He'd tried to cut Jonah's head off and would have succeeded if he hadn't been interrupted. He'd wadded towels round the boy's chest to soak up the overflow and put more under his buttocks, maybe in case his bowels opened.

'It's him.' Under the table in her peculiar freeze-frame, Flea had seen the jug, the blood pooling round it. 'It's him,' she muttered. Slowly she raised her eyes to the underside of the table. 'Isn't it? It's Jonah.'

Caffery looked over to where a video-camera on a tripod was tilted down at the body, its record light flashing on and off. He's dead, he told himself, trying to force himself to scan the rest of the room, to see beyond the horror on the table. There's fuck all you can do. You don't know him. Get your priorities right. Forget Jonah and find the bastard who did it.

Flea grunted and scrambled out, like a dog,

461

from under the table. '*Christ Christ Christ,*' she said, when she saw the body. '*Fucking Christ.*' Slipping in the blood she got to her feet, her hands out tense at her sides, staring at the body.

'Sssh,' Caffery said, trying to work out where the noise had come from. '*Be quiet.*'

He went to the sofa, put one hand on the back, leaned over and saw instantly what he was looking for. From waist height down, another hole had been dug into the wall. He dragged the sofa back and tried to listen, but behind him Flea was talking to herself, breathing hard.

'Ssh,' he whispered. 'I need you to be quiet, for fuck's sake.' It had been cut out with an angle-grinder, maybe, or a hacksaw. A dim blue light, daylight perhaps, was filtering on to the floor. 'Be quiet. This is it.'

When she didn't answer he turned. She was still at the table. She'd planted her feet solid and wide, had pulled Jonah's head back and had her hands locked together on his chest, squeezing down on him, each compression pushing a half-hearted dribble of blood out of his neck.

'*Christ!* Stop that.'

But she went on pumping.

'Hey.' He came back from the sofa and grabbed her arm. 'He's dead. Now stop the fuck what you're doing.'

She froze, her hands on Jonah's chest. Her face was grey, her pupils dilated.

'Remember what we're doing,' he growled. 'Remember.'

'What?' she murmured, her mouth moving slowly.

462

'Fuck's sake. Keep with me, Sergeant Marley.' He dug his fingers into her arm. 'Keep with me. We've got to get going.'

She turned her eyes to the sofa, the gap behind it. Then she looked back at the corpse. He was about to shake her, when something in her face changed. Her forehead creased, and she seemed to snap back into herself.

'Yes,' she said, wiping her bloodied hands on her vest. She bent down, put both hands on her thighs and breathed fast through her mouth. 'Yeah, I'm OK. Let's do it.'

Caffery held up the CS canister in front of his face, the knife in his other hand, and ducked into the gap. It opened into a small passage with a similar gap cut at the other end. This one had a gate welded into it, like the one they'd seen before, but it stood open.

He scrambled towards it, squat-walking, the hand with the knife hitting the floor at every other step. For a moment Flea wasn't with him — she was still in the room getting a grip on herself — but before he reached the end of the passage she'd caught up and he could feel her breathing behind him. For some reason he remembered something in the files from the Met — that the Tokoloshe could become invisible if it put a pebble in its mouth — and had to check over his shoulder that it really was her behind him. And it was. Her eyes were shining, her small face set and determined.

At the far wall they stopped in crouches by the gap, and listened again. On the other side of this wall someone was breathing, hot, panicky breaths.

'Three-sixty sweep,' she mouthed.

'What?'

'We do a three-sixty sweep. Check the room.'

He copied her, turning slightly to the side in the crouch, pressing his left hand on the inside of the wall and mirroring her by pushing his right foot ahead of him into the opening. 'Now,' she whispered. '*Now.*'

Holding the CS gas and the ASP in front of them, they craned their necks and scanned the room fast. It was small — there were two other doorways in it and a boarded-up window — and filthy, full of flies and used food containers. On a sofa pushed up against the opposite wall sat two men, one skeletal and white, one short and black.

'Police!' Caffery yelled, pointing the CS gas into the room. 'Police!' The two men shrank into each other. One was the guy they'd chased, the little witch doctor in the jacket; the other — Caffery didn't have to see the stumps of his arms to know that it was Mallows. Alive. They'd cut off his hands. They'd taken his blood. And he was still alive. The fucking Crime Scene Manager. He'd been right, the bastard.

'Hey — you,' Caffery said. 'Mallows? Ian Mallows?'

Mossy tried to raise his filthy, bandaged arms, but the effort seemed to half kill him. He sat there, gazing at Caffery with heavy eyes. 'How d'you know my name?'

'How do you think I know your fucking name? You all right?'

'No, I'm fucking not.'

464

'Well stay there. I mean it. Don't move.'

'Do I look like I'm going anywhere?' He wiped his nose on his shoulder. 'Jesus,' he muttered. 'Jesus fucking Christ.'

'You,' Caffery shouted at the black guy. 'You. Why did you run? Eh?'

'I'm sorry, sir.' He put his hands up, cringing. 'I'm sorry.'

Caffery waved the canister at him. 'Get up — off the sofa. Against the wall. *Move it*.' He did as he was told, dropping down off the sofa like a child, making Caffery think of what the waitress in the restaurant had said: *He was so tiny . . . He'd of only come up to here*. 'Against that wall. That's it — stay there. Hands where I can see them. Spread them against the wall.'

Caffery stepped into the room and straightened. Flea came after him and they stood, both instinctively with their backs against the wall, holding out their weapons, eyes darting around.

'Where is he?' Flea said. 'Baines? Where's he gone?'

'Eh?'

'Where's Baines? Where is he?'

Mossy half raised his head, his eyes rolling. 'In the bathroom,' he said, as if he couldn't give a shit any more. As if the police being here to rescue him was an inconvenience that might go away if he was patient. He gave a vague wave in the direction of the window.

Caffery turned and realized they must have come all the way through to the back of the building. The boarded window was in an unlit corridor that led towards the side of the tower

465

block. Outside he heard distant, wavery sirens. The other support-unit serials arriving. Flea's eyes were watery. He knew what she was thinking. Did they have to go into the bathroom or could they just stay there and wait for the other units?

'Is there a way out of the bathroom?' Caffery snapped at the witch-doctor guy. 'A window — another door?'

'I don't know. Maybe a window.'

'Shit,' he muttered. 'Shit, oh, shit, oh, shit. There would be a window, wouldn't there?'

★ ★ ★

In a previous life, before it had been boarded up by the council, this had been a bedroom — a woman's, from the ornate plastic wardrobe in the corner. The door into the bathroom, shabby now, the veneer peeling off it, still had the crystal-cut glass handle that must have once been someone's pride and joy.

Flea and Caffery stood in the corridor. Flea had her back to the wall, alongside the boarded-up window. She took her eyes off the door, bent slightly, craning her neck up under the grille, peering through the gap where the corrugated-iron covering had been ripped back, seeing the cars parked outside. She pulled her head out again and looked back at the room they'd come from: the hole wasn't big enough for Tig to get through, but the little black guy, he could make it through if he wanted. She should have handcuffed him to Mallows or shut him in a cupboard. Too late now. The sirens were louder — the first of the support-unit serials would be pulling up outside.

'Ready?' Caffery mouthed.

She nodded, remembering a protocol she'd once trained in: the 'deranged-man' tactic. It needed at least three officers with shields, not just her and Caffery sharing one person's equipment. Fuck only knew what would happen, but she racked the ASP anyway, flicking it up and bringing it to rest on her shoulder. 'OK,' she murmured. 'Give it a hoof.'

He smiled at her sideways, ironic. Then he aimed his foot at the door. It flew open and they threw themselves forward, Caffery first, then Flea, coming in too fast behind him, half tripping, righting herself by putting a hand on his arm, getting balanced and snapping into the combat position: weight low, knees unlocked, presenting her side, left hand in front of her face.

And then what happened was nothing. Silence. They blinked a bit, their faces yellow in the dim light from the grille on the window. It wasn't like any bathroom either of them had seen. A St Andrew's cross had been welded with workmanlike durability on to the cracked tiles above the bath, and where the toilet had once been there was a powder-coated, galvanized-steel cage that stood tall enough for an average man to get into but not to stand up in. Otherwise the bathroom was empty. No hidey-holes, no exits. Nothing could have got through that tiny window.

'Fuck,' Caffery said, dropping the knife

wearily. 'Lying little shits.'

'Listen,' Flea said, catching his arm, looking back at the boarded-up window in the corridor. If the skinny guy tried to climb through it he'd see him, and if he'd already tried going back through the flats he'd be mopped up by the serials coming round the front. But Tig — Tig could be anywhere. 'I think he's still somewhere in here,' she said. 'There's another door out of that room, leading back into the middle of the flat. Let's go back in and, if they're still there, I target the black guy. 'K?'

He turned to her. For a split second their faces were so close she could see details of his skin. 'OK,' he said. 'Yeah — OK.'

'Right,' she said, holding up a finger. 'When I count to five, we're going to do it. Yes?'

'Yes.'

'One. Two. Three. Four . . . '

The words died in her throat. She went still. Very still. A drop of water had appeared on Caffery's shoulder, a perfect, clear, tearshaped drop on his white shirt — and for a moment she couldn't do anything but stare at it, while the drop ran down and spilled on to his chest. He watched it, too, then raised his eyes to hers. Neither spoke, because they knew, even before they turned their eyes upwards, what they'd see.

★ ★ ★

He was above them. Hanging from D-rings bored into the ceiling, spreadeagled, sweating and trembling with the effort of holding himself

468

in place. Dressed only in black combats, his body glistened with sweat and blood. His mouth was open, his teeth were bared and the blood pooling in his bad white eye made it bulge out at them. An avenging angel.

Flea felt a sound coming into her throat, a voice in her head screaming, *You didn't follow your training, you effing idiot*, and she had time to think, *The 360-degree sweep should take in the ceiling too.* And then Tig was falling from the ceiling like a hawk, nails outstretched, landing with a sickening crack on Caffery's shoulders. His knife and the CS gas spun away across the floor and the two men tumbled backwards on to the tiles, colliding with the bath panel, coming to a stop against the wall on their sides, facing each other like lovers, grappling at faces, ears and hair.

She wrenched her Quikcuffs out of the body armour's front pocket and threw herself down next to the men, trying to push the ASP between them, but she couldn't get at Tig's hands.

'Flip him,' she yelled at Caffery. 'Flip the bastard — let me get the cuffs on.'

'He's trying to fuck me first,' Tig hissed. 'Wants to give me one before you cart me away.'

Caffery gritted his teeth and used his elbows to lever Tig's hands down. Flea reached out to grab his legs but he yanked them away, drumming his feet on the floor. 'Did you hear me?' he screamed at Caffery, saliva foaming at the corners of his mouth. His bad eye was flicking from side to side. 'I said, do you want to give me a little hand-job while we're down here,

469

you City Road whore-fucker?'

On top of him Caffery went still. Sweat ran down from his forehead into his eye, but he didn't blink or move.

'Let me get at his arms,' Flea shouted, trying to find a good place on Tig's arm to bring the ASP down. 'Let me get at him!'

'Hey, *filth*, answer me,' Tig roared up into his face. 'Yes, *you*, you fucking filth john.' He thrust up at him with his hips. '*Answer* me. Come on! Say you want it.'

Time seemed to stop. Then, in an instant, it accelerated forward with a jolt. Somewhere behind her, Flea could hear voices, a radio cackling, someone in a far-away room yelling, 'POLICE', and Caffery rocked back, grabbed Tig's ears, pulling his head up. Tig screamed, trying to wrench himself free. Flea had to change sides, stepping over them, banging her legs on the bath, trying desperately to reach under and get Tig's arm, but this time it was Caffery who was stopping her. Without a sound, not a sigh or a word, he released Tig's ears, letting his head crack down on to the tiled floor.

'Jesus!' she yelled. 'Stop it! You'll — '

But Caffery wasn't listening. He hauled Tig's head back again, and slammed it down, harder this time. Something shot out across the floor — a tooth, maybe. Blood pumped from Tig's nose in a thin fountain, the width of a straw. '*I will fucking kill you.*' Caffery knelt back to adjust his grip on Tig's ears. He was going to do it again.

'Stop it. *Stop it!*' She grappled at him, digging

470

her fingers in, trying to get him to loosen his grip, but he shouldered her away, scuffling on the floor so his back was to her. Under him Tig's feet were kicking for purchase. She rolled back, got on to her haunches, not enough time to get the position right, just enough to choose a target — not the ribs, because of the body armour, but his ankle. That would do: his ankle. His feet in the smart Loakes shoes and grey socks, trousers snagged up enough to show a bit of dark hair on his shins. She muttered a prayer and brought the ASP down fast, just once, on the bone.

There was a split second's silence — absolute quiet. Caffery went very still, his head held back. For a moment she thought he wouldn't move, thought he'd snarl at her, but instead, with a long exhalation, he loosened his grip on Tig and rolled away in a foetal curl, clutching his ankle. She expected him to scream at her, but he didn't, just lay on his side with his back to her, holding his foot, his ribs rising and falling, rising and falling under the body armour.

She had two or three seconds of surreal silence, just long enough to study the back of his neck, to look at Tig with blood over his chest, curled up, his hands clamped to his face. Then there were shouts, and flashlights, and radios. The Support Unit guys were swarming over the place, and the whole thing, the whole bloody thing, was over.

56

Caffery was peeing when it happened. He was standing in the trees, steam coming off his urine because it had got cold now the sun was going down, when the noise came from his left, slightly down the slope, making him stop. At first he thought it was the Walking Man, picking up sticks for the fire, but when he glanced behind him through the branches he could see that the Walking Man was where he'd been earlier, silhouetted against the twilight sky.

He shook himself, zipped up and, hand in his coat pocket to check that his penknife was still there, limped a short way into the trees. He stood for a moment, trying to disentangle the shadows, make sense of them. On the distant road the traffic droned, low and steady, but in the trees there was no noise. After a while he went back to the camp.

The Walking Man was standing next to the unlit fire, eyes bright in the new moonlight, staring in the direction of the noise. 'Jack Caffery, Policeman,' he said, not taking his eyes off the trees. 'What have you brought with you to my fireside?'

Caffery didn't answer. There had been no cars on the track that led into the wood, no noises. Whoever it was must have come on foot. The Walking Man clicked on his lighter. He bent and put a flame to the fire, which flared and sprang instantly to life, bathing the area with red light, throwing the branches and brambles into stark relief. Then he pocketed the lighter and went to the edge of the trees. There was a long, long silence while he seemed to be listening to the night. Then, as if he was satisfied, he grunted and shook his head.

'It's gone now.'

Caffery was still studying the edge of the firelight, the edge of the night.

'Don't worry,' the Walking Man said. 'It's just curious. At the moment, just curious. It's still scared of you.'

'"It"'? And what the fuck is 'it'?'

'Who knows?' The Walking Man smiled. 'A devil? A witch?'

'Fuck off.'

The Walking Man gave a nasty laugh. 'Yeah — of course, you're right. It's none of those things. It's a figment of your imagination.'

Caffery looked past the Walking Man at the trees. He couldn't say why but suddenly all he could think about was the little black guy at Tig's. It had turned out he was an illegal immigrant, one of the many who hadn't been sharp enough to claim asylum. Like a lot of illegals in the Hopewell area, he'd fallen in with Tig, whose head had started ticking when he'd heard the Tanzanian police were after the skinny little African for trafficking human skins. It didn't take Tig long to see the mileage there: selling *muti* to other Africans in the city, selling the ritual, selling the goods. There was money, big money, in a scam like that.

473

Earlier in the afternoon, while Tig raged and bellowed like a caged minotaur from a custody-suite cell, Caffery had stood quietly at the skinny guy's door, watching him through the observation hatch, trying to picture him standing naked at a lakeside. It had been him at the harbour, he'd sworn it had been him, wearing the ridiculous dildo thing to scare the women. He'd told them about the grease he'd rubbed over his body, about the way he poured water over himself to make it seem he'd come out of the river. It all tied up, in its way. And yet Caffery couldn't shake the lingering feeling that something was wrong — that he'd missed something. It wasn't the Tig side of things — they fitted perfectly, he'd be in the can for the rest of his life — no, it was something about the skinny guy, the notion of him creeping around the streets when it got dark. Still, Caffery knew he should drop it. The guy was in custody and he should stop thinking about it.

'That's right,' said the Walking Man calmly, reading his mind. 'Stop thinking about it. No one comes near our fire without me knowing.' Caffery watched him walk slowly back to the camp, bending to pull two cans from under his bedroll. He used his Swiss Army knife to puncture the lids, then pushed them into the heart of the fire, jostling them with a stick until they were upright.

Caffery came and sat on one of the squares of foam and tried not to look at the trees. But it wasn't easy. While the food heated, while the Walking Man drank cider and counted the crocus bulbs in the paper bag over and over again, he kept thinking about it. He'd come here with a sleeping-bag, planning to spend the night under the stars, but it was colder than he'd thought and the inhospitable little cottage near the Neolithic circles suddenly seemed like a pleasant place to be. It was only after they'd eaten and he'd drunk half of the jar of scrumpy that his pulse returned to normal. The fire flickered on in the night, and eventually the sounds became more familiar, the shadows staying where they were meant to stay.

When they'd cleared up they went to their sleeping-bags. Caffery pulled his round his shoulders and settled down with his back to the old watering trough, his injured ankle straight out in front of him. The Walking Man pulled his round his knees and sat at the base of a tree.

'Well, now,' he said, opening his jar of scrumpy. The cork made a sharp popping noise that echoed round the camp. 'Mr Policeman has seen a lot today. I know that from his face. Please tell me your stories. I love to hear about death and destruction.'

Caffery grunted. 'There are no stories.' He thought about Tig, never changing since he'd half killed that old lady, never letting the violence go. He thought of himself, of how convinced he'd been that he'd never lose control as he had years ago. He thought of what would have happened if Flea hadn't been in that bathroom today. And then he thought about Penderecki, the person he was really hitting, over and over again. 'Except I've worked out you're right.'

'That I'm right?' He raised his eyebrows. 'I can hardly believe it.'

'You said once you'd never believe in redemption and now I see you're right. There is no such thing.'

The Walking Man laughed. He settled back against the tree-trunk, hands behind his head, and watched him, waiting for him to go on. Caffery knew he was enjoying seeing him discover truths that he, the Walking Man, had known for years. He reached inside his pocket and began to roll a cigarette.

'So if there's no redemption what's left to us? Revenge? Revenge and then death?' He put the cigarette into his mouth and lit it. He met the Walking Man's eyes. His face, he thought, wasn't very lined. So why did he always seem so old? 'I asked you before and you didn't answer. What did you mean when you said I was looking for death?'

The Walking Man snapped a pick from his Swiss Army knife and began to clean his teeth carefully. 'You have two children in your life, Jack Caffery, the one that is dead and the one that doesn't yet exist. The child that could be.'

'Yeah,' Caffery laughed. 'What crap.'

'You had a woman in London, you told me, who wanted a child but you walked away. So you have to ask yourself, is that the last chance you had?'

Caffery sighed. He rubbed his sore ankle, bruised by Flea and her ASP, and looked out at the valley, to a line of poplars on the horizon. He had a sudden picture in his head of a woman. She had fair hair and was wearing jeans, but he couldn't see her face. She had her back to him and was gazing into a pool of water, hardly moving. He wanted to make her turn round. He wanted to know if she was Flea. But whatever he did she wouldn't move.

'No,' he said. 'There won't be any children.' He took a long drag on his cigarette. 'You?'

The Walking Man chuckled. 'Look at me. I could father a child but could you imagine anyone mothering it? It's different for you. Maybe you still have a chance.' He found something on the toothpick and wiped it on the grass. Then he buried the pick in his mouth again. 'When I said you're looking for death I meant that you've chosen to follow the child that's gone. Every step you take in your job, every move, is you making gifts to him — to Ewan. Every case you solve is just something else to lay at his altar. And so you have chosen death. On this course it will not be a painful thing, your death.'

'What does that mean?'

The Walking Man didn't take his eyes off him. His voice was very quiet when he spoke, but every consonant and vowel came lightly through the clean air. 'It means . . . ' he whispered. His eyes reflected the firelight. For a moment he looked all things at once: he looked monstrous, he looked sad. He looked old and he looked wise. 'It means that it's not too late. It's not too late for you. You can change your mind. You can still care about a different child. You,' his eyes locked on Caffery's — inescapable, an inescapable truth, 'you, Jack Caffery Policeman, can still care. You can care about the child that might be.'

477

57

It was dark when she got home, and the clouds moving across the moon were sending predatory shadows to patrol up and down the hill, slipping across it like wraiths. Exhausted and hungry, Flea parked her car with its back to the valley so she didn't have to look at them. Her PPE body armour and the jeans she'd been wearing had been taken by the CSI team: they'd loaned her a police sweatshirt and combats and there wasn't much left in her car except a set of overalls. She shoved them into the holdall and was getting out of the car when she noticed a wavering square of artificial light on the gravel.

She stopped what she was doing and turned to look at the towering face of the Oscars' house just in time to see a light go out, leaving the windows blank, reflecting the gathering night. Dark now, but she thought she saw the movement of a curtain at one. Just a faint shifting of form and colour. Earlier, when the team had been bringing Tig out of the flat, strapped into emergency restraint belts — in spite of Caffery he was alive — she'd noticed one member of the unit standing on the scrappy little piece of grass outside the flat, staring up at the windows in the tower blocks. When she'd asked what he was looking at he'd shrugged, given a little shudder and said something like, 'I dunno. I feel like I'm being watched. It's the windows.'

At the time, her first thought had been of the boarded-up window outside the bathroom — the way the corrugated iron had been torn up just enough to allow someone small to crawl through. Stupid to think it, because everyone who'd been in the flat was in custody now, but it came back to her, that window, and the words: *I feel like I'm being watched.*

Another movement of light from the Oscars' — someone stepping back from the window, maybe. She had an impulse to walk round to their front door and hammer on it — demand to see Katherine, demand to know when she was going to stop spying. But she didn't. Instead she took a few calming breaths and, with all the control she could muster, raised her hand, acknowledging them, letting them know she knew and that it wasn't going to get to her. Then, she calmly pulled the holdall out and closed the door.

The electronic key fob must have broken; it wouldn't open the boot, so instead of slinging her kit in there overnight, she let herself into the house and dropped it inside the front door. As she straightened she saw a light on in the kitchen at the end of the corridor. There was a smell too, of cooking, of ginger and citrus and molasses. She knew who it was — there was only one person who knew where the spare key was kept, wedged in the branches of the wisteria. Kaiser.

She should ignore him, go upstairs, get warm, get washed. Instead, pulling the police sweatshirt down over her cold hands, she came down to the kitchen. Kaiser was standing at the table, using his fingers to lever muffins in paper cases into a tin.

'Hello,' he said, not looking up at her. 'I've left the molasses tin out on the side to remind you to get some more.'

'Why are you here?'

'Oh,' he said lightly. 'Because you want to talk to me. There are things you still haven't talked about.'

She sighed and sat down at the table, next to the window, her hands tucked in her armpits. She watched him work. He was so familiar to her, so familiar and yet so unfamiliar. He was still wearing the stained white shirt from earlier, and although he kept his enormous African goat face turned from her, she could tell he'd been crying. She noticed Dad's safe from the study was on the table next to the tin. Kaiser must have taken it off the shelf and put it there. She reached over and touched it.

'Kaiser?' she said. 'It's got something to do with Nigeria, hasn't it? Whatever's in here is something to do with the experiments.'

Kaiser stopped what he was doing and looked across at her. 'It was my project, Phoebe. David was simply an observer. Don't blame him too much. He saw nothing in what we did to be ashamed of, but when I was thrown out of the university he knew he had to hide his involvement. I am sorry we didn't tell you, but it was long before you were born and we never thought you needed to know.' He put the last of the muffins away and leaned on the lid to close the tin. 'The safe contains his notes. I don't know the combination, but now he can't speak for himself I think he deserves his privacy, don't you?'

He turned, took the baking tray to the sink and ran the tap. She took her hands out from her armpits and rubbed her tired eyes, looking out of the window to where the moon hung low in the sky beyond Bath, the clouds cruising past it lit grey and yellow like bruises. The nightmare that had started with the hand in the harbour was over. She could put it to bed, everything that had happened: Jack Caffery on the bathroom floor with a light in his eyes that shouldn't be in any police officer's eyes, and Jonah, his neck leaking, his dead eyes on hers as she tried in vain to start his blood-parched heart. Tig was in custody and it was over, the whole thing was over. She should feel a weight lifting. But she didn't. Instead she felt heavier.

'Kaiser,' she murmured, not taking her eyes off the valley. 'When you say ibogaine can let you talk to the dead, do you really believe that?'

He scrubbed at the tray. 'What about you, Phoebe? Do you really believe it?'

'I saw Mum. I didn't tell you but I saw her that night. She told me two things: she said she and Dad were going to be found — soon. She said when they were found I shouldn't try to bring their bodies up. And Kaiser . . . ' She hesitated, her voice smaller, almost inaudible. 'This is the part I can't understand, the part I haven't told you about. *It's happened.* Just like Mum said it would. Someone's found them, Kaiser. Someone's found them in Boesmansgat.'

There was a beat of silence while she wondered if he'd heard her, then he laid the tray down in the sink, wiped his hands on his trousers and took a handkerchief from his pocket. He blew his nose. 'Yes,' he said, his voice muffled. He shovelled the handkerchief back in his pocket and raised his head to look out of the window. 'Oh yes. I know.'

'You *know*?'

'I know. David was my only friend, Phoebe. I've waited two years for them to be found. I check every day.'

'But *I* don't. Not any longer. So how did *I* know, Kaiser? I'm sure I didn't really speak to the dead.' She paused, thinking about it, then added, more faintly, 'Or did I?'

He turned to look at her. 'Maybe you did, maybe you didn't. But you knew the bodies had been found because you went on the computer during the ibogaine trip.'

'I'm sorry?'

'You looked at the site. I came in from the kitchen and found you at the computer.'

'I got on to divenet?'

'You were crying.'

'But I . . . ' She put her fingers on her forehead, frowning, trying to understand how she had forgotten, trying to understand how neatly the ibogaine had excavated her memory.

'I know what you're thinking — that it's impossible. But you don't give the ibogaine enough credit. And you don't give your instincts enough credit either.'

'My instincts?'

482

'Your need to see your parents again.'

Your need to see your parents again. The words made her bite her lip. Suddenly, unexpectedly, her throat was tight and there were tears in her eyes. 'Kaiser,' she murmured. 'Oh, Kaiser. I keep thinking we should try to bring them up. Do you think we should try?'

'Only you can answer that. You and Thom. And maybe . . . '

'Maybe . . . ?'

'Maybe your parents. What did your mother say to you in the hallucination?'

'She said to not bring them up. She said whatever happened to leave them there.'

He shook his head, pulled back a chair and sat with his elbows on the table, looking at her steadily. She saw the way the skin crinkled around his eyes and was reminded that he was old. As old and as mysterious as the continent he came from. 'Then don't you think you should listen to her? Let them rest? Let David's past rest, let their bodies rest?' He paused. 'And, Phoebe, more importantly . . . '

'Yes?'

He smiled. He reached over to cover her hand with his. 'Don't you think you should let yourself rest too?'

She pulled her hand away and wiped the tears from her eyes. *Let yourself rest. Let yourself rest.* The words rolled through her head. She turned her eyes to the window. Yes, there was pain — things from her past she didn't want to face. Yes, there were things in the future that would make her cry, probably.

In the distance some lonely wayfarer on the other side of the valley, where the Warminster road ran, must have lit a fire because she saw a small light flare red inside a canopy of knotted trees. It was too far away to see exactly, but she focused on it, and slowly, slowly, something about the light, something about Kaiser's words, began to settle inside her. She closed her eyes and sat back in her chair.

'What are you thinking?' Kaiser asked. 'What's that smile for?'

She didn't answer. She shook her head and just held on to it: the image of the small flame in the distance, the sound of his words repeated over and over, the beginning of something like peace. She was smiling because she now knew he was right. She could allow it. She could allow herself to rest.

Acknowledgements

Thank you to all those at Avon and Somerset Constabulary who helped me get the procedural details to approximate reality; everyone at the Underwater Search Unit, especially Sergeant Bob Randall, whose contribution to this series cannot be underestimated. Also to DI Steven Lawrence, CID training unit; DSupt Steve Tonks; PC Kevin Pope, Road Policing Unit; Alan Andrews and the Major Crime Review Team. And to Cliff Davies of the Homicide Review Team, Metropolitan Police.

To all my friends at Transworld including, but by no means limited to: Alison Barrow, Larry Finlay, Ed Christie, Nick Robinson, Simon Taylor, Claire Ward, Danielle Weekes, Katrina Whone, and especially Selina Walker, my awe-inspiring editor.

To Jane Gregory and her team: Jemma McDonagh, Claire Morris, Terry Bland and Emma Dunford.

For their help, their friendship and their inspiration: Christian Allis, John and Aida Bastin; Linda and Laura Downing; the Fiddlers; Tracey and Eddie Gore; the Heads; Mairi Hitomi; Sue and Don Hollins; Patrick and ALF Janson-Smith; the Larkhall girls (Kate, Karen, Rebecca and Ness); Lee the woodsman; Mel and Chris Macer; Margaret OWO Murphy and E. A. Murphy; Misty Marshall Welling for lending me her name; Selina Perry; Helen Piper for being outrageously brainy; Keith Quinn; Karin Slaughter for tirelessly devoting herself to weirding me out; Sophie and Vincent Thiebault; all the Vaulkhards, but particularly Gilly for her grace and friendship; Mark Watson; and to Tracey and Jo Waite for giving me a glimpse of what true courage means.

Most of all, thank you to Lotte Genevieve Quinn, my daughter, who is beautiful and keeps my world turning even when nothing else is right.

We do hope that you have enjoyed reading
this large print book.

Did you know that all of our titles
are available for purchase?

We publish a wide range of high quality
large print books including:
Romances, Mysteries, Classics
General Fiction
Non Fiction and Westerns

Special interest titles available in
large print are:
The Little Oxford Dictionary
Music Book
Song Book
Hymn Book
Service Book

Also available from us courtesy of
Oxford University Press:
Young Readers' Dictionary
(large print edition)
Young Readers' Thesaurus
(large print edition)

For further information or a free
brochure, please contact us at:
Ulverscroft Large Print Books Ltd.,
The Green, Bradgate Road, Anstey,
Leicester, LE7 7FU, England.
Tel: (00 44) 0116 236 4325
Fax: (00 44) 0116 234 0205

Other titles published by
The House of Ulverscroft:

WHITE NIGHTS

Ann Cleeves

Midsummer in Shetland, the time of year when the birds sing at midnight and the sun never sets . . . When an unknown Englishman turns up in tears at an art exhibition hosted by Bella Sinclair at the remote Herring House gallery and claims not to know why he is there or even his own identity, the evening ends in farce and confusion. The next day he is found dead, hanging from a rafter in a boathouse, a sinister clown mask on his face. When a local musician is also found murdered, Detective Jimmy Perez becomes convinced that the killer is local. But are his personal relationships clouding his judgement? Or is it just this unsettling time of year, the time of the white nights?